RAINCOAST
CHRONICLES
FIRST FIVE

RAINCOAST CHRONICLES FIRST FIVE

Collector's Edition

**Edited with an introduction by
Howard White**

**Foreword by
Bob Hunter**

Harbour Publishing
Box 219
Madeira Park, B.C.

Copyright © Canada 1976 Harbour Publishing

First printing — 5,000 copies January 1976
Second printing — 5,000 copies March 1976
First paperback edition — 5,000 copies January 1977
Second paperback edition — January 1979
Sixth printing — November 1983
Seventh printing — September 1987
Eighth printing — June 1989
Ninth printing — August 1991
Tenth printing — March 1995

Dedicated to Joe Simson

Design pages 4-201 Cal Bailey, 210-262 Stephen Jackson.

Illustrations and line work pages 67-69, 80, 81, 108, 114, 144, 156, 157, 159, 161-163, 169-171, 173, 175, 190, 207, 215-217, 219, 224, 225, 236, 237, 250-253: Stephen Jackson. Illustrations and line work pages 93, 94, 96-98, 122, 123, 176, 177, 181, 185, 200-203, 220-223, 249: Linda Prine. Illustrations pages 19-26, line work pages 42, 43: Stefan Brunhof. Illustrations pages 151, 152: James Schwartz. Illustrations pages 104, 106, 110, 126, 127, 130: Gordon Labredt. Illustrations pages 204-206: Paula Wainberg. Illustration page 246: Cal Bailey. Map page 32: Steve Holecka. Photographs pages 113, 114, 116, 117, 119, 120, 136: Cal Bailey. Photograph page 210: Hubert Evans. Photograph page 245: Jone Paine. Historical photographs courtesy B.C. Provincial Archives, Vancouver Public Library, Vancouver Maritime Museum, **The Fisherman**, Mike Poole, Rex Padgett, W. G. Dolmage, Martha Warnock, Harriet Helliar, Elsie Klein.

Printed and bound in Canada

Table of Contents

Foreword

Truck drivers, fishermen, loggers, miners, whalers, Indians, Norwegians, Scots, mechanics, gamblers, boozers . . . the flesh and blood people of a strange wet land that was at the end of the world, the mists of which parted to reveal mountains and woods and totem poles. Fogs that could swallow whole civilizations.

Raincoast Chronicles is essentially a no-bullshit book that opens up the past of those of us living along the West Coast of Canada in a way that no other magazine has ever succeeded. No glossy tourist nonsense. No political monkeying with the facts of life. Sweat and grease and silver and salmon. Lovely yellowing old photographs. Steam engines. Diesels. Oars. Easthopes. Rigging. Donkeys.

Without doubt the Chronicles is the most engaging and funky published matter to appear in this corner of the planet. Almost from the first edition, it became a cultural event in its own right, the sort of thing you realized, the moment you saw it, that you had been waiting for it all along. History that wasn't as dry as the tobacco in an old man's pipe. Good solid writing without pretense and without being obviously designed to score brownie points in somebody's thesis.

What Raincoast Chronicles has done is fill a very special need. The age of monocultures has passed away and a new time of acute sensitivity to one's immediate terrain is taking shape. Simply, the Chronicles tell about the real British Columbia of Haida potatoes, petroglyphs, rum running, leper colonies, towboating, you name it. Whatever the past was, here it is again, gathered like a rich mellowing harvest.

At one level, the "book," as everybody involved in its production calls it, is essentially a historical journal. One of its articles — still my favourite — goes back to 499 A.D., telling how a Buddhist priest from China probably travelled along this whole coast. The book includes such staid-sounding down to earth titles as Pioneer Steamers of Vancouver Harbour, Lighthouses of the B.C. Coast, and articles of Tsimsyan myths, cargo hulks and page after page of old photos the likes of which you haven't seen since the last time you crawled through Grandpa's attick, grubbing through mildewed boxes, showing great old boats and trains and trucks, all the rockbottom stuff of which our history is truly fashioned. A mechanic would get off on it as much as a mystic.

That's one level. At another, the Chronicles are a vehicle for the expression of some distinctly West Coast sensibilities, featuring poems by Peter Trower of Gibsons, for instance, who is a people's poet if there ever was one.

Dragging our past for an image that will let us like ourselves a little better — Editor Howie White says that's what the Chronicles is about. What emerges clearly from the pages of the book is an identity which is deeper and truer to these tremendous landscapes than anything else yet published. If "sense of place" is important, then the Chronicles is important. That's all there is to it.

For me the Chronicles has been a joy to discover. It is already part of the landscape. Earth coloured. You can almost smell it. It appears, almost predictably at this stage, on the counters of funky little shops and book racks almost anywhere you go in B.C. The only trouble has been, once you get a copy of one edition you immediately want the rest, and back copies are rare as nuggets — and often as costly. Reissuing the whole works under one strong cover was a break for all of us. Glad it happened.

Bob Hunter

Introduction

Much as I'd like to tell a story of long-suppressed historical forces on the west coast drawing inexorably together in the formation of **Raincoast Chronicles**, the truth is the thing was conceived on a rainy Pender Harbour afternoon in September of 1972 as I sat at the kitchen table casting about for a likely fantasy to plug into that year's LIP grant form. But in those days when the epochal romanticism of the sixties was still strong upon us, enlivening everyone's outlook from the country's rose-toting prime minister down to the lowliest college dropout, filling out a grant form tended to be a lot like forming a wish for the thing you'd most like to happen, so my fantasy took the form of some quite real personal yearnings.

Essentially what I longed to do at that point was to return to my childhood. I had grown up following my logger father from one hard-luck gyppo show to another, not learning much in the way of reading and riting but forming my imagination permanently in the shape of the lichen-bright bluffs, wicked tiderips and miragical horizon-haunting islands of the upper coast.

Later, so that the kids might have school, we settled in Pender Harbour. Pender Harbour did not begin to get seriously involved with the twentieth century until the mid-fifties, when the road from Vancouver came in with the first automobiles, followed shortly by electricity and telephones. Television has still not fully arrived. Shopping and visiting was done exclusively by "kicker" — open clinker-built skiffs with 3-horse Briggses — and the most prominent families were second and third generation fishermen who could count on one hand the number of times they'd been "out" to Vancouver but couldn't remember all the times they'd shot the Yacultas or bounced around Cape Caution. In the sixties I still had high school friends who'd never been "to town", though many spent their summers in fish camps on the Queen Charlotte Islands.

The point is it was a very close and independent community, with the peculiar home-made culture that implies, and it extended northward, through all the identical steamer stops, fishing villages and Indian reserves up coast. Loggers hopped camps from one end of the coast to the other, fishermen yo-yoed between fishing grounds from the Fraser to the Skeena, and the daily passage of the steamers kept Pender Harbour and the other communities of the coast in touch like families along a common road. Men like Charlie Klein, who could lift a full gas drum, and women like Sidney Sauderman, an iron-fisted ex-madam who ran her own camp around Minstrel Island were legends that fired childish imagination the length of the coast.

One speaks of the things when one means the spirit, but how is the spirit to be pictured otherwise. There can be no nostalgia for things, only the use of things and the spirit of that use. Grown up and living in cities, it seemed to me there had been great spirit inhabiting that world known in childhood, as any matured culture comes to possess an élan, a genius, a soul that is like all souls immortal and worthy of awe. It was tied to the place, the B.C. coast, and the uses, fishing, logging, farming, hiding, people had put it to, but it was more than that, the west coast experience. It was the people who'd been there, their reason, and what the place had done to them. The more I tried to talk about it, especially around city academic circles where the B.C. coast was considered to have about as much historical character as a new concrete apartment block, the more I began to feel like some obsessive proponent of the Sasquatch. The idea of a rural west coast culture in the city context seemed a rich fantasy indeed. But I couldn't give the idea up without giving up on what I discovered I unalterably was, as soon as I started trying to be a city boy — an upcoast boy — so I moved back to Pender Harbour and started a community newspaper, thinking to become involved as deeply in that left-behind reality as I could. Of course it was too late. The fishermen were trading their waterfront property to marina builders and moving into bungalows nearer the new shopping centre. The kickers had been entirely replaced by cars, although it is only half a mile across the harbour by kicker and 15 miles around the shore by car. No one wore gumboots to weddings anymore and the social diseases of the suburbs were increasingly evident. This shook my faith in the existence of indigenous west coast folk culture more than anything had, and just as I began to realize any contact with that vanished world of childhood would of necessity be a historical study, the LIP grant form came into my hands.

The magazine I envisioned would not merely detail the stages of local settlement, counting arrivals and births and *things*: it would drive through that easy chronicle for the flavour, the *spirit* of the B.C. coast story. Its founding assumption would be that there was a contiguous coastwise community which could be described in general terms.

To my breathless astonishment the grant came through and the onus was suddenly on me to make the fantasy real. I realized with panic I had no idea how to do it. I had some notion of things I would like to deal with, Pender Harbour as a typical steamer stop and the Nootka whaling story, which had originally reversed my notion of Northwest coast Indians as a society of shiftless clam suckers, but I had no notion of how to go about the presentation. Apart from a handful of dry community histories and a few professional books by Alan Morley and Roderick Haig-Brown, very little serious writing had been done on what the west coast was and there was no satisfactory established modes to work from. The only two books I felt I could really look to were **Woodsmen of the West** by Martin Grainger and Hubert Evans' **Mist on the River**.

The project was really saved by other people. Mary Lee, who'd been the managing editor of the newspaper, soon assumed the task of administering the grant and doing all the work, a function she has filled with increasing appetite to this day. Lester Peterson, the community historian of Gibsons and probably the greatest source of unwritten social history of the coast to be met anywhere, gave the project his blessing and helped with ideas and sources.

I went to see the most respected of my old university profs, Warren Tallman, and he put me in touch with Scott Lawrance, a Roberts Creek writer who came up with the name **Raincoast Chronicles** and was the magazine's strongest contributor up to the fifth issue. Our biggest break apart from actually getting the grant was picking up a hitchhiker near Sechelt who turned out to be Cal Fingers Bailey, a mad genius photographer who had just finished three years in the New York design studio of Martin Petersen — learning how to lay out magazines. It was he who bundled our disorderly scribblings into a bag and came back with the handsome, almost professional-looking product that was our first issue. Without Cal, **Raincoast Chronicles** would have been a one-issue wonder.

As it was, we hit the jackpot. The 3,000 printing sold out in three months and we got 500 letters, many of them from old time coast residents who said things like, "Our family has been here 102 years and this is the first time we've seen anything about what it's really like in a book . . ."

We now have enough material in sight to carry us to our 100th issue. The weak point remains financing: circulation has levelled off around 5,000 which leaves us still dependent on government largesse for the money we pay to our writers and artists — at, in spite of what **MacLean's** magazine says, the best rates in the province. We have taken some criticism over this grant dependence, but the way we figure it, the consumer subsidizes you whether by advertising (which is ultimately billed to him) or by grants (which are ultimately billed to him). The only difference between the two systems is that advertising makes a mess. In any case we have now been accepted as authentic culture by both the Canada Council and the B.C. Cultural Fund — to whom our thanks are sincerely given — and our future seems secure.

Howard White

Rum Running

By Ed Starkins

Early in the year 1920, an obscure Canadian vessel leaving port on a trip to American waters missed a chance for a notation in a volume of maritime lore by failing to publicize the destination of its cargo. The name of the ship and its home port are unknown, but its quiet, unheralded voyage marked the anonymous beginning of the colorful history of rumrunning along the Pacific Coast.

From 1920 to 1933, more than 60 Canadian ships, including some of the best known vessels operating in coastal waters, would participate in the grand effort of carrying contraband liquor to millions of Americans who had little respect for the moral dictates of the Prohibition period. Although loosely tagged as "rum runners", the fraternity of rum ships dealt mainly in bourbon although beer, rye, wine, rum, gin and nearly every other variety of liquor was well-represented.

At the top of the rum running hierarchy were the "mother ships", the schooners, steamers and yachts which could literally carry a fortune in liquor in their holds in a single sailing. Among their ranks were the *Malahat*, *Quadra*, and *Coal Harbour*, vessels which were to provide their share of dramatic headlines in the rum running period.

Beyond a large concentration of Indian names, the smaller rum runners bore nameplates which might be found in any modern harbour:*Principio*, *Nobie*, *Skeezix*, *Zip Ruth B.*, *Temisconda*, *Speedway*, *Gertrude*, *Audery B.*, *Fitz Hugh*, *Ouchewaw*, *Fisher Lassie*, *Chief Skugaid*.

Throughout the 1920's and early 30's, the rum running armada was usually arrayed in berthing areas nicknamed "Rum Row" by its inhabitants. Both Vancouver and Victoria had their respective Rum Rows during the 12 years of American Prohibition.

M.V. Truicella, one of the originals owned by the so-called "father" of Rum Row, Archie McGillis

The birth of rum running can be viewed as the simple response of Canadian businessmen to a highly rewarding market south of the 49th parallel. The market appeared, of course, when the U.S. Congress passed the Volstead Act as the finishing glory of roughly thirty years of antiliquor agitation by suffragettes, church groups, politicians and others. Although over 90 per cent of the country was already under prohibition initiated by local agencies, the Volstead Act made prohibition national, forbidding everything but low-proof beer. With an eye to the future, American merchants were able to stockpile a modest cache of spirits before the curtain fell for "John Barleycorn" on January 16, 1920.

Carrie Nation, who led the U.S. into prohibition with her attacks on saloons and cries of "Smash, for the love of the lord, smash!"

Canadian rum running did not seriously begin until 1921, at least a year after the last official bottle of liquor was sold, because this "secret reserve" and local moonshine more or less sustained the nation's speakeasies.

When the hidden supplies dried up, Canada sprang to the rescue by delivering liquor via two oceans, the great lakes and along most of its border.

Dubbed a "respectable trade" by one of its practioners, rum running was at no time illegal in British Columbia and most other Canadian provinces. Alberta, Saskatchewan, and Manitoba were in the midst of their unsuccessful experiments with outlawing alcoholic beverages while British Columbia itself had just concluded a brief period of being "dry". If the rum runners were dealing in moonshine or had not paid the required Canadian duties on bonded products, they were treated as violators of the criminal code. To create even more of a profit, many outfits did operate outside the law of both the United States and Canada by either setting up their own stills or ducking the necessary duties on factory produced liquor.

The rum trade was tacitly condoned by the Doninion government which in 1920 decided to take full advantage of the "new industry" by creating a "special" $20 a case export duty for liquor cleared to American ports. The rum runners easily slipped around this provision by claiming that their shipments were bound for some other country which would, of course, never receive the consignment in question.

It is curious to note that customs officials would often clear a cargo for the United States where its receipt would be in clear violation of that nation's internal laws. The more common ruse, however, was to clear the shipment for a Mexican port such as Ensenada or La Libertad.

Within a few years, the Canadian government grew exasperated with the duty evaders and levied a general $10 a gallon excise tax on all liquor being exported from the Dominion. The new tax was not considered particularly stiff and was absorbed into operational costs without much disgruntlement.

The rum runners often claimed that they provided a genuinely helpful service to the "alcohol impoverished" human beings south of the border.

It is hard to separate sincerity from self-rationalization in the comments of Captain Charles H. Hudson, a leader of the Rum Row commercial enterprises:

"We considered ourselves public philanthropists!," he said. "We supplied good liquor to poor thirsty Americans who were poisoning themselves with rotten moonshine. We brought prosperity back to the Harbour of Vancouver."

Hudson also claimed that Vancouver was "in the midst of a real depression" in 1922. "It took rum-running to keep industry going," he explained, "...with logging, fishing, mining, etc., in the doldrums." This was a time when business in Vancouver was at its lowest ebb.

A former Q-boat captain in World War I, Hudson became a central figure in Rum Row operations after assuming the post of "marine superintendent" for Consolidated Exporters, the principal rum running combine.

Another enduring myth of rum running is that most of its wealthier entrepreneurs, upon retiring from the practice when Prohibition ended in 1933, immediately moved en masse to the more aristocratic suburbs of Vancouver and Victoria.

A legend which persists into the 1970's claims that there are uncounted numbers of these "Rum Kings" still residing in some exclusive area of the city, usually pinpointed as West Vancouver's British Properties high above Burrard Inlet or the elite Beacon Hill in Victoria. Supposedly these aging liquor barons cannot enter the United States for fear of arrest.

Although it would be hard to take a poll of the surviving rum runners, it is obvious that only a handful still live in affluent districts like the British Properties. There is some truth in the myth, however, since a few "rum barons" could be apprehended in the United States for nonpayment of duties rather than any infraction of the long dead Volstead Act. Although there is no statute of limitations on duty evasion and violators are still held liable, it is doubtful that the American law agencies are still much concerned over the "crimes" of half a century ago. Most of the Rum Row businessmen are now dead, but their ship crews, salesmen and other personnel, generally a younger group of individuals, are still a viable part of the community. A few are at the tiller of large corporate or personal fortunes obtained partly through their Rum Row careers.

While the Rum Row economy was an undeniable source of jobs, money and added prosperity for Vancouver, it nevertheless failed to assume more than a marginal economic significance. Rum running accounted for only a bare fraction of the overall shipping industry -possibly because most of the money involved went into the pockets of the handful of organizers and top men who ran the trade.

There was certainly no Vancouver "depression" of 1922 and, in fact, the evidence is slim to support the existence of any recessive economy in that year. A 1927 City Council survey of local industry shows an almost dizzying upsurge in almost every kind of economic indicator from 1920 to the time of the report. The year 1922 is one of the less energetic periods in the pre-Depression era, yet the whole Vancouver economy was still in optimum condition at that time as may be judged from bank clearings and other statistics.

As far as a "low ebb" is concerned, British Columbia has experienced less attractive conditions both before 1922 and after that year of so-called "depression." It seems likely then, that Hudson recalled old times with a few added touches of his own - an entirely normal process when people reflect on the past. Rum running, undeniably spared "poor thirsty Americans" from the poor, sometimes poisonous quality of their home brew yet the "philanthropy" of the suppliers is still very much in question.

Hudson was interviewed, it should be noted, some 45 years after the "depression" of 1922 by Ruth Greene for a chapter in a popular volume, *Personality Ships of B.C.* His remembrances can be regarded as an example of the rationalizing process which attributes to rum running somewhat more of a social conscience than it actually had.

There were two distinct routes for the rum fleet to follow in bringing their merchandise to the States. Monopolized by larger, swifter vessels, the ocean route from B.C. harbours to rendezvous points along the coast of California was the most lucrative passage.

The smaller ships and boats were the mainstays of the second major route, the relatively short trip from Canadian waters to destinations on Puget Sound or, less frequently, the seacoast of Washington.

The operations of the steamer *Quadra* were typical of the coastal voyages of the bigger rum runners. Commissioned in 1891 for use as a coastal lighthouse tender and survey vessel under command of the famous navigator and historian J.T. Walbran, the *Quadra* was a steel-hulled beauty of 265 tons register, quadruple expansion engines and 120 horsepower. Her top speed of 11 knots and heavy lifting gear made her an ideal candidate for admission to Rum Row.

The *Quadra* was chartered in 1924 by a large rum running cartel in Vancouver and it made several voyages that year before it encountered the United States Coast Guard in one of the most celebrated incidents in the history of rum running.

The Quadra employed the usual scheme of clearing its cargo for Mexico and, usually before it ever left port, would obtain papers from Mexican officials to show that it had properly deposited its consignment at Ensenada, sixty miles south of the California-Mexico border. The Mexican bribery fee, called a *mordita* (little bite), was generally 50 cents per case.

The steamer could carry a huge number of cases on a single journey. A full manifest might include some 25,000 cases of beer, whine, and whiskies - enough to stock several of today's Liquor Control Board stores. The value of the load would fluctuate somewhat as the demands varied in stateside speakeasies but the *Quadra*'s take for a voyage often ran from several hundred thousand to well over a million dollars.

The *Quadra* customarily worked its way down the coast somewhat in the manner of the Hudson Bay Company's old trading ships which would visit numerous points when navigating Canadian ribers. The steamer would slip down the coast making a series of discreet late night stops off the shore near such cities as Portland, Eureka, Astoria, San Francisco and Los Angeles - or almost anywhere else that a customer wanted to pick up a few dozen cases of prime liquor.

Great rum runners like the *Quadra* would stay a considerable distance beyond the threemile limit and preferred to go no closer than necessary to make its deliveries. As a rule, avoidance of the three mile statutory boundaries of the United States made rum running a perfectly safe livelihood for ships like the *Quadra*. Yet the U.S. Coast Guard, which was lobbying in Congress at that time for a 12 mile limit, frequently acted as if their desired legislation was already on the books.

When the Coast Guard seized the *Quadra* and, a few months later, the three-masted schooner *Coal Harbour*, both ships were well past the 12 mile "danger zone" and, according to their logs, more than 20 miles from shore when captured. Although the Coast Guard acted beyond the limits of American jurisdiction in both instances, the ship owners were never cleared from criminal charges because of any dubious constitutionality in the arrest procedure.

The *Quadra* would transfer its cases of liquor to the small swiftly moving motor launches which were used to bring the liquor cases to the beach. Effective at darting through the patrol areas of the cutters, some launches were designed and built for the speeds and maneoverability required to

avoid the Coast Guardsmen.

The *Quadra* and the launches would establish their mutual identities by matching halves of a dollar bill which had been divided during the earlier negotiations for the liquor purchase. If the pattern of the launch crew's torn half matched the other half on the *Quadra*, the liquor was then unloaded.

On October 24, 1924, the *Quadra* ended its career as a "rummie" when the cutter *Shawnee* captured it near San Francisco. The *Quadra*'s second engineer, George F. Winterburn, recalled in 1957 that the ship had been involved in a minor accident while loading on liquor cases from the huge "mother ship", the *Malahat*. The *Quadra* supposedly collided with the *Malahat* in rough seas, incurring a large hole in a bulkhead just above the waterline.

Whiskey on deck awaiting the contact boat. The *Malahat* could haul 60,000 cases, a value exceeding $1,000,000.

According to Winterburn, the crew member who was supposed to be watching for approaching ships came down to help stuff up the hole with mattresses. The *Quadra*'s first mate, Charlie Coppins, gave a different version of the incident by claiming that there had been no collision with the *Malahat* at all.

In any case, the *Quadra* soon found itself being towed into San Francisco harbour. Winterburn hid seven cases of whisky in the engine room's double bottom tank, then flooded the tank so the crew would "at least have some fortification against melancholia and seasickness" in case the cargo was destroyed but the ship allowed to return to Vancouver.

Although the litigations over the legality of the seizure lasted for years, the American courts were prompt in giving Captain George Ford a two-year jail sentence along with a $1,000 fine. Twelve other defendants were fined and given short sentences, but they all jumped bail along with Captain Ford and returned to Canada.

For rather obscure legal reasons, the *Quadra's* owners back on Rum Row retained the entire crew on full salaries for eight months following the seizure. The crew members spent their seemingly endless shore leave enjoying the glories of San Francisco's Barbary Coast, which offered numerous pastimes for any sailor in the Roaring 20's.

While the legal battle continued, the *Quadra*, which was not drydocked, gradually rusted in the harbour and eventually sank at its moorings. The ship was sold for scrap to a local salvage company. The estimated $1 million in contraband liquor evaporated by the time the courts decided that the seizure had been legally carried out.

It was later alleged that the captain of the Coast Guard cutter had received a huge bribe from a rival Rum Row outfit to bring in the *Quadra* from beyond his country's territorial waters. In 1925, the captain was convicted of perjury in the *Quadra* litigation apparently because he accepted a $20,000 bribe from an agent of Rum Row.

In addition to its typical patterns of operation, the *Quadra* can be viewed as representative of the high caliber of seamanship present on most of the rum runners. In the popular view, the rum fleet was a sort of modern pirate society with wild,greedy crews brawling over money, liquor and women.

Ironically, most ships forbade the consumption of alcohol on board after leaving port and many crew members were teetotallers by personal choice.

The Vancouver Rum Row had nearly 60 vessels in semi-permanent status and nearly all were run with the same businesslike standards that one might have found on a stately CPR liner. Because its cash rewards were high, the rum fleet attracted the best crews on the coast. Ship personnel were usually capable of the highest standards of maritime performance and seamanship.

One of the more illustrious outfitters of Rum Row was H. W. Hobbs who later was a prime mover in the creation of the Marine Building in Vancouver. Hobbs began his career by buying a ship in England, stocking it with choice quality Scottish whiskies and later selling the entire cargo on the California market.

His decision to buy the luxurious yacht *Stadacona*, once the flagship of the New York Yacht Club, was a distinct embellishment for Rum Row. The *Stadacona* was a plush, beautiful ship with a clipper bow, raked smoke stacks and a streamlined hull that made her one of the most elegant vessels in existence. She had been owned by the head of the Singer Sewing Machine Company, had an admiral's flagship in the Spanish-American War and had recently been a volunteer cruiser in World War I.

After Hobbs purchased the *Stadacona* and sent her to England for high proof merchandise, he set about looking through Lloyd's Register for a name that did not exist under British registry. With a playful impulse, Hobbs suddenly looked up at a map of British Columbia and picked the name of an isolated mountain peak near the Alaskan border as the new name for the *Stadacona*. In this random fashion, the *Kuyakuz Mountain* was brought forth - only to endure another name change by equally accidental means.

The abbreviated form *Kuyakuz Mt.* was supposed to have been on the new nameplate but a confused drydock painter lettered *Kuyakuzmt* on the bulkheads. The name remained, it is said, because Hobbs felt it might hamper any Coast Guard wireless operator trying to transmit the odd-sounding syllables over the airwaves.

The *Kuyakuzmt* was a swift, maneouverable ship that worked with remarkable efficiency in the rum running operations. Hobbs prospered from her long years of service.

The schooner *Malahat* became the most famous ship on Rum Row, the Queen of its small navy, by virtue of her enormous supercargo capacity. It was not unusual for the *Malahat* to carry 60,000 cases of liquor on board when leaving Vancouver. Much of her trading was done in the Farralone Islands near San Francisco where a virtual open sea marketplace for smuggled liquor existed until it became "hot" with U.S. cutters in the mid-20's.

The *Malahat* began its career as a windjammer in 1917 but soon afterwards was equipped with powerful Bolinder engines. Capable of operating with either sail or engine power, the vessel was uniquely capable of staying out of the clutches of the Americans. The *Malahat* would often ride the winds out to sea in order to run the engine powered cutters out of fuel. When being tailed by the Coast Guard, her crew would sometimes dump decoy rum cases, actually bags loaded with sand, into shallow water so the Coast Guard would drag for it as the *Malahat* vanished over the horizon.

Owned by Archie Gillis of Vancouver, the *Malahat* used a ship board radio transmitter to receive its instructions from Gillis' key man, Capt. Charles Hudson. Under U.S. pressure, the Canadian government eventually suspended the *Malahat's* wireless license. Gillis countered the suspension, however, by installing a secret shortwave transmitting system in the *Malahat* and most of his other ships. A Vancouver short wave ham was called upon to create the radio network clandestinely operated from Capt. Hudson's Vancouver office-residence.

Victoria's Rum Row was a less ambitious undertaking in most respects than the corresponding row in Vancouver. It was the staging center for the smaller trade which kept high proof cargoes moving down Puget Sound. Most vessels only operated as transfer ships which would remain in Canadian waters when handing over their bundles of liquor to American rum runners. Some ships from B.C. would occasionally take the risky journey down the sound to lonely transfer points where American smugglers awaited them.

For rum runners of both nationalities, the Puget Sound area, entirely within American territorial waters, was a dangerous place to frequent with contraband liquor. American cutters, oddly enough, were never able to mount an effective blockade of the relatively small Puget Sound entrance. More feared than the Coast Guard, however, were the marauding hijackers who usually behaved in the classical tradition of pirates.

A rum runner operating in Washington waters could often assume that a cutter would not venture very far from a safe cove when one of the Sound's frequent squalls was lashing up the water.

The rum runners often took advantage of the large number of fishing vessels which would dot the inland waters during much of the year. Mingling with the collection of fishing boats, a rum runner like the *Speedway* might make a pretense of trawling the area and thus boldly pass under the eye of a watching cutter.

The Pither and Leiser wharehouse, situated across from Kingston Wharf in Victoria, was the main liquor wholesaler for Rum Row. Located on Wharf Street, the building still has iron bars on its basement window which once protected thousands of cases of liquor stocked there during the heyday of rum run-

ning. Many of Victoria's small craft were involved in liquor smuggling. An altogether respectable business as in Vancouver, Victoria's Rum Row even featured the son of a city policeman.

There is an apocryphal story that the term "six pack" originated in Victoria. One Swede Peterson, a crewman on the steamer *Emma Alexander*, supposedly was in the habit of sewing six bottles of Scotch in burlap while aboard ship. In a U.S. port, the story goes, Peterson would slip the six pack through a porthole to some eager recipient waiting below in a dinghy. Like many legends of the rum running era, this six pack tale may be pure fantasy or, however improbable, the truth.

In addition to the legal liquor which was cleared for coastal trade in Victoria, there was a healthy business in moonshine products. A truly remarkable distilling plant on Texada Island produced enormous quantities of whiskey before an R.C.M.P. raid shut it down. A three-story building housed several huge vats which apparently were capable of turning out several hundred gallons of liquor a month. Remnants of the vats and underground conduits for piping the moonshine to shipboard may still be seen on the island.

Almost every island in the Gulf was a way station for smugglers at one time or another. The smuggling operations not only dealt with moonshine but extended to more exotic forms of contraband such as opium and stolen jewels.

The cove at Clo-ose on Vancouver Island's west coast was well known for harbouring rum runners and other smugglers. The lady proprietor of the village store, a sort of "thieve's market" featuring all kinds of smuggled goods, aided the rum runners with such courtesy that she became wealthy enough to buy a Vancouver hotel in the late 1920's.

Both the moonshiners and "legal" rum runners were particularly fond of little D'Arcy Island in Haro Strait northeast of Victoria. A leper station for most of the 1920's, the island was normally avoided by Canadian lawmen although they raided it after several years of use as a stopover point for the rum runners. The station keeper was friendly with the rum fleet and even guarded cargoes for one Washington rum runner.

High production still on East Coast of Texada Island. Note pole frames (left) which carried track for rolling barrels to shore.

Inside of Texada still showing boiler.

The most prominent rum runner in the B.C.-Washington trade was Roy Olmstead, an Olmstead, an American who began his rum importation activities while serving as a lieutenant on the Seattle police force. Olmstead's methods for bringing contraband liquor into the country had the sophistication and intelligence of the masterminds in a James Bond novel. He still managed to get caught, however.

Arrested for the first time in 1920, Olmstead was tossed off the Seattle police force with a great flurry of newspaper publicity but he forged ahead in spite of this minor setback. When he was finally imprisoned in 1928, the former policeman was the head of a rum running empire rivalling the Capone gang in Chicago in the scale of its activities. The New York Times described his efforts as "one of the most gigantic rum running conspiracies in the country."

By buying in large volume and "clearing for Mexico", Olmstead undersold his competitors by 30 per cent or more. He owned a small fleet of rum runners which contacted the Canadian delivery vessels north of Puget Sound. He also maintained a small army of telephone operators, dispatchers, checkers, collectors, salesmen and other personnel. According to a federal judge, he was able to sell 200 cases a day in Seattle alone and "there was evidence of transactions that each month amounted to nearly $200,000."

Although he had been thrown off the Seattle force, the rum runner managed to act as virtual "Chief of Police" by maintaining most of the city's law enforcement agents on his payoff list. Olmstead was even able to bribe Coast Guard crewmen and federal officials, both usually beyond the reach of bribes.

A true "Rum King" if there ever was one, Olmstead bought a beautiful mansion in Seattle's high-prestige Mount Baker suburb and threw extravagant parties for the city's social elite. He started the first radio station in Seattle, now known as KOMO, over which Olmstead and his friends were reading children's bedtime stories when raided by federal agents in October, 1924.

Audacious enough to organize such an empire, Olmstead never balked at the most flagrant and incautious ways of conducting his business. Shipments of liquor were sometimes brought into Seattle harbour in broad daylight for his men to unload in trucks marked "Fresh Fish" or "Meat". This sort of bravado earned the Rum King a certain respect from Washingtonians who were also appreciative of his store policy of not selling moonshine or adulterated liquor.

According to one authority, Olmstead "was in many ways the best thing that could have happened in the Northwest." He maintained a high standard for his own business and fought practices like gambling and prostitution which were repugnant to his own moral code.

Olmstead managed to control the hijacking problem to a limited degree by pressuring Seattle buyers into not taking the stolen consignments. He forbade his boats to carry weapons and, although his business suffered from the hands of the masked gunmen who hid in remote coves and backwater, Olmstead preferred to use fast boats and evasive tactics rather than direct confrontation.

When Olmstead was arrested for "conspiracy to barter, sell, deliver and furnish intoxicating liquors," his case turned into the biggest court trial in the history of Prohibition because of a controversy on constitutionality of wiretapping as well as the complicity of large numbers of public servants. Federal agents introduced massive transcripts of wiretapped phone conversations into the court record and, after a lengthy challenge to their methods, the Supreme Court ruled that the evidence was obtained through legal means.

In the courtroom, the Rum King often smiled knowingly at the United States Attorney's young assistant to whom he supplied a personal stock of Canadian bourbon as the trial continued.

After serving 35 months at McNeill Island Prison in Washington, Olmstead was released from custody in 1931, shortly before the end of Prohibition. Within four years, he received a full pardon from President Franklin Roosevelt because of a complete "change of character" towards a more law abiding, moralistic outlook.

Rum runners like Olmstead sometimes came close to attaining the stature of folk heroes in the public mind. Since Prohibition was an unpopular institution in the United States, its violators were often highly regarded by the public.

Capt. Robert Pamphlett of Vancouver became a true hero to the anti-Prohibitionists following a strange incident involving his ship, the *Pescawha*. The son of veteran captain Thomas Pamphlett, the *Pescawha's* skipper was delivering a load of whiskey to a contact off the mouth of the Columbia River when he encountered a raging storm. Safely outside the 12 mile safety margin for Coast Guard cutters, Pamphlett noticed a derelict ship through his binoculars as it was being driven by high winds towards the rocky coastline. This vessel, the *Caoba*, was completely out of control with both its masts broken and the sails shredded to tatters.

The *Pescawha* quickly entered the forbidden waters and, with what must have been expert handling, managed to remove the crew before the *Caoba* hit the reefs. On its way back to open sea, the slow-moving *Pescawha* was overtaken by a cutter and, although he possibly could have ignored the Coast Guard's order to receive a boarding party, Pamphlett hove to. He took the courteous action of transferring the men to the cutter rather than bringing them to Vancouver for eventual repatriation through the American consulate. The cutter probably had seen the rescue operation and was not suspicious of the *Pescawha* for other reasons, Pamphlett felt.

The Coast Guard commander noted the gallantry of the rum runner's crew but, despite the enraged protest of the *Coaba's* men, impounded the ship and towed it to Portland. A general outcry followed from the city of Portland and it was echoed by other communities along the coast.

Public meetings, newspaper editorials and other measures of support did not prevent the United States government, however, from forfeiting the vessel to public ownership, destroying the smuggled liquor and jailing Capt. Pamphlett.

Upon release from jail a year later, the *Pescawha's* captain received an inscribed gold watch from the residents of Portland who appreciated his courage in rescuing the *Caoba*. Pamphlett's action proved even more costly since he apparently contracted tuberculosis in jail and died in North Vancouver within two years of his release.

Pamphlett's poignant story, the fate of the *Quadra* and the *Kuyakuzmt's* grand entrance onto Rum Row were high points in the story of coastal rum running, but all have been overshadowed by the gruesome event that took place on the little *Beryl G*. The boat's tragedy assumed the proportions of a latter day Manson case or Jack the Ripper story in B.C. newspapers in the 20's and, since that time, it has been recounted so often that it requires mention only for the uninitiated.

By the time of the *Beryl G.'s* ill fated encounter hijackers had become so much of a problem that some boats were equipped with armour plating and automatic weapons to discourage hostile boarders. William J. Gillis and his seventeen-year-old son, Bill, had not, however, achieved such sophistication in their modest Rum Row operation. When boarded by three hijackers as they were preparing their dinner, the Gillis men fought with their bare hands before being murdered by the attackers.

An Inspector Forbes Cruickshank of the B. C. Provincial Police infiltrated the waterfront hangouts of the hijackers in Washington and, through an involved bit of police work, eventually secured the arrest of the *Beryl G.* hijackers. Within a year and a half of the murders, two of the hijackers were hung at Oakalla Prison. Before his execution, one man noted they had carved up the bodies "into strips to make them sink better." The third man was initially sentenced to death but later was given life imprisonment.

Such brutal behaviour as may be inferred from the disposal of the *Beryl G.'s* occupants was typical for the hijackers. An infamous family of ne'er-do-wells named the Eggers, remembered for various acts of hijacking and generally underhanded activity, were among the most feared of the Gulf Island marauders. One Egger accidentally killed his own brother in an escape attempt and, somewhat later, was himself found floating in San Francisco Harbour with his head and four limbs missing. How the police identified his body in this condition is not recorded.

Despite the deprecations of the hijackers, the deaths on the *Beryl G.* are apparently the only murders committed by these infamous men in Canadian jurisdiction. By transferring their liquor in B. C. waters, the Canadians were within the framework of the law and hijacking was considered an act of piracy punishable by death. It was less risky to hijack cargoes in United States waters because the legal issue of piracy was rather

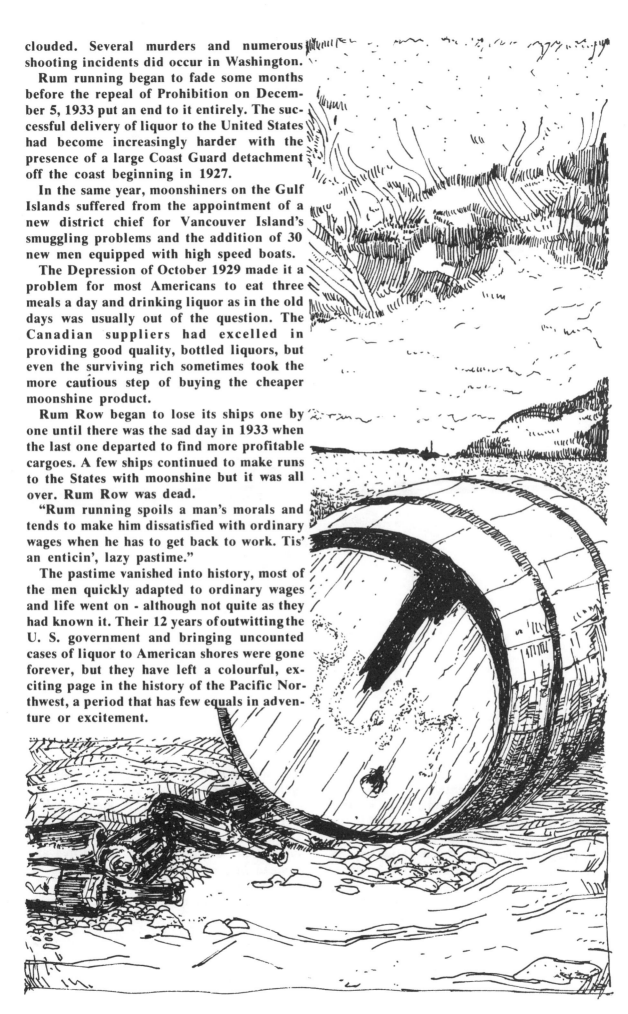

clouded. Several murders and numerous shooting incidents did occur in Washington.

Rum running began to fade some months before the repeal of Prohibition on December 5, 1933 put an end to it entirely. The successful delivery of liquor to the United States had become increasingly harder with the presence of a large Coast Guard detachment off the coast beginning in 1927.

In the same year, moonshiners on the Gulf Islands suffered from the appointment of a new district chief for Vancouver Island's smuggling problems and the addition of 30 new men equipped with high speed boats.

The Depression of October 1929 made it a problem for most Americans to eat three meals a day and drinking liquor as in the old days was usually out of the question. The Canadian suppliers had excelled in providing good quality, bottled liquors, but even the surviving rich sometimes took the more cautious step of buying the cheaper moonshine product.

Rum Row began to lose its ships one by one until there was the sad day in 1933 when the last one departed to find more profitable cargoes. A few ships continued to make runs to the States with moonshine but it was all over. Rum Row was dead.

"Rum running spoils a man's morals and tends to make him dissatisfied with ordinary wages when he has to get back to work. Tis' an enticin', lazy pastime."

The pastime vanished into history, most of the men quickly adapted to ordinary wages and life went on - although not quite as they had known it. Their 12 years of outwitting the U. S. government and bringing uncounted cases of liquor to American shores were gone forever, but they have left a colourful, exciting page in the history of the Pacific Northwest, a period that has few equals in adventure or excitement.

B.C. Whaling: The Indians

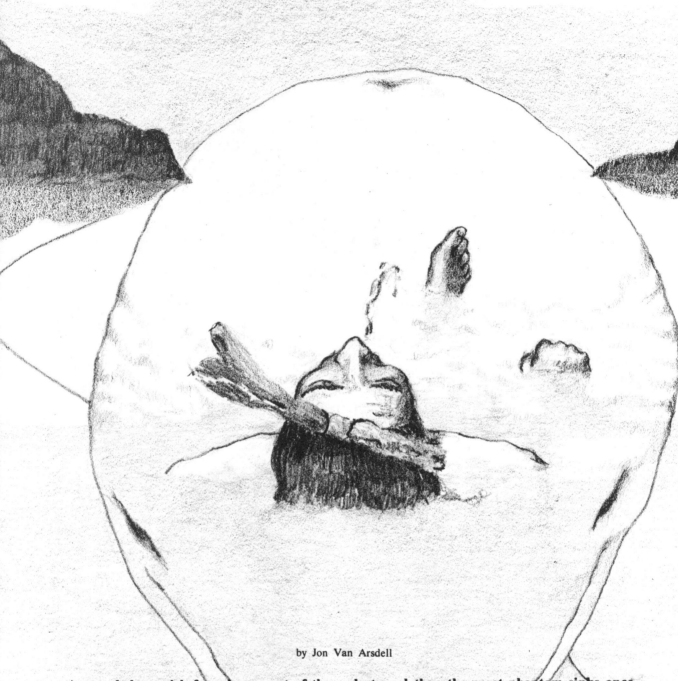

by Jon Van Arsdell

A rounded, greyish form looms out of the ocean depths near the entrance to a wooded cove on Vancouver Island's west coast. Sliding through the billowing surge of foam, the shape grows larger and larger to the eye, revealing the presence of something beyond the breakers - enormous, frightening, magical. Just before this strange shape seems about to leap from the waves, it sinks back into the curling surf.

A sudden burst of spray. The great, sleek hulk surges once again from its place in the sea. A huge gasp bursts forth, the explosive gasp of a diver who held his breath to the last, and then the great phantom sinks once again from sight.

It is a whale at play. A medium sized sperm like the one the Russian explorer Adam Johann Von Krusenstern accidentally bumped off Alaska in 1803. It turned and rammed his vessel from below, "raising the entire ship three feet at least out of the water." On November 20, 1820, another sperm whale, angered by the harpoon, rammed and sank the 238-ton whaling ship Essex off Clipperton Island in the South Pacific, providing Hermann Melville with the idea for his whaling epic, Moby Dick.

When the Indians of the Pacific Northwest hunted the whale in coastal waters during bygone days, the tribes evolved an elaborate ritual which featured spiritual communion with the great creature they sought to kill. Based on a form of "sympathetic" magic designed to influence the whale's behaviour, the Indian ceremonials were also sincere expressions of human empathy. Before rendering the death blow to the whale, the chief of the tribe would sing a eulogistic song of respect, telling the whale that its own wish was to surrender to the canoes.

This approach is in obvious contrast to that of the "civilized" whaler, whose only thought on sighting a magnificent blue was the quantity of oil it contained. In this time of ecological anxiety, there has been a reawakening of interest in the sensibility of the Indian - hopefully a sign of more fundamental change in modern man's attitude toward nature.

The term Nootka is now applied to a loosely-knit family of tribes which range from Kyuquot Sound at the northern end of Vancouver Island's ocean shore to the tip of Washington State's Olympic Peninsula in the south. Not all of the Nootka were whalers. Only the Ahousat of Clayuquot Sound, the Moachat in Nootka Sound, the Makah living on Cape Flattery and the Tofino Inlet group made it a major part of their lives while others like the Hesquiat and Kyuquot were periodic whalers, acting whenever an opportunity presented itself.

The Indians' ostensible motive for whaling was food but there was more than a little of Melville's "hell-driven" Ahab in men like the famous whaling chief Maquinna. Competition between neighbouring chiefs and the great personal challenge of the hunt undoubtedly made their efforts more elaborate and time-consuming than strict economic reward could justify.

Accounts of splintered chase boats with their harpooners batted hundreds of feet through the air by the flukes of enraged whales abound in whaling literature. In 1956, the American cetologist Paul Dudley White had a close brush with death while trying to plant an electro- cardiograph on the back of a comparatively small grey whale. The monster rose up on its flukes, turned about and flung itself down on the scientist's boat, smashing his instruments and sinking the craft.

This is the gigantic being which has come for a brief visit to the shoals of Vancouver Island: the whale, creature of romance and science, source of food and industrial products, and an animal of great beauty and little-understood intelligence. Two years ago, Dr. Roger S. Payne put out a long playing record of the poignant calls of these remarkable animals. Listening to these haunting, musical sounds, man seems to glimpse another reality, what *Scientific American* calls "the other world of the mind."

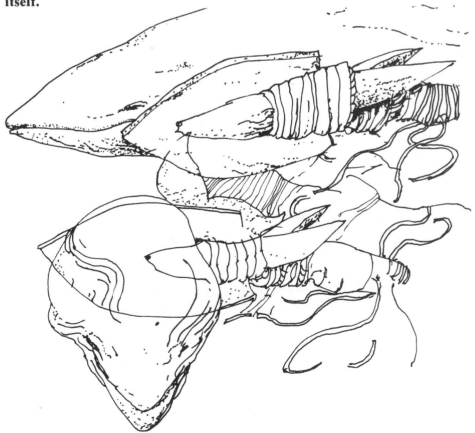

When Captain Cook touched land at Nootka Sound in 1778, he found the Indians there engaged in methodical and effective whaling operations which they told him their forefathers had begun ages before. Technologically, these Nootkas were living in the stone age. The methods of their whaling industry bear witness to a capacity for adapting primitive technology to the most complex and demanding tasks.

The challenge of the whale hunt, it should be noted, was one European man avoided until after the development of ocean-going ships and the discovery of America. The industry did not really become efficient until the development of the American whaling ship in the early 1800's, a vessel described by Charles Olson as "one of the most successful machines developed up to that time."

When the reader comes across the details of Indian whaling methods related in this article, it may be worthwhile for him to imagine himself in the role of a native whaler, attacking a beast five times the size of the greatest dinosaur with minimum safeguards to his own person and with heavy odds against his success.

The canoes used in Nootka whaling varied little from tribe to tribe. The main body was hewn from a cedar log with fitted pieces bow and stern. Days might be spent wandering through forests far from the village in search of a suitable tree. Only in thick stands did the trunks grow straight and free of limbs. If a likely candidate were found, a hole would be chiselled into the stump to test for soundness. On rare occasions the entire tree might be felled but this was very hazardous. More often a scaffolding was erected around the trunk to the height desired in the canoe and a cut made halfway through the tree, top and bottom. A vertical split was started at the top with hard wood wedges and a pole inserted in the crack. The carver would then return home to other business. As the tree swayed, the pole would work its way down the trunk until a half-round block of just the right size broke loose. If the whole tree was being felled, surrounding timber was cleared away, limbs cut, and the chips of the cut scattered in the direction intended for the drop. After doing everything physically possible to assure a soft landing the carver sang out, imploring the tree to go gently.

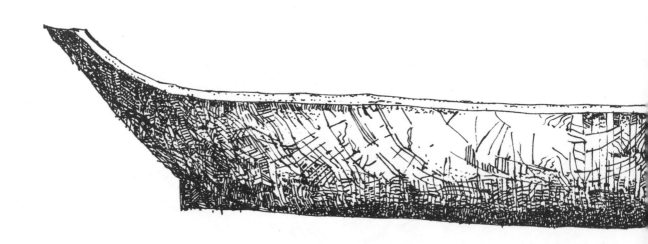

For the rough shaping heavy stone mauls and nephrite or jade chisels were used. For the finer work the carver had stone or bone adzes and chisels of mussel shell. While he was working on a canoe the carver had to be very watchful of his own behaviour. He dared not touch women or rotten spots would appear at crucial points in the log. If he combed his hair, or dropped a hair, splits would appear.

When the outer hull was finished, holes were bored at all the critical bends and plugged with carefully measured coloured dowels. The hull was then righted and the hollowing begun. When his adze shaved the tip of a dowel, the carver knew he had dug far enough. This technique assured even thickness throughout the hull. The hull was humped up in the middle so it would level out upon spreading, which was accomplished by inserting long crosspieces anglewise between the walls and banging them straight after the wood had been softened with hot water. If the carver had been anywhere remiss in his duty, from choosing a cross-grained tree to winking at a girl, the canoe might at this point snap in two. No one but he dared look until the spreaders were firmly fixed and the wood dried. The bow and stern pieces were tightly fitted then laced down with spruce roots set in pitch.

When all carving and fitting was finished, the hull was singed with a torch flame to remove tiny slivers and sanded with dogfish skin. A final finish of seal oil and red ochre was baked on with torches. Narrow with straight gunwales, long prow and square stern, the Nootka whaling design greatly impressed early white shipmen with its speed and, according to some scholars, inspired the famous "clipper bow" so popular in the mid-19th century.

The canoe was carried to the water on fir poles padded with cedar bark. It was never dragged or touched on the ground. The Nootka standards of craftsmanship were such that the largest 60-foot dugout, brought through such involved labours by purely instinctive judgement, was expected to float in perfect balance. There were no excuses and no ballast.

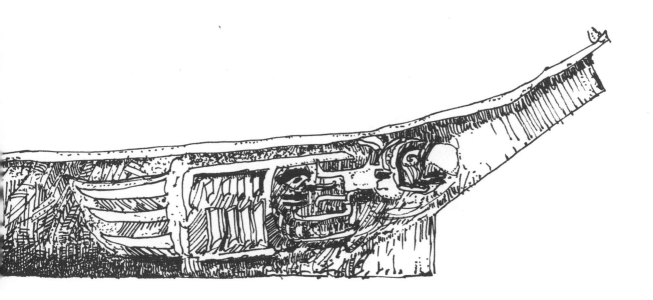

The Nootka harpoon was an awesome weapon four inches in diameter and eighteen feet long. It was made of two or three pieces of yew wood joined with interlocking curves and wrapped with whale sinew. The sinew was sewed together with yellow cedar bark, creating a tight binding that held the segments into a rigid whole. The harpoon head was made of a mussel shell with two carefully fitted pieces of elkhorn as barbs, and connected to a lanyard of whale or sea lion sinew covered with yellow cedar bark and, finally, overlayed with cherry bark.

The lanyard was spliced and served with nettle fiber string on a 240-foot length of line nearly one and a half inches in diameter. This line was spliced on to a second line of lighter cedar rope 360 feet in length. The combined strength of these lines was greater than a hemp rope of similar dimensions; also, the line had a certain rigidity which prevented it from fouling when played out after a strike.

Floats were the key of the Nootka method of whaling, and a special person was assigned to prepare and maintain them. Es entially they were whole sealskins sewn up and inflated like balloons.

Fresh skins were scraped with a pecten shell and tanned with warm urine. The hair was left intact and apertures closed with yew wood plugs, the skin was turned inside out and left with a small opening for inflation later on.

Other equipment included paddles of yew or maple which were tapered to lessen noise when striking the ocean's surface.

The canoe also carried bailing scoops and boxes for food and water supplies. Special bags filled with cedar shavings held human excreta which, it was believed, would anger the sea spirits if placed in the ocean. A large lance was included for administering the *coup de grace* . All of the canoe's gear was maintained in perfect order by the crewmen since inefficiency might spell disaster or result in the loss of a whale.

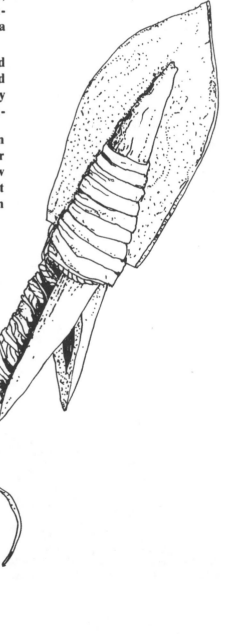

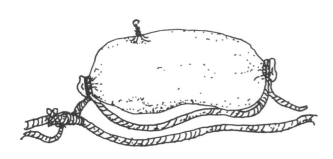

The Nootkas were hunting the seven species of whale which frequented coastal waters at the time of European contact. The largest variety of cetacean was the blue or sulfur-bottom whale. The largest animal ever to live on earth, blues measuring 100 feet in length and weighing over 100 tons have been recorded. By comparison, the largest of all dinosaurs attained a length of only 60 feet and weighed a paltry 20 tons.

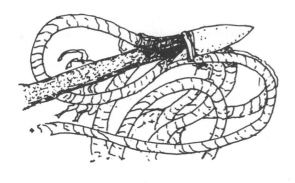

The smaller, more common types of whale hunted by the Indians included the California grey whale (50 feet), sperm whales (60 feet), right whales (50 to 60 feet), humpback whales (45 feet), finbacks (80 feet) and the killer whale or blackfish (30 feet).

Sperm whales and killer whales are true carnivores with predatory habits and fully developed teeth, but the other species are baleen whales which filter microscopic plants and animals called plankton through the myriad rows of whalebone lining their mouths. Normally very difficult to catch, killer whales were sometimes taken by young Nootkas out to assert their prowess at whaling. The killer whale's flesh was considered a delicacy with a rich flavour like that of porpoise.

The whaling season lasted from the beginning of May to the end of June, corresponding with the whale's migrating habits.

The principal figure of every whaling expedition was the chief, who served as harpooner on the lead canoe. Supposedly having inherited his powers from his father, the chief was considered the greatest whaler of the tribe and all whaling equipment belonged to him. The strictest rituals of preparation for the hunt were reserved for the chief and his wife, who were required to live separately and abstain from sexual contact for weeks prior to the whaling excursion.

The couple spent days in singing and praying to the whale before the canoes actually disembarked, and rubbed each other's bodies vigourously with hemlock branches until the plant's needles had been torn off. With blood flowing freely from their scratches, they entered a special fresh water bathing pool. Submerging and surfacing four times, the pair spouted water in imitation of the whale and moved in the direction that they wished the whale to follow after being harpooned. The wife repeatedly chanted a chorus of "This is the way the whale will act" as her husband sang to the unseen animal. The ritual reflected their great concern to have the whale stay close to the village after being struck. If it headed out to sea it might take days of laborious paddling to bring it back, or it might run out of range, taking the prized harpoon head with it.

Besides living apart from his wife, the chief was required to avoid contact with all women during his preparations because of possible association with women who were ceremonially unclean. Both the chief and his wife tried to avoid thought of sex as a means of obtaining further purification.

When the whaling canoes finally left for the long expedition, the chief's wife retired to her house, laid down and was covered with a cedar bark mat. She could neither move, eat nor drink until her husband returned.

The chief's whaling regalia included a bundle of hemlock twigs tied to his forehead, a bearskin robe and a ceremonial whaling hat woven for him by his wife. His hair was tied in a knot at the back.

The expedition left before dawn in order to arrive at the main whaling grounds at daybreak. The lead canoe carried the chief and his massive harpoon, a steersman and six paddlers. The second canoe was usually captained by a relative of the chief. Sometimes a small, fast-moving sealing canoe accompanied the other boats; it would return quickly to the village if a strike was made so the Indians on shore could offer prayers and sing as the men in the canoes struggled at sea with their giant catch.

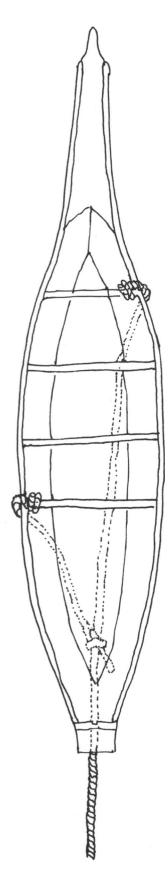

Towing hookup

The whaling grounds were often a shallow area such as a bay or cove where the whales were lazing near the surface. The animals would often select these quiet, sheltered waters to briefly rest on the annual migratory journeys from South Pacific regions to the icy Arctic waters.

After reaching the proximity of the whaling grounds, the Indian crews sat with all eyes trained on the horizon for the telltale spout of water marking the presence of a whale resting on the surface. The steersman, often an older and more experienced whaler, had a firm understanding of the whale's sounding habits and could predict with some accuracy the creature's underwater movements.

A whale resting will normally submerge and swim between 200 and 300 yards before surfacing again. These short periods of submerging and reappearance may be repeated three or four times before the creature finally sounds, disappearing beneath the surface for as long as 20 minutes.

The steersman was required to make a calculated judgement where the whale would surface and then direct the crewmen to row there with maximum speed. The striking position had to be exact because the cumbersome harpoon was thrust from above, never thrown. Close wasn't good enough; the canoe must be exactly positioned or the harpooner held his hand.

The account of John Jewitt, an English sailor who spent three years as a slave of the Moachat chief, Maquinna, gives an idea of a Nootka whaling party's day to day chances of success. According to Jewitt, Maquinna diligently hunted whales a total of 53 days between 1803 and 1805. His crews harpooned nqne whales but only managed to kill one and bring it to the village. The greatest whalers of ancient times, according to early informants, might have reached ten catches a season.

The best striking angle was to the whale's left with the harpooner having relatively free access to the area under the animal's left flipper. The crew tried to approach from the monster's rear where they would be out of its field of vision. At the exact moment of the strike, each crewman had a specific function which had to be carried out with clockwork precision.

The steersman shouted out to the harpooner when the tail was exactly the right distance under water for the strike to take place. Since the whale's flukes usually flipped up when the harpoon hit, the steersman would have to judge when the tail would miss the canoe if it made a sudden movement out of the water.

Responding to the steersman's call, the harpooner would ram his weapon down with all his strength into the whale's body below the left flipper. The harpooner immediately flattened out in the front of the canoe to avoid the wildly careening shaft.

Three pairs of paddlers sat between the harpooner at the bow and the steersman at the rear of the canoe. The starboard paddler occupying the most forward position, directly behind the harpooning chief of his tribe, would throw over the first float after the strike. The third starboard paddler, next to the steersman, played out the line for this float with his paddle to avoid fouling.

Paddler number two, occupying the middle position between his fellows and also on the starboard side, steadied the canoe with his paddle. The paddlers on the port side of the canoe backed water to port to keep the canoe away from the walloping flukes of the wounded beast.

After the canoe was backed out of danger and the floats and lines secured, the harpooner returned to his role of chief and sang to the whale, imploring the thrashing, angry creature to head towards the shore.

"Whale, I have given you what you are wishing to get - my good harpoon. And now you have it. Please hold it with your strong hands and do not let go. Whale, turn toward the beach of Yahksis and you will be proud to see the young men come down to the fine sandy beach of my village at Yahksis to see you; and the young men will say to one another 'What a great whale he is! What a fat whale he is! What a strong whale he is!' And you, whale, will be proud of all that you hear them say of your greatness. This is what you are wishing, and this is what you are trying to find from one end of the world to the other, every day you are travelling and spouting."

The whale's initial struggle was a violent, dangerous period of the hunt in which the animal often would jump completely out of the water in attempts to escape the stinging harpoon. The line flew from the boat as if snagged on a runaway locomotive; crewmen careless enough to get in the bite might have an arm torn from its socket. The canoe itself would often be capsized or split in two by a blow of the flukes. Cases have been recorded where a split canoe was righted, bound together, the chase resumed and the whale ultimately overcome.

If no accidents occurred, the second canoe usually moved in for another strike.

Ideally, the whale would swim towards the village but often it broke for the open sea.

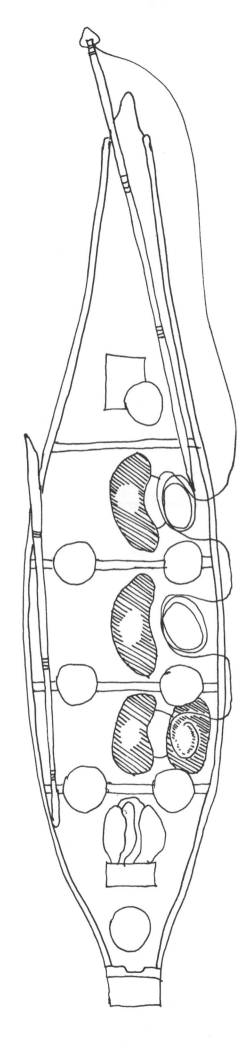

The crew regarded this as a sign of some error in their preparations. As the whale tired and surfaced, the crew would make attempts to turn it around by poking its head or eye with a shaft. If nothing could be done, the forward paddler on the starboard side used the canoe's lance to slash the main tendons controlling the flukes. The paddler then drove the killing lance under the flipper. The great creature spouted blood and died.

A crewman would then dive into the water and hack holes through the snout and lower jaw so the mouth could be sewn shut. This prevented the dead carcass from filling with water and sinking. Additional floats would also be attached with small harpoons. Then the long tow back to the village began.

The entire tribe responded to the arrival of the whale with the ceremony and celebration of a great religious event. The whale was welcomed by a chorus of tribe members who praised its greatness in song as the chief's wife made offerings of water and eagle down.

The "ceremonial hump", a wide piece of choice meat taken off the back near the fin, was presented to the chief. Considered taboo for eating, this blubber was hung on a rack outside the chief's house and decorated with eagle feathers and down. He also received a small piece of the tail for eating purposes. In order of their supposed "gourmet value" other pieces were presented to visitors, crew members and visitors who assisted in the hunt.

Ritual singing and formal chants of praise to the whale were made in front of the carcass continuously for several days.

Blubber was boiled in wooden boxes and the oil skimmed off for storage in bags made from the whale's stomach and bladders. The meat and blubber were dried, smoked and stored. The bones and waste protions of the flesh were left on the beach for scavengers.

Five days after the hunt a blubber feast was given. Visitors received gifts of choice cuts but neither the chief nor his wife could partake lest their luck in future hunts be affected.

Whaling among the Nootka Indians fell into a decline around 1860, probably owing to the greater attractions of white sealing. However, a revival of Nootkan culture renewed activity early in this century and some west coast tribes were taking the occasional whale as late as 1940. When Phillip Drucker made a study of contemporary Indian whaling in 1951, he found eight remaining whalers on the coast, only two of whom had been successful. One, named Ahousat Amos, had taken one whale and another, Aliyu, had taken three.

It is difficult to say now whether the final demise of the art was a result of the ultimate deterioration of Nootkan traditional culture or of the west coast whale population itself. Perhaps in some cosmically ironic way it was fitting that both hunter and prey fell victim to the age of technology about the same moment in history.

Noticias de Nutka

by Scott Lawrance

Our land was founded as part of an imperial conquest. That is common knowledge, but many of the details of our origins are forgotten. *Noticias de Nutka*, a journal of Spanish botanist Jose Mozino, is an engrossing reminder of part of this story. In the last years of the eighteenth century the

Pacific Coast was still up for grabs. Participating in the treasure hunt were Britain, Spain, Russia, America, and insignificantly, France.

The great showdown came between Britain and Spain arising from a dispute on the West Coast of Vancouver Island, in Nootka Sound, about territorial privilege. A Spanish captain seized British lands and ships and thus began a legal battle between the two countries that was to last for five years. Had history moved differently we may now have been living in Spanish Columbia.

Spain was unique amongst the European powers in its policy of making detailed studies of not only the lands, plants and animals that were discovered for the first time, but also of the people. The Catholic church found knowledge of the native's languages a great asset in winning converts to the faith while the Spanish crown found it profitable to adapt native customs, such as a tribute to the chief, to their own advantage. Spain's scientists were as important to its colonial policy as were the discoverers and explorers themselves.

In 1792, one of Spain's most prominent young scientists, Jose Mariano Mozino, born and raised in Mexico, arrived at Nootka to help determine whether Spain should defend this northern outpost. He rapidly acquired sufficient skill in the Nootkan language to leave us a comprehensive view of the native culture before it was much corrupted by European contact. Up until Mozino's visit, various white explorers including Captain Cook had made observations of the Indians' material culture, making notes on their clothing, their houses, "totem poles" and weapons. The great importance and interest of Mozino's work comes from the fact that he was able to understand not only the material culture and describe it in great detail, but that he explains such things as the native religion, their government and social system.

Doctor Iris Wilson's translation marks the first time that this work has been available to an English speaking public. Her copious footnotes supplement the lack of depth of Mozino's ethnography, working as he was as a pioneer in the studies of other people. For example, rather than examining what he sees as part of an inseparable cultural fabric, things remain separate and unrelated. This academic simplicity is one of the charms of the book. Though trained as a scientist, his contact with the Nootkas is fresh and untainted with a distracting theory. Much of the book is composed of observations that intrigue his more sophisticated eye. "I doubt that they like garlic because, even though they came in their canoes to sell it, it annoyed them greatly to see it on our tables."

Mozino's broad cultural background and connection with the church become readily apparent in the typical tone of this paragraph:

"They are all generally fond of singing, either because the music enters into part of their rituals, or because it constitutes one of the demonstrations of their courtly ceremonies. Their natural voices create the harmony in unison on the octave. They are accompanied in place of bass, by a noise which the singers make on some boards with the first solid object they find, and by some wooden rattles whose sound is similar to that of the Mexican ayacaztles (Aztec gourd rattles.) One of the singers constantly gives the tone and all the others follow it successively, forcing their voices unevenly, in almost the same manner customary in the Gregorian chant of our churches."

In similar depth and style he treats such things as whaling practices, women's puberty ceremonies, house building, poetry, and class division. As well as the volume of research on the life of the Nootka people, Mozino made a detailed list of unknown plants found in the area, a vocabulary of the language and a thorough history of Europeans in the area. This covers the period from 1775 when Juan Perez first discovered the sound to 1792, when Captain Vancouver met Commander Bodega y Quadra to discuss settlement of the Nootka Sound controversy. Though of course biased to Spain, Mozino is not slow to denounce the actions of Martinez who had through his brutal behaviour precipitated many crises, not only with the British, but also with the Indians. His sound judgement is also apparent in his summation that the Spanish would be best off to vacate the northern post of Nootka to the British or Americans and concentrate on consolidating their position in California, which his government subsequently did.

Whoever ultimately gained the rule of the area, one thing was clear. The Indian's time honoured ways of life were doomed to extinction. The years to come held acquiescence to the whites at the very least and genocide at the worst. Mozino, just one actor in this process, enables us to see what was destroyed and gives hints about now cultures change generally, wherever they are. His journal at once announces the death knell of a culture and nurtures a vision of its reality. It remains for us one of the innumerable possibilities of man's existence which have flourished and failed on this planet, a victim to a "superior" technology.

Jose Mariano Mozino *Noticias de Nutka* translated by Dr. Iris Higbie Wilson, McClelland and Stewart Ltd., Toronto, 1970

Union Steamships' *S.S. Comox,* docked at Irvine's Landing in 1911

Pender Harbour: A Steamer Stop

by Jackie Holecka

In motion past a dome of grey granite, gnarled runt of fir tree there, a sign on it weathered and silvered, CABLE, foot high letters. Rounding the point, eye moves with the ship, the outlines of a sheltered bay unfold. On a hill above the beach, in a clearing won by bucksaws from the fir forest, sit several silver storage tanks - oversized upright kitchen cannisters. A large building framed against the bluff below advertises its use across its roof of red - STORE. The foot of a pier rests here and strides on creosote piles some way into the bay. The T-shaped end of the wharf and brown metal roof shed are transfigured by nets of light cast by the sun on sea. Small ramp slants to float bobbing cedar logs and planks speckled with caulk boot spike marks.

Scattered around the bay, more buildings, some perched on brush-covered shoreline, some strung-out over the water on deeply imbedded piles, heron-like habitations govering over tides. A dingy cod boat labours across the foregound, its Easthope engine sluggishly sputtering, wheezing and coughing its way toward open sea. Oil smell, trail of smoke.

This scene could be any one of many. The coastal stops of Union Steamships were as alike as railroad stations on the endless CPR prairies. The communities all shared the coastal forest, its damp and rampant growth, the constant wash of the changing sea. Refuge Cove, Grantham's Landing, Stuart Island, Cracroft, Halfmoon Bay, Roberts Creek,

Myrtle Point, Irvines Landing, Lund, Blubber Bay. Communities of shared economies, shared ecologies.

The similarity of these ports to railroad stops is strong - links on a chain. Early settlement of the coast took place along the routes of the CPR and Union Steamship lines the way the continent was settled along the narrow band of railway. Economic life centered at freight shed or grain elevator, social life of coming and passing of loved ones at steamer landing or railroad station.

Just as the railroad stops owed their existence to the resources of the prairie, wheat in particular, the steamer landings served pulp mills, or logging operations, or in rare cases mines. These were the coastal camps which died when the resources ran out or no longer brought profit to the Vancouver and Victoria businessmen. The first communities with permanently established families grew up in places like Minstrel Island and Pender Harbour., which were supply centres for varied activities - small logging operations, shingle bolt cutting, canneries and salteries. In these landlocked little centres developed a breed of person and style of life that has now virtually disappeared.

Looking at the small group of communities lying within a few miles of Pender Harbour in the early part of this century, we get a glimpse of that way of life. Lying at the head of a long island dotted fiord, Pender Harbour is now a burgeoning fishing and resort village of over 2,500 people. In the early 1900's however, the village was a much smaller place. A handful of families dominated community life.

In 1905, Pender Harbour, was known as the "Land of Portugese Joe". One of the several Portugese Joes known to B.C.history, Joe Gonsalves and his son-in-law Theodore Dames owned the two large buildings at Irvine's Landing, the first hotel and the saloon. A large house to the rear of these two structures was the home of Dames and his wife.

From all around the harbour, people paddled, rowed, and chugged to Irvine's Landing for business and pleasure. On a steamer day a large crowd would arrive for the socializing which accompanied the arrival of the boat from Vancouver. The baseball games and dances of these days were like large family picnics. Mrs. Dames presided over the gathered celebrants like a benevolent aunt. Only the worship services occasioned by the arrival of Presbyterian minister George Pringle, in his boat "The Sky Pilot", could equal the festivities of the boat welcoming parties.

For years, Pender Harbour was known as "the Venice of the North". Since there were no roads all life was centered on the sea, giving the people a strangely amphibious character. Fishermen and loggers, attracted to the sheltered coves, became the first inhabitants of the area. Like most of the people who settled on the coast, they came because they saw an opportunity to live and raise a family by the work of their own hands. Some families lived on float houses following the fish or logs with the company to new

places of harvest. The standard of living of the early settlers varied greatly but the land was so abundant that everyone was well fed. Deer were shy animals but their curiosity often drew them to the sun-splashed knolls where they were seen. Every bay yielded good fish dinners.

On Francis Peninsula, where the settlers began to acquire land, fruit trees and gardens were planted. Fighting continually with encroaching bush and the stubborn ever-creeping salal, the men and women carved out toeholds on the land and moved away from the float houses.

One of the first families in the area was the Warnocks. They settled in Bargain Harbour around the turn of the century. Martha Warnock, 78, thinks back on those days - "Years back in Pender Harbour there were ever so many logging camps in ever so many bays. Logs everywhere. All logged along the beach. Beautiful big timber everywhere. There were always big booms of logs being made up and anchored in the bays. Nice to see the tugs come in and tow them away. Then about 1914 some fish company, Samson, I think it was, towed a big herring saltery barge up to Donnely's Landing. That's when the herring fleet came to the Harbour. At that time Pender Harbour was polluted with herring. You would be killing them with the oars as you rowed along."

Always a land of abundance, this coast drew white men to it with the whisperings of a promised land, suggestions of a golden profit. With the herring saltery came Scottish fishermen and their families to settle around Whiskey Slough. Naturally they weren't too popular with the old timers, who regarded them as "them bunch over at Hardscratch!" "The Scots were gillnetters," Mrs. Warnock recalled, "and the seiners and handliners figured they just got 'too damn many fish.' There was some justification to the charge, because gillnetting was virtually unrestricted for many years.

Within the community there were always clans and families who became figureheads and mainstays. Their signatures can be read in the place names and geography of the Harbour area. One of these men was John Wray who worked as the government Road Foreman and widened narrow Canoe Pass between Bargain and Pender Harbours which formerly could be navigated only by boats the size of Indian canoes. He was the first white settler in Pender Harbour, arriving with his young family around 1894 after a stay of several years in Vancouver. He had been a schoolmaster in England but wanted to break into the wilds of sea and forest and he became a fisherman in Egmont and then on Nelson Island where he settled permanently.

At the head of Pender Harbour, or Kleindale as it is now called, three brothers, Bill, Charles, and Fred Klein established a logging camp of about 30 men in 1912. Here they cut the original trees of Lumberman's Arch, a monument to the industry in Vancouver's Stanley Park. Unlike many lumber men who stayed in one place only as long as the timber lasted, the Kleins cleared land, dyked saltmarshes and settled permanently in the area.

P.B. Anderson owned another large logging group. It maintained several camps in the Pender Harbour area, one of them over a hundred men. Many others were employed to build a railway line through the forest almost to Halfmoon Bay, traces of which can still be seen.

Though these men lacked female companionship and doubtless spent much of their time and money at the saloon, when the communal gatherings took place you could count on them being there to whup up some fun and games, mixing well with the growing number of families.

Even though it had its divisions, "the Harbour" was a pretty tight little community. Everyone knew everyone else's business in fine detail, and new developments went around at the speed of sound. The local grapevine provided such a comprehensive and colourful communication network none of several attempted newspapers was ever able to compete.

Outsiders, especially "dudes" (city slickers), were considered snooty and treated to a round of rustic put-downs whenever they tried to make conversation. They were kept to their own tables in the saloon and their wives were excluded from the gossip sessions in Portugese Joe's store. The ice might melt a little after ten years, but in some cases twenty didn't help.

Distrust of authority was universal throughout the community. A local would hide his worst enemy from the police without thinking, and if a newcomer were seen getting chummy with a cop his chances of winning acceptance would be set back another decade.

Frank Lee, whose family put ashore on Lee's Bay in 1917 remembers a little Mexican log-pirate who came chugging into the harbour one day with the police boat hot on his

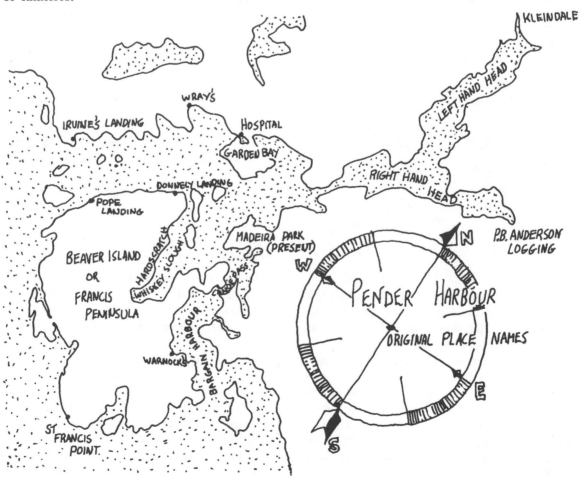

32

tail. Some fishermen pulled his boat into the bush at Farrington Cove and for two weeks the local kids were cautioned by their parents not to speak the fellow's name or cast their eyes in the direction of his hideout. Everyone in the community soon knew, except the police, who finally gave up the search for lack of a lead. The fugutive was then promptly put back in the water and sent on his way.

No one paid attention to hunting restrictions but fishing regulations were a more serious matter. No one agreed with them, but if a man passed up a good catch on their account, he was very concerned that his neighbour did the same. A sunk-netter might be concealed from the government fisheries inspector, but he ran a great risk of being punched out by the village fathers as he attempted to land his ill-gotten catch at the buyer's scow.

Irvine's Landing has the oldest history of the Harbour. Old-timers have vague memories of the first person there being a Chinese who ran a cannery. The landing takes its name from Charlie Irvine, who arrived there about 1880. This pipe-smoking, bearded Englishman sold his small log cabin home and store to John and George West. They in turn sold out to Joe Gonsalves and Theodore Dames in 1904.

Many of the stories about this Portugese Joe disagree but it is certain that he was born in the Madeira Islands and left home as a stowaway while still a young boy. After travelling to many different parts of the world, as all good seamen in those days did, he landed in Vancouver and squatted in Stanly Stanley Park. He moved from there to Irvine's Landing, where he and his son-in-law bought up large tracts of land including the site of Irvine's Landing and Madeira Park, which takes its name from the islands of his birth.

Besides running the hotel with its large dining room and saloon, the post office, and the general store, Joe also traded in fish. He owned a seine boat, "the Hermosa", which was skippered by a black from the Azores. This huge man, Joe Perry, was well liked by the settlers, especially the children who used to sit on his knees and listen to tales of far away ports and islands. Besides running the boat, Perry was Joe's handyman, gardener and bouncer. At the saloon, he enforced Joe's rules, discouraging drunken brawls and making sure the liquor stayed locked up after the men had had enough.

The population was increasing and more families were appearing on the scene. A dogfish oilery and a herring kippery were added to the industries. The Union Steamships called more regularly. By 1929, their visits had increased from once every two weeks to three times a week, or six times if they put in on their return run. Among the boats putting in were the *Chasina*, the *Comox*, the *Lady Cynthia*, *Lady Evelyn* and the *Chelosin*. As time passed new stores were established at Pope's Landing and Donnely's Landing on Francis Peninsula.

"Lady Cecilia" grounded Pender Harbour

Al Lloyd, in his column in the *Peninsula Voice*, gives an idea of the trasportation situation in those times:

"To get out of the Harbour there was the Union Steamship boat sailing south, three times a week, or a fish boat. The choice was more or less yours. The Union boat would phone Bill Matier at Irvine's Landing with an ETA, which was at best an approximation and at worst a downright lie. The Boat mostly got here when it got here. Waiting for hours on the wharf on a hot summer day could and did get pretty tedious. I remember a time when I took a guest over to catch the boat at noon, having previously checked that it was expected about 12:30. We waited for a long while, roasting in the sun, finally I took our guest home for a swim, and then back again to the wharf, another long wait and I took her home for supper, back to the wharf again and the boat finally arrived at 8:30 p.m. Never did have the heart to enquire when it got to town.

"Anyhow the trip could take anywhere from 5 to 10 hours, and it was a brave person who asked friends to meet them at the boat, or made an appointment for the same day.

"The old community hall at Irvines Landing didn't have one parking space," Mr. Lloyd says. "And what's more it didn't need one.

"Local travel was latgely a matter of taking a boat as far as you could and walking the rest of the way.

"Coming home after one of our local 'dos' could be a little hazardous, it was not uncommon for no one to be steering the boat, as the men folk made for the bottle or the babe according to their taste, in the happy illusion that Joe or whoever would see they were busy and would take the wheel.

"There was the very odd car around and a trip to Gibsons and return was a hard days work. The road was mostly a car and a half wide, so you drove down the middle, but traffic was fo sparse that it made little difference. The only blacktop was a couple of blocks in Sechelt, which was so full of sharp potholes that 10 mph was as fast as you dared go.

"All in all, transportation was slow to the point of being leisurely, and the calendar was more useful than the clock. When you went visiting you made a day of it and if the weather turned bad, it might be a night too. This was a pretty nice way of doing things, after all you could read your mail or the paper while you steered the boat, and if you had to wait when you got there, there was no hurry and lots to talk about over a coffee or a beer if you were lucky."

As time passed new stores were established at Pope's Landing and Donelly's Landing on Francis Peninsula. Mr. Lloyd, himself a Pender Harbour storekeeper for many years, remembers what they were like:

"So off to the store. Timing was important as there was not much use going on other than a 'boat day' for anything but staples. You tried to arrive long enough before the boat so that you could have a good visit with other customers before the freight got to the store. You never shopped until the freight got to the store, as you would miss out on the fresh stuff if you did. When you finally got to the shopping, you stood at the counter and called out the items you wanted one by one from the list clutched in your hot little hand, and the clerk climbed shelves, dived under counters, and into the back room to get what you wanted. This was a slow process as each item was written laboriously in your charge bood, or a cash book.

Waitin' at the steamboat dock.

34

"Despite the long delays everyone was quite cheerful and the store would be the scene of endless discussions on the topics of the day.

"Selection was not quite what it is today. Tea was Nabob green label in one or half pound packages, coffee the same, take it or leave it. Fruit was apples, oranges and bananas and very rarely grapes. Vegetables were spuds, onions, cabbage, turnips, and carrots. Tomatoes, lettuce, celery, etc. were only for special occasions like Christmas, and you had to order ahead.

"Most everything was in bulk; even sugar was made up into 2, 5 and 10 pound bags at the store, likewise rice, prunes, and so on.

"By the time the customers were served after the boat came in, the meat, milk, bread and any 'goodies' were all gone and for the next two days you were out of luck for them.

"Your shopping completed and final good-byes said to friends you were faced with getting the groceries, packed in boxes tied with string which fell off as soon as you picked them up, down to the boat and home. Depending on your age and disposition, this you did yourself, or numerous gallant men would carry them down for you. It was not unknown for a wife to be ftruggling down the wharf with a heavy box of groceries while her husband was gaily packing down a light box for some other gal.

"Howeber you got them down, whether by brawn or beauty, the grub was not to be left unguarded; they had to be covered against the rain, but it wasn't always raining. The other hazard was the wily seagull. While you went up for another load, the seagulls would ruin a dozen loaves of bread and a package of hamburger, as well as leaving gooey thank you notes over everything in the boat. You'd never believe how fast those gulls could work until it happened to you.

"Back home, probably wet and cold, knowing the fire would be out in the house, and all you had to do was tie up the boat, get the kids up to the house, back to the boat for the groceriesbefore the gulls got into them, or they dissolved into the bilge. One note of caution, 'Watch the bottom of the box'. Many a load of groceries went into the chuck at the home float, twixt boat and float.

Around 1920, it became obvious that the growing number of children needed a school. Bob Donnely, a local resident, donated his tiny store on Francis Peninsula for that purpose. Children came by boat from all over the harbour, braving the worst types of weather to season their p's and q's with a good dash of seamanship.

Within a few years, the people of the Harbour got together and built another school on the land above the converted store. In their usual enterprising manner they beachcombed the logs for this school and towed them to Vananda sawmill to be cut into lumber. The little school wouldn't hold the ever-increasing number of children and three more were built. The new schools were at Kleindale, Irvine's Landing and Silver Sands.

A picnic party in 1914.

Another big step was made in the early 1930's with the opening of the Columbia Coast Mission Hospital at Garden Bay. The hospital was built by public subscription and the excavation and all preliminary work was done by the citizens themselves.

As the area continued to grow, trails began to connect to different settlements. Then, in the 1930's, the Sunshine Coast Highway was begun. The work was done by some of the men from the armies of unemployed. Stationed at Woods Bay and Silver Sands, working at barely tolerable wage and living standards, they pushed the highway through to Garden Bay and Irvine's Landing by 1936. It remained unpaved until the 1950's

Until this time, Pender Harbour stayed pretty much as it had always been. But slowly, the small logging operations gave way to monopolies and the outlying canneries were shut down in favour of the improved packing boats. Travel had shifted from the water to the land as the road was built and now the pavement accelerated the change. The Union boats lost their reasons for living. They ran now on government subsidies and abandoned their northern ports one by one. No longer was the landing the centre of social and economic life. In 1959, Irvine's Landing finally joined places like Stillwater, Land Bay, and Port Neville, as it lost its service. No longer would the friendly whistle resound through the fir and cedar, or the wake of the large boats wash through the kelp onto rock shores. The community once centered in the presence of these shuttling social clubs was hearing its death-knell.

The centre of Pender Harbour, one time Venice of the North, shifted inland to Madeira Park, while Irvine's Landing slowly drifted into the comfortable obscurity of its past joys, the whispers of celebration and communal work becoming fainter and fainter. With the coming of the road, coastal communities as far north as Lund increasingly became adjuncts to Vancouver, places where the city dwellers could retreat from the hustle of growing city life. Though Pender Harbour still hosts a little fleet of gillnetters and trollers, its future lies in real estate and tourism, dependent on investor's whims and the fortunes of high finance capital. The sense of altruism, simplicity, and generosity of community which characterized the early settlers exists only in the memories and good faith of some of the old-timers.

George Bowering's "George Vancouver"

A few years ago George Bowering wrote his most extensive historical poem, *George Vancouver*. In other places he has drawn from Kwakiutl ceremony and legend and one whole book, *Rocky Mountain Foot* was rooted in the history and geography of southern Alberta. In all these poems, Bowering has been trying to find his place in the history of this land, thinking to find roots without which his life remains unnurtured. He is a poet and a Canadian well worth listening to.

George Vancouver is a series of short poems which finally and vitally link the lives of the explorer and the poet. Both are confronted with new territory, an open frontier, and if either fails in his mission of charting the ground, it will result from the nature of the coast that confronts them.

> *To chart this land*
> *hanging over ten thousand inlets*
> *and a distant mind as of many narrows,*
>
> *an impossible thin -*
>
>   *no music*
> *sounds as many changes with such*
> *common theme.*

This is the problem whether the chart is to be made of the physical coast of this province a search for a waterway to the continent's heart, or the metaphorical coast of the imagination seeking a passage into the continent of the soul, in search of the Grail.

> *The North West Passage*
> *is the waterway*
> *to the Kingdom of God,*
> *the New Jerusalem deep inland*
> *up Cook's River.*

This is the search, emerging, forming and changing, the fancy becoming real and the real fading into dream or memory. It is the charting, by Vancouver on the maps or by Bowering in the poems, that permits a steering through the shoals.

The King has ordered Vancouver to go on a fantastic voyage, to discover a passage which does not exist so as to consolidate his military strength on the coast. There is no such waterway but other discoveries are made on this ship Discovery. Menzies, the botanist, is the practical man, no imagination, who notes with great care and love the plants and animals of the new land, foreshadowing its eventual settlement.

The poet starts on a similarly difficult voyage of discovery. What he seeks is a living history, a sense of his place in the continuum of people who have developed this coast from its beginnings.

I keep losing sight of the subject,
Captain Vancouver seems lost in the poem.

Lost in the trees.
Lost between small islands.
Obscured in the dark Indian house.

I'm looking for Jesus
but my faith needs support

Trusting himself to the Inland Sea,
forgetting stories of the Strait of Anian,
setting foot among actual salmonberries.

It is the reality of the coast that he keeps stepping into, a reality that permits very few of his own fanciful desires to remain. On a waterski trip to Passage Island, "to look for the rumoured snakes / on the island's one acre." all he finds is "washed up Burrard sewage."

But the coast that confronts Bowering and denies him a renewal of faith and defeats his hope of charting a place which he desires does much to show him the scope of human life. It is never a closed thing and the poems lead into many openings, all possible, all real.

The savages, all of us, moving through the ripples of history, the King's fancy thrown like a pebble into the pool of history.

Let us say
this is as far as I, George,
have travelled,

the line
obscured still, the coast
I mean, touched, sighted,
mapped to some extent,
the islands
noted.

Now on this side, east,
it is that much,
water, pines, the Spanish
and their names, the savages
on the edge of the water.

I have seen some
of what lies in the mind,
the fancy of the British king
gone like fish odour
into the life-giving fog of that coast.

The vast range of material assembled in these poems would suffice to recommend it to anyone with an interest in the history of this coast. But it is the poet's coherence that enables us to grasp these facts and relate them to our lives, one way or another. The poets of this country have a lot of singing to do before they become as vital to our culture as Homer to Greece, or Shakespeare to the national pulse of England, but people like George Bowering are making a start.

Bowering, George. **George Vancouver,** published by Weed / Flower Press, 756A Bathurst St., Toronto 179, Ontario. 1970. 39 pp. $2.00.

by Scott Lawrance

Petroglyphs

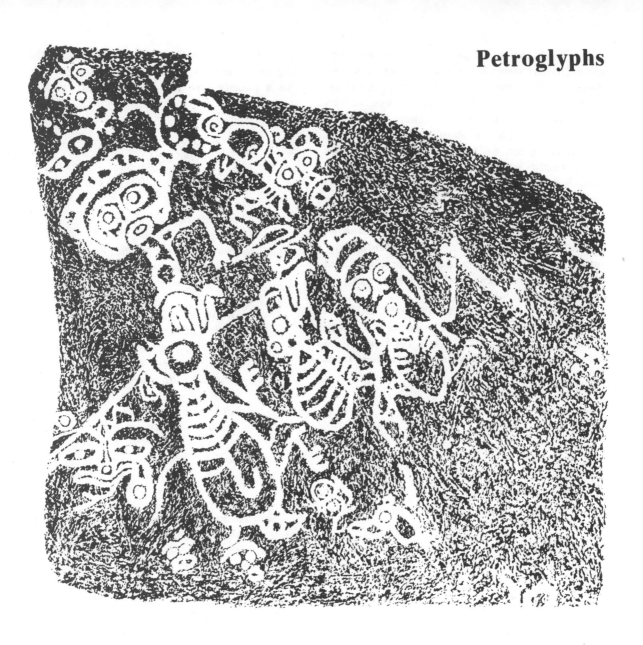

by Scott Lawrance

You round a sweeping curve of beach. The sun is out and glistening on the bay, gulls wheeling and crying in the sky overhead. There, immediately in front of you is a grotesque figure on a rock, composed of swooping lines and a large round head, carved into a large sandstone beach boulder.

The figure is large, maybe two feet long and its lines are cut over an inch deep into the rock. You could be looking at a primitive abstract painting hung in a New York gallery, but this creature stares stonily from a humble chunk of the B.C. Coast.

Here and there, throughout the length of this coast, on storm pounded beaches or in secluded forest haunts where the sun plays hide and seek with shadow, is the rock art of our predecessors in this land. These petroglyphs and pictographs (carvings and paintings) are part of a world wide heritage of primitive art. They are a record of humankind's hopes, fears, and fulfillments before they had a written language, before they had a history.

This art provides access to a world lost to us, subordinated to the implacable demands of civilization. It is the voice of the ancestors of the native peoples of British Columbia, speaking from the time when people and nature nourished each other and formed one body. Their desires and fears were those of the elements. Animals and spirits were as much a part of their body as their blood and moved through their thoughts and lives as they moved across the gulfs and inlets in their dugout cedar canoes.

The myths and legends of the tribal societies of this coast provided the people with a knowledge of who they were and how they could best live in this land. The beings represented in the rock art brought order and meaning into the universe, spreading peace to the hearts of the people. Today, we have lost touch with our history, forgetting the lives of people in other times and places. Such history is the record of what humankind has been and done, and is all we have to show us who we are now and what we might become. Rather than the dates of wars and the names of succeeding kings, history could be the living fabric of our lives, linking us to our vast family, when and wherever it has been born, flourished, and died. Once we forget our history we are as if dead, for our infinitely varied memories become replaced by an inflexible succession of repeated activities, done day to day without giving us any sense of peace or fulfillment.

It is good to begin a search for such meaning by looking at people in a "natural" state, living close to the land, not separated from it by a complex technology. This way of life, the primitive, is the common denominator of human experience. It is here that we find what is essential to being "human". The early dwellers on this coast possessed the requisites for the life of any animal, food, shelter and clothing, but they possessed something more. With art and myth they gained a sense of who and why they were, a sense of connectedness with the life of the world, the universe. Looking at the rock art of these people, we can catch glimpses of that harmony.

Rock art is found throughout the world wherever a place was associated with a surge of power, the voice and presence of supernatural forces. Rocks everywhere have been linked with solidity, permanence and eternity. The sites of rock art have frequently been separated from the daily life of the tribe, given a special, sacred importance. Most people are familiar with the famous Paleolithic cave paintings in Europe, at Lascaux and at Trois-Freres, where one has to crawl on hands and knees for forty-five yards before entering the cavern of the paintings. Caves have often been associated with mystery and reverence, as anyone can understand who has ever entered one. The caves and the drawings are linked in their magic to the deepest and barely formed thoughts of our minds. Early hunters shot arrows and hurled spears at the animal paintings in the caves to give them power in the hunt. They danced for visions of success under the painted eyes of a shaman masked in a stag's skin, the man who knows the secrets of the spirit and animal worlds.

In British Columbia there is a clearly defined culture area running the length of the coast from above the Alaska Panhandle to the Puget Sound area of Washington. The petroglyphs and pictographs in this area may some day provide clues to the migratory routes of the first discoverers, explorers, and settlers of this country. It is the petroglyphs, or rock carvings, that will occupy our attention from here on. Few petroglyphs have been discovered thus far in the interior of the province, probably because at the time of the first carvers, ice and snow from the last great glacial age still covered most of B.C. The interior of Washington is the first area away from the coast where carvings are found. These are a different style than those on the coast and seem continuous with those of the Great Basin area, in Idaho and Utah, home of the Shoshonean peoples. The break from coastal style is abrupt, ending near the mouth of the Columbia.

In the north, the coastal style begins on the Alaskan coast, but no carvings have been found on either the Aleutian Islands or in the interior or Arctic regions of the Eskimaux. These patterns may help answer the questions of primitive migrations that are still unsolved by prehistorians. One thing that is sure is the great antiquity of petroglyphs. This is verified in some areas of North America by the depiction of animals that are now extinct. Some petroglyphs have been done since the coming of the white man, witnessed by the carvings of horses and in one case, a sailing ship.

Sometimes the carvings at one site come from a variety of periods, judging from varying amounts of erosion and different styles. This suggests that the same rocks were regarded as locations of spiritual power over many generations. Many rocks which appear to have good working surfaces have been passed over in favour of the particular sites used. At Port Neville, near Port Hardy, are three distinct styles, varying greatly in age.

The location of the vast majority of petroglyphs on the coast provides some clues to their age. Many of the carvings found on beaches lie at least twelve feet below the high tide level so the artist would have had to be constantly interrupting his work for the tide. It is more likely that tidal fluctuations have raised the tide levels well above where they once were. Geological surveys indicate that there were world tidal fluctuations several times within the possible time span of the petroglyphs, some occuring two, three, and four thousand years ago, consistent with the melting of glaciers and snow caps which permitted deeper access to the interior of the continent by the first hunters.

Surveys on this coast have revealed that 8,000 years ago the tidal level was fifteen feet lower than today, but it is doubtful that the carvings are quite that old. Dating by location is complicated by the fact that forces of erosion have dropped many of the carvings nearer the water than they originally were, having been undermined and slipped down.

In some places, such as at Sproat Lake, the artist either had to stand in a boat or else erect a complex wharf and stage from which he could carve his work, which sits on a cliff face seven feet above the water. At some places in North America, the carvers have gone to considerable trouble to give the carvings an impressive, inspiring position. One can imagine them working on stages high on a cliff face, pecking at the granite or basalt with their quartz and chalcedony tools, and rubbing wet sand into the grooves with sticks to smooth the line, sweat running down their faces as they sought to give form to the forces which shared their lives. At Lake Chelan the petroglyphs are thirty feet above the water. At some sites the artist may have climbed to his carving on stone wedges driven into the wall. Other places, he used nature's helping hand, climbing columns of scree and talus to the site. After the carving was finished he removed the crumbled rock or let the rains and winds carry it away.

Neither present day Indians nor the informants of the first anthropologists have been able to tell us anything of either these methods or the meaning of the petroglyphs. According to the Kwakiutl, visited by Franz Boas in the early 1900's, the carvings were made before the animals were turned into humans. Other tribes of North America had created mythologies and gods to explain the existence of the carvings, ascribing to them a supernatural origin.

In accordance with this, some petroglyphs were said to be describing destined events of the future, for example, the coming of the white man. The sailing schooner carved at Cape Avala, in Washington could have had such a function, but it is likely that the shamans who interpreted these carvings were also the ones who carved them. There is, however, a singular lack of caucasian elements in the petroglyphs suggesting that the most recent of them are no later than 1800.

Whatever function the carvings had, oracular ceremonial or magical, it is clear that they were never the work of "doodlers", as was once suggested. The pioneer Mr. Sproat said of the petroglyphs beside the lake which now bears his name that they were "nothing more than the crude representations of a natural event that impressed itself strongly on the imagination of the natives."

It is important to remember that the peoples of the petroglyphs lived in a substantially different universe than we do and that we should be very reluctant to attribute our motives to their actions. In a world in which all activity is ritually defined and sanctified, where there is no "leisure time" as we know it, it is highly unlikely that these people had any idea of "doodling".

The time and labour required for the carving speaks eloquently for seriousness and purpose of the petroglyphs. Perhaps several generations of shamans worked at the same site, carving figures which one man would never be able to complete, or see finished in his lifetime. The similarity of style and motif over large areas of the coast also suggest that the carvers were working out of a particular cultural context. The "cannibal spirit" of Bella Coola bears a striking resemblence to that at Yaculta Bay, some 200 miles distant. The spirit and animal figures, sometimes clan symbols, and the geometric patterns of circles and dots all show a great range and common elements. Personal guardian figures show the greatest disparities from area to area.

Also, there is a rather distinct and uniform style found only in Southern Vancouver Island, notably at Naniamo and Sproat Lake. Whatever the style, the carvers favoured similar sites the length of the coast. Many of the carvings are on prominent headlands, high cliffs, commanding wide and generous expanses of sea, islands, and coastal mountains, giving them a sense of majesterial power and beauty. Other sites are equally impressive but in a much different way. They are hidden away in quiet secluded groves of the forest, sometimes beside pools or small streams. Here, the shaman and his initiates could fast and commune with the spirit beings far away from the profane activities of everyday life.

These sites acted as centers of power and cohesion, not unlike Canterbury or Jerusalem, drawing to themselves shamans and carvers for generation after generation. Though the rock itself may have originally been the subject of devotion, or the place, they have been sanctified and given meaning by the carvings, which represent the spirits which inhabit the place. A man would go alone to one of these sites where the gods of the sky, the demons of the sea, forest and earth entered into the world of men. Man would meet all the beneficient and destructive forces of the cosmos; all the helpful and malevolent beings of his dreams would meet him here. These sites functioned as the center of the world, the sacred places where life was charged with power and meaning. They were the places where man could feel his life and the life of his tribe blessed by the powerful forces of the land and sea.

We can see this functioning well into the nineteenth century in the puberty rites of Quinault Indian boys on the Olympic Peninsula. They would retire to secluded places where they painted pictographs of the sea monsters they had met in their visions. Sea monsters, along with snakes and and dragons, represent primordial and chaotic forces wherever they are found. With the Quinault,

they are linked to the onrush of sexuality during adolescence which must be directed to the goals of the tribe to maintain the order of the universe. To paint these forces gives the youths magical power over them through appeasement or coercion and protects them from the disintegrative aspect of sexuality.

In the winter ceremonies of the northern tribes, youths are abducted from the village by the secret societies. They may have been taken to petroglyph sites to come in contact with the spirit powers resident there, and to undergo a spiritual rebirth into the society. Shamans were recruited and initiated in the same way. Some of the body painting used in the ceremonials is found carved into the rocks.

Another possible function of the petroglyph sites was as an aid to hunting; the hunter appealing to the spirit of the animal to come near his spear, or invoking its population to increase so the people would not go hungry in the winter. Such motivations were clearest among the paleolithic tribes of Europe where marks of arrows were found in the paintings.

At many sites, bowls are carved into the rock alongside the carvings. At pictograph sites they were used for mixing paint. At petroglyph sites they are either for sacrificial offerings or represent the world axis, a passage from a former world to the present, through which the ancestors arrived long ago. The pueblo people of the southwestern U.S.A. call these holes sipapu. They are carved in the floor of the kiva or ceremonial house where they represent the center of the universe.

At many of the sites is a design composed of an encircled dot, known as the "eye". It is possible that this design also represents an earth center, as may a spiral design that is found from place to place. It is important to remember this sanctifying sacred character of the sites, which are the places that order enters the world to impregnate it with power.

One of the truly amazing things about living in British Columbia is our accessibility to a natural area where less than two hundred years ago people lived and loved in what amounts to a different universe. That universe did not end with the death of the old shamans but stays alive wherever we acknowledge the power of the elements and partake of them as essential to our well-being. The sacred places of the first inhabitants are still accessible to our reverence though thousands of years have passed since they were carved. Some sites have been defaced by vandals who lack a living connection with the land and seek to immortalize themselves by carving their initials and graffiti in immortal art. Erosion, too, has taken its toll of petroglyphs, but the carvings at most sites are still clear.

The petroglyph trail of B.C. is part of a cultural area extending from coastal Alaska to the mouth of the Columbia River. The British Columbian petroglyphs begin in what is now Tshimshian country, the north coast area of the Skeena and Nass Rivers. Many of these northerly sites are remote and guides are necessary to find them.

In this area, the ardent seeker will find sites near Metlakatla, on Ringbolt Island in the Kitselas Canyon of the Skeena, at Gold Creek, on Pitt Island in Grenville Channel, and on the Nass River, near both Canyon City and Greensville (Lackalzap). Near Prince Rupert, on Robertson Point, is an intaglio carving of "the-man-who-fell-from-heaven". This carving the entire body of which is carved deeply into the rock, represents one of the ancestors of a creation myth. At Kispiox is a slab on which is carved several large and unmistakable mosquitos, testament to that very noticeable animal hundreds of years ago. Today, there is a Mosquito clan of Tshimshian Indians, whose ancestors may have carved the rock.

Moving south into Kwakiutl and North Salish country the petroglyph hunter enters his most bountiful fields. There are more sites in the area of Bella Bella and Bella Coola than in any equivalently sized area on the coast. The watchful observer may be able to detect an interesting difference between the carvings on the coast itself and those found further inland, toward the heads of the inlets. There, life was somewhat harsher as the winters were colder and the salmon did not run as prolifically as on the coast.

Some of the more noteworthy sites here are on Meadow Island, Return Passage, and Namu Lake. The site on Meadow Island is remote and hidden, requiring a guide to show the way. This is one of the carvings accompanied by a stone bowl. At Return Passage, the carvings are located below high tide line on a wooded point jutting into the inlet. There are representations of human figures, fish, spirits, and masks, similar to those in the Bella Coola canyon. Halfway up the north shore of Namu Lake is a petroglyph telling the story of a grizzly bear hunt. A canoe loaded with four men returns with only one, a typical ending for the four brothers of many a northern tale.

At Elcho Harbour in Bella Coola country is the "cannibal spirit". This is very similar to a carving which is located at Cape Mudge

in the Gulf of Georgia. Harlan Smith, one of the early anthropologists working on this coast with Franz Boas for the Smithsonian Institute, suggested that this was an important site to the members of the Hamatsa society. Here, the novice would be initiated into the ritual of symbolic cannibalism and thereafter participate in the colourful winter ceremonies. The Hamatsa ceremony suggests the acknowledgement of powerful forces and channeling those forces for the social good.

Other sites are found at the mouth of the Nootasum River and in the Bella Coola River canyon. One of the latter is about a mile south of the bridge on the Mackenzie Highway over the river. It is a large granite dome almost completely covered with figures, a fantastic work which must have required many generations of carvers.

On the Queen Charlotte Islands, Haida country, there is only one known site. Consisting of human heads and mask faces, it is about a mile from Skidegate. Questioned in 1900, the local inhabitants had no idea of its origin or meaning.

The sites in the southern Kwakiutl territory around Fort Rupert were some of the first investigated by Boas and the white anthropologists, in 1897. There are two groups of carvings near Fort Rupert, one is three-quarters of a mile down the beach from the old fort site, the other is immediately in front

of it. Both groups consist of a series of faces, free-flowing, dynamic and alive. They abstract the faces into fields of energy rather than depict them naturalistically. In the same style is the large Cluxewe stone which was literally fished from the mouth of the Cluxewe River by two seiners. This stone is carved into a head with sharp, intriguing features. It was possibly a totem stone in a ceremonial canoe, lost in a storm or fight.

On the West Coast of Vancouver Island, Nootkan country, are four sites which blend well with the rugged beauty of the open Pacific Coast. At Nootka, there are two human figures, one male and one female. Unlike most petroglyphs, these two are outlined with a double peck line. They seem lifelike, perhaps happy with their long life together. Between Wickaninish and Florencia Bays, there is the carving of a whale at Quisitis Point. The whale is chasing a smaller fish. South of Barkeley Sound there are two sites located on the West Coast Trail. The first is in a cave at Pachena Point, near the beginning of the trail, and the second is further south at Clo-oose. There several seabirds, perhaps puffins, quietly observe the changes being wrought in their environment

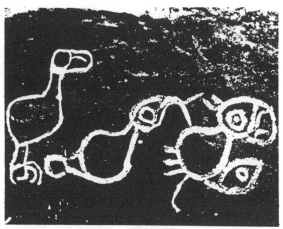

by huge logging companies.

Back in the Salishan country of the Gulf of Georgia, sites dot many islands and run the length of the east coast of Vancouver Island. Once south of the intricate labyrinth of islands and passages which terminates at about Desolation Sound, there are no petroglyphs on the mainland until nearly into Washington.

One of the most interesting sites in the Georgian Salish area is a Port Neville. On a large dome of bedrock granite on the west side of Robber's Nob, there are three distinct styles. It is a protected site, so the carvings have suffered little from erosion. The oldest style, known by its deep, smoothly incised line, is similar to that at Cape Mudge, a little to the south. A more recent but more primitive style is marked by the roughness of its line. Finally, there is what has become known as the "northern" style. This shows a greater concern for form and symmetry than the two preceding styles. It is thought to be the antecedent of the typical North Coast style of the Kwakiutl and Tshimshian. A good example of this is the expressive "deer's head" with its large round eyes and open mouth. One senses the reverence held for the deer by the carver and his deep love for the spirit of the animal. At this site are many geometric designs. There are three simple circles, two of them bisecting, which seem to have been done by the same person who carved the deer. One could speculate for many hours on the meaning of such symbols. Perhaps they represent the union of man and woman, or earth and sea, which bring forth the creatures of the world.

Cape Mudge and the village of Yaculta has the greatest number of carvings at a single site. Two hundred yards north of the village along the beach are twenty six boulders all carved with at least one figure. The rocks are covered at high tide and heavy storms have battered many of the carvings badly. Still to be made out are a great variety of humanoid

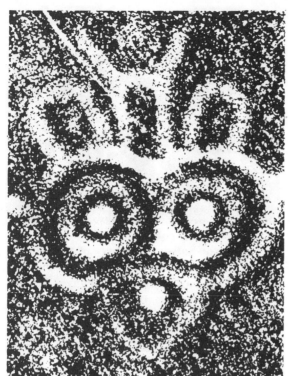

spirit figures and spirit being heads, mask faces, peck marks, and one lone bird figure. One rock has been carved into a bowl. The peck markings are similar to whose found along some South American rivers and on the Amur in Siberia. Merely dots chipped in the rock, they may represent in some places the faces of the ancestors.

The Cape Mudge band has recently received a government grant to enable them to move their petroglyphs away from the destructive effects of the weather. They will be housed in a shelter in the village itself, safe from both natural elements and vandals Hopefully the removal from the natural setting will not detract from their beauty.

On both Quadra Island and Cortes Island there are carvings which have suffered from vandalism. On Cortes, midway between Smelt Bay and Manson's Landing, is a large whale or fish over which an early settler carbed his name and whose lines are partly obscured by mortar. On Quadra, there are carvings at Francesco Point, the site of an old Indian summer village, and a half mile north of the point, at dogfish bay. There, a sea serpent gazes wistfully out to sea.

Further down the Straight of Georgia are the numerous and delightful carvings of Yellow Rock. Just south of Deman Island, these petroglyphs are carved near the lighthouse. There are figures of whales and fish, birds, suns and stars, spirits and humans, both full figure and mask, There seem to be two different styles here. On the western part of the rock the human figures have square or round heads with rectangular

closed bodies, while those on the east side lack a line outlining the trunk, similar to the figures on war clubs collected by Franz Boas on the West Coast. The faces of the Western group are stylized with large ringed eyes with eyebrows connected to the nose and lacking mouths. Those on the east are pictorial with distinct eyes, nose and mouth. Some of the figures have arms attached directly to the heads like some of the masks used in the Kwakiutl Hamatsa ceremonial. One face, with a bump or tusk on the forehead, is reminiscent of a mask used in Fort Rupert ceremonials.

On Hornby Island, there are four sites, all near Whaling Sation Bay. One of the most striking petroglyphs of the coast is found on the east coast of Vancouver Island a bit to the south of Parksville. On exposed bedrock near the top of the Englishman River gorge is a bear whose free and flowing lines make him unique. He is the only figure on the coast who is carved in profile rather than fullface frontally. Truly majestic, this must be an exceptional piece of primitive art anywhere.

Somewhat further south, Nanaimo appears to be the site of a shaman's centre. At Petroglyph Park, two miles south of the city on a ridge near Chase River are many carvings done in a style which is unique to the southern part of Vancouver Island. They are highly stylized and non-naturalistic. They are pecked and abraded into the rock, cut deeply from one to two inches. Represented here are humans, halibut and other fish, a crab-like animal and several canine figures. The site is inscribed with a series of bisecting lines up to 40 feet long. These suggest a primitive map or maze, perhaps symbolic of spiritual journeys in the land of the spirits.

Also in the Nanaimo area are carvings on Harewood Plain and on private land owned by the Monsells of Wilkinson Road. On the plain is the carving of a dancing man and a snake. This suggests parallels with both the snake dancing cult of Washington and of various tribes in the American Southwest. There is also a unique hermaphroditic figure, with hair on the right side of its head, a female breast on the right side, and male genitals. Many tribes used hermaphrodites as shamans, feeling that a person who combined the traits of both sexes could more readily understand the secrets of the world.

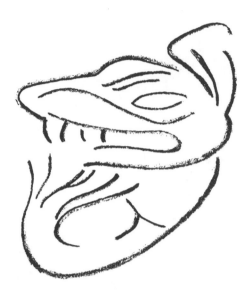

The carvings on the Monsells property were not discovered until 1969, when clearing on the land revealed thirty-two glyphs. Some of these are phallic and several of the human figures wear headdresses. All the carvings are free-form, expressing great movement. Another carving from the Nanaimo area now resides in the Nanaimo Town Museum. Jack's Point Rock, named after where it was discovered, is the same style as the Petroglyph Park carvings. It represents several fish, a flounder, a spring, dog, humpback and coho salmon. In one part of the carving can be seen the beak of a pelican. Local legend explains that it was erected by a shaman after his daughter was turned into a dog salmon.

In the same style are the carvings on Sproat Lake, not far from Port Alberni. The petroglyphs are on the eastern shore, near the southern outlet, seven feet above the surface of the lake.

This is one of the first carvings recorded in anthropological texts. The figures represent fish and sea monsters and are similar to the Nanaimo petroglyphs in that their bodies contain many incised lines, perhaps representing ribs or digestive organs, not unlike the depiction of animals in the Kwakiutl style, which always seem to see through the skin of the animal. One of the figures resembles Haietlik, a monster used like a javelin by Thunderbird, to spear whales. Unfortunately, part of the carving has been cleft by a deep fault, which has destroyed some of the figures.

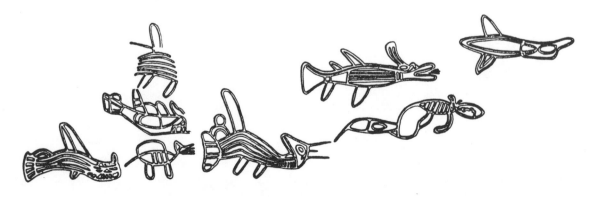

The last large site in southern B.C. is at Kulleet Bay in Ladysmith. On the north side of the bay, between Deer Point and the head of the bay, some thirty yards into the bush is a remote shaman's site. There, on a sandstone ledge, are twenty-one figures: humans, shrimp, birds, fish, and a frog-man. On the south shore, two miles from the head of the bay, is a figure of the rain god, spectacularly alone on a single sandstone boulder. Further south still, there are petroglyphs on Salt-spring Island near Fulford Harbour and at Centennial Park on the Isabella Point Road. On the mainland, though some distance from the coast, is a petroglyph at Doctor's Point on Harrison Lake known as Kaiyama, or "little doctor". His body is the same shape as the power boards of the Central Puget Sound Indians.

With a little patience, perseverance, and a "little help from our friends", anyone can see these carvings in their natural surroundings. They should be viewed as far as possible in a mental state uncluttered by the worries of home or office or workshop, letting the power of the place gently pervade one's being. Care should be taken to disturb the sites as little as possible, mentally or physically. The spirits are apt to frown on those who leave disposable bottles and cans as offerings.

The sites should be regarded as pages in a book open to whoever is fortunate enough to live on this frontier and willing to take the time to seek them out. There we will find not museum piece curiosities, but a record of humankind's history. If we see what we have lost we may come to question what we have gained. The petroglyphs are as much a part of our history as the balls that James Douglas used to throw in Victoria for the officers of the British Navy, or as the rush to carve open the ground and haul gold out in Barkerville, or our present pillage of the wilderness to provide power to American cities, metal and oil to American cars, and wood for Japanese sawmills. We know what today's life is composed of. Perhaps these ancient rock carvings will give us a glimpse at a world we still have much to learn from.

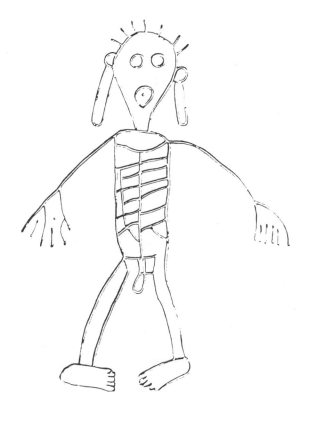

Afterword - Much of the meaning of each carving must remain for some time little more than speculation. The great antiquity of the pieces makes it impossible to state with scientific accuracy much more than their location and appearance. Those wishing an excellent account of the sites, with a good many otherwise unavailable photographs and good working bibliography, are directed to Ed Meade's *Indian Rock Carvings of the Pacific Northwest*, published by Gray's, in Sidney, B.C.

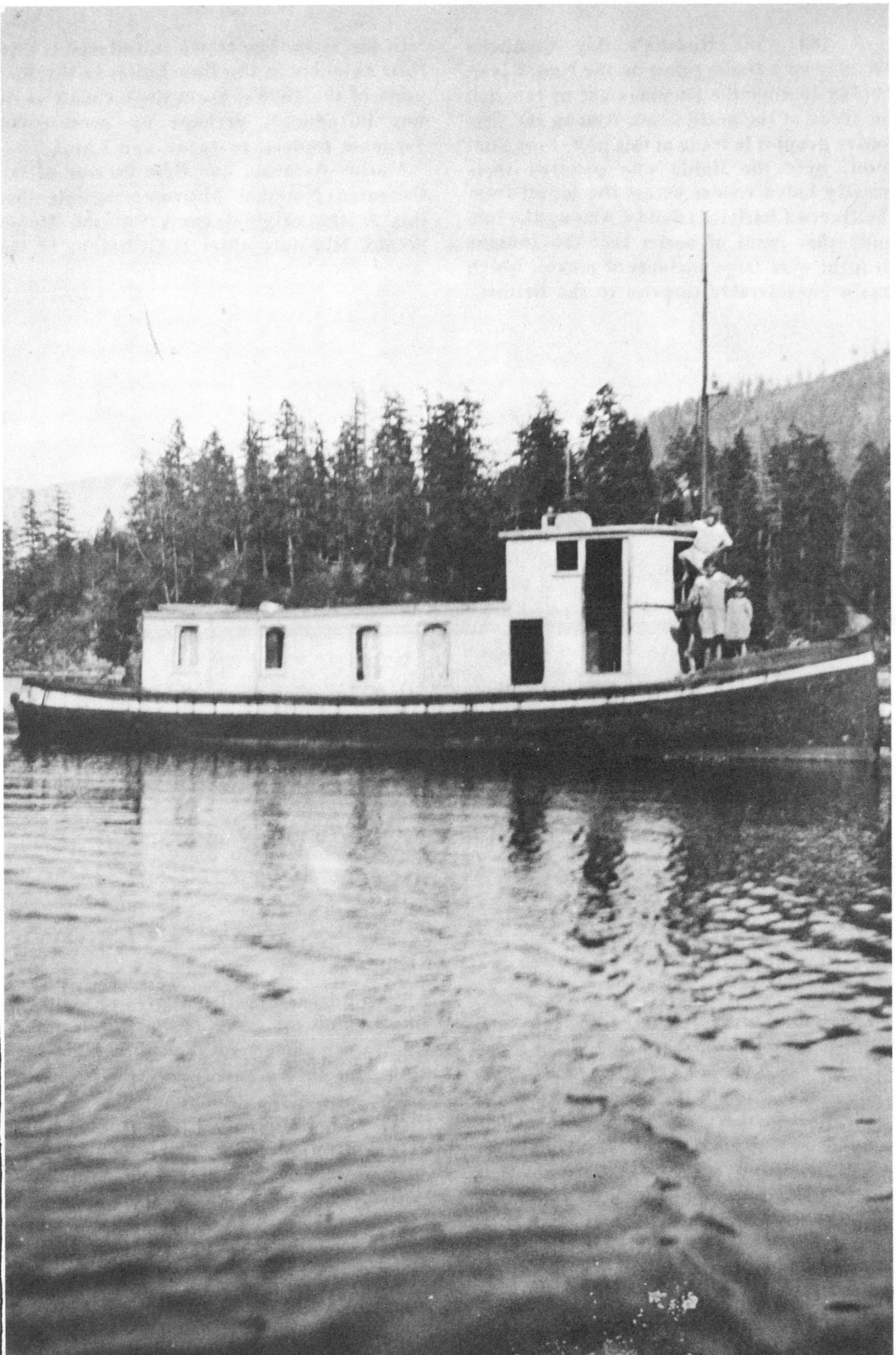

The Haida Potato

by Scott Lawrance

In 1831, the Hudson's Bay Company established a trading post on the Nass River, hoping to edge the Russians out of the rich fur trade of the north coast. Among the first native peoples to trade at this post, Fort Simpson, were the Haida who paddled their heavily laden canoes across the sound from the Queen Charlotte Islands. Among the furs and other items of barter that the Indians brought were large amounts of potato, which was a considerable surprise to the British.

into Malaysia. The Dutch introduced it into their colonies in the East Indies in the first years of the 1600's. From these countries, it was introduced, perhaps by ocean-going Japanese traders, to Japan and China.

Marius Barbeau, one time curator of the Canadian National Museum, suggests that this is the original source of the Haida potato. Old-time chief H.F.Clinton, of the

The potato was discovered by the early Spanish explorers in the highlands of South America, in Peru and Chile. Christopher Columbus had found the sweet potato under cultivation in the West Indies and brought samples back to court with him in 1493. The potato itself was brought back to Spain, where it was to be cultivated, no later than 1570. In the years between 1570 and 1830, the potato followed a long land and sea route around the world to arrive again in the hemisphere of its discovery.

It was taken by Spanish and Portugese colonists through Africa, India, and out to the Far East, where it was introduced by Spain into the Phillipines, and by Portugal

Kitka'ata tribe, recalled stories of his tribal elders about the early days of Haida travel. Once, when a band was out fishing, they were blown far to sea and finally discovered an island where the inhabitants ate maggots (rice) and were called Kakayoren. These strange people took the Haida in and taught them new ways, one of which was the cultivation of the potato, which they brought back with them and cultivated when they returned home. Thus, sometime between 1600 and 1800, unwitting Haida explorers were plying the waves of the North Pacific in their dugout cedar canoes, weaving a mystery for the British at Fort Simpson which would leave them scratching their heads for many days.

A B.C. Leper Colony

by Ed Starkins

D'Arcy Island is a small, evergreen covered point of land lying among numerous islands which are scattered like pieces of an unassembled jigsaw puzzle between the Saanich Peninsula and the mainland. The island is not usually regarded as one of the more northerly Gulf Island group but as part of a vague Canadian continuation of the U.S.-owned San Juan archipelago.

Bordered on three sides by a rocky, inaccessible shoreline, D'Arcy Island gives no outward sign that it once was a colony for victims of one of mankind's most horrifying diseases.

From 1884 to 1925, D'Arcy Ispand was a government leper station.

Although leprosy is popularly regarded as a foreign affliction which is unknown in North America, there have been sporadic cases of the disease in Canada and the United States. For example, there are around 1,000 known cases in the United States and 150 in Canada at the present moment.

Around the turn of the century, the Canadian government maintained "lazarettos", as they were then called, (the modern equivalent is "leprosarium") in Tracadie, New Brunswick and on D'Arcy Island.
young
Island's lazaretto were Chinese immigrants who had apparently become affected in the Orient where leprosy was widespread. When Ernest Hall and John Nelson wrote an 1898 pamphlet on the island, there were also white patients who probably were exposed to the disease in Asia or Africa.

In their short stay on the island, Hall and Nelson noted that the lazaretto was less of a hospital than a quarantine station. The situation was apparently unchanged in 1905 when C.J. Fagan, secretary of the Provincial Public Health Commission, visited D'Arcy Island.

"There is no pretension made to give medical treatment," he wrote in a report to the British Columbia Legislature. "There is no effort made to relieve pain," Fagan added.

Beyond generous supplies of food, there was no nursing care or unusual provisions for the lepers at all.

Fagan recommended "that an effort be made to send the patients to some place where regular and systematic treatment is given." In the dry language of his report, there is compassion but only passing reference to the extreme pain which the more severe cases must have endured and to the general horror of the patients' lives.

Of the six patients on D'Arcy Island in 1905, Fagan wrote that "two are in the advanced stage of the disease, and are indeed pitiable sights, both eyes in one case are attacked, and the pain, now considerable, is bound to increase as time goes on."

Fagan noted that the island had six small cabins with verandahs to house the lepers. Each cabin had a bed, a chair and a stove.

The government apparently failed to take Fagan's recommendations although some effort at providing a nurse was made a few years later. In Fagan's day, none of the moderately effective modern drugs such as the sulfone compounds were available, but remedial chemicals such as chaulmoogra oil were widely used. There is no evidence any of these treatments were ever employed on D'Arcy Island.

Because of the government policy of rapid and complete quarantine of cases, the incidence of leprosy in Canada fortunately grew smaller until, in the 1920's only one young man remained on the island.

In 1925, the leper station was closed and the sole inhabitant transferred to the new station at Bentinck Island, 12 miles from Victoria.

In 1947, one writer could say that a "black aura of gloom" lay over D'Arcy Island because local people apparently avoided it without exception. It has been 45 years since the last sufferer from leprosy resided on D'Arcy Island and many people now are unaware that the place was ever used as a "lazaretti". Uninhabited in the winter, D'Arcy has lately been the summer home of young persons camping out amid its heavily forested reaches. The gloom seems to have at last departed.

They Don't Make 'em Anymore Dept.

This column of personalities significant to the story of the B. C. Coast, will be a regular feature of Raincoast Chronicles. If you know someone who should be here, get busy and write it up, or if you prefer, gather the information together so we can write it up.

The subject may be famous or unknown, male or female, dead or alive, animate or inaminate. For a finished piece we'll pay $25, for unfinished $10.

We are starting off with a visit to Pender Harbour pioneer Martha Warnock, who is an interviewer's dream: her memory is as clear as a mountain stream, her language is rich, and she doesn't have to be asked anything twice. She begins on her own:

"Dear Book,

"As to gathering all my memories of the old Pender Harbour days from July 4, 1909, on our arrival at what is known as Earl's Cove today ...

"My father, William F. Rouse, in his late sixties, was forced to quit work on account of his health. He was head feeder in smelter work. He decided to buy this small forty foot steam tug, sold our nice house in Ladysmith, loaded all our belongings aboard the tug. We pulled out July 2nd for our new destination. After a very frightening trip across the gulf we sighted land which was St. Francis Point, known as Francis Peninsula today, and then passed Pender Harbour and continued up Agamemnon Channel and landed at this deserted log cabin. ...no windows or doors... at Earl's Cove. When we finally seen our new home we all felt terrible upset. You could hardly see it for ferns and bushes. Our first night we put all our mattresses in a row on the floor. In those days there were plenty of deer, grouse, cougars, bear and fish. That night a cougar almost got our dog, Shepherd. We could hear cougars killing fawns on the bluff and in the woods. That put the fear into us kids and Mother. On the third day we got some boards and blankets and nailed them over the doors and windows to keep the wild animals out, so we thought.

"About ten days after we finally got settled we took our first trip down to Irvine's landing to shop and get our Post Office address. What a small settlement it was - a few houses, a hotel and a Post Office and store and a couple of small cabins. But we were glad to meet the people as we were so isolated at home."

William and Maryann Rouse and their family of eight stayed in Earl's Cove for a little over three years before they hooked the family tug to their float house and towed it down to Bargain Harbour where they had purchased 12 acres for a permanent home. Mr. Rouse was a beachcomber. Maryann Rouse had been a midwife in Vananda, Texada Island and continued the practice in Pender Harbour.

"Mother delivered around forty babies here - never lost a case. There was no nurse or doctor to help her. She got $15 and spent two weeks with each case."

In 1912, after a three-year courtship, Martha Rouse married Martin Warnock.

"Martin and I first met in 1908. Martin was working on boats at the time. He had worked on several CPR boats and about five tugs. Oh yes! We went to Victoria for a four-day honeymoon. We came back on the Union Boat *S.S. Comox*. We were on our way to the P.B. Anderson logging camp where Martin worked on the mainland across from Flat Island (Harness Island). The captain and crew of the Comox waited until I got aboard the camp boat, then cut into a 50-pound bag of rice - poured the whole sack on Martin and I. They bailed rice out of that boat for months after."

For several years Martin held various jobs ... logging, trapping and beachcombing, and the Warnocks lived in a float house in various places. By this time they were well started on their family of nine children. Finally they bought their present property on Bargain Harbour. Martha Warnock still lives in the house her husband built at that time. It was around this time that Martin started fishing.

"He fished at every kind of fishing and packing for about forty-eight years."

After moving to Bargain Harbour the Warnock family worked together and except for staples managed to live off the land. Martin fished in the summer and later on built his own sawmill which he worked in during the winter. Sounds a bit like the land of milk and honey, but it wasn't all that sweet. The family worked hard. The boys worked in the garden—a very large one. Anyone who has cultivated a garden at the edge of the coastal forest knows how much stamina that takes. There were numerous chores to keep them busy. The girls helped their mother in the house and the end of summer would find them in the kitchen putting down boxes of

canned goods for the winter ahead. The War-nock's planted a number of fruit trees.

The hardness of the life taught them to count things closely. When their chickens were laying well they sold the surplus and according to one former customer Martha sized every egg and pencilled an individual price beside it on the carton. Another neighbour tells of the time he was helping Martin seine herring when a tourist came by and bought five dollars worth over the side. The help was puid on a share basis and when the cheques were made up weeks later each deckhand received a dollar for the tourists's boxful beside his several hundred for the regular load.

"Finally came the day we had to get a school in Pender Harbour. Then the battle began. Where was the new school to be built? Donnely's Landing won out, as it was the most central place for all the children. This is where my husband came in with our forty-foot boat *Luella May*. He beachcombed the logs, towed them all up to Vananda sawmill to be cut and then towed them back to Donnely's Landing. A big building bee was formed. Our family, all of Hardscratch, and the Klein families came to carry the lumber up that hill. All the ladies brought lunches and coffee and within a short time the school was built. Short time after that it was burnt down on a Saturday night. So, we repeated the whole process and built another school in the same place."

For years Pender Harbour was called the "Venice of the North" because all travel was done by boat. Martha remembers those days vividly.

"I used to have quite a time with that old Canoe Pass! No roads or trails. In all kinds of weather when Martin was away I had to take all my kiddies with me and hurry over and back oo Irvine's Landing for my mail, then to Donnely's Landing for groceries and then row like mad to get back into Bargain Harbour before the tide got too low in the pass. Many a time we had to get out of the boat and pull and tug it all the way through."

As the Warnock boys grew they went fishing with their father and gradually became fishermen in their own rights. Ed, Bill, and Jim Warnock own some of the sturdier boats of the Pender Harbour fleet today. There were two other boys. Malcolm was lost by drowning when he was three years old. Fred Warnock, also a fisherman, died in his thirties. There was quite a fleet of boats tied up at the Warnock float at one time.

Of the girls, two still live in Pender Harbour, Luella and Cledia - both Duncans now. Nina Warnock lives in Nanaimo where she runs a pet shop. The fourth girl, Agnes, kied when she was twenty-eight.

Before the hospital came to Pender Harbour Martin Warnock ran a sort of sea-going ambulance. He had the fastest boat and would run the sick into Vancouver. He was also a school trustee for twelve years and one of the organizers of the local Credit Union. He now rests near his home in the acre of ground he gave for a community cemetery back in the Harbour's early days.

Martha, now 78, still plants a big garden and tends the old family orchard. Meighbours and passers by still come on summer days to buy the fruit and few pickers get away without a greatly enlarged knowledge of the community's past glory.

EDITORIAL

Chokerknob. Rockcod. Floatcamp. Stumpranch. Steampot. Campboat. Netfloat. Down the channel. Catch the tide. Pacific Milk. Store boat. Across the bay. Salal bush. Japweed. Just when the fire is in the water. Windigo. Widowmaker. Gyppo. Union boat. Mission boat. Fishing boat.

Stumps. Hard white stumps with cowlicks. Soft brown stumps leaking powder and bugs.

Up North someplaces there's a band of black almost like black paint along the rocks between the edge of the bush and the high tide line. Either it's lichen or else stain from all the rain seeping through the leaf mold. Kelp leather.

As things pass into memory what was most normal becomes most unique.

*   *   *

We are pleased that so many of the letters from our first issue came from people of the coast, and that so many spoke of its filling a need.

We received approximately 300 subscriptions and the printing of 3,000 was oversold (though many were given away.)

While boom towns sprouted like morning mushrooms along the banks of the Fraser River and the tent metropolis of Victoria careened with her gold-crazed thousands through the early eighteen-sixties, the shores of Burrard Inlet still lay under that uninterrupted blanket of green timber which has so depressed its discoverers the century before. A few croaking ravens, a few camping Indians—noises that blended invisibly with the evolutionary seethe of the wilderness. Alberni, or even Sooke, were showing more promise than this future site of the Pacific Coast's most busy port.

The establishment of two sawmills began to change all that. On the north shore, a San Francisco business man bought out the Burrard Mills, owned then by some men in New Westminster. The new owner, Sewell (Sue) Moody, established the settlement of Moody Mills, later incorporated in 1871 into a townsite, which became Moodyville, and which, of course, is now the City of North Vancouver.

On the south side of the inlet, Captain Edward Stamp, working for the British Columbia & Vancouver Island Spar, Lumber & Sawmill Company put into production another mill. This became the settlement known as Hastings.

These two operations brought to the wilderness a touch of civilization and industry. Inevitably, along came the steam boats, small vessels that contributed much to the lives of the early loggers and settlers in the Pacific Northwest.

Until 1866, all ships entering or leaving the inlet were towed by Victoria-based tugs, but on July 28 of that year James Trahey of Victoria launched the 142-foot sidewheel tug *Isabel* for the Stamp Mills. *Isabel* was the first steamer to call the inlet her home port.

At the time of her launching, the Victoria Colonist described her as..."A remarkably handsome model, and a most serviceable craft for any purpose, being, in fact, almost too good to be engaged as a tug at the Burrard Inlet Mill for which she was designed".

Pioneer Steamers of Vancouver Harbour

Isabel's function was to tow the sailing ships through First Narrows, and to and from the Mill's wharf. In this occupation she ran for several years; her sole mishap occurred when she ran ashore in dense fog, 500 feet from Nine Pin Rock - now known as Siwash Rock. She was holed, but patched up and back at work within two months - and eventually became something of a heroine.

On May 26, 1868, the British barque *Moneta*, under Captain W.H. Turpin, was loading at the dock of Stamp's Mill. Suddenly flames began to spout from the vessel. It was Queen Victoria's birthday and most men were still celebrating, so few were available for fire-fighting, especially aboard a ship. Disaster was imminent when the *Isabel* hove in sight with a ship in tow.

Captain Tom Pamphlet, then in command of the *Isabel*, immediately assessed the situation. He cast off his tow, got a line aboard the blazing ship, towed her away from the wharf, and scuttled her. Except for his prompt action, and the effort of the *Isabel*, the entire settlement of Hastings might have gone up in flames.

Isabel was later sold to the Starr Brothers, who used her on the Port Townsend - Victoria route for a few years. She then passed into the ownership of the Dunsmuir interest ... and ended her career as a coal barge.

From New Westminster about this time a road had been built as far as Brighton in the east end of what is now Vancouver, near the Second Narrows. From Brighton a ferry service was operated across the inlet to Moody Mills. The ferry was a rowboat, and the owner was John Thomas, who became known locally as Navvy Jack. Later he operated a gravel pit west of the Capilano River.

But population in the area was increasing, and a clamour began for more adequate service to both sides of the inlet. In 1868 a Captain Van Bramer, somewhat of an adventurer, and born in New York, brought his small screw-driven steamer *Sea Foam* into the inlet.

Capt. Van Bramer originally ran *Sea Foam* on the Fraser during the days of the gold rush, but with activity in this field lessening he put his vessel into the ferry business, running between Brighton, Stamp's Mill, and Moody Mill. *Sea Foam* had an undistinguished career. Once, while embarking passengers at Brighton, she blew her steam tubes, scalding the Moody Mill doctor, Dr. A.S. Black, and a Mrs. Bloomfield and her young daughter. The following year she caught fire, destroying her upper works entirely. But she was patched up, and continued on her merry way. *Sea Foam's* sole bid for fame was that she was the second steamer to call Burrard Inlet her home.

By 1869 the lumber business was booming. That year, customs records show Moody loaded five ships, eleven barques, two brigs, two barquentines and a sloop. Stamp loaded five ships, fourteen barques and a schooner.

Gastown came into being with a population of 65, finding its spiritual center at "Gassy" Jack Deighton's famous hotel.

The first steamer ever to be built on the inlet was at Moodyville in 1873 by the great pioneer logger Jerry Rogers, who also introduced oxen and skidroads to the local lumbering scene. He was then logging the south shore of English Bay and Fairview. Rogers' 72-foot sidewheel tug *Maggie* under Captain William Rogers, was the first tug to tow log booms on the coast.

In this same year Van Bramer augmented his ferry service with the addition of the 37-foot steam launch, screw-driven, *Chinaman* - so called because her hull had been brought out from China on the deck of a sailing ship. This craft scampered about the inlet for several years, until sold to the Royal City Planing Mills. From there *Chinaman* passed into oblivion.

In 1874 Capt. Stamp sold his mill to the Heatly Company of London, who renamed the operation Hastings Mill, and about this time a second steamer was built at Moodyville. This was the 82-foot sternwheeler *Ada*, built by Henry Malony for James Robinson. *Ada* was employed mainly in freighting to settlements in the Lower Fraser Valley. On her last trip she towed the newly launched hull of the S.S. *Robert Dunsmuir* from New Westminster to Victoria. There, *Ada's* engines were removed - and installed in the *Robert Dunsmuir*.

Meanwhile, Capt. Van Bramer continued to add to his ferry fleet. *Sea Foam* had been dismantled, but her engines were recycled to the new 43-foot screw steamer *Lily*.

One of the most remarkable steamers the waters of the inlet ever knew was launched in 1874. This was the 54-foot steam scow *Union* ...better known as the *Sudden Jerk!* She was a side wheeler, built of bits and pieces for J.C. Hughes, who used her for freighting and log towing. *Union*, or *Sudden Jerk*, was powered by a threshing machine engine - to which was attached a line, and buoy, to assist in locating the engine's position, if it fell through the bottom of the ship!

This unique vessel had no reverse gear in its threshing machine engine. When approaching a dock, and in order to slow her down, a sack was flung into the gears!

The manner in which the *Union* came to her end, may be described as a true epic of the sea. Under command of Captain Hugh Stalker, she was on passage from New Westminster to Moodyville, with a load of hay. Then, and this was reported in the August 3, 1878 issue of the New Westminster *Mainland Guardian*..."When she reached a point about 6 miles down the North Arm, it was discovered that her steering was out of order. When the cause was looked for, it was discovered that the rope, attached to the tiller, was burned through, and that the cargo of hay was on fire, this probably due to sparks from the smoke stack. The vessel was rendered helpless, and with the current carrying her around, the fire spread.

"The anchor was let go, but the fire spread with such rapidity that the crew were compelled to take refuge on the anchor chain in the water, from which unpleasant position they were ultimately saved by one of the hands, who had succeeded in recovering the small boat, the painter of which had been burned through. The vessel was completely destroyed." So, through fire and water, *Union* came to an end.

In 1874, Moody Mills purchased the American built *Etta White* for towing ships, and log booms. This 93-foot screw-driven tug was built at Freeport Mills - now West Seattle. The *Etta White*, built in 1871, was well known up and down the coast. She burned and sank at Fraser Beach in 1920.

No discussion of steam on the inlet prior to 1900 should be concluded without some mention *Spratt's Ark*. The Ark was a big scow 140 feet long

and 33 feet wide, built by Joseph Spratt, who had made his fortune with the Albion Iron Works in Victoria.

Spratt's idea was to make a floating cannery and oilery, which could follow the fishing fleets and eliminate the problem of long distance, warm weather fish packing. On the main deck was a two-storey building, with the canning equipment below and quarters above. The principal disadvantage in this was that the accomodations were continuously bathed in clouds of steam whose piquant bouquet eventually permeated the glass in the windows. Ahead of this superstructure was a mast with jib and mainsail, and behind it was the stack, which quickly blackened the white sails. In the hold was a 30 H.P. engine with two 50-inch boilers. The shaft went straight out the stern.

As a cannery she was a failure. One of the reasons was that she was almost impossible to navigate. One story tells of the time that she was crossing between Vancouver and Victoria when she was hit by a nor'wester and swept sideways down the Gulf of Georgia. Thirty-nine hours later she miracuously limped into Victoria Harbour. To overcome this problem it was necessary to have a tug accompany her on future expeditions. This was fairly effective but greatly inflated expenses. Modifications were attempted in order to make her economical. The fish oil refinery was removed to make more room for canning and storage. The oil had only been a nuisance. By the time the vats were full, the oil had turned rancid, and Spratt thoughtlessly drained it overboard, making English Bay unbreathable for many days.

After two seasons of unmitigated failure, Spratt abandoned his $75,000 investment and the *Ark* sat useless and forgotten at the foot of Burrard Street in Vancouver.

It was in this downcast state that the hapless barge became a heroine.

On the tranquil blue-skyed Sunday afternoon of June 13, 1886 a dry west wind dropped suddenly upon Vancouver, exploding sails on the inlet and blowing slash fires on the south shore into a wall of flame that swept across the crisp townsite in less than half an hour. On the inlet shore terrified housewives, storekeepers and schoolchildren gathered like a great drop of sweat, then broke in dinghies and rafts for the great *Ark* sprawling out in the water. A first aid station was set up aboard, and many families camped on until their homes were rebuilt weeks later.

This ushered in a happier chapter in the history of the vessel. Shortly after, she was fitted with an additional engine and placed in the freighting business. She brought bricks from the Island for the new Vancouver and stone from quarries up the

Inlet. She did salvage work on the old *San Pedro* and even survived a few trips to Wrangell during the Klondike rush. She was last seen working as a ferry back on Burrard Inlet.

Before 1900, two more steamers were built on the Inlet, both for Van Bramer's ferry service. In 1876 the screw steamer *Leonora* was launched, named after Van Bramer's two daughters, Louisa and Nora. This vessel was 57 feet in length. Four years later, Van Bramer built, or had built for him, a 55-foot vessel which was christened the *Senator*.

Together with the *Skidegate*, 76 feet long, 12 feet wide, launched in 1879, these two vessels passed into the hands of four Vancouver men who formed the Burrard's Inlet Towing Company.

This company, sensing the great potential for expansion wrought by the newly extended Canadian Pacific Railway, sent Captain William Webster overseas to search out financial backing and a vessel suitable for upcoast travel. In England he met John Darling, former superintendent of the Union Steamship Company of New Zealand, and through this alliance in 1889 began the Union Steamship Company of B.C. The desired vessel was found in Bombay, India and brought to Vancouver by way of the Indian Ocean and China Sea. This was the 324-ton *Cutch*, built in 1884 for an Indian rajah.

The next three additions to the Union fleet were built on order in Scotland and shipped around the Horn in sections. First assembled, and the first steel ship launched in B.C., was the 101-foot S.S. *Comox*, which entered the Inlet October 24, 1891. In December the company launched the 120-foot *Capilano*, and in April the next year, the *Coquitlam*. Another storied "Union boat", the *Cassiar* (No. 1) was rebuilt from the burnt-out Seattle steamer *J.R. MacDonald* in 1893.

A towing company that was to ride the young port's spiralling growth through the next half-century, the Vancouver Tugboat Company, was formed in this decade by H.A. Jones with his 50-foot tug *On Time*.

On April 28, 1891 a ship cruised through First Narrows and brought with it a new age in B.C. shipping. An enterprising photographer caught her gliding past the wreck of the H.B.C. steamer *Beaver*, and that about said it. The hull was glistening white and 485 feet in length. Her beam was 51 feet, gross tonnage 5700. She was owned by the C.P.R. and her name was *Empress of India*, first of three "White Empresses" that were to make Vancouver a station in the "All-Red" shipping route that encircled the globe. From this period on, the ships of Burrard Inlet became lost amongst the ships of the world.

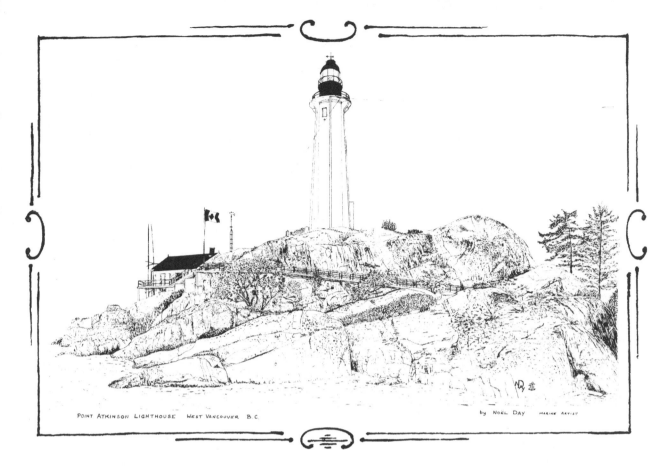

POINT ATKINSON LIGHTHOUSE   WEST VANCOUVER B.C.   by NOEL DAY   MARINE ARTIST

LIGHTHOUSES OF THE B.C. COAST

When white men first sailed to the Northwest Coast they were so bewildered by its manifold passages, which unpredictably butted into the bases of mountains, or dumped them into boiling rapids, or opened into placid gulfs, that they hardly dared go forward. Captain George Vancouver, who charted many of them in 1792, had to scout ahead of his ships with longboats; even so the *Discovery* spent ten days on a reef near Cape Caution. The initial British venture into pelagic sealing here in 1786 found the market rich but the hazards of navigation prohibitive. In the first year they lost two ships and a hundred men.

The first attempt to mark a path through this "sea of mountains" was made almost two centuries before, by the region's discoverer and greatest publicist, Apostolos Valerianos. Valerianos was an energetic and eccentric Greek of the 16th century whose talents attached him to Spain, the ascendant imperial power of the time, and like his countryman El Greco, the Spaniards gave him a nickname, Juan de Fuca. His itch to whirl in the vortex of discovery floated him across the ocean to the thin edge of European civilization at San Blas in Western Mexico.

Between battles with the English marauders Francis Drake and Thomas Cavendish, he persuaded the local commandant to trust him with a small caravel and sailed north to search for a western outlet of the Northwest Passage. Sometime in the summer of 1592 he rounded Cape Flattery and began sailing east into the strait we name for him, bright with the expectation of coming out on Hudson's Bay. Returning three weeks later, confused and disappointed but impressed with the great inland sea he had stumbled upon, he noted for the benefit of those who might follow that the entrance to this new waterway was marked by "a headland or island, with an exceedingly high pinnacle or spired rock, like a pillar thereupon."

While many of the things the Greek later said about his "western sea" were terrible lies, seafarers have always recognized this as an accurate description of Tatoosh Island and Juan de Fuca Rock, which stand at "the corner" of Juan de Fuca Strait and the open ocean 1 1/2 miles off Cape Flattery. (Even the old Greek pilots' lies had their use - the French cartographers' new map of the world, showing the Strait of Georgia stretching clear to Winnipeg, touched off a series of western explorations by the seafaring nations of Europe that brought the coast its first settlers).

The trouble with landmarks is that they're no good in the night, or in fog.

Captain Cook, following Juan de Fuca's tracks on a foggy day in 1777, saw Cape Flattery differently, snorting in his log, "It is in this very latitude where we now are that geographers have placed the pretended Straits of Juan de Fuca. But we saw nothing, nor is there the slightest probability that any such ever existed."

That Britain's greatest navigator was so convincingly fooled might have been seen as an ominous portent for future sailors to the coast: in the succeeding 200 years the channel has been mistaken more times, with more loss of property and life, than perhaps any other in the world. It is understandable that before long men would try to erect in the place of Juan de Fuca's landmark something that could be seen in the dark and heard in the fog.

The earliest navigational lights were all manned lights, because there was no other way. The evolution of lighthouses has been from the great to the small. The original lighthouse at Pharos on the Nile delta, consisting of an open wood fire on top of a great spiral tower, had a staff of one hundred weary-legged men and was considered one of the Seven Wonders of the World. The newest lighthouses are squat concrete boxes with short radio masts and no men.

HOLLAND ROCK LIGHTHOUSE
SOME THREE MILES OUT OF PRINCE RUPERT B.C. WHERE NOW STANDS A WHITE STEEL SKELETON TOWER

The first lighthouse on the west coast was built during Cortez' time at Salina Cruz in Mexico. It also was of the raised bonfire type, housed on a square adobe building at the Harbour mouth. Judging from helmsmens' gripes that have filtered down the years it was not a model of efficiency: it was only tended when important boats were expected and a prevailing breeze to seaward obscured the flame in its own smoke.

The next effort to guide ships at night was made by the next people who established settlements on the West coast - the Russians. Housed in the cupola crowning the governor's castle at Sitka the Russian beacon, a decided advance on its predecessor, was fuelled by seal oil held in four round bowls with floating wicks. The beam was directed to sea by a large copper reflector. It flickered and guttered away from 1837 until the castle burned down in 1894.

Quaint as the Sitka lighthouse was, pilots elsewhere on the coast would have been happy to have it. With a booming fur trade and growing English settlements on the south end of Vancouver Island, shipping into the trap-infested in-

side passage increased rapidly during the 1840's and 1850's. The only channel markers of this dark period were the bones of broken ships.

The busy Hudson's Bay Company steamer *Beaver*, which began a regular circuit of the coast in 1837, bounded from rock to rock like a football. When a ten-pound boulder was discovered imbedded in her keel during a refit, the crew could only guess where it had been contracted.

The British government was not about to remedy the situation. Generally speaking the home office displayed little enthusiasm for this "sterile and rock bound coast" which had come so easily into its possession, and in 1851 was refusing to provide a salary for its governor, let alone sponsor frivolities like lighthouses.

The U.S. government seemed more attentive to the area's possibilities and in 1854 decided to build two lights in Juan de Fuca, one at Dungeness Spit directly opposite Victoria and the other on Tatoosh Island. The Americans were not shipping into Puget Sound at this stage, but the act was not just neighbourliness either: San Francisco was trying to entrench itself as a supply centre for the whole continent west of the Rockies, and improved shipping routes upcoast would head off competition from the new English port at Victoria.

Construction of the lighthouse at Tatoosh ran into an immediate snag. The treeless, storm-torn crag was supposed to be deserted, but a party of workers approaching its one good landing beach in 1854 found it jumping with mean-looking savages, who had war-canoed down from the north like aboriginal Hell's Angels on a mission of terror and plunder amongst the milder tribes of the south. They had adopted the castle-like Tatoosh as their base for the duration. The workers judiciously landed at another part of the island, but nothing could be accomplished against the mischievous and violent young outlaws, and work on the lighthouse began only after months had been spent erecting a guarded blockhouse around the site.

CARMANAH LIGHTHOUSE   by NOEL DAY
SINCE 1891 HAS LOOKED AFTER THE CANADIAN SIDE OF THE MOUTH OF JUAN de FUCA STRAIT

When the northern raiders left, the Cape Flattery Makah moved aboard and turned the island into a whaling station. The blockhouse was a good defense against bullets but not odour, and sometimes the air became so heavy with month-old whales that the crews had to flee to the mainland.

The original structure, a round brick tower 65 feet high and 12 feet in diameter rising from the centre of a sandstone keeper's residence, is unchanged today.

Unlike the Russian beacon at Sitka, which focussed its beam by means of a metal reflector, the great iron lantern of the Tatoosh light contained one of the new refractory lenses developed in France by Jean Augustin Fresnel. The Fresnel system utilizes concentrically arranged glass prisms which gather the diffuse lightwaves into a single polarized beam. Though expensive, fragile, and hard to keep clean, they can produce a powerful beam from a weak source and are still used in most high-powered lights. The rotating Fresnel lens at Point Atkinson light, which is about four feet across, generates 250,000 candlepower from a stationary five-hundred watt incandescent bulb. Lighthouse lenses are arranged in a standard order of size - first order being the largest, second order the next, and so on down. At Tatoosh, light was originally supplied by a wick flame using lard oil. In 1885 kerosene was introduced, and later, electricity.

The Tatoosh light was finally lit in December of 1857, but the first return of the supply boat found the four keepers waiting at the dock with packed bags. On top of the endless work of packing oil up the cliffs, continuing harassment from the Indians was too much to bear. It was another year before the light could be kept in constant use.

The Indians of Tatoosh have long since shrunk away to distant reserves, their places being taken by the families of mild-mannered weathermen and Coast Guards, who man large stations on the island, and over 100 years of unbroken service have established Tatoosh light as one of the corner posts of Pacific shipping.

Dungeness lighthouse, situated on a long hooked finger of sand that wags back and forth in the current and periodically detaches from the mainland, was also the site of Indian battles, but not with white men.

The flat spit turned out to be the traditional battleground of two continually warring local tribes, who occasionally put the new light to use for clashes in the night. At first greatly disconcerting, the slaughter went on so long the keepers learned to close their shutters and ignore it.

James Douglas, the second governor of Vancouver Island, understood timing. In spite of the terrible losses being suffered by local shippers, he didn't waste his breath while his London superiors were not prepared to listen. In 1857, however, Esquimault became a temporary supply depot for the British Navy's Pacific Squadron, which spent much of the Crimean war in the North Pacific waiting for permission to attack Russian settlements in Siberia. It would be a dreadful thing to lose a 1400-ton man o' war on one of the rocks around Victoria, just for the want of a few well-placed lights, Douglas suggested. The Lords of the Admiralty were truly horrified at the thought, and immediately agreed to erect two light stations, one on Fisgard Island at the entrance to Esquimault Harbour, and the other at Race Rocks, a cluster of low tide-rounded islets blocking the Harbour approach 20 miles to seaward.

Befitting its duty, the Fisgard light was an elegant structure of imported English brick and boasting an ornate wrought-iron staircase fabricated in San Francisco. Completed at a cost of 3000 pounds sterling, B.C.'s first light was lit on December 1, 1860 by a Mr. George Davies.

Great was the consternation when the HMS *Bacchante*, Flagship of the Royal Fleet, thundered into the rocks and swamped almost at the foot of the tower in July of 1862.

Rough-faced granite blocks for the Race Rocks light were cut to size in Scotland and brought under sail around the Horn. When they were pieced together they formed a tapering 105-foot tower that even American maritime writers concede to be the finest looking on the Pacific Coast. Originally unpainted, it was done up in black and white stripes after complaints that it was invisible against the surrounding landscape. Race Rocks was lit, also by George Davies, in November, 1861.

As at Fisgard the new light did not signal an end to local mariners' troubles. In succeeding years over 39 vessels came to grief in its vicinity. Only comparatively recently was it established that a silent zone existed on the Vancouver Island side of the Rocks, where the fog horn couldn't be heard by boats attempting the inside passage or leaving the quarantine station at nearby William Head.

Race Rocks became the scene of B.C.'s first lighthouse casualties when a boat trying to land a party of relatives on Christmas Day, 1865, capsized in a tide rip. All five passengers were drowned as Davies and his family stood watching from the rocks.

The north side of the Juan de Fuca mouth was illuminated in 1891 when a first order light was installed in a square wooden tower atop the sheer bluffs of Carmanah Point. Only 55 miles from Victoria, the awful exposure of this site made it one of the least accessible on the coast, and before the advent of helicopters the keepers were sometimes left on their own for six months at a time. It used to be muttered around amongst lightkeeping circles that the Marine Service would let you run out of anything but fuel for the light.

The path started by Juan de Fuca is today a virtual marine express-way, with twenty lighthouses lined like streetlights along the shore. Victoria's growth as a port brought four more lighthouses to that vicinity; the busy quarantine station necessitated one at William Head in 1930 and the grounding of the *Empress of Canada* on Albert Head in 1929 was responsible for one built there the following year.

In 1909 the American government placed the bright yellow *Lightship Number 93* on Swiftsure Bank, completing the job of marking the Strait's entrance. This light, now replaced by a buoy, serves as a point of departure for ships setting out on the Great Circle Route to the Orient.

The early lights at Tatoosh, Race Rocks and Fisgard began sweeping the Strait just in time to find it crowded with vessels steaming neck-and-neck for the gold sands of the Fraser River.

"HOMAS F. BAYARD"   by NOËL DAY
                                                      MARINE ARTIST
SEEN HERE IS OLD FAITHFUL TO MANY A CANADIAN FISHERMAN
AT THE ENTRANCE TO THE FRASER RIVER FOR NEAR 50 YEARS

These hard-pushed little craft, which boosted B.C. population from a bare 2,000 to 20,000 in two years, found the unmarked river channel with little trouble; the only notable wrecks there in the early sixties were both the result of bursting boilers. Nevertheless they started local authorities pondering ways of marking the river channel. The actual entrance was six miles offshore in a shifting silt bank, which seemed to rule out a stationary light, and illuminated buoys were yet to be developed, so they opted for a lightship, which was duly anchored off Sand Heads in 1866.

One of the problems of being the first lightship on the entire Pacific Coast was that there were no stand-ins, and after 13 unrelieved years on station the hull of the *Fraser River Lightship*, as she was officially named, was so full of dry rot the boat had to be scrapped, and it was decided to build a lighthouse after all.

In April of 1913 another ex-sealer was fitted for the job. This was the 86-foot *Thomas F. Bayard*, a beautiful schooner originally built as a pilot boat on the East Coast. As *Sand Heads Number 16* she was painted bright red with her station in huge white letters on both sides and fitted with a kerosene light on a 40-foot mast. She had a crew of two and the only boilers ran the fog horn; her keel was never bored.

This third Sand Heads lightship more than atoned for the shortcomings of her predecessors, toughing it through 44 years of storms, groundings and collisions. It wasn't until November 10, 1957, when a gale drove her up on Point Roberts, that the D.O.T. decided the 75-year-old hull had taken enough. Some thoughtful soul snapped her up for a houseboat, and she is moored at this moment at the Mosquito Creek Basin in North Vancouver. According to her present owner, Mr. J. Parke-MacKenzie, she is the oldest floating hull on the Pacific Coast, and he swears the only water in her bilge is rainwater.

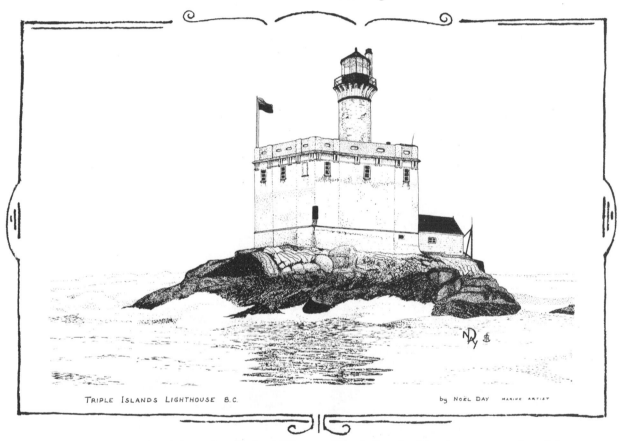

TRIPLE ISLANDS LIGHTHOUSE B.C.   by NOEL DAY MARINE ARTIST

Screw piles were twisted into the silt in 1879 and a wooden building placed aboard, but by 1905 the snaking restless channel had shifted so far away from the boxy tower that it was leading more ships into the muck than it was helping so the Department of Transport went shopping for another ship.

Their choice was the *Mermaid*, an ex-sealing schooner that owned the distinction of having been slapped by a whale while cruising off Japan in 1893, "snapping two ribs off clean and turning the bowstem to one side like a rudder." In 1899 she had been expelled from the fleet as unseaworthy, afterwards being rebuilt for the Klondike trade. She was on her new job only a short time before a storm opened up the old wounds for good, and it was back to the lighthouse.

The bulwarks have been removed and in some places the forged nails can be picked from their rusty holes by hand, but you can't compare her with the flimsy, boxy vessels around her without marvelling at what has been lost to the art of building ships since 1880.

Meanwhile, back at the Sand Heads, there is a new lighthouse.

Burrard Inlet lay dormant through much of the Fraser Gold Rush, but in the late 60's began a harvest that was to prove more enduring. The Moody Mill on the north shore cut 5,832,000 board feet of lumber in 1868, loading 34 ships, while the Hastings Mill across the water loaded 14 ships. First Narrows began to be known to windjammer skippers of the world.

The light at Point Atkinson was lit in 1875; the one at Brockton Point, which was originally manned, in 1890. Before the turn of the century a manned light station was also built on Prospect Point, and for a time there was one across the narrows from it at Capilano on a little shack on stilts.

Even before Vancouver came on the scene, lumber exports had begun flowing out of Port Alberni on Vancouver Island, and in 1874 a square wooden tower with a revolving reflector-style beacon was built on Cape Beale at the entrance to Barkley Sound.

This was the scene of an incident in 1906 which has since become one of the legends of the West Coast. On the stormy night of December 6 the keeper, Elmo Patterson, saw his beam sweep the hull of the American barque *Coloma* - decks awash, demasted, lifeboats carried away. He knew the supply ship *Quadra* was lying around the point at Bamfield, but he could not leave his light so his wife Minnie set out through the whirling sleet to give the alert. With a small lantern she stumbled and crawled through several miles of bush and snag-filled gullies, and got the *Quadra* away. It had time to rescue nine crewmen before the derelict dropped in splinters among the rocks,

but Mrs. Patterson's health was broken by the ordeal and after three years of lingering illness she died.

As late as 1898 the coast north of Cape Beale on the outside and the Sisters in the Strait of Georgia was still without a beacon.

Ships of the Canadian Pacific Navigation Company made a policy of anchoring at nightfall on the West Coast, and Captain J.K. Warren of the pioneer passenger freighter *Boscowitz* refused to move after dark in waters north of Campbell River.

Agitation for lights on the upper coast had been rising for some time, but it took another gold rush to make the point.

News of the steamer *Portland* and her ton of Klondike gold exploded upon John Citizen's sense of caution in June of 1897 like the declaration of war. Men who one day would hesitate to row all the way across the local millpond were the next day coaxing grey old hulks off the mudflats and setting out for Alaska, coming down to the realities of navigating B.C. waters only as the Strait of Georgia began to squeeze them into the swift gorges of Discovery Passage and Cordero Channel.

CAPE ST. JÀMES LIGHTHOUSE   by NOËL DAY
                                        MARINE ARTIST
SITUATED ON THE SOUTHERN TIP OF THE QUEEN CHARLOTTE ISLANDS
NOW THE HIGHEST LANTERN IN USE ABOVE SEALEVEL IN B.C.

In October, 1898, the schooner *Viva* intercepted three gentlemen scudding along 250 miles west of Vancouver Island in a tin rowboat with a burlap sail. The interesting thing was that the three were sailing south, not north. They had been to the gold fields, lost all their money, and were returning home from Dawson the cheap way. They had descended the Yukon and crossed the Bering Sea, covering almost 3,000 miles and weathering several of the storms that claimed larger vessels.

But the losses were as appalling as the successes were colourful. The wrecks of two large passenger steamers, the *Clara Nevada* taking 100 lives in 1898, and the C.P.R. *Islander* taking 42 lives in 1901, made the hazards of upcoast travel a cause of national indignation, while dozens of lesser mishaps focussed the need for navigation aids on specific places.

The northbound California steamer *Corona* struck Lewis Island near Prince Rupert in 1898. The Schooner *Alexandria* sank with ten lives on Goose Island in Queen Charlotte Sound during the same year. A short time later the steamer *Thistle* sank at Cape Mudge, taking nine lives. The schooner *American Girl* was wrecked near Cape St. James at the lower end of the Charlottes in 1900, taking seven lives. The number of small boats destroyed can only be estimated, and of the freight tows started from the south in 1898 only half reached Dawson.

In 1899 a light was stationed on Cape Mudge, and on Dryad Point, Egg Island and Ivory Island in Queen Charlotte Sound.

The Egg Island station, built on a rock slightly apart from the main island, was swept away by a storm in November 1948. The keeper and his wife managed to scramble to the main island just as the footbridge tore loose, and had to remain huddled there in the open storm for a week before help came by. As soon as they hit dry land they quit the lighthouse service and never returned. A few years ago part of the Pine Island light in Queen Charlotte Strait was also wiped from its perch by a storm.

During the gold rush period lights were also established at Ballenas Island, Pointer Island, Boat Bluff, Lawyer Island, Holland Island, and Scarlett Point. In 1902 the American government built two lights in the Alaska Panhandle, the first since the Sitka castle burned, and by 1905 they had added seven more.

The arrival of the Grand Trunk Pacific Railway in 1916, creating a deepsea port at Prince Rupert, led to the building of a light on Triple Island in 1920.

On January 22, 1906, a passenger ship of 1,595 tons, the S.S. *Valencia*, bound for Seattle from San Francisco, lost her way in fog and struck the West Coast of Vancouver Island near Cape Beale. She quickly settled and slid stern first into deep water. Of the 154 aboard, only 37 found their way to shore, no women or children among them. It was the worst shipwreck in B.C. history, and resulted in a light being built at Pachena Point the next year.

In the same year a lighthouse was finished at Estevan Point, guarding the approach to Nootka Sound. The 127-foot octagonal tower, designed by Colonel W.P. Anderson, is still the tallest on the Pacific Coast, and carries one of the largest lens assemblies of any B.C. light.

But it is not size that Estevan is famous for. On June 20, 1942, a Japanese submarine surfaced two miles offshore and at about 10 p.m. commenced firing at the light, the first and only hostile shells to land on Canadian soil in this century. The keeper promptly extinguished the target at the start of the firing, and no damage resulted, but the incident loosed new floods of Pearl Harbour paranoia up and down the coast and had far-reaching effects.

The most immediate was that the lighthouses were ordered blacked out, resulting in a number of serious shipwrecks. One of the more notable was the 10,000-ton Russian supply ship *Uzbekistan*, which crashed below the darkened Pachena Point light on April 30, 1943.

Undoubtedly the most ambitious lighthouse project attempted on Canada's western seaboard was the one begun in 1909 on Triangle Island, a totally desolate block of stone 25 miles into the ocean from Cape Scott at the northwestern tip of Vancouver Island. The tower itself was only 46 feet high but the total elevation from sea level was 700 feet, twice that of any other light on the Pacific. This was matched by a million candlepower lantern, theoretically visible 34 miles on all sides. In reality it spent most of its time buried in the local fog bank, which seemed to anchor itself whenever the wind wasn't blowing on the island's peak. But the fog was preferable to the wind.

Month-long storms carried the radio tower over the cliff and blew concrete buildings off their foundations, and on one occasion sank the temporary supply tender *Galiano* with a loss of 27 lives. In 1920 the D.O.T. gave up on the light and moved the radio towers to Bull Harbour.

The northernmost primary light in B.C. was built on Langara Island at the northwest tip of the Queen Charlottes in 1913, capping a network of 43 manned and 815 automatic lights which stretch around the coast like a chain of hands, each within the reach of another, waiting to lead the fisherman, tugboater, freighter captain or yachtsman away in any direction he desires to go.

What will undoubtedly turn out to be the last manned lighthouse ever built in B.C. was the belated replacement for Triangle Island, established on Cape Scott in 1960. The increasing success of high-powered automatic lights and foghorns, and the development of electronic navigation in general has given the Marine Service occasion to adopt a policy of "personnel reduction", and automation of all the remaining manned stations is only a matter of devising some politic way of doing it.

So far complete automation has been restricted to stations where the keepers leave on their own or retire but this spring 11 stations on the outer coast were fitted with automatic fog horns and continuously operating lights on a "trial basis" and it is a safe bet you will have to pay admission to see a real lighthouse by 1977.

The original B.C. light at Fisgard Island, automated for some years, was recently turned over to the Fort Rod Military Museum and arrangements have been made to heli-lift the lantern section of the Point Atkinson light at Vancouver across the bay to the Maritime Museum in Kitsilano.

BUDDHIST COLUMBIA

Had you been standing near the Air Terminal across from the Art Gallery on Georgia Street, Vancouver, on May 2nd, 1972, you may have witnessed a curious sight. Had you asked any of the young, long-haired, baby-toting, smiling, bead-garlanded men and women who those Japanese were in the long orange and purple robes, they would have said "They're not Japanese, they're Tibetan, monks, lamas, and a nun, and they're on their way back to Northern India via Samye-Ling monastery in Scotland."

It is a long way in time and space for those Tibetans from pre-invasion Tibet where cars, electricity and running water were unknown, to the world of jet travel. Tibetans, Indians, and Japanese have been travelling to modern North America in increasing numbers in the past few years, spreading the word of the Buddha and other spiritual teachers to the open-eared young of the West.

When several groups of businessmen, teachers, artists and writers working for the Tibetan Relief Fund attempted to obtain permission for the displaced Tibetans to establish in the B.C. Rockies, Welfare Minister Gagliardi gave one of his familiar gruff replies. "We've already got too many deadbeats in this province." He would be surprised to know that the spiritual forefathers of these same "deadbeats" had preceded his countryman Chris Columbus to North America by at least ten centuries.

That, at any rate, is the speculation surrounding one of the greatest adventure stories of this coast. Little is known of this story, however, and its validity has yet to be established, but with a few concrete facts and a bit of imagination, we can probably fill it in.

In the early nineteenth century the discovery of some early Chinese texts stimulated a raging controversy among European scholars. The writings, in a work by Ma-Twan-lin, record the travel story of Huei Shan, a Buddhist priest who returned to China from a land far to the east in 499 A.D.

He told of a land named Fusang, and of two lands before it, named Wan Shan (the country of marked bodies) and Ta Han (Great China). In Fusang, which derived its name from a tree which produced food and clothing for the inhabitants, houses were made of planks, people wrote on tree-bark, bartered for goods, and had a very clear system of rank, being led by a king treated with much pomp and ceremony. Of Wan Shan, it was said that the inhabitants marked their bodies to indicate tribal rank and lived in houses surrounded by moats filled with "yin shui", a term difficult to translate but suggesting silver-water, now considered to have been oelachen in process of having their oil extracted.

In an exhaustive study, the nineteenth century scholar Edward P. Vining draws strong arguments to place Ta Han in the Aleutian chain, Wan Shan on the North Pacific coast, and Fusang in Mexico. His deductions are simple and mechanical. The distances stated in the Chinese texts, though a point of contention, place the countries in the areas he suggests. The argument for a water crossing through the Bering Strait is highly possible. The greatest water distance on that crossing is under two hundred miles. Even simple seal-skin craft could have weathered it. Well into the last century, Japanese junks were blown off course to appear adrift off the coast of Washington and British Columbia.

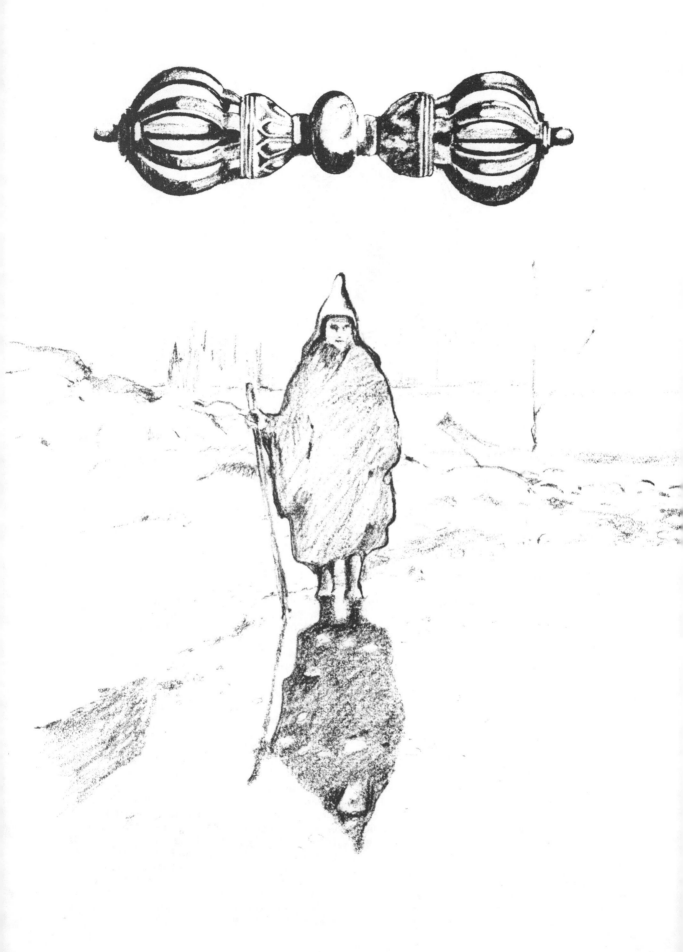

Next, Vining compared the texts with known anthropological data, finding, for example, the use of caste tatooing by the Point Barrow esquimaux and body painting by the Haida and Kwakiutl. In Mexico, he found many parallels with Fusang. People did have written script, ate a fruit resembling the pear (from cactus), made cream from deer's milk, did not have iron, though copper in abundance, all of which are stated in the Chinese.

Also he cites many cultural and religious parallels between Asia and Mexico. In Pre-Columbian Central America, many priests lived in monasteries said to have been established by "the Revered Visitor" Quetzalcoatl. *Tlamacazque*, or more simply *Tlama*, the name of those priests is suspiciously like the Tibetan *Lama*. At Uxmal, above the entrance to the House of Priests is a seated cross-legged figure bearing striking resemblances to a meditating Buddha. Representations of various gods correspond to those of China and Japan and there are parallels of dress, bridge construction, calendars, armour and anchors.

Of Fusang, the Chinese texts said "In olden times, they knew nothing of Buddhist religion, but in the reign of T-ming, of the Emporer Haio Wu-Tu of the Sung Dynasty (A.D. 458), from Ki-Ping five beggar priests went there. They travelled over that kingdom, everywhere making known the laws, canons and images of that faith. Priests of regular ordination were set apart from the natives, and the customs of the country became reformed."

One of the most interesting, if not vitally important studies of history is of such movements of cultural traditions and ideas. British Columbia's position in relation to Asia made it a possible main highway for Hwei Shan and his fellow monks. Buddhists in particular had a tradition of widespread travels, spreading the Dharma (or Way), meeting with other practitioners, and seeking instruction. Buddhism was originally carried by such wandering mendicants from its home in India, to China, Japan, South-east Asia, Tibet and Mongolia. There are records of Buddhist monks reaching as far west as the Black Sea area sometime before the first century A.D.

It is interesting to imagine these early Buddhists making their way past the islands of British Columbia in small boats, stopping here and there to propagate the word of Buddha, having become conversant with the Indians' tongue. Lending credence to these conjectures are a number of finds at various sites in B.C. In 1882, the October 25th issue of the *Weekly Colonist* in Victoria ran a story on the discovery of a string of bronze coins which were up to 3,000 years old. They had just been found by some miners working a creek bank near Telegraph Creek. When they were hauled up from their resting place several feet below the surface the wire holding them together disintegrated. The newspaper suggested "whether the Chinese miners who went to the Cassiar seven or eight years ago deposited the collection where it was found for the purpose of establishing a prior claim to the land - may never be known." Some years later, while prospecting in the same area, the Chinese court interpreter from Victoria met Indians who showed him several ancient Buddhist silver ceremonial dishes and a number of brass charms. Though they were reluctant to part with any of it, the Indians did give him one of the charms, which was estimated to be at least 1,500 years old. It had been found, along with the other objects, buried in the roots of a large tree.

Also discovered in the roots of a tree, when the townsite of Powell River was being cleared, was a small statuary Buddha. At the Planetarium Museum in Vancouver, there is a stone ceremonial figure closely resembling a seated Buddha. It was taken from a Fraser midden. In Nanaimo, layout workers found an ancient Japanese sword in a copper-bound wooden scabbard. It was lying eleven feet beneath the earth's surface.

Though there is a possibility that such items made their way to the coast via Russian or Spanish trade routes, the evidence for a Chinese origin are equally strong. Marius Barbeau, long time curator of the National Museum of Canada and noted ethnomusicologist, entertained theories that the Northwest Coast tribal music was strongly flavoured by Buddhist temple chanting, which would certainly not have been introduced as a trade good.

It is doubtful if Huei Shan would care too much about being the "discoverer" of a land which he felt to be "illusory". One place is much the same as any other to a person who finds his reality centered in the workings of the mind rather than in his history. Doubtless, the North America through which Huei Shan and his monks wandered was less foreign, economically and culturally, than today's North America is to the refugee Buddhists of Tibet. Similarily, Shigetsu Sasaki, later known as Zen Master Sokei-An, would have found himself in a more familiar environment hiking the backwoods country of Puget Sound in the early 1910's while he was living around Lummi Island with Indians for neighbours. Patterns repeat themselves and echo. The mind of man plays infinite variations on countless themes, but here on the Northwest coast, Buddhist wandering monks inject an element of continuity, one more thread in the tapestry of our history.

TOWBOATING

On the West Coast here we see tugboats chugging around the seas and harbours every day. Tall rounded pilot houses, low afterdecks, short on the freeboard. Brightly painted - yellows, reds, greens, black. There's something comical about them, and something curious. Towing a raft of logs or a chip barge. B.C., with its vast expanse of protected water has often been called the tugboat capital of the world. The population at last count was nearly 500, ranging in size from 30 ft. to 230 ft., in horse power from 150 to 4800.

Tugs have been busy in the sea around here for a long time, say since 1836. That's when the *Beaver* first came to the coast. Of course she wasn't a tug, she was a steamer, passenger and freighter. But as the only power boat on a coast full of sailing vessels and sheltered water she ended up doing a lot of towing.

The handsome schooners would be escorted to Cape Flattery - if the wind was blowing offshore. If the weather was bad, they would be towed maybe sixty miles further out to sea, until it was safe to raise the sails with no danger of drifting inland.

The days of steamboats.

There's not too many folks around who worked on steam tugs but those who did remember them fondly. Man, they were *quiet*. Puffing along at a few knots. There was no privacy because everyone would hear what everyone else was saying. Of course they were dirty too. Built big so as to be able to carry enough coal to get there and back. There weren't coaling stations in every port. There was one at Nanaimo, at Union Bay and Wellington and Vancouver. One of the big towing jobs in those days was the barging of coal to various outlets for the needs of passenger steamers and freighters.

You didn't necessarily use coal. The Thulin family of Lund cut wood for their homemade ship, the *Niluht*. One way or another it took a large crew to keep the fires hot. In the end of course they all got hooked on oil.

Most of the old tugs had Chinese cooks and reportedly everything was cooked in grease so it all tasted the same. And something about steam tugs seemed to make them a real stronghold of bedbugs.

Of all the old steam tugs built in the late 1800's and early 1900's (few were built after about 1923) only one still has her boilers intact - the *Master*. She was built in 1921 (91 tons, 70.5 feet). Today she's owned by the World Ship Society of Western Canada. It's an expensive proposition to keep steam tugs alive and the towing companies around Vancouver take turns putting the old girl up.

There are a few old steamers besides the *Master* still around, but they've long been converted to motor power. The *Fearless* (75 tons, 71 ft.) was built at New Westminster in 1898. She's still there and her present owner uses her on his shake claim. Mention should also be made of the *Sea Lion* (1905). From *McCurdy's Maritime History of the Pacific Northwest*: "The handsome steam tug Sea

Lion, 218 tons, 114 feet in length with triple expansion engine was built at Vancouver B.C. for Captain G.H. French. She was noted as the only tug on the coast to boast a piano in her saloon and also for her melodious thirteen-note chime whistle which could run up and down the entire musical scale." The *Sea Lion* was the *Sudbury* of her day, always in the news with deepsea rescues, or things like escorting the embattled *Komagata Maru* out of Vancouver Harbour.

Steam tugs were good vessels. The slow turning engine made for dependability. Repairs were easy. And, they were quiet.

A 1200 b.h.p. diesel engine. Encased in a 20 gross ton steel hull. A vibrating steel echo chamber of noise. That's the modern tug. Diesels are also cleaner, more economical, require less crew and they start immediately.

Gas engines played a short-lived role in tug propulsion. The first heavy duty gas engines were brought up from San Francisco - like the Frisco Standard, the Atlas, Imperial and the Union engines to name a few. These companies were soon producing diesels.

They were huge uncomplicated beasts and apparently if anything went wrong it was easy enough to fix. Just carry a bit of wire aboard.

The first full diesel tug built in Vancouver was the harbour tug *Radio* constructed by Captain F.A. Cates. (The Cates family have been involved in the towing trade since the beginning. Today Cates Towing in North Vancouver is the oldest family-run tugboat service in B.C.) This was 1922 - one year after the last steam tug built on the coast.

These years also saw the beginning of the change from wooden hulls to steel. Wooden hulls are still built for tugs occasionally - they have many fans. Wood absorbs engine noise. Wood is dependable - with steel you never know when a plate is going to crack or a weld open up. If rot is promptly replaced to keep it from spreading the wood hulls last for years and years.

There are a few, says Captain Bill Dolmage, like the *Ivanhoe* built in 1907 and still active, with hardly an original piece of timber in her today. On the other hand steel is easier to repair, quick to build.

I've mentioned the major changes - steam to diesel, wood to steel. Of course there are continuous improvements in material and design by naval architects, engineers, ship builders as aids in propulsion, maneouverability, stability, safety.

A 1972 coastal or harbour tug though is basically the same as a 1922 tug. The work load - that's a different matter. According to the old-timers, "It's not like it used to be. These young fellers now get a day off for a day on. Only work half a year. We used to work 24 hours a day 363 days a year. Take a couple off for Christmas. You might get a night in town once every 3 or 4 weeks." And after a month or so at sea out of sight and sound of all but your mate, town was a veritable carnival. A place to spend all your money and stay juiced. Often the skipper had to go out and round up his men himself (with a wheel barrow, as Capt. Jack Ryall puts it). One thing - he always knew where to find them. A lot of old skippers were extremely fond of rum and whisky and carried it aboard the ship. One never knew when one would have to tie up in a bay during wicked weather.

Naturally there wasn't much home life. The crew was your family. That may only be two men if times were tough. One captain recalls a skipper who ran his tug by himself. He could undo knots and boom chains with a pike pole. Tricky business. There were no rules or regulations about crew numbers like now, so an independent tug boater would only take one or two deckhands to help. They usually stayed together for years on the same tug. She was theirs and great pride was taken in her appearance. Polished brass. Scrubbed decks. Clean engine. A new deckhand was put through the ropes and if he wasn't busy at another task he was scrubbing.

A tugboat captain had to be well versed in many sciences. Foremost he was a seaman. He had his master's papers from the Canadian Merchant Marine - and to obtain his papers meant an apprenticeship. First as a deckhand, then as a mate. A deckhand keeps the boat clean, the engines clean, cooks the meals, washes dishes, counts logs, takes his turn at the wheel. The mate is at the wheel from midnight till 6 a.m., the captain from 6 a.m. till noon, the mate from noon till 6 p.m. ten the captain again from 6 p.m. to midnight. This apprenticeship must have 4 years sea time. But years ago it wasn't uncommon to be in your late thirties or forty before becoming captain.

The captain was also the navigator in interior waters. (A tugboat captain is happy in sight of land, a deep sea mariner is happy out of sight of land), a weatherman, a mechanic, a salvage rescue operator. And a shrewd businessman in days of individual strong competition.

There were hosts of gyppo logging outfits. Captain Len Higgs figures in 1948 there were 78 logging camps in Sechelt and Jervis Inlets, Blind Bay, down as far as Halfmoon Bay. Now there are

sixteen. It was a lot of fun then. You'd pull in to a logging camp and stay there a little while, talking to the boom man, everyone would be taking it easy; the boss would come down and you'd have a cup of coffee and he'd tell you about that next logging camp up there - they'd be the worst bunch of no good bastards around. So you'd leave, making plans to come back in three days or so. "You'll have the boom ready, then, Yep. Fine. Okay."

Then you'd go see that bunch up at the next camp, sit there and have a cup of coffee and he'd be telling you about the guys you just left. This'd go on all the way around the coast. Used to have to keep quiet. Couldn't say a word. Had to be a real diplomat in the inlet when you were yarding years ago.

There'd be three or four towing companies and they all had camps in the inlet and all were trying to get each other's camps. The skippers would be talking to a camp boss with a well trained ear for another tug's lost logs. If you arrived around 4:30 or 5 o'clock, well usually the boss's wife was in the cookhouse you know and she'd yell out "Tell those guys on that tug to come down here and have something to eat - they must be starved." So you'd oblige, fill yourself full of steaks and coffee. It was a lot more fun than being shunted around by the company dispatcher, or being greeted by a gruff preoccupied foreman yelling about where've you been, you're late, and get this boom loaded, the way it is today.

Competition brought out lots of salty characters you had to deal with. Like Pete the Sneak. Pete the Sneak always liked to be on the outside in tie-ups. Even if he arrived at a dock first Pete would untie and let the other tows tie up next to the float. Come about 2 a.m. if the sea was calm and the

wind blowing a little offshore Pete and his mate, they'd been together for years, they'd unlash the boat and drift a mile out of the harbour and be cruising down the Stretch a solid four, five hours before the sleeping skippers behind.

All the captains knew one another and their vessels - it was a fraternal, competitive, friendly society. Everyone had their own special record - like towing the biggest boom through the "hole-in-the-wall" or having the cleanest boat or cursing the loudest and longest on the marine telephone band. And then there were the records you didn't talk about, like running into Bowen Island, asleep at the wheel.

Of course navigation was a very different proposition before the advent of sophisticated electronic equipment - ship to shore radios, radar, depth sounders, remote control steerage. When the fog was too thick to see you sounded out the shoreline with your whistle. Speed travels at about 1000 feet a second, so if it took one second for the echo to return you were 500 feet offshore, but don't picture someone bent over a stopwatch. In those days all the instruments were in your head. You read the weather by the expressions on mother nature's face.

Later on when radio phones were introduced a captain could phone up Cape Lazo for the weather condition in the straits. And Robbie (he was the weather man, and everyone knew Robbie) would say "Just a minute, I'll go have a look. Aw sure, she's fine out there."

It was around 1923 that communications at sea began to take over. From *McCurdy's Maritime History*: "B.C. tugboat operators pioneered in the use of radio telephone communications at this time. For many years the coastal telegraph lines had been relied upon for more or less rapid com-

munication in emergencies but in 1923 the Vancouver Merchant's Exchange and B.C. Towboat Owner's Association began working towards acceptance of radios on tugs and ship to shore radio telephone was established. Stations were built at Cape Lazo and Merry Island and ten tugs were fitted with radio telephone equipment. Within a short time a hundred Canadian tugs could thus maintain constant contact with home ports." Increased communication made things easier at the cost of independence, like all modern conveniences. It was safer. Production ran smoothly. But before when a tug went out her whereabouts were unknown until she reported back. The captain and crew were trusted to know what to do. They ran their own schedule - parametered by weather conditions and the occasional good poker game. If the weather got bad you'd have to tie up till it got better.

Captain C. Andrews remembers when he was stranded for 90 days in Deep Bay. Finally they decided to tie *all* the logs together and put all the tugs on them to pull them in. Reportedly there were 500 acres of logs floating.

You were lucky if you were near a community. But if it was in a outlying bay ... Of course if you were tied up chances are others would be too and you could usually get a poker game happening. At any rate the weather always cleared eventually and the logbooms delivered.

Tugboats are towboats. In B.C. the towing of logs was and is their prime task. This is a land of lumber - fir, hemlock, red cedar, spruce - sometimes 200' high and 9' in diameter in the old days. Since wood floats, flat rafts were the first timber transportation structures. The old steamers could tow 4 or 5 sections, that'd be over 10,000 feet of logs. (Today tugs can tow 150 sections)

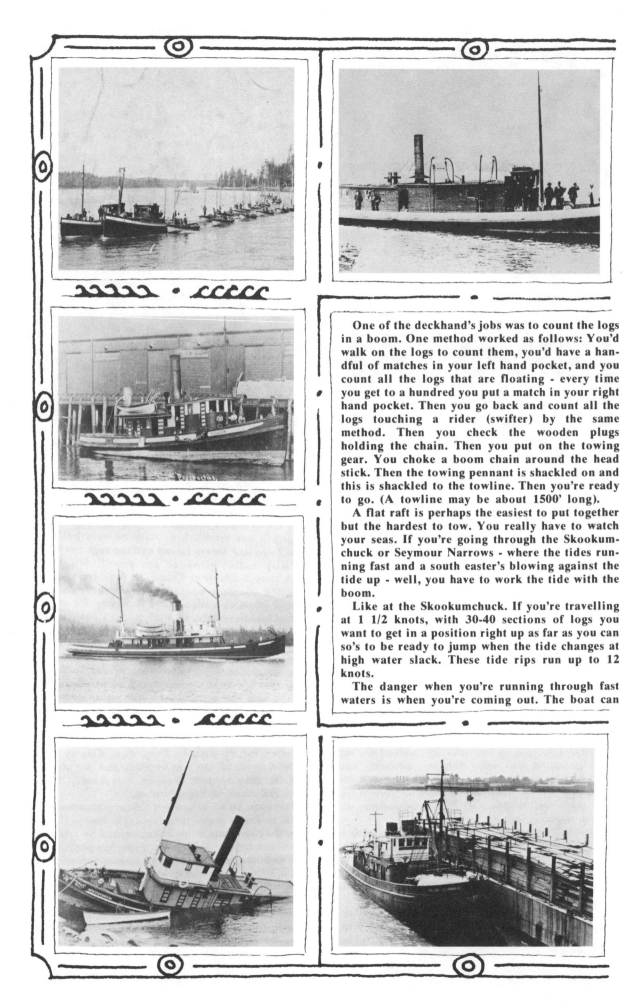

One of the deckhand's jobs was to count the logs in a boom. One method worked as follows: You'd walk on the logs to count them, you'd have a handful of matches in your left hand pocket, and you count all the logs that are floating - every time you get to a hundred you put a match in your right hand pocket. Then you go back and count all the logs touching a rider (swifter) by the same method. Then you check the wooden plugs holding the chain. Then you put on the towing gear. You choke a boom chain around the head stick. Then the towing pennant is shackled on and this is shackled to the towline. Then you're ready to go. (A towline may be about 1500' long).

A flat raft is perhaps the easiest to put together but the hardest to tow. You really have to watch your seas. If you're going through the Skookumchuck or Seymour Narrows - where the tides running fast and a south easter's blowing against the tide up - well, you have to work the tide with the boom.

Like at the Skookumchuck. If you're travelling at 1 1/2 knots, with 30-40 sections of logs you want to get in a position right up as far as you can so's to be ready to jump when the tide changes at high water slack. These tide rips run up to 12 knots.

The danger when you're running through fast waters is when you're coming out. The boat can

hit an eddy that'll made the tug stand still - while the cargo's still moving at 10 knots. And it's impossible to buck the wind with a log raft, you've got to be running with it but not over about a 15 m.p.h. blow. In other words, flat rafts work in calm waters.

As logging spread further up the coast and rough water had to be crossed, the Davis Raft came into play. It was a "cigar-shaped bundle" bound with cable and chain, and could withstand heavier seas and winds. Today transported logs are usually bundle booms. They strap together a bundle of logs of all different species, the cedar will float the hemlock, leaving the sorting grounds to arrange specific loads. (All the booms are yarded to a central yarding station). Most recently log carrying barges prove to be the most efficient rapid means of transport.

Dangers. There's lots of close calls in tugboating. Even well seasoned skippers have sometimes had occasion to figure it was all over and many a tug has gone down in the perilous sea. There doesn't seem to be one prevailing cause, just endless combinations of the elements at work. Think of the equipment on a tug - towbitts, winches, hawsers, poly lines, tie-up wires, shackles and boomchains, spikes and pike poles ...All this must be shipshape. You always get a new deckhand who gets his foot caught in the middle

of a towline. Or getting caught by the swing of the line from the winch to the tow. The law requires four men on a continuously operating boat - two awake at all times - you don't want the ship running aground with a fatigued skipper at the wheel.

The worst thing that can happen on a tug is fire. There's no place to go. You've got to head the boat into the wind to blow the flames away from you. There's usually no way to get down to the engine to shut it off, so it must burn itself out. Always the lifeboat is on top of the house and the house has got years of paint on it so the first thing to burn off is the lifeboat.

The tow, too, can be a potential disaster. Towlines must always travel directly behind a tug. If the tow takes charge and starts pulling you backward through the water, nine times out of ten it'll shear off (the towbitts are a third of the way back from the stern) until the towline comes over the corner of the tug. A good skipper won't let this happen but you've got many tide rips and gales to contend with in these waters.

The First International Tug Conference was held in London, England in 1969 with representatives the world over. *Ship & Boat International* published the proceedings from the conference. One recurrent theme was that of tugboat safety. Foremost was noise pollution. A large diesel engine in a steel hull is a conductor of noise of the first order. A number of tugboaters mentioned the fact that it can cause considerable irritability after too many hours at sea. Ear muffs and remote control are attempted solutions. But a comprehensive solution has yet to be arrived at. (A *feasible* solution - one of those parametered by economics).

Another safety problem is the size-to-horsepower ratio encountered in some tugs. Again a number of captains have expressed the opinion that putting high powered engines in boats under 90 feet or so is a dangerous proposition. You now get over 1000 h.p. in the same space you'd only have 125 h.p. years ago.

But there's another side to tug boating. Interwoven amongst the many tug tales are those of rescue and salvage. There's a high element of camaraderie in towboating - if the weather's bad a large tug will go in and tie up his boom and come back to help a smaller horsepower tug bring in his. There probably hasn't been a skipper who hasn't been involved in helping out a companion tug or a fishing boat or more than likely a floundering American yacht in unfamiliar waters or ripening weather.

Marine Rescue, the first organized service of its kind, operated by the B.C. Towboat Owners Association begun by Capt. C. Andrews, worked as follows: All the tugs and eventually all the fishing boats and other sea craft were alerted through radio telephone as soon as there was trouble on the coast. Marine rescue would broadcast on a given frequency that a vessel needed help - say in the vicinity of Trail Islands. If a tug was close he would answer and be given exact location. But say he might be towing a log boom. Then, if another tug was tied up at Halfmoon Bay or Selma Park, he would take over the boom and safeguard it while the most powerful tug performed the rescue. Naturally lives come first, and this is all done free of charge. The service today is Air Sea and Rescue.

Tugs not only transport logs. There's lumber products - like woodchips, wood pulp, newsprint, and cargoes of sand, gravel, limerock, cement, salt sulphur, petroleum products, chemicals, general cargo and rail cars. Importing, exporting, berthing freighters. Serving the Island, small communities, government camps. The "Lifeline Industry."

There'll *never* be roads where tugs travel - take Jervis Inlet. Or Howe Sound. You'd have to go way the hell up to Squamish and down the other side. Or through the mountains. No, there'll always be towboating, according to Captain Bill Dolmage.

Some say its hard work - you know, rugged and resourceful. Others say its easy - lying on a raft of logs in the sunshine making a slow 1 1/2 knots. I sat in the friendly cabin of a harbour tug (Kleeman's) for most of one bright day, drinking coffee and more coffee, talking to the skipper and the deckhand - waiting for calls. Waiting for the jimmy six to shudder to life. We did go out - for ten minutes, escorting a huge cement barge to the foot of Burrard Bridge. Some days it's real relaxed.

TSIMSYAN MYTHS

Canadian government publications are another source, easier to locate or order. These include several works by Marius Barbeau, one-time curator of the National Museum of Canada. They are on north coast legends and myths and are illustrated with fine argillite carvings. As well as the one at hand, *Tsimsyan Myths*, there is also *Haida Myths, Haida Carvers in Argillite*, and *Medicine Men of the North Pacific Coast*.

These books do for our cultural environment what the B.C. Government wildlife bulletins do for the natural environment. Assuming that people live in a cultural-historical matrix as well as in a particular landscape and climate, an understanding of one will be as important as the other in understanding our place in the whole. The Indian mythology deals with the central events in a person's life, seeking to find an ordering process at work.

That is discovered in the web of life itself. Raven, Mountain-Goat, Grizzly Bear and Frog are all crucial symbols in the lives and interactions of the Indians. The important events of one's life are echoed by events in the animal world. A knowledge of the stories of that world helped the tribesman know his responsibilities.

Each of the tales in *Tsimsyan Myths* pivots on this interweaving of worlds.

"They made full preparations. As they were good seal hunters, they had many seal-skin robes and sea-otter robes and much food. They set out. As they had learned the direction from their elders, they were sure of themselves. Early in the morning they started, and soon all land was lost sight of. They grew alarmed as to what direction to take, for the wind had changed and there were no landmarks to guide them on. Suddenly a large Eagle came upon them. It had on its back and wings ten small eagles. It flew ahead of them and they followed as they knew the Eagle was guiding them. They were aware that they belonged to the Eagle Larhskeek clan, so now they were being guided by their crest, the Eagle."

Indians found themselves living in a world in which human and plant-animal realities were interwoven with the immediacy of dream. Only recently have scientists, thinkers, and poets begun to appreciate the enormity of the gap between this way of thought and our own and begun a move to bridge that gap, which is after all, not eternal. Poet Charles Olson stated the problem precisely in a poem from the "Maximus" series, a great modern epic work.

Land of darkness and the people grope for food.
Raven, flies through the narrow place,
Slips into Sky-Princess' water,
becomes child in her, grows up in
Sky-Chief's Palace, headwaters of Nass.
Howling and crying til he plays with the sun-ball,
Then one day
Laughing and flapping
Over the hill.
"Hey, ghost people, give me some food
Or the sun-ball will blast you all away"
They didn't believe him.
All the ghosts are gone now.
The sun gives light to live by.
Feed our friend the Raven,
All the animals are brother-sister to us all.

"....that the objective (example Thucidides, or the latest finest tape-recorder, or any form of record on the spot

-live television or what - is a lie

as against what we know went on, the dream; the dream being self-action with Whitehead's important corollary: that no event

is not penetrated, in intersection or collision with, an eternal event

      The poetics of such a situation
are yet to be found out."

I've always found it hard to find collections of genuine native mythology, written in language which captures the spirit it was spoken in. There are a few, Ella C. Clark's *Indian Legends of the Pacific Northwest* for one, which help fill the hole. Generally, I've had to search through libraries and resort to source material in the Memoirs of the Smithsonian Institute, American Anthropological Society, Museum of Natural History, and other such hard to locate, academic tomes. Specific volumes by individual researchers such as Franz Boas on the Kwakiutl, or, further afield, James Mooney on the Ghost Dance tradition are similarly difficult to locate.

It was such poetics that primitive people were indeed working with. In the "Strong Man Who Holds Up The World", the hero is the younger brother of four, who is seemingly a lazy good-for-nothing who sleeps in his own excrement. Actually, he is a supernatural being undergoing training for the most difficult of all tasks. Again and again he saves the family and tribe from disaster and embarrassment but is never fully accepted. Finally he is called to the other world where his Uncle is old and tired, unable to hold up the world any longer. Aemaelk, the younger brother, uncomplainingly takes up his task, for which he has been so painfully trained.

These stories are rooted in the physical environment of the North Pacific Coast, making them easy for us to approach. "At that time, the mountains were all at the water's edge. They planned to push Aemaelks' village into the ocean so they began to slide into the village." The animals of the stories are familiar, but rather than being trophy-figures they are heroes, transformers and teachers. Always, the emphasis is on an ecological tapestry. If the sanctity of natural forces or animals is threatened by man, he will rapidly experience the results. In this sense, the North coast mythology approaches the Greek idea of *hubris*, or Buddhist *karma*, when the people attempt to over-reach themselves and threaten other forms of life.

In one story, the Indian princess marries a dark stranger who comes to her every night. She has chosen him for the roughness of his hands, which denoted a hard working, honest man. He was the sea-bear, a grizzly from the sea who wore a large dorsal fin. If anyone knew of his identity he would die. Finally, the princess' grandmother discovers him. He dies and with him goes the tribe's prosperity.

In another story is the origin tale of the Mountain Goat clan who, over the years travelled down the Nass to the coast. "The people had become sinful. They no longer observed the rule of the Sky according to which animals must be an object of respect. They recklessly slaughtered herds of mountain goats on Stekyawden (now Rocher Deboule, near Hazelton) and made fun of a young goat, which they had taken home as a trophy. A young man adopted the goat as a pet and saved it from abuse. The offenders were invited by Goats to feast at the mountain lodge. There they perished by falling down the cliffs at night, all but the young man who was led down the peaks to safety by his grateful pet."

Finally, there are the stories of Raven, the foremost culture hero of the north coast, who brought the Sun back to the Earth after the sins of the people had caused it to be hidden away. The message of these tales is one that we are hungry for. They take man out of the concrete-and-asphalt, mental cities of isolation and alienation of his head and reveal a mode of living, natural to this same environment which emphasizes the natural harmony of living things.

The underlying philosophy of flux, change and transformation, expressed by the Raven story, is antidote to a wide-spread rigidity. In one story, Raven is at first a prince, miraculously born in a seaweed patch after having drowned. He shoots and skins a raven, whose skin he wears. He becomes a Raven and after flying to the Sky-Chief's palace gains entrance by turning himself into a pine needle and floating into the princess' mouth, becoming embedded in her womb. As a boy, he steals the sun, becomes Raven once more and flies back to his people bringing with him the Light. This was the first of his many adventures.

Barbeau's workings become increasingly vital to people interested in re-establishing a harmony, both personally and culturally with the world we live in. Fascinating reading whichever way you look at them, they can be taken as Freudian or Jungian, or ecological, or just plain fantasy, good stories for children. They present a different view of history than ours which moves through figures and dates and names. It's a view we'll need to familiarize ourselves with, somehow or other, if we're to be left with any history at all.

Tsimsyan Myths, Marius Barbeau, National Museum of Canada Bulletin No. 174, Anthropological Series No. 51, 1961, Ottawa. ONLY ONE DOLLAR!

THE CARGO-HULKS

Beaten barges
limp the coastal moats
ferrying hogfuel and sulphur
to the castles of the mills -
food for insatiable
bellies of the digesters -
ammunition for the smokestacks
to vomit at the gulls.

Cargo-hulks
stripped of mast and superstructure
name, rank, identity
and any vestige of esteem,
they flounder through the waves
like great gutted whales
behind the strutting tug-boats
and they dream

of full-sail -
horrendous high-seas thundering -
fanged antarctic gales -
the white challenge of the Horn -
shrouds under full-stress bulging
like a trumpet-player's cheeks -
the pitching - the nearly-foundering -
and the going-on

to dolphin-country
in the long rolling warm
past stark coasts where volcanoes growl
like old men in beds -
equatorial becalmments -
the deckboards cracking in the sun -
parched voices croaking for a wind
on the hard green road.

Blowing north again
before a good kicking gust
through starhung climbing nights
and new-minted days
to drop anchor at last,
winner of the harrowing marathon
before newraised cabins smoking welcome
in the pioneer bays.

Memories melting
in the cold reality of the rain,
they wake to ultimate winters by wharves
in the crucifying stink,
become shells
for the same caustic cargo
that fouls the water brown and foaming
along their flanks.

Peter Trower

Voyageur-route, to the Western ocean, he follows. Paul Kane, in 1846, penniless wanderer "with no companions but my portfolio and box of paints, my gun, and a stock of ammunition", is granted free passage with the Hudson's Bay Company brigades by George Simpson. After passing trials of ordeal, Kane the early artist and first tourist, has the road, of muskeg, bog, channel, river, lake, forest, mountain, at his feet, open.

He comes, in air ringing with songs in patois jargon of Cree, Iroquois, French and English, songs of the bright-shirts, sash-wearers, wolf-slayers, buffalo eaters. He follows: paths opened and paddled through wilderness, sky of clouds clearing, the songs ringing to hand now preserved in canvas hangings, parliament halls, and museums of Canada, waiting for voice.

Kane, latter-day Cain wandering with knowledge of exile, a homeland somewhere in the past, a Europe and Britain beyond the great grey sea, images recently burnt into his head on trip there, but now no man to put an end to the curse, that he wanders never to cease, seeking a country of his own. There is no release into clear sky of prairies or salt wash of north-west breaker, save in the imagination when the search is suspended in the art to record.

Kane, brother's keeper, of a brother recently discovered, by French philosophers, named noble savage by Rousseau, eulogized by new world poets, the *Huron Chief* of J. Mackintosh in 1836, recognized by a few as human, and now fought for by the artist in quiet ways, ways too quiet to avoid the decimation and demoralization that follows. He, Paul, enters the new world, an exile self-consumed by a passion to record what remained of the garden that was aboriginal America.

But as his paintings and journal show, his senses and craft remained locked in the Old World, the France and Italy of the Old Masters, so he is strung out, straddling ocean, spread across time, a bridge between sensibilities. Though commonly acknowledged to have been born September 3rd, 1810, his biographers confuse his birthplace, unsure if it be in the new world of York, Upper Canada, or old, of Mallow, Cork County, Ireland. It is the latter.

He comes to Canada to live with his family in York, in 1820 and lives now in this dirty little town through which hundreds of Indians move to trade. Not enjoying it, he leaves school early and apprentices with a furniture maker, then works a while as a sign painter. On June 8, 1841, he sets sail for Europe where for two years he travels through France and Italy, Switzerland and England, studying the profession that he has chosen, artist.

When he returns to North America, he heads almost immediately for the frontier. From the orderly cities of Europe to the backwoods of North America is a leap beyond time and space. Paul Kane is wandering through the remnants of paradise, a world of fantasy and imagination. The scenes he sees and records are of a different order. "I have seen many men on the northwest coast of the Pacific who bore frightful marks of what they regarded as honourable distinction; nor is this the only way (bites taken from their flesh) in which their persons become disfigured. I myself have seen a young girl bleeding most profusely from gashes inflicted by her own hand over her arms and bosom with a sharp flint, on the occasion of losing a near relative. After some time spent in singing and dancing, Chea-clach retired with his

The Wanderings of an Artist:

people to the feast prepared inside a large lodge, which consisted principally of whale's blubber, in their opinion the greatest of all delicacies, although they have salmon, cod, sturgeon, and other excellent fish in abundance."

Having spanned the continent at the same time as the settlers crossing the Oregon trail, this first tourist is a herald of the advancing civilization. With it comes measles, yellow fever and smallpox. His wish to find the flower of the unknown and to capture its colours before it fades is involved with a race against time. Kane himself sees the last great herds of buffalo. In 1846, the Metis have their last grand hunt in which over fifty thousand of the hairy brown earth-shakers are destroyed, victims of the advancing tide.

"I again joined in the pursuit; and coming up with a large bull, I had the satisfaction of

PAUL KANE

bringing him down at the first fire. Excited by my success, I threw down my cap and galloping on, soon put a bullet through another enormous animal. He did not however, fall, but stopped and faced me, pawing the earth, bellowing and glaring savagely at me. The blood was streaming profusely from his mouth, and I thought he would soon drop. The position in which he stood was so fine that I could not resist the desire of making a sketch. I accordingly dismounted, and had just commenced, when he suddenly made a dash at me. I hardly had time to spring on my horse and get away from him, leaving my gun and everything else behind."

AT THE PACIFIC

◄ ━━━━━━━━━━━━━━━━

Meanwhile, in London, Ottawa, and Washington, politicians hatch visions which will force the buffalo further afield: railways and settlements to divide the continent in behemoth parcels. On June 14, 1846, the continental boundary line was set at the 49th parallel, ceding to the United States the vast Oregon Territory of the Hundson's Bay Comapny. This change of territory does not hinder Kane's passage and he proceeds to the coast with the dual passport of Sir George Simpson's letter and his easel and paints which have aquired him a reputation of medicine man amongst the Indians.

"I was indebted to the superstitious fears which they attached to my pictures for the safety and ease with which I mingled amongst them. One of them gave me a great deal of annoyance by continually following and watching me wherever I went, for the purpose of warning the other Indians against my sketching them, telling them it would expose them to all sorts of ill-luck. I repeatedly requested him to desist out in vain." Finally, threatened by Kane with the magic he had been warning against, the Indian does desist.

Magic, not white man's government and laws of territory, determines Kane's passage through this wilderness. Having arrived on the west coast, quest end, he continues recording what it is like to be on the advance edge of civilization, the knife edge limits of the known world. His eyes are alert to detail but a foreign lens remains between him and his subject. Colours and forms from the old land hinder his vision: sights of the Bay of Naples, Florentine skies, the Spanish Steps of Rome beside which Keats died only twenty years before, scenes painted by Raphael, Murillo, Rubens and Dolci; these dance in his memory and filter through his dreams. Reflections of "exercises to improve (his) colouring" executed in the grand galleries of Europe echo in every landscape.

Kane's paintings are a sharp contrast to George Catlin's, which he had recently seen in London. Unlike Kane's they show a lack of sophistication and technique. Catlin travelled to Europe after his trip west. He had taken news of the new world to the old, pleading the plight of the Indian people: "I love a people who have always made me welcome to the best they had....who are honest without laws, who have no jails and no poorhouses...who never take the name of God in vain...who worship God without a bible and I believe God loves them also...who are free from religious animosities...who have never raised a hand against me...or stolen my property where there was no law to punish either...who never fought a battle with white men except on their own ground...and oh ! how I love a people who don't live for the love of money." A plea to Europe and white America that the aboriginal beauty of person and land be not destroyed in the name of either God or commerce, a plea we know to have gone unheard.

Kane has less of the moral sense, is more a wanderer, strung out. His "native town of York" is not truly his own, nor is the Europe to which he attempted return. All the old world offered him is the mastery of his craft, that he might record a world in which his imagination would find himself a home. Strung thus between two rare flowers locked in a battle to the death, he carries the conflict within himself. The world of the "noble savage", in its own way far advanced from the decadent European culture, though in its death throes, spreads seeds which will inevitably bring the while world down. In a fit of vision, at Taos, New Mexico, novelist D.H. Lawrence sensed the invisible presence and power of the Indian spirit, a restless ghost waiting to reclaim its own. The west Kane moves through is still populous with the living source.

In Europe, a craving for rejuvenation of commerce and spirit gives rise to increased interest in what are now known as third world countries. While Europeans, enthralled by the curiosities of the new worlds, attend exhibitions and fairs featuring "wild men", strange plants, animals and artifacts, American settlers are pushing across the continent, transforming the world they pass through. Hungry for gold, adventure or open land that can be turned to farm, orchard, or vineyard, they stream out to the Pacific Coast into Oregon and California.

As Kane arrives, the numbers are accelerating. In 1843 only five settlers made the trip to the coast across the Oregon trail. By 1848, 4,000 hungry, blue-eyed, calico-clad, wagon borne settlers arrive after the perilous journey through high mountains and hostile tribes. Most of them survive the epidemics they carry with them as gifts to the natives. Kane wanders into villages decimated by these diseases, villages of bones where none were left to bury the dead, villages changing, never to be the same, in the floodpath

of virulence. An epidemic of measles brought on the Walla Walla indian uprisings of 1847 which culminated in the Whitman massacre in which several of Kane's newly acquired friends were killed. His journal shows no understanding of the times and their omens. His details are fixed in convention. The immensity of the change he is witnessing is obscured by his attention to the details, which are never seen as they are, but always as by a tourist, a wanderer, rooted in a distant culture.

Kane's arrival on the coast has been preceded by hard traveling. Coming through the Rocky Mountains, Jasper Valley, in late December he was nearly deserted by a boat company at a rendezvous on the Columbia River when they presumed he was lost in the mountains, the harshest land he travelled through; "nothing, therefore, remained but for me to take off my snow shoes, and make the traverse. The water was up to my middle, running very rapidly, and filled with drift ice, some pieces of which struck me, and nearly forced me down the stream. I found on coming out of the water my capote and leggings frozen stiff. My difficulties, however, were only beginning, as I was soon obliged to cross again

four times, when, my legs becoming completely benumbed, I dared not venture on the fifth, until I had restored the circulation by running up and down on the beach. I had to cross twelve others in a similar manner, being seventeen in all, before I overtook the rest of the party at the encampment.
... We no longer had to toil on in clothes frozen stiff from wading across torrents, half-famished, and with the consciousness ever before us, that whatever were our hardships and fatigue, rest was

sure destruction in the cold solitudes of those dreary mountains." The primitive encampment of Fort Vancouver is a welcome haven to the worn traveller, arriving in time for a replica British Christmas dinner at this outpost of empire.

On the coast the scenes are of great stability, the Indians as sure of their position with the whites as they are of the forces of their environment, living in a peace mediated by a rich fur trade. So far, they have not come into contact with settlers and prospectors who have no use for them and desire only the land they live on. Living in small groups, they come together in time of winter scarcity to villages of cedar lodges. Into these, Kane is welcomed, as medicine man, a welcome addition

to the winter activities of the bands, bringing power and honour to the people he visits.

The winter is cold, down to seven degrees at Fort Vancouver. The Columbia has frozen over for the first time in memory. Cattle, which chief factor McClaughlin had taken great pains to nourish and increase, freeze to death by the hundreds and become wolf food by the river. As the days begin to lengthen Kane joins the local youths and British sailors on rides onto the flatland surrounding the fort, chasing and throwing calves for sport, having shooting matches, waiting for the sun. On January 4th, the settlers and visitors are treated to theatre aboard H.M.S. *Modesto*, gaily bedecked in flags and painted sets. They see "High Life Below Stairs", "The Deuce is in Him", and that "laughable comedy 'The Irish Widow'". While they shiver on deck of the ship-cum-theatre some miles north the Clallums and Makahs are battling with stone age weapons over the possession of a whale whose body, pincushioned with Clallum spears, has washed onto a Makah beach.

The two chiefs, Yellow-cum and Yates-sut-soot fight "with great bravery hand to hand, with nothing but their knives, until they are separated in the melee." Kane sees one of the surviving Clallums who was forced to run a gauntlet, bearing "shocking gashes." "Yellow-cum took eighteen prisoners, mostly females, who were made slaves, and he had eight heads stuck on poles placed in the bows of the canoes on his return."

The two worlds clash. Beneath a peaceful surface they are locked in deadly struggle. London theatre and tribal battles vie to define the real world. Kane straddles both, part of the advancing and victorious civilization yet in spirit on the side of the Indian. He is a rock in the surf of history, being polished in tidal suck and wash. He wears Indian clothes and is photographed in them when he returns to Toronto. He approaches a total transformation but can never affect it. The new world does not co-incide with the perspectives of the old.

"One day, a tall, large-boned Indian came on board the *Modesto* while I was sitting below with some of the officers. The Indian was dressed as usual in full costume, as they would call it in California (where it is said, a shirt collar and spurs are considered the only clothing indispensably necessary); that is to say, he had his paddle in his hand, and walked about the deck with great gravity, examining the cannon, and other things equally incomprehensible to him, much to the amusement of the idle sailors. The purser, no doubt from a feeling of delicacy, took the Indian below, and gave him an old swallow tailed coat of his, which was adorned with numerous brass buttons. The Indian, highly delighted, struggled into the garment with the greatest difficulty, as it was infinitely too small for him, the cuffs reaching but a little below the elbow, and the front not meeting within a foot... seldom has the deck of one of Her Majesty's ships been the scene of such uproar - ious and violent laughter."

Flux and juxtaposition describe the limbo of the coast. What Kane sees with his classic eye is novelty. The stable, sedate and noble world of the Indian becomes so much froth on the advancing wave of the white. The artist finds great interest in the physical types of the Indians he visits, the

flatheads of the Salish and the coneheads of the Nootka; their clothing of blanket and bark; their medicine - shamans singing over patients, sucking on their bodies to draw disease out; their habits and foodstuffs. Much he abhors. They pick lice from each other hair and eat them in revenge for the discomfort they cause. They eat acorns which have soaked in urine in earthpits several months - "however disgusting such an odiferous preparation would be to people in civilized life, the product is regarded by them as the greatest of all delicacies."

The physical environment too is violent, alien and threatening. Mount Saint Helens, the Indians believe, "is inhabited by a race of beings of a different species, who are cannibals, and whom they hold in great dread; they also say that there is a lake at its base with a very extraordinary fish in it, with a head more resembling a bear than any other animal." As Kane passes it, the mountain erupts, spewing a cloud of white smoke which hangs in a curious shape over the peak in an otherwise brilliantly clear sky. "About three years before this mountain was in a violent state of eruption for three or four days, and threw up burning stones and lava to an immense height, which ran in burning torrents down its snow-clad sides."

On both canvas and in the journal such natural wonders are portrayed with an element of the grotesque. Kane's perspective is sometimes faulty, as if the land defies attempts to make its true proportions known. Between Fort Vancouver and Nasqually lies Mud Mountain. "The mud is so very deep in this pass that we were compelled to dismount and drag our horses through it by the bridle, the poor beasts being up to their bellies in mud the tenacity of bird-lime." Also lying on the route to Fort Victoria was Prairie de Bute, formed of "innumerable round elevations, touching each other like so many hemispheres, of ten or twelve yards in circumference, and four or five feet in height. I dug one of them open, but found nothing but loose stones, although I went four or five feet down. The whole surface is thickly covered with yellow grass. I travelled twenty-two miles through this extraordinary looking prairie."

Kane is alive to these wonders, his nose sniffing with excitement at the scent of the extraordinary. He craves the energy of the wilderness and finds it. "The Indians on board now commenced one of their wild chants, which increased to a perfect yell whenever a wave larger than the rest approached; this was accompanied with blowing and spitting against the wind as if they were in angry contention with the evil spirit of the storm. It was altogether a scene of the most wild and intense excitement: the mountainous waves roaming round our little canoe as if to engulph us every moment, the wind howling over our heads, and the yelling of the Indians, made it actually terrific." This is the Straight of Juan de Fuca, with the mighty Olympics towering over shoulder.

His stay on the coast is somewhat of a rest period. One hundred of the five hundred oil sketches composed on his trip are from the coast. He stays in Fort Victoria for two months, making excursions on foot and by canoe to neighbouring villages. He is about ready to start the return voyage which will return him to York in the fall of 1848. He has accumulated enough rough material for his life's work, which will mark Paul

Kane as one of the first Canadian artists to draw directly from the nation's soil for inspiration. His coasting travels become mopping up operations. As he continues painting the Indians, the ugly, the handsome, the noble and the grotesque, his travels take him into further adventure and discovery, but one imagines he is making preparations to leave. "As our canoe neared the land, I observed them hurrying toward the bastions, and shortly afterwards heard several shots. Supposing this to be intended as a salute, we drew still nearer, and were astonished at hearing more discharges, and seeing the balls fall near the canoe. My Indians immediately ceased paddling and it was with the utmost difficulty that I could prevail upon them to proceed."

Landing at one of these villages, he records the tribal funeral practices. The husband's body is placed on a funeral pyre with his wife lying on the corpse, compelled to stay there as long as possible while the flames mount, then to descend as best she can to safety through the smoke and flames. "No sooner, however, does she reach the ground than she is expected to prevent the body from becoming distorted by the action of the fire on the muscles and sinews; and whenever such an event takes place she must, with her bare hands, restore the burning corpse to its proper position."
Into this rediscovered world of the familiar he brings the butterfly net of his sketchpad and brushes, with a hand and eye trained by European collectors of old world specimens.

Of the world to be recorded for the eye of posterity, a burning corpse, to put its body back in place, Kane climbs the pyre of history. Into the forms and perspectives of Delacroix he pours the horses of plains Indian warriors. It is impossible to put the body into its former shape. The flame consumes it and transforms it. Kane leaves us a legacy which we have much work with yet. In a wilderness, such as Canada remains, a new approach to the environment is necessary. Kane's work prefigures much of the difficulty we have had adjusted to this coast and this continent. Later artists, such as Emily Carr, will continue the work that Kane began, the attempt to place oneself fully in his environment and history, whether it be regional, national, or universal context.

He will return to Toronto and spend the bulk of his life in studios mounting these specimens for "posterity" and "future generations of Canadians." This taxidermy of place and event keeps his own childhood alive, finding his innocence not in one place but in many scenes: fish drying on racks by the Columbia river, stenching in sun; women weaving Salish rugs on vertical looms, with hair clipped from dog raised for that purpose, mixed with cedar-root shreds and goat wool; shamans chanting over naked girl, cedar incense rising in smoke; medicine men in masks dancing, masks of fright, masks of mourning, wooden two pieced moving chewing cannibal bird masks, forest shrieker spirit masks; foods of camas, bulb, wopatoo, deer and elk, acorns pickled in urine: each is a moment of ecstasy as the artist stands outside of time, free and affirmed. Kane is thus curiously absent in his art, either paint or journal, from the scenes he depicts.

Notes & Queries

Send questions, discoveries, unidentified photos or interesting facts to Raincoast Fact Finder, Box 119, Madeira Park, B.C.

The rock carving in this photograph was found at a remote place on the north end of Vancouver Island about 50 miles from Alert Bay by Stephen Lablosky of 12320 Old Yale Road, Surrey. The figures are about 8 inches high and 1/4" deep on the face of a large granite boulder. What interests both he and I about this carving is that it can't be Indian, nor is it feasible that a logger would have the skill to do such work. Because of the religious symbolism and because of the skill necessary to carve in granite, we tend to believe that early Hudson's Bay explorers left it ... but for what reason?

Charles Lillard
4697 West 4th Avenue
Vancouver 8, B.C.

It is certainly not a typical Indian petroglyph, although styles varied immensely in that area. Whether Indian or white it is a curious find, and we can locate no previous record of it. If any of our readers has knowledge or interesting thoughts about it, we invite them to write in.

Lying on the beach at Long Bay, Gambier Island is the very fascinating hulk of a large sailing vessel. It is copper fastened and the planks appear to be treated in some way to resist rot and teredoes. The name still readable on her bows is *Sir Thomas Lipton.* Is it possible this might be the remains of the famous tea clipper depicted on labels for many years as the symbol of the Lipton Tea Company?

E.E. Armstrong
2445 West 8th Avenue
Vancouver, B.C.

It would appear not. Lloyd's Register shows her as a very late four-masted schooner built by the Brunswick Marine Company in Brunswick, Georgia in 1919. The hull was salt treated and she measured 209.1 feet long with a 41.8 foot beam, gross tonnage 1193. She was originally named the E.T. Marshall. In 1921 she was transferred to Honolulu for the Northwest lumber trade, but was laid up in Astoria from 1924 until 1940, when she was acquired by Island Tug & Barge for use as a sawdust scow. Her binnacle can be seen in the Island Tug & Barge offices in Victoria.

Raincoast Place Names: The Nawhitti Country

A glance at a map of British Columbia's coastline shows a seemingly endless proliferation of place names. A closer scrutiny reveals the fact that these names fall into three main derivations: Native Indian, Spanish, and British.

On a present-day map or chart, these names are objectively mingled throughout much of the coast, as if all appeared simultaneously.

Of course, they did not. Far back through the veils of time, aboriginal peoples gave appropriate designations to every body of water, every rocky point, every significant mountain. Today, such appellations as Saanich, Kitimat, Qualicum, Kitsilano and Chemainus are used without a thought as to their origins. Others—Okisallo, Wickanninish, Bella Bella, Coquihalla, Mamalilacula—roll so mellifluously off the tongue that they cannot conceal their aboriginal beginnings

Where native terms had arisen out of imaginative or harmonious qualities, British and Spanish mariners decided that significant landmarks and waters should commemorate their saints, their national personages, and themselves.

Interspersed among the majority of British names, our charts still show Malaspina Strait, Quadra Island, Laredo Channel, Espinosa Inlet, Estevan Point, Camano Sound, and many more terms to remind the traveller of the Spanish mariners who once sailed this coast.

In 1789, activities at Nootka Sound brought Britain and Spain to the brink of war. In 1790, signing of the Nootka Convention left most of the Pacific North-West Coast of North America open for claims by either Spanish or British naval commanders.

Prior to the Nootka controversy, Captain John Strange, in 1786, had travelled by small boat from Sea Otter Cove, around Cape Scott, and down the east coast of Vancouver Island. He had gone ashore, so he wrote in his journal, on an island off the shore, at a place he called Bay of Whales. There he had climbed a hilltop and, looking southward, had concluded that the channel he saw continued on, and made an island of a great section of the coast. Captain Strange also named Queen Charlotte Sound.

In 1792, Captain George Vancouver explored parts of the Gulph of Georgia, as he called it, in the company of Don Dionisio Galiano and Don Cayetano Valdez. The expeditions separated at Toba Inlet, Vancouver continuing along the mainland coast, in search of the mythical North-West Passage, and the Spaniards along the Vancouver Island shore.

With, apparently, no thought that theirs would be the last expedition along this coast by their countrymen, the Spaniards travelled at a leisurely pace, visited native villages, and added place names to the charts they were compiling.

One of their main halts on their way northward would seem to have been at the same locality that Captain Strange had reached on his trip southward from Cape Scott. The island Captain Strange had climbed six years before the Spaniards named after Don Galiano. The channel between this island and Vancouver Island appeared on the Spanish charts as Goletas, after the schooner-type vessels; and the names of these tiny craft, *Sutil* and *Mexicana*, were given to the two points that mark the northern limits of this channel.

At Cape Sutil, they visited Nahwitti, the chief village of that territory. While the explorers mention having given beads and other gifts to native peoples as far south as the present Galiano Island, they seem to have been most lavish in their giving at their nothernmost anchorage. While metal corrodes and cloth decays, glass remains immune to natural disintegration. Although not many Spanish simulated amber beads have been recovered at other places along their route, many thousands have been found on sand beaches in Goletas Channel. Other beads reclaimed from there indicate the fact that fur-traders from Britain, from the United States, and from Russian Alaska also left gifts among the Nahwittis.

Occupying the coast from Shushartie Bay to Scott Island, and quite friendly when first visited by Europeans, the Nahwitti people later received nothing but grief from such contacts, as the number of sea-otter furs decreased in proportion to the increase in traders. In 1811, prompted perhaps by injustice suffered at the hands of some previous trader, natives of—so the story has come down—Nahwitti village surprised and killed the crew of the Astor America Fur Company's *Tonquin*. On going below, the attackers accidentally detonated the ship's magazine, destroying the vessel and themselves in the process.

Twice within the space of a year, the village was destroyed by naval gunfire; by HMS *Daedalus* in 1850, and by HMS *Daphne* in 1851. Both attacks were ordered by Richard Blanshard, first Governor of the Crown Colony of Vancouver Island, in retaliation for the deaths of several seamen. It would appear that natives of this village were not clearly known to have caused the deaths for which they paid most dearly.

Although the Nahwittis apparently rebuilt their village, by 1879 they had moved to a spot they called Mel-oopa, on Hope Island. Troubles of a changing world beset them there, and the remnants of this once-powerful people finally removed to Alert Bay. They are commemorated on today's charts by Nahwitti River, Nahwitti Bar, and Nahwitti Point. Nigei Island takes its name from their hereditary chief. Shushartie Bay and River represent a slightly Anglicized native term for "place of good cockels". Captain Strange's Whale Bay is now given the melodic Kwakiutl name Loquillilla Cove.

For fifty years, the Spanish name Sutil was lost, that point having been re-named Cape Commerell by Captain George Richards, Canadian Hydrographer. In 1909, Captain John Walbran asked the Hydrographic Service to reinstate the Spanish name. The name Commerell was relocated at a point on the west coast of Vancouver Island.

Bull Harbor commemorates a visit paid to the anchorage by George Simpson in 1841, when the Hudson's By Company Governor apparently noticed a great number of sea-lions disporting themselves there. Hope Island bears the name of an Admiralty officer who kept the flag flying far from this remote piece of what is now British Columbia.

Extracted in part from the forthcoming Cape Scott Story, Mitchell Press.

It is a rare sight nowadays to watch a sperm whale (or any other variety for that matter) fountaining defiance in the B.C. coastal waters. Finback; Blue; Humpback; Sei - all the species of that ponderous tribe have virtually vanished through overkill or a sense of self-preservation, from the sounds and straits where they once abounded. With them has vanished the industry for whose mills their blubber, flesh and bones once provided the grist. Coal Harbour, last of the whaling stations, was closed in 1967 and lies deserted with its sheds, fading stinks and bloody memories. The whaleships have been scrapped or converted to other purposes and the harpoons and flensing knives are finding their way into nautical museums. It was a hardluck trade from the very beginning, and not only for the whales.

The first men to hunt whales on the B.C. coast were the Nootka Indians, but their activities have been detailed in a previous article and, in any event, what they practised with their spears and flimsy canoes, could scarcely be described as an industry. They killed only from neccessity and took no more than they needed. Their infrequent forays did little to deplete the great herds.

Hot on the heels of Captains Cook and Vancouver, British whalers began working the North Pacific in a sporadic fashion, as early as 1790. Commencing in 1809, those doughty sailors from New Bedford and Nantucket, immortalized by Melville in *Moby Dick*, began to assert predominance and several hundred Yankee whalers hunted sperm in B.C. waters over the next forty years. In 1834, there were so many American ships on the coast that Sir George Simpson of Fort Victoria envisioned a profitable new provisioning trade. Two whaleships passed the winter of 1842 at Nawhitti at the North end of Vancouver Island, making H.B.C. Chief Factor John McLaughlin, who regarded B.C. as his personal back yard, suspicious that they were cutting into the fur trade. In 1845, four whalers wintered at Victoria. New England ships visited the Queen Charlotte Islands on numerous occasions and from these salty men, the Haida Indians learned the intricate method of bone-carving called Scrimshaw which was to have a profound influence on their manner of designing totem-poles. Apart from this bit of cultural impingement, the American whalers left little tangible record of their comings and goings. Their home-ports lay round the Horn, thousands of miles remote from the fog-haunted shores of British Columbia.

There were no whaling-stations as such in this distant period. The New England men simply dragged the dead beasts up on gradually-sloping beaches by means of capstans and flensed and rendered them on the spot. There was no market at that time for anything but the oil; the rest of the carcass was left there to rot and provide a banquet for a thousand scavengers till nothing but the gargantuan bones remained.

One of the first local white men to practise the trade was a half-legendary character called Peter the Whaler. Little is known about the background of this strange man. He hunted the giant mammals with a wild crew made up of Kanakas and Indians. The blubber was rendered at Deadman's Island and later near Deep Cove, providing oil for the sawmills then burgeoning along the shores of Burrard Inlet, and later for household lamps.

The earliest recorded attempt to establish a local whaling industry was launched in 1868, when an enterprising Scotsman named James Dawson joined forces with a group of San Francisco men, including a Captain Abel Douglass, to form the Dawson and Douglass Company. Early in August of that year, they purchased at auction a schooner named *Kate* and commenced operations in Saanich Inlet, near Victoria. Foul weather conditions and heavy fog hampered this initial effort but despite the inclemencies, the *Kate*, under Douglas' command, managed to bag eight whales that yielded 2400 gallons of oil.

In the Spring of 1869, the Company moved operations up the Gulf of Georgia and established a station on Cortez Island, nearly in a line with the mouth of Bute Inlet. This, in time, would become the settlement of Whaletown and here, in the more favourable location, their luck improved.

During this same period, a Captain Roys arrived on the brig *Robert Cowan* from the Sandwich Islands with a party of experienced whalemen to head a second company called the Victoria Whaling Adventurer's Expedition. On March 1, they set off in the steamer *Emma* for Barkley Sound "to cruise in search of the oleaginous monsters of the deep", as some waggish reporter of the period most picturesquely phrased it.

All was optimism as the Roys' expedition steamed staunchly north. They were modernly equipped with two whale-boats, six guns and a plentiful supply of bombs and lances of the most approved style. One can imagine the stout Captain Roys striking an Ahab pose in the wheelhouse as he searched through binoculars for any of several schools of whales, reportedly sporting in the vicinity. Oil was worth 87 cents a gallon, by God!

Back in Victoria, a groundswell of scepticism regarding the expedition was roundly criticized by the irrepressible *British Colonist.* It argued with much conviction in the Captain's favour, stressing his experience, superior equipment and the fact that other hunting areas were already becoming worked out. What more shining endeavour than to work these near-virginal waters to honest profit?

On May 20, a Mr. John Kreimler arrived from Nanaimo, the bearer of somewhat discouraging news. The *Emma,* with Roys and his party, had arrived at the up island port empty-handed some days before. They had been unsuccessful in their search, having spotted only two whales, which evaded their clutches. While at Nanaimo, a report was received from Knight's Inlet which stated that

brief, glum item, five days later, The Victoria Whaling Adventurer's Company announced that it had decided to disband. It is presumed that the disillusioned Captain Roys returned to the Sandwich Islands to ponder on the perverse nature of fate and whales.

Perverse indeed! The very day after they had dissolved the company, a dozen great whales darted into Victoria harbour to sport, spout and fight like mad all day long. One of the impudent mammals ran aground and lay beached over one tide in huge mockery before floating away again. Little over a month later, a similar event occurred that is worth quoting verbatim - "Six enormous whales passed Clover Point yesterday morning - saucily spouting and sporting in their native element within a short distance of shore. The oily rascals seem to be aware that Roys has abandoned his whaling enterprise and gone away."

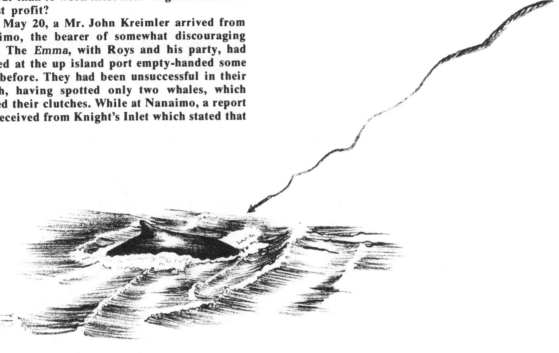

a large school of whales was sporting near shore in that northwest coast vicinity. The still hopeful Captain Roys obtained a map-tracing of the largely uncharted inlet and - to use again the long-gone correspondent's exact words, "started immediately to attend that school, confident that he will be enabled to give not a few of the scholars a lesson they will not be apt to forget in a hurry."

Alas for poor Captain Roys. He seems to have been born beneath an unlucky star. A number of whales were observed disporting off Knight's Inlet as per the intelligence but they were too far out to be reached. The *Emma* returned in disillusionment to Nanaimo, picked up some passengers from Sitka and headed for Victoria to get refitted. As if to add insult to injury, the boat broke her propellor off Trial Island and was towed back in complete ignominy to her point of origin by the steamer *Fry.*

Apparently, the stockholders and backers were none too overjoyed by this state of affairs. In a

There is one final postscript to the whole, sad fiasco. On February 20, 1870, scarcely a year after its inauguration, a Mr. Davies announced a sale by auction of the complete effects of the illfated Victoria Whaling Adventurer's Company. The best laid plans of mice and men ....

It is not recorded whether the unlucky Captain Roys ever crossed paths with the Dawson and Douglass Company. Paradoxically enough, their luck was running high during this same period. By July 27, 1869, the Scotsman and his partner had taken five whales in the vicinity of Cortez, yielding 13,000 gallons of oil. Two or three more whales killed were lost and picked up by outside parties. There is a suggestion that whale-rustlers were at work.

Fortune continued to smile on Dawson and Douglass. The *Kate,* working as far south as Comox and Cape Lazo, harpooned and secured seven more whales, all humpbacks. This breed of whale averages a length of fifty feet. The estimated yield from these operations was 9,450 gallons of lucrative fluid.

Captain Douglass kept in regular touch with the editor of the *Colonist*, apprising him both of the statistics of the catch and the hazards that were an integral part of the business. The big beasts seldom died quickly or easily and were capable in the throes of their passing, of inflicting severe damage on the small boats that hunted them down. There were certainly safer ways of making a living.

Three more whales were added to the tally-sheet by August 11. They were killed off Cortez under extremely difficult conditions involving high northwest winds and heavy seas. Despite bad weather, the Company prospered. One season produced 20,000 gallons of oil which the *Emma* freighted to Victoria and returned promptly to Whaletown, her holds empty, hungry for more.

By November of 1869, a further 15,000 gallons was shipped south to market from Cortez. Since the *Kate* was engaged in cruising the Gulf for telltale waterspouts and more greasy profits, a steamer called *Otter* was engaged to haul this late autumn cargo. Another 14,000 gallons was hauled to Victoria in mid-December and then the whalers took a well-deserved break, having completed a most rewarding season. It is not documented how the whaling men employed their leisure time but one can picture them in saloons, regaling the landlubbers with roaring yarns of the stormy hunts they'd survived.

After a short layoff, they joined forces with the Lipsett Whaling Company, whose shore works were located in Howe Sound. The two companies working in concert, cruised the Gulf of Georgia for six weeks and produced 150 barrels of oil. This was shipped to Victoria and business suspended for the season.

In June, 1870, the company moved their station from Whaletown to a fresh base on Hornby Island and operations were recommenced from this point. Encouraged by another successful season, the Scotsman and his partner decided to expand. Two wealthy Victorians joined forces with them and they were registered on July 27, 1870 under the Joint Stock Companies Act with a combined capital of $20,000. With an eye to widening their activities, arrangements were made to purchase a 200 ton vessel.

Things progressed satisfactorily and by May of 1871, the Lipsett Company incorporated with Dawson and Douglass, to form the British Columbia Whaling Company Limited. They operated that year in Gulf of Georgia waters but signs of change were already becoming evident. Catches were smaller than in previous years and whales were scarce south of the Yaculta Rapids.

The writing was on the wall for the British Columbia Whaling Company. The schooner *Kate* struck a reef off Mary's Island during a violent southeast gale and considerable damage was sustained.

She was repaired and returned to the hunt but more grief ensued. A large whale, furious in its death agonies, came up under its tormentor's small boat, capsizing it and spilling the crew into the rough and chilly water. It was sorely wounded from a lance and three bombs but continued to hurl itself about in a leviathan struggle for life. Eventually, a second boat which had a line on the plunging beast scored a mortal hit and put the whale out of its misery. It floated inert at last,

staining the waves crimson with blood. Whaling was a cruel and messy business.

And these were ill-omens for Dawson and his associates. Whale-sightings became less and less frequent. Catches dwindled to a point of virtual non-existence and the company slipped rapidly into a different sort of red from the whale-gore that had sustained it.

In January, 1872, scarcely three years after its auspicious beginnings, the British Columbia Whaling Company went into liquidation. Two months later, in March, the effects of the Company, including the brave schooner *Kate* and the hundred-acre pre-emption claim on Hornby Island with its wharf, sheds and other buildings, were sold at auction. Dawson's dream was dead.

The Scotsman turned his back on the seas that had betrayed him and became a prospector, travelling throughout the province in search of minerals. He was not notably successful at this new career and died some years later of general debility in Victoria. What happened to Captain Douglass is not known. Perhaps he sailed off to the Sandwich Islands to join Captain Roys. Thus ended the first period of whaling in British Columbia.

Now came a long hiatus. There is no reference whatsoever to Whaling in the Newspaper Index between 1873 and 1886. On September 19 of the latter year, the ever-vigilant *Colonist* reported that the Messrs. Gutmann and Frank of Victoria planned to establish the industry afresh by purchasing a complete whaling outfit in San Francisco and using it on the west coast of Vancouver Island. Evidently nothing came of this scheme. Four years later, on August 2, 1890, a Captain T.P.H. Whitelaw disclosed a bold plan to reanimate the industry for "there has been no whaling done in the Gulf of Georgia for the past 17 years". Once more it was a false alarm although Whitelaw's method of killing was said to be "new and thoroughly scientific in contrast to the old-fashioned methods which could never be made to pay in the past."

The "new methods" referred to by Captain Whitelaw undoubtedly involved use of the highly effective and more humane explosive harpoon, invented by Svend Foyn in Norway some years earlier. This device had revolutionized the industry. It killed quickly and cleanly, eliminating much of the turmoil and butchery that cruder methods had involved.

Late in 1898, Samuel Foyn, nephew of the inventor, was in Vancouver in hope of establishing a series of modern whaling operations, directed from B.C. ports. "I am here," he said at the time, "to engage capital and am not yet bound to anyone. As to whether Vancouver or Victoria will be the home port of the projected whaling business, I am indifferent, as a whaler is seldom in port."

Foyn's visit was to draw no immediate results. A year later the *Colonist* reported that although one of the biggest whale catches on record had been made that year off the B.C. coast, not a single Canadian vessel had participated and all the profit had gone elsewhere.

It took until 1905 for the Norwegian's vision to materialize in practical reality. In that year, a Captain Sprott Balcom in company with his brother Captain Reuben and a Captain William Grant, formed the Victoria Whaling Company.

They purchased two whalers, *Orion* and *St. Lawrence*, and steamed seaward in quest of spouting signs. For the first time in over thirty years, B.C. had a whaling industry.

The newborn Company opened its first whaling station in September 1, 1905 at Sechart on Barclay Sound. This served its purposes sufficiently until 1907, when a second station was established in Kyoquot Sound on the south side of Narrow Gut Creek (now known more mundanely as Cachalot Inlet.) A post office was established there in the same year and a 1909 Gazeteer describes it as "a whaling station, Indian village and P.O. on the east side of Union Island in Kyuquot Sound". In 1919 a separate post office was opened at the station itself and was called Cachalot. This factory was operated successfully for 17 years until a shortage of whales caused its abandonment.

At about the same time, a third factory was set-up at Page's Lagoon on the southeast end of Hammond Bay near Departure Bay. This operation did not fare well. A disappointing dearth of whales in the Gulf of Georgia resulted in its closure the following season after an abortive attempt to run it as a plant for converting dogfish to fertilizer. Sometime before March 31, 1910, the factory was dismantled and rebuilt on Moresby Island in the Queen Charlottes where it was operated with somewhat more success. The relocated plant was in a bay called Rose Harbour, a rather inappropriately-named site for such a foul-smelling endeavour.

In 1911, the Company constructed yet another factory on the west side of Naden Harbour on Graham Island, also in the Queen Charlotte group. A steamship timetable for April, 1914 shows regular service between the station and Prince Rupert so it appears to have been a fairly profitable venture for a few years. By August, 1917, however, it seems to have been phased out. A contemporary report mentions only the Sechart, Kyuquot and Rose Harbour plants as being in operation by that year. Despite the apparent bit of belt-tightening, the Company was prospering in this period. Its annual income frequently exceeded $1,000,000 and in 1918, three new steam-whalers were purchased from an American Company.

The original Company underwent several name-changes during its almost 40 years of operation. At various periods, it was known as Canadian Northern Fisheries, Pacific Whaling Company and finally, the Consolidated Whaling Corporation. The reason for this ambivalence is lost to posterity but another incident involving names has been recorded by T.W. Peterson in his article "Foreign Competition, Too Much Hunting Threat To Whalers" (*Daily Colonist*, July 4, 1965).

At an early period in the Company's career, the directors came to the decision that the Norwegian type of whaler, a small trawler-style steamcraft, would be best suited to the shore-whaling methods employed in B.C. waters. As a result, $300,000 was allotted to have six of the 102-ton vessels built by a firm in that Scandanavian country and shipped to Canada.

While the boats were under construction, a German scientist called Reismuller was enlisted in Newfoundland and brought to the west coast to supervise a revolutionary method he had developed for the extraction of whale-oil.

When the ships were nearly completed, the builder wired the Company, asking what they should name the new vessels. Professor Reismuller immediately spoke up, insisting, with Teutonic fervor, that they be called after various rivers of his beloved Fatherland. His suggestion was challenged by Lt. Col. J.M. McMillan, a Vancouver shareholder. The Scot had no objection to using the names of rivers as long as they were rivers like the Afton and the Clyde. The newspapers got in on the controversy and the whole business got quite out of hand. The exasperated Norwegians threatened to launch the boats incognito.

This would not have been in the interests of good luck or practicality and the directors arrived at a compromise that would offend no one. The ships were christened by colour - *Green*, *Blue*, *Black*, *Brown*, *White* and *Rose*. The last was undoubtedly in deference to Rose Harbour and equally inapt in this new context but, despite criticism, the title stuck.

Since this was before completion of the Panama Canal, the spanking new whaleboats were forced to make the tedious and storm wracked journey around the Horn, a fitting test of any ship's mettle. At the risk of making an outrageous pun, it is recorded that they came through with flying colours.

These sturdy vessels formed the nucleus of the Company's whaling fleet for most of the years it existed and must have paid for themselves many times over. 92 feet in length and powered by triple-expansion steam engines of 45.6 horsepower, they prowled the coastal waters at a top speed of ten knots with their bow-mounted harpoon guns at the ready. They carried a crew of eleven men including a Chinese cook and the skipper who doubled as gunner and could generally estimate a whale's length within a foot of accuracy. The taken whales were tagged and inflated with compressed air to prevent their sinking. Then the boats moved on after fresh prey, leaving the huge corpses to be picked up by the following tenders and towed to whichever station happened to be closest.

Unlike the wasteful early years when oil was the sole product, virtually every part of the creature was now utilized. Certainly, the main profit still lay in the blubber and many new uses had been found for it in munitions and leather-currying but now the bones, with the passing of corsets, were ground for fertilizer and the meat packaged for table-use, mostly in Japan where it is considered a great delicacy, as well as for animal food. There was little left for the scavengers now.

The Company, under its several names, prospered for many years and was infinitely more successful than the brief, jinxed era of Captain Douglass, James Dawson and their ill-starred contemporaries. Gradually, however, the same fate began to overtake them. The catch began to drop off year by year in an inexorable downgraphing until it had dwindled from 1,200 a year in slaughterous peak times to a pitiful 163 whales in 1942. The valuable Japanese market, too, had vanished with Pearl Harbour. There seemed little point in continuing in that third, gloomy year of World War Two and with little fanfare, the Consolidated Whaling Co. breathed its last. The fleet lay rusting at anchor near Point Ellis for the next three years and the whales swam unmolested for the first time in decades.

At the cessation of hostilities in 1945, the boats were examined and found to have deteriorated from disuse and neglect to a point where it was impractical to refit them for use. In April, 1947, two years later, all holdings of the bankrupt Consolidated Whaling Corporation were placed on the auction block. The *Brown, Black, Blue* and *White* were sold for scrap at $273 each. The *Green*

was sold to one of Victoria's original sealers, Max Lohbrunner, for conversion to a fishing station but nothing ever came of it and she ended up rusting into oblivion at another dock.

About a month after the auction and nearly six years to the day since a whale had been taken in B.C. water, a final whaling company was formed. Incorporated as Western Canada Whaling Company, it set up a station at Coal Harbour and with three ships, the *Nahmint, Saanich* and *Carruthers*, and $500,000 capital, commenced operation. Like its predecessors, it enjoyed considerable success at first. The Japanese market had reopened and the whales had returned in sufficient numbers to make a profit possible. In 1962 it merged with Japan's Talvo Gyogyo Company and in 1964 realized a record year. But it was the last. Once again, the whales began to vanish from the coastal waters as though in response to some secret signal and by 1967, they too were forced out of business by sheer lack of quarry.

There has been no whaling in B.C. since that time and it is highly doubtful whether it will ever be revived. Perhaps the whaleherds have learned their lesson at last, for they avoid these once-deadly waters like the plague. And perhaps, man is learning his lesson too.

They Don't Make 'Em Any More
Department

ON THE PASSING OF BASIL JOE

1

The church is chill in keeping with the day
But, shouting loud, its tolling tongue shatters
The brittle silence. The church is chill but
Rising soft as smoke, its windless choirvoice
Veers a southern breath, then dies.

Waxen, as in death, cold candles strive
A feeble flame. The lenten-shrouded
Deities, roused from Thursday drowsing,
Wait only for the celebrants to leave.

Led by an embroidered priest, the twelve-legged
Casket crawls its deathweight to the waiting wagon.
The bilious building vomits a sprawl of mourners,
Halted on the moulding steps, they look beyond
The coffin-color, elevate above the cursed hearse;
They squint the thin light April, scent
The salted weedwash of the sea,
As if reprieved.

Agleam with simonize of mourning, the
Cadillac houses its empty tenant and silently
Purring, slides and glides the country track
That sinuates from church to charnel ground.
A tail of dragging silence shuffles in its wake.

2

Within the gate the holed ground gapes and
Waits to claim again the clay it loaned.
The seawind, winter-whetted, fingers lean
Unleavened trees, drifts the sifting sunlight
Upon the mossgrey heads of dumb and drunken stones.

Beside the hole the hillocked sand drinks down
The holy rain; the holy words are mumbled to
The mud. The stoic circle tightens as
The earth reclaims her own. Idle spades
Made resolute, are manned by grieving Chiefs,
Rained gravel thumps the coffin-cage... hollow,
The thudding of a final, quiet drum.

It is over then.
The dying of a last archaic man;
Banana-fingered, oak-legged, caskchested,
Leather of lung... cut from the living flesh
Of native stone. A stone-age man, born
In the weathered longhouse, terminal son of
Aristocrats; progenitor of captive sons...
A fenced and ghettoed tribe.
Climber of mountains
Hunter of goats
Catcher of silver salmon,
Host to a horde of spectacled scholars,
Firemaker, toolmaker, teller of tales... old
Old as time. Wrinkled, toothless,
Massive. A brook of
Sunshot brightness, a well of
Midnight brooding...bemused,
Amused, whimsied.

It is finished then.
The expectant hole is filled... but
Filled with more than the husk
Of a worn and harried primitive.
With him a language passes, fashioned
by ten thousand generations, molded
From these hills, these trees, this
Sea and earth and sky...grown
From the growing of a people.

The lips of this land are sealed,
The tongue of its talker, stilled.

Buried too, the knowing of unwriting generations
The bunched and hoarded wisdom of survival... back
To a misted genesis, back to the brink of forgetting;
Buried the magic words, the affective incantations,
The rituals of living and of death.
Buried the invested symbols, the pantomimes
Of power, the dramatic demonstrations
Of courage, evil, wealth. Buried
The knowing of wilderness foods, miraculous
Uses of root and leaf...(his children
wander the market place, buy their
health at the pharmacy).

The mind of this land is cut down,
Its thought lies dormant as seed.
Buried the stern unsmiling gods, the
Animistic energy, gone the old totemic power
Back to the sea and sky, back to
The timeless time that gave them birth.

Gone the last ecological man, vanished
The last participant...the last who
Wandered still outside the fences, the last
Who shared the earth with all of life.

D.G. Poole
Grantham's Landing

EDITORIAL

You can look out almost any window in B.C. and see logging in the very shape of the landscape, but you can search libraries in vain for a book about logging.

You find little sign of logging in the province's official emblems or insignias, and when we celebrate a centennial we put up pictures not of the pioneer loggers who really made a place for the whiteman to live here on the west shore of Canada, but of more gold miners.

Maybe logging is just too obvious to see, like one's nose, or maybe it's that old inferiority complex, suppressing our own quite serviceable reality to imitate other people's myths.

The truth is, when we stop to see it, logging was one of the founding industries of the New World, and surely one of the most colourful, and here in the Pacific Northwest is where it reached its final glorious climax. The story of logging is not only one of great physical adventure, it is the story of a certain kind of man, a true-breeding North American species that evolved through 300 years of lonely and brutal confrontation with the continent's wilderness, to be swallowed in the end by the civilizing tide that followed it west.

It is to this story that we have devoted Issue Number 3 of *Raincoast Chronicles*.

FROM THE HILL TO THE SPILL....

The British Columbia coast has not always presented the patchy aspect we are familiar with today. Once the great trees pushed clear to the tideline in a green wall, broken only by the odd natural clearing, gouged out by landslide, flood or fire. Most of the fires then were the result of lightning strikes but it is said that on occasion the native Indians would set them deliberately, this being their only method for cutting some sort of hole in the infinite conifers. Apart from this, they lived in peaceful coexistence with the trees, using the natural fibres of the cedar bark for clothing and other practical purposes. The forbidding appearance of the primeval rainforest so oppressed Captain George Vancouver, one of the first whitemen to cast eyes on it, that he deemed it mournfully in his log as being totally unfit for human habitation. Many of the places he named, like Devastation Channel, Desolation Sound, reflect the dark sense of melancholy that possessed him. But of course the settlers came anyway.

The very first trees deliberately felled on the coast were probably for shipmasts. With the arrival of the first pioneers however, it became necessary to clear land for settlement and cultivation. The timber was dropped laboriously by means of axe and crosscut saw, a truly gruelling process that was not to alter substan-tially for many decades. Some of the trees were so enormous in girth it took several men an entire day to topple a single one. Metal-tipped springboards set in notches were used by the early fallers to climb above the butt-swell where the diameter of the tree narrowed and there was less wood to cut through. They would balance precariously on these slim platforms like stubborn acrobats as they plied their backbreaking trade.

The original logs were dealt with where they fell, rough planks being sawn and split from them by hand. Very shortly, sawmills began to spring up along the lower coast and it became more practical to transport the logs to these points in some manner. Floating them there was the obvious method, and wherever possible the trees were felled directly into the sea down steep shoreline cliffs, and even on the flatter beaches where the trees grew close enough to the water. This simplest method of getting logs to the sea was known as hand logging. It required little initial investment beyond a good saw and axe, a Gilchrist jack and a capacity for hard work. The jack was used to pry the logs free when they became wedged behind stumps. Most of the timber suitable to this mode of logging was rapidly gobbled up but there were still a few old timers working the more remote inlets in the early 1950's.

As soon as handy foreshore timber began to run scarce, it became essential to devise ways for getting more distant trees to the saltchuck. This was first accomplished with teams of oxen - as many as sixteen animals yoked together - hauling the logs from the woods along greased skid roads. These roads consisted of small logs laid crosswise like rail ties, only much closer together. The skids were greased before each haul by a grease dauber, frequently a young boy, who walked along the road with a bucket of fish oil, usually rancid and foul-smelling. The logs, to facilitate sliding, had all knots chopped off and the front ends sniped or undercut by two axemen known as the knotter and the sniper. A third man, called a rider, hooked up the logs for hauling and frequently barked them, except on steeper grades where the bark served as a natural brake. Highest paid man on the show was the teamster or bull puncher, who drove the oxen to exert themselves by means of a goadstick and a ready repertoire of thunderous cusswords. The bull skinner's trade called for much skill and could net him $125 per month.

Oxen were very strong, but they were also stupid and slow and required constant supervision by their poisonous-tongued drivers. As the sawmills grew in number, it became apparent that some faster method must be devised to feed them wood. The first step in this direction was the advent of horse logging around 1890. Huge cart horses of the Clydesdale variety were generally used. The logs were hauled in essentially the same manner as with oxen, the advantage lying in the considerably greater intelligence of the horse teams and their ability to work steeper grades. The horses could not pull as heavy loads as the bulls but they made up for it in speed and savvy, learning the route of haul like a book and knowing exactly when to knock off for lunchtime. The team - generally of twelve horses - could adjust to the speed of logs on inclines and knew enough to take to the brush if a turn ran away on them. A lead horse and driver controlled the operation, working in partnership. The drivers, for the most part a more humane breed than the blasphemous ox jockeys, often had true affection for their

Ox logging had its heyday roughly between 1865 and 1890. The original loggers were simply homesteaders who undertook the work along with their numerous other chores, but as the population increased and the timber was cut further from the settlements the first actual camps began to spring up. These were extremely primitive affairs where the men slept on straw bunks, provided their own blankets, ate chiefly beans, bacon and hardtack and worked twelve hours a day, six days a week. The rates of pay varied from little to less and a good axeman made only one dollar per shift. It was an extremely hard life, which separated the men from the boys in short order.

animals. The loads averaged five or six logs up to two feet on the butt, hooked in line. Where the roads bent sharply, huge steel rollers were fastened on stumps, enabling the logs to negotiate the turn more easily.

An alternative mode of getting wood to the sea that also came into use around this period was chute or flume logging. This method, used primarily in quite steep country, was tedious and time consuming to initiate and never achieved the popularity of animal hauling. It involved building a wooden aqueduct down which the logs would ride to the sea at ever increasing momentum. Some, such as the famous Pokegama Chute in Oregon, were of immense length, and the logs

would be literally on fire from the friction by the time they hit the bottom. Such a flume once existed on the northern shore of Howe Sound, and an old time hooktender who was working the area during its operation has told me of seeing the logs come down off the hill like bobsleds, hit the water in an explosion of spray and travel underwater for for an amazing distance before they finally leaped to the surface. Woe betide any passing boat that happened to be in their path. Assumedly such stray vessels were warned clear of the area while it was operating. Much smaller flumes were employed in like fashion to transport shingle bolts.

In none of these early non-mechanical systems of logging were anything but the very best trees taken. Any wood but number one cedar and fir was considered trash and left behind. Hemlock was deemed particularly worthless. With the opening of the first pulpmills around the turn of the century, this situation rapidly altered. The same ground was re-logged as once discarded trees acquired sudden value. The industry, relatively small up to this point, began to expand by leaps and bounds and with this expansion came an entirely new approach to moving logs.

It began with the advent in the woods of the steam-operated donkey engine. The first of these came into use around 1890 and were extremely crude. Contemporaneous with horse logging, they employed the same sort of skidroads but were set at the bottom of the road and pulled the logs from the brush by means of a cable wound on a windlass or capstan.

This very early system of mechanical logging was the germ from which all later techniques of yarding timber evolved. Power was only used to pull the logs to the landing. To return the rigging to the bush a line horse was employed. This astute animal was considered one of the crew and actually wore caulked horseshoes like any other brush ape. He was the first and last four-legged rigging man, however. The enormous gears of progress were already in motion and vast changes lay in store for the woods. Steam was the thing. The Industrial Revolution was coming late to the rough-hewn forest tamers but it was coming with a vengeance. Before very long some ingenious tinkerer deduced that it would be far more practical were a second or haulback drum installed on the donkey and both drums set horizontally, one above the other, in a steel frame, rather than vertically. This second, lighter cable ran through a couple of blocks out in the brush and attached to the mainline rigging, thus eliminating the need for line horses, who were put, perhaps gratefully, out to pasture. Later a third drum holding a lighter cable yet was added. This was called the strawline and was used to string the two heavier cables. Thus was the first true donkey engine born, and while it has changed radically in many aspects since those pioneers pots first built up steam and went ahead on her, the basic details remain the same to this day.

While skidroads were still used for a time after the animal teams were phased out, it soon became apparent that they were no longer necessary. With the new-fangled steam rigs, the logs could be yarded clear out of the underbrush along the line that ran from the machine to the first corner block. As each road was finished (for they are still known as roads in 1972 in unwitting tribute to the long gone first loggers and their sturdy animals) the block or blocks were moved and the line restrung. In this transitional period between the old and new the modern day rigging crew took form. Undisputed boss was the hooker or hooktender who took his name from the guy who hooked together the five or six log loads on horse hauling shows. In temperament however, he was generally a direct descendant of the old bullwhackers, a tough and formidable man with a loud voice and sulphurous vocabulary, who was not above using his fists if threats or inprecations failed. His chief function, apart from terrorizing the crew and supervising road changes, was to fight hangups when the log being yarded became stuck behind a stump, a frequent occurence in these early days of ground lead yarding. This was effected by various kicks and rolls, achieved by changing the position of the choker on the log and accompanied by the most ear-blistering curses the hooker could devise.

The choker was and is a short piece of cable with a steel knob or ferrule at either end and a sliding bell into which one of the knobs fitted to form a slip noose around the log and thus strangle or choke it. In the earliest days chains were used, but chokers proved much more effective. The worthies who performed this task were known as chokermen. Gradually an intermediary job called rigging slinger evolved. A sort of strawboss for the chokermen, he picked out the log or logs to be taken and was also an apprentice hooktender, expected to stand in for his boss should the occasion arise. Rigging slingers, provided they had the command of profanity for it and the necessary savvy, were generally promoted to full-fledged hookers in time.

Lowest man on the totem pole was the whistlepunk, although he generally sat on a stump. His job was to relay to the engineer the frequent signals that the rigging slinger or hooker shouted at him. Originally this was done semaphore style by means of flags, but as the machines began to extend their reach it was not always possible for the donkey puncher to see the punk and a better method had to be developed. This occasioned the invention of the jerkwire system, whereby a length of clothesline was attached at the machine end to the valve of a steam whistle and strung through the bush from a series of small saplings about six feet from the ground or whatever height suited the punk. Providing the line was tight enough, he could by hauling on it open the steam valve. This system was used for many years until it was replaced by electric whistles; latterly, transistorized transmitters carried by both the hooker and the rigging slinger have eliminated the job altogether. But for decades the punk was very much a part of the rigging crew, despite his lowly rate and status and the invective he was often compelled to endure. Although the job was usually performed by young boys or spindly men unsuited for heavier work, it sometimes fell to ancient hooktenders who had exhausted their furies. Sometimes a man would describe the whole cycle and end up in his old age, right back on the whistles where he'd begun.

The other members of the crew were the engineer who operated the donkey, a fireman, a couple of woodsplitters and a chaser who unchoked the logs at the landing. This was the basic crew structure of a yarding operation and it has remained substantially the same, although ad-

ditional men were used on the larger and much more complex systems that were to evolve when spar trees came into use. The fireman and wood-cutting jobs, of course, died with steam but that event was several decades distant.

The area being logged in B.C. up to the turn of the century was pretty much confined to coastal country south of Knight Inlet. It had spread out originally from such early settlements as Victoria, Esquimalt, Nanaimo and Port Moody. As late as 1883 the area where Vancouver now stands held only a very small scattering of cabins and was so heavily wooded that men despaired of its ever being logged off. The task was finally undertaken by the old Hastings Company, grandaddy of all the big B.C. logging outfits. With oxen, horses and ground lead yarders, plus a large crew of hard slugging woodsmen, they finally brought daylight to the swamp at the mouth of Burrard Inlet and the city began to take shape. Having completed this formidable job, they extended their operations to the North Shore and later on up into Howe Sound, where they removed much of the choice foreshore timber to feed their busy and ever-burgeoning sawmills. The largest and oldest stumps to be found in this area, with their high springboard holes, still bear witness to the staggering labours of the men who toiled for Hastings long ago.

Logging up to this point, and even after steam donkeys were introduced, was a slow and tedious business. Ground lead yarding was all very well, but the logs were constantly becoming hung up behind stumps or giant boulders. It seemed there was no way to speed up the process beyond blasting the obstacles out with dynamite and this was scarcely practical on a wholesale basis. It was necessary to innovate once more, and after several years of struggling with the unsatisfactory ground lead method and spurred on by the ever in-creasing demand for logs, some ingenious soul came up with the answer.

It consisted of hanging two lead blocks high in a topped tree, a huge one for the mainline and a smaller for the haulback. This provided the missing element of lift, enabling the logs to clear the stumps in most cases. The original high riggers must have been adventurous men to say the least, for they had to invent their new and dizzy trade as they went.

There was virtually no precedent for spar trees. Decapitating a standing fir often one hundred and eighty feet from the ground was a harrowing business, particularly when the top let go and, as though in outrage, the tree whipped back and forth across the sky. It could not have been easy at first to find men daring enough to attempt such madman's work, and for this reason, plus the general sort of reaction that sets in against any radical notion, the high lead method spread slowly. Another factor that delayed the accep-tance of the new system was the initial lack of a suitable climbing method. The belt and spur technique of mounting poles had not been inven-ted when the initial spars were rigged and their conquerors were obliged to scale them the best way they could. *Woods Words,* the invaluable source book produced by the University of Oregon, tells of two such trees that were still stan-ding in 1953. One of these, at Coos Bay, had spikes driven clear to the top. Another at McKen-zie Bay had been mounted by faller's springboards. How it was possible to have topped these trees without the use of a climbing rope for support and safety when the tops kicked loose has not been left to record. It is conceivable that the trees were beheaded by the use of dynamite and long fuses, a method not uncommon in later years on difficult or dangerous jobs where there was a possibility of the tree splitting.

The spar tree system, in any event, appears to have been first tried in Oregon as early as 1906 at Discovery Bay, by the Gardner Timber and Lum-

ber Company. A few years later it was in general use all over the west coast. It is uncertain precisely when high lead logging came to the B.C. woods. The first newspaper report of such activity came in 1911 when a correspondent for the Colonies Federation newspaper described quite graphically the operation of a Lidgerwood skidder, the first high lead machine, developed for swinging cypress out of the Louisiana swamps but not used in the northwest until 1904.

Shortly before the development of high lead systems came locomotive log hauling. As shore timber became scarcer, the huge companies then coming into being, such as the Bloedel, Stewart and Welch operation, forerunner of MacMillan and Bloedel, began working their way farther and farther from the beach into the incredible valleys and vast interior timber stands of Vancouver Island. In those times the primary tool for overcoming distance in the quickest and most practical manner was the railroad, and as the logging operators pushed inland they began to lay track. In a locie show, everything centred around rails. A line was pushed into a virgin stand of timber, the timber felled, the spar trees rigged and everything within reach yarded to this central artery to be loaded on flatcars. These enormous log trains, sometimes a hundred cars long, would chuff seaward, drawn perhaps by a Shay, most famous of all the logging locies — over trestle bridges and through canyons till they hit the great pier of the dumping ground that jutted like a finger from the beach. One trainload of logs was sufficient to keep a good sized booming crew jumping for some time.

The boom men took care of the aquatic end of the business. It was a prerequisite of this job to be nimble on your feet for you were fated to spend a good deal of your working day leaping from log to floating log some of which were prone to roll violently or sink away under you. The principal work involved sorting the logs into species and making them up into rectangular rafts or booms for transportation to the mills. The principal tool was the pikepole, with which you pushed or pulled the logs through the water. Flat booms were used in the protected waters. To weather the open seas around the outcoast camps, hundreds of logs were woven together with cables to form giant cigar-shaped structures called Davis rafts. Building these was a fairly complex business, requiring a special crew. Today the Davis raft has been supplanted by the self-dumping log barges, and men in dozer boats have taken the place of the pikepoled stowing gangs who were the mainstay of the trade for so long.

Those were the wide open years. The demand for lumber was increasing by leaps and bounds. At last the logging moguls had the power and techniques to effect enormous production, and this they did. It was a far cry from the relatively easy-going days of horses and oxen. Highball was the name of the game and highball they did. Log production doubled, tripled, quadrupled. Safety regulations were virtually non-existent, and quota-crazed hookers drove their crews like galley slaves. Don't walk, don't run. . . fly! they'd scream at the chokermen. The fatality rate was considerable. Only the best was taken - the rest left to rot. The rape of the coast had begun.

Completely unregulated logging can destroy the balance of nature in short order, wrecking the watersheds, fouling salmon streams, leaving the land a sacked shambles, and this was exactly the picture in the early years of the century. The advent of effective machines and improved methods had caused the industry to mushroom overnight into a huge and highly lucrative business with virtually no legal safeguards to curb its depredations. There were fortunes to be made in timber and countless men anxious to make them. It is no exaggeration to speak of the coast being raped in that greedy and careless period. They creamed the prime stands with their hungry steam donkeys, left fire-hazardous wreckage and half-logged country in their wake. It was a get-rich-quick proposition with no thought whatsoever for posterity. Speculation and graft abounded. It became obvious to certain farsighted people that disaster would be the only long-range result if this wholesale looting of the forest resources continued unchecked. In 1912 the first Forestry Act was drawn up and passed into law. It served to put a series of restrictions on the books that generally curbed the irresponsible plundering, and its basic precepts are still followed today. Logging continued apace but in a slightly more restrained manner.

FAIRBANKS-MORSE
UNDERWRITER FIRE PUMP
18 × 10 × 12
CAPACITY
1000 GALLONS PER MINUTE OR 4 GOOD
1⅛ INCH SMOOTH NOZZLE STREAMS
FULL SPEED 70 REVOLUTIONS
PER MINUTE

NEVER LET STEAM GET BELOW
50 POUNDS NIGHTS OR SUNDAYS
OR AT ANY OTHER TIME

There were numerous variations on the basic high lead system, most of them involving the use of a skyline. Usually this meant a stationary cable strung either between two spar trees, or from a spar tree to a large stump in very steep country. A carriage rode back and forth along this line, to which the end of the mainline was shackled. A heavy fall block hung in the bight of this, to the neck of which the butt rigging (a series of shackles and swivels from which the chokers hung) and then the haulback were attached. It was possible by this method to lift the logs completely clear of the ground and thus eliminate the hangup problem entirely. In the case of a slack line, the skyline itself was on a special large drum and could be lowered up and down when needed. This was useful for yarding out of canyons or deep gullies. The skidder was another skyline variation, as was the Tyler gravity system. Skylines of one form or another were an integral part of the cold-decking process, whereby timber too far from the rail lines or roads was yarded and piled at a separate spar tree and then swung out to the trackside trees for loading. Often in unusually rugged territory the distance was too great for the logs to be brought out in a single operation and an intermediary or swing tree was employed, where the logs were unhooked from one set of rigging and hooked up to the next. Perhaps the most outlandish skyline set-up ever used in the woods was the skyhook. It required as many as eight spar trees and a double skyline, which the donkey and its steel-nerved engineer rode like an overhead crane, moving from tree to tree with their suspended loads by means of a by-pass system. This giddy contraption was considered so hazardous that the Compensation Board refused to cover the reckless operators who rode it. This factor, plus the complexities and time involved in rigging it up, kept its use to a minimum. Another curious variant was the Wisen line, a Swiss importation. This was a very light, strong cable that was purportedly capable of taking out logs in a single swing over twice the distance of an ordinary skyline. It worked fine with small logs but the Swiss simply hadn't reckoned on the sheer weight and size of much B.C. timber. "Okay for swinging cuckoo clocks around in the Alps, I guess! a scornful old hooktender remarked as he watched one such failed device being forlornly dismantled by its Swiss exhibitors.

From almost the very beginning of large-scale logging on the B.C. coast there were two distinct types of camps, the big ones and the gyppos. The former employed as many as six hundred men and were invariably locie shows. They were located primarily in the vast timber stands of Vancouvdr Island and the Queen Charlottes, although they were found in the mainland valleys too, where the ground was suitable. These large outfits were like gigantic roofless factories, systematic, tightly organized, fussy as to regulations, geared for high production, relatively impersonal. Their campsites were fair-sized villages, with quarters for married men and their families and often a one-room school. These camps, as a rule, had a hard-core crew of home guards who often worked there for years in as close to a stable situation as could be found in the woods. Few loggers gave much of a goddamn about stability however, rejoicing in their independence and the privilege of quitting a layout at the drop of a hat (usually a bone dry canvas hat in the days before hardhats became compulsory). They varied in their itinerant habits from two or three camps a year to thirty or more in the case of the notably footloose breed known as camp inspectors. Perhaps the most famous of this group was Eight Day Wilson, king of the short stake artists, who was a good as his name. To his eternal chagrin, he was once cajoled on a bet into staying sixteen days at the same outfit. These restless characters rapidly became persona non grata with the big companies and spread their talents out among the hundreds of small gyppo camps which were considerably less fussy.

The gyppos were a different proposition altogether from the big outfits. They proliferated in astounding number along the steep shores of

the upcoast inlets and among the islands. Gyppos varied in size from minimal operations where a couple of partners slugged it out alone to fairly elaborate set-ups employing as many as forty men. The majority of these places were float camps, both for the sake of mobility and for the fact that along much of its shore area the B.C. coast plunges steep and beachless into the sea. The big interests had cornered the market on flat ground. The gyppo operators were left mainly with the mountaingoat shows, and more often than not they logged them by means of an A-frame. In this mode of yarding, the donkey sat on a raft held off-shore by a stiff-leg and made stationary by shore guys or guylines. The place of the spar tree was taken by two trees leaning inward, lashed together in the shape of an A and guylined erect. The high lead blocks hung from a cross brace. An A-frame could be used either for straight yarding or in conjunction with a skyline. It was both the most common and the most practical method for logging precipitous shorelines.

The big camps were fairly well standardized and you knew pretty much what to expect when you hired out to one. Not so the gyppos. They varied from excellent to execrable with every gradation between. Working in a good small camp could be

as pleasant an experience as you were likely to have in the woods. Working in a bad one where the grub was poor, the crew surly and chronically short-handed and the equipment worn out was a sobering business indeed, especially since such ill-run places frequently went bankrupt and did you out of your wages. The gyppos were a gamble and you took your chances.

Caterpillar tractors were another method of hauling logs. A very primitive ancestor of the cat, with two tracks on the back and a single front wheel for steering, was in use as far back as 1912 but these early machines were slow, cumbersome and limited to flat country. The counterpart of the present day cat did not come into general use until the early thirties. This versatile machine, with its ability to both bulldoze roads and, with the addition of an arch, to yard logs, was widely used on suitable shows from the thirties until quite recently. In latter times it has been more or less replaced in the log hauling department by the giant-tired Timber Toter, although it is still widely used on clearing and earth-moving jobs. In their manner of hauling both cats and Timber Toters are the direct mechanical descendants of the horse and ox teams.

109

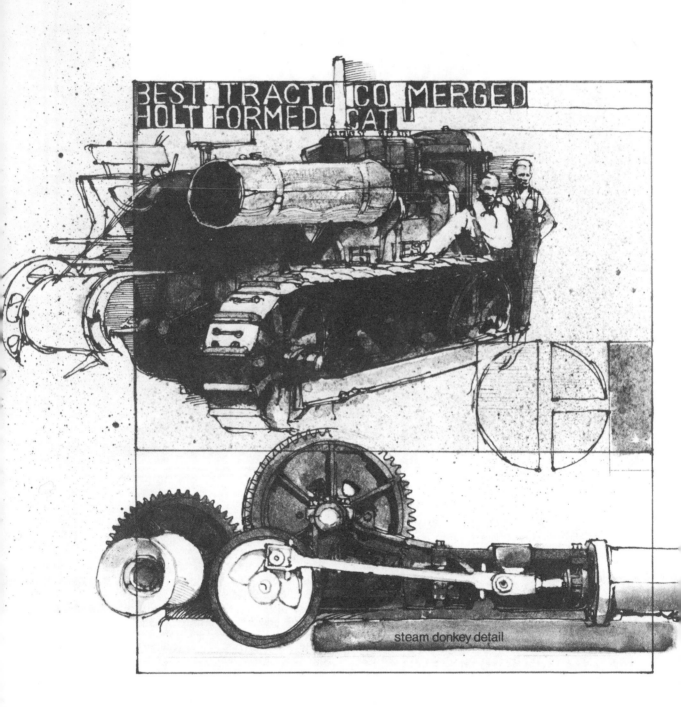

BEST TRACTOR CO. MERGED HOLT FORMED CAT

steam donkey detail

The primary mode of transportation back and forth to the camps, and virtually their only point of contact with the outside world in the days before aeroplanes and radio telephones, were the once familiar black, white and red boats of the Union Steamship Company. Just how many stakey loggers climbed those getaway gangplanks after months of sidehills and bunkhouse walls for a well-earned blowout in the Big Smoke, it boggles the mind to imagine. Thousands upon thousands. And thousands upon thousands made, wet weeks later, the morose return journey to servitude, hammered silly by the city flatter than a steam rollered pancake, hung over beyond human comprehension, sure they'd never do it again but always doing it, hard-done-by, toughluck tame apes chasing their tails round a squirrel cage to nowhere until they were too damn old to cut it anymore. Of course not all loggers were roary-eyed drunks, but the majority were. It was something in the very nature of the trade. No matter how wet those bitchin' sidehills got, they still made you thirsty. Oh, there was always that quiet gink in the corner bunk who saved up his money and bought his way out of the slivery, slovenly rat race but there were always ten goofs like you to every one of him. In the bull pen of the *Cassiar*, safely hidden from the more respectable passengers, you toughed out the shakes and the snakes again and again. The old Union Steamship Company had your number. Their passenger lists read Men, Women and Loggers as though you were a member of some other species entirely. And maybe you were.

The Golden Age of Steam in the woods lasted from perhaps the turn of the century until after the Second World War. It was a brawling, dangerous era when the donkeys roared full tilt and the locies snorted dumpward with their mighty gleanings. Blood, toil, sweat, logs and no time for bullshit in the beginning. Then the union organizers began to infiltrate the camps, preaching the seditious gospel of the forty-hour week and a decent basic wage. And time-and-a-half for overtime. And a lot of other things the logger had hardly even thought of before. At first it was the Wobblies with their war cry of a World Union. Sure, their teachings didn't take. They were blacklisted and run off the claim with their Commie notions, but they sowed the seed. And finally the boys got organized, and stood up for their rights and altered their lot forever in the end. And Compensation was established and Unemployment Insurance and they cleaned the bedbugs out of the bunkhouses and steam began to die.

The jig was actually up for the big locie shows with the appearance of the first logging trucks with their open cabs and hard rubber tires. Not many people realized it at the time but those almost laughably crude vehicles would metamorphose into the giant diesel rigs of today and supplant the roaring Shays. For trucks could go where trains couldn't and chase the timber into the hills when the flat country ran out. They could negotiate grades that no locie without a snub line on it could ever hope to attempt. The tide began to turn around the end of World War Two and it was purely a matter of time for the logging railroads after that. Trucks were simply a faster and more practical method of hauling wood as the easy shows petered out and the country got

hairier. There were a few locie shows still operating in the early sixties but they were the last, and running one jump ahead of the boneyard. It was purely a matter of time.

The big steam pots went even earlier. They outlasted the Second World War with its fuel shortages, but as soon as the conflict was over and restrictions relaxed spanking new diesel and gas donkeys began to appear on the market and were fast adopted by the operators. Steam pots were all very well but you needed three or four men to run the goddamn things. None of that nonsense with these new babies and they were much less trouble to move.

Even the fallers, those men apart on whose sweat and knowhow the industry depended and whose hardway method of dropping timber had not altered appreciably since the ox team days, began to get a break around 1940 or so with the introduction of the power saw. At first it wasn't much of a break. The earliest chain saws were enormously cumbersome and temperamental and required two men to operate them. Many an old Swede stuck stubbornly to his crosscut, unwilling to even consider using such an unsieldy device. But just as with the steam pots and locies, progress was bound to triumph in the end. The power saws, benefiting from the technological quantum leaps taken during the war, were to improve by leaps and bounds, increasing in cutting efficiency as they grew lighter. For a time electric saws were tried, four or five of them attached by cables to a portable power plant but the drawbacks of this system were self-evident from almost the beginning and it was soon abandoned. Gas saws were the ticket and the poor old hand-fallers simply couldn't compete. They were compelled either to adopt the new methods or retire and a good many took the latter course. I saw a team of ancient Norwegians working a setting with crosscuts and springboards as late as 1954 but they must have been some of the very last. Today a single faller, using one of the light and highly effective chain saws presently available, can fall and buck twice the number of trees as three men could in the past. Falling remains the most dangerous and highest-paid job in the woods but it's a far cry from the old days.

The loading of logs, too, has undergone considerable streamlining. Originally, in the earliest days of high lead logging, chokers were used to load the logs while tongs were used on the rigging to yard them to the tree, but this illogical system was soon reversed. There were two basic loading techniques. In the Maclean Boom method, two tongs were used. The log was tonged at both ends, lifted completely clear of the ground and swung onto the flatcar or trailer truck. This system often used five men - an engineer, a head loader who stood on the truck cab and built the load, two second loaders who set the tongs, and a third loader who stamped or painted the logs. In the hay rack or heel boom system has evolved into the grapple loader, a sturdy crane offshoot. The entire process is accomplished by a single operator who picks up the logs by means of a steel-jawed grapple and builds his own loads. Since, in effect, one man has taken the place of five, this could be offered as a prime example of automation at work.

Until 1952 logging remained a pretty reckless and haphazard affair, quite loosely regulated. In that year, however, a bill was passed, imposing a yearly log quota on the logging operators. They were allowed to take out a set number of board feet in a twelve-month period but no more. This effectively put an end to the avaricious behaviour of some operators who were chewing up the forests at a staggering clip. It also made the woods a safer place to work, since it cramped the style of the highball artists who were still maiming and killing their fair share of men. In addition to the quota, settings were required to be logged off much more cleanly than before and extensive reforestation programs were undertaken. The freebooting era, now referred to wistfully by some old loggers as the Glory Days, had officially come to a close.

And the changes were not over yet. Wooden spar trees, for so many years the mainstay of any high lead setup, were shortly fated to go the way of the dinosaurs. Compact yarding units, mounted on tank tracks or flatdeck truck bodies, complete with folding or telescopic steel towers, were rapidly being developed. These units carried their own guylines and took only a fraction of the time to rig up that the wooden trees had traditionally demanded. The practical gains were enormous and the new system was adopted as rapidly as the manufacturers were able to turn out the towers. Toward the end of the sixties, it had become a rare thing indeed to see a wooden spar tree in use and today they are virtually non-existent. With the passing of the spars the high riggers were no longer needed to ply their giddy craft and one by one those steeplejacks of the tall timber hung up their belts and spurs for the final time. To some perhaps it came as a profound relief, but others must have felt like Wyatt Earp hanging up his guns. There was a certain class connected with being a good high climber that few other jobs could offer.

Logging today is carried on almost entirely by steel spars and track loaders, another crane variant that both yards and loads. The skylines are gone along with the cold-deck piles, the whistle punks, the A-Frames, the springboards and all the other vanished men and methods that once made the woods unique. Present day yarding is a pretty sedate affair in comparison with the roaring highball sides of times gone when the steam fakes ran wide open and merciless hookers howled for more wood. Safety regulations are quite religiously observed. It's almost a gentleman's game, but a trace of the old romance still lingers here and there on wet, windy days when you fight a big paylog out from behind a stump, using the same hold they used in ground lead times, and send it kicking and crashing safely home. At such moments it is possible to feel a definite sense of continuity, for not quite everything has changed.

What the future holds for the industry is difficult to assess at this point. Doubtless it will grow progressively smaller and more selective. Automation will continue to eliminate the traditional jobs. Already, a grapple yarder is in use that requires only one man in the bush with a walkie-talkie, thus dispensing with the chokermen and the rigging slinger. Balloon logging has been tried with some success and helicopters, although expensive, have been employed to log stands of timber previously considered inaccessible. One thing certain is that the old days of roughnecking it and slugging those logs out any which way, damn the cost! are gone forever. It's all good and proper and sensible and inevitable and somehow, rather sad.

"Highball"

RAILWAYS
IN THE WOODS

"Late one night and colder 'n hell, standing on the lower running board where I usually stood, flyin through the black night, I did something I rarely never did, got a notion to climb up beside the boiler and huddle there, gather some of that locie's heat; pulled my jacket tight around me and sat there shivering. Wham! We come around a corner and there beside the track's a boulder big as a room. Faster'n I can say it, it tore hell outa that side of the engine, ripping off the running board where I was standing a mile earlier. Woulda cut me off about where I buckle my belt."

One man is telling a story about one of the things that happened to him as an engineer on a logging railroad. Many men, many engines, more trains, hundreds of lines and countless stories make up the saga of railroad logging, one of the most memorable and thrilling occupations in the history of the coast.

I've heard old woodsmen say that in the 1930's and '40s it was every young man's dream to get out into the woods for the money and glamour of logging. If they did get into the woods, you can bet they thought now and then of how they could get a job as hogger or fireman, to ride the puffing, snorting, whistling steam engines. The trainmen were the elite of the woods.

The job went through a lot of changes since the first locie was used around 1900 at either Chemainus or at Hasting Mills up at Quadra Island and Thurlow Inlet. It started out with rails tacked onto the old skidroads recently vacated by oxen and horses, an adaptation of the rig used by the first big donkey engines which hauled the logs with one-and-a-quarter-inch wire cables.

They called it skidder logging. The logs'd be hitched one to the other and a whole string of them, up to twenty big logs at a time, would be dragged along the track, sliding on their bark-stripped stomachs. Outfits used this haywire rig, rails laid on skidroad, till as late as about 1910, by which time all had switched over to regular rail.

When the demand increased, Eastern American companies started supplying detached trucks, sets of four wheels each, like the trucks on railroad cars today. The logs'd be slung from one to another and blocked in place with wedges of wood or metal. Each of the trucks had its own brake, manual or steam, which had to be set separately.

That was the job of the brakeman. He'd course up and down the moving train which would be hitting speeds of thirty miles per hour, jumping on and off the loads to set the brakes. Going up hills at a grade of nine per cent, they could still manage about ten miles per hour. A guy had to be pretty quick on his toes to keep em all set right. The engineer'd have a system worked out to tell how tight to set em: one whistle, a half turn; two whistles, three-quarter; three, damp em right down.

A native carver out near Port Renfrew, Charlie Jones can remember those early days. He used to be head brakeman at Renfrew and Jordan River around 1908. He recalls that in the four years he worked on the trains there were five brakemen killed and a bunch more bashed up, losing arms and legs. But the brakemen got good pay, all of four seventy-five a day, or three dollars if you were second brakeman. It was obviously before the Wobblies happened along.

It was the engineers and firemen later on, white folks running on rails laid by Chinese crews, that saw the glamour and glory in it. They seem to like rubbing up against adverse conditions and though they got a little less by the hour than the other woodsmen, they made up for it with lots of overtime, especially if there'd been a wreck or a big fire threatened.

Working the trains really seemed to get into some men's blood. They talk of the thrill of being known up and down the coast, to ride through camp in the cab and have folks wave at you, to sit in and work a shining black Shay, coaxing it up hills with a load no crew had managed before.

Everyone remembers the Shay as their favourite locie. With its three side-mounted cylinders and geared drive-shaft it easily stood apart from its biggest competitors, the Climax and the Heisler. It was called "the eggbeater" and "the cadillac of the locies". It was the pioneer in its field and was made by the Lima Locomotive Works in Ohio. Shortly after the American Civil War, a Michigan sawmill operator named Ephraim Shay designed her to haul logs through the heavy northern winters. She was to see action in a lot of countries, trucking far across the seas to serve in places like Taiwan, the Philippines, Japan, Argentina and Chile.

For Ephraim, "the big problem in logging was, and still is, how to get the logs out of the woods." By 1877, he was using a tram-way to log on, but it was many years and modifications before his engine attained the classic proportions of the Pacific Coast Shay. What set these locies apart from mainland engines was the drive system, which was geared rather than fitted with straight shafts. Universal joints on the shaft let the engine navigate sharp curves. The Shay could turn a 32-degree curve and the Climax, because its drive was right in the center of the axles, could take a 50-degree turn. The Shay with its three cylinders was a better steamer; it had more draft, a more constant torque and better starting power. Then there was the works, which were all out in view. It didn't need a pit to do repairs; most jobs could be done in the woods.

The Climax engines were a beauty to watch but rough to run. There was a piston on each side, and as these fired alternately it moved something like a sprinter. Waddy Weeks, who now drives truck for Canadian Forest Products at Port Renfrew, recalls "They were the hardest damn thing on a fellow's body; banged yer kidneys around, shook up yer lungs. It was like riding a jumping horse. You couldn't sit down on em. You got aboard, tucked yer shirt up tight to you, pulled the throttle and you were off, bucking and snorting down the line."

When the Climax Company experimented with a couple of big 100-ton engines, the action was so heavy it shook the things apart. They only made two and one was used over at Port Renfrew. They called it a white elephant and fitted it with heavy counter-weights. Then they said it had boxing gloves on.

The Heisler was a good engine but was a late-comer and never dented the Shay's market. Like the Climax, its drive was under the engine. There were V-mounted pistons encased in a box on either side of the boiler. Also like the Climax, it needed a lot of maintenance work done back in camp. There were only two things which could cripple a Shay, a broken shaft, or a broken wheel.

shay drive gear detail

If one of its three cylinders went, it could still move on the two remaining; not so the other engines.

Some of the companies on the coast used all three engines. Others used haywire rigs like the Fordson tractor with its wide flanged wheels, readily accomodated to the small track rails. One was used till 1940 by Dot Brothers up near Cape Scott. On really steep grades, some outfits used a funicular railway which could operate up to forty-three per cent! Washington Iron Works made a special twelve-foot drum mounted on the front car, around which cable was wrapped, connected to a pulley at the moutain top. If one of these got loose, like it did up at Englewood, it would pick up a lot of speed before hitting the lake below. One of the last of these used on the coast was at Jeramiason's show at Goliath Bay up Jervis Inlet.

Usually a steam operation would consist of a number of steam donkeys to do the skidding and loading, some small engines to shift the loads from the shows to the main road, maybe some forty or fifty-ton Shays or Climaxes, and a larger engine, a hundred-ton Shay or a big Baldwin, rod driven, to haul the train down to the pond or salt-chuck.

In the early days of detached trucks, the logs'd be bound together with chain. Later, with flat cars rented from the mainline companies, wooden stakes would hold em in place. When they got to the dump those stakes would be whacked off and the load'd slip down an incline into the slough. Any logs that hung on there to the bunk would be jettisoned, or "jillpoked" off by a log stuck into the ground as a lever. They'd move the car for-

ward into that log and pop the lazy ones off.

If the engine was powered by wood there'd be about five men on a train. There'd be a couple guys to cut and stack the wood; the engineer to direct the operations and drive the train; the fireman to fire the engine, shoving wood into the furnace; and a couple of brakemen to see to it that the train wasn't going to run away down the hill. To get his license to run a train, an engineer had to serve eighteen months firing time. To become a fireman, you had to know someone, and that meant you'd either been on trains before, or you'd been around the woods long enough to make friends.

Charlie Jones started out firing steam donkeys. Then he got a job on the trains. He went to Vancouver a couple times to try for his engineers ticket but one question on the exam stumped him - how much pressure is there in a nine by ten cylinder head. "I never was much good at arithmetic." he says.

The closest most guys got to the trains was sitting in the speeders, heading out in the morning and coming back at night. In the big days of company logging of the '40s and early '50s, the speeder would haul a trailer and both of em would hold thirty or forty men. The speeder was usually a gas driven rig with a chain drive and a reversing gearbox. It was frequently a place of relaxation and rambunctiousness. Jim Crickney told me about a time when there were two crummies hooked onto a long train of empties. They stopped at the powder shacks to pick up a hundred cases and must have been kind of sloppy loading it aboard. They hadn't pulled out for very long when the

—note triple cylinders and drive shaft—

black powder was spewing all over the tracks in front of em like porridge. Some one pulled the brake and they swept it up and continued on, nervously happy.

Another story I heard about some careless fun concerns a fellow called "The Bishop" up at Elk River. He was well known up and down the coast for having one of the friendliest establishments around. When the locies'd pull into the dumping ground, "The Bishop" 'd be there with a couple cases beer and some bottles of hard stuff. By the time the trains were dumped the engineer and the boys'd be ready to fly back up the hill. They'd hide the booze in the firebox.

Working up there once, Waddy Weeks noticed both the fireman and engineer getting "drunker 'n skunks." The train was running out of water and getting low on fuel. It looked like the boiler might blow any minute so Waddy and a young guy along for the ride left the front of the train and scrambled down the line. Pretty soon, the train's still steaming along, chug, ka-chug, ka-chug and both the hogger and fireman are passed out cold in the cab. There's one on either side, heads on the window still going ka-bump, ka-bump, ka-bump, smacking with the rhythm. Pretty soon they get a whistle from the super and they brake it down. There's a couple guys in hot water mighty quick. But the hauls at night would be pretty cold and lonely.

Few people realize just how many logging railroads there were. After 1930, it was pretty well just the big outfits that had them, but before that they were all over the coast, with the greatest number on Vancouver Island. There were outfits

on the West Coast dumping into the Pacific at Port Renfrew, at Point No Point near Jordan River, and at Serrito Camp near Bamfield. On the east coast of the island, trains hauled their loads down to Chemainus, Crofton, Ladysmith, Nanaimo, Comox and Elk River. The interior was dotted with them, at Englewood, at Cowichan Lake. The geared engines saw action as far north as the Queen Charlottes where five of them were used above Cumshewa Inlet at Skidegate Lake on Moresby Island. That's right above an ancient village sight of the Haida, perhaps the first loggers on this coast.

There were probably at least a hundred railways over the years from 1900 to today, when only one bona fide logging road runs up at Englewood. They dotted the inlets and logged the lower mainland before the city of Vancouver was built, chugging through heavy forest behind Jericho Beach. On Texada, Gambier and Quadra Islands logs were steam hauled to make the lumber which built the coastal towns and cities.

Between 1928 and '34, there were a hundred 42-ton Shays in operation on the Pacific Coast. Thirty-five 90-ton Pacific Coast Shays have seen action here since the first one was sold fresh from exhibition grounds to Bloedel, Stewart, & Welch, of Menzies Bay, in 1928.

The first engine hauling logs in B.C. for sure was a 45-ton Climax working down from Miller Creek at Chemainus in 1900. Some folks say that maybe the first one was *Curly*, operating up at Hastings Mills, on Quadra and Thurlow Islands. It was being used there by 1901 by a fellow by the name of Saul Reamy. He picked it up from the

CPR when they'd finished laying rail with it. They bought it cheap when it was finished work down in Panama when the canal was being dug. Now the little fellow sits in Vancouver's Hastings Park, just one of the places you can still see these old time locies. There's others here and there along highways and in towns, at Crofton, Ladysmith, Duncan and Port Alberni, to name just a few.

The same time *Curly* was working on small islands up in the gulf, outfits on Vancouver Island were experimenting with large steam traction engines fitted with "bell-shaped wheels" that ran on round poles spiked end to end on existing skidroads. Though most operators switched to regular between 1904 and 1910, the skidroad models were used till 1930.

The Department of Transport started calling the shots early and had a lot to say about design and safety features. They outlawed the narrow three-foot gauge railway under a number of mishaps, the last of which happened on Mount Sicker when a Shay flipped over and killed its driver. They also stepped in and made the air brake mandatory, though Hastings Mills used steam brakes till 1928, eight years after they were outlawed. It seems that one of Hastings Mill's bosses was none other than Lieutenant-Governor Humber. But that's nothing new in this province. The air brake saved a lot of men's lives but must have cost the operators a few dollars initially.

An interesting adaptation on the logging railroads was the use of regular rod engines fitted with water tanks which sat directly over the drive wheels. Called saddle tanks, they greatly aided the driving power.

The heavy grades of the coastal mountains made such power vitally necessary. One of the longest and most spectacular runs was out at Jordan River. It was seventeen miles long running on grades from nine to fourteen per cent. That was in 1908 and it would take three hours to complete the run. With grades like that, a good brakeman was essential. If the brakes weren't on tight enough it meant derailments; if they were too tight, the train'd get flat feet, the wheels'd skid instead of roll and there'd be inches of metal burnt right off them.

At Port Renfrew, there was over a hundred miles of track. B.C. Forest Products by 1950 had three hundred miles. Some of the bridges in that west coast area where huge, among the largest in the world. The Bear Creek trestle was about 250 feet high and 700 feet across. It was supported by three Howe trusses, each 90 feet long. The lower San Juan trestle was 154 feet high and 600 feet long, supported in the center by an A-frame.

One of the biggest outfits on the east coast was the Comox Logging and Railway Company, originally built by Minnesota logger J.D. McCormick, who rafted the logs in Comox Bay and towed them to mills in Vancouver. By 1911 they were still using skidder logging, but soon the big trains became central to the valley's economy. At one time there was a million board feet a day pouring out of the forests through Courtenay and Headquarters. At twelve dollars per thousand, that works out to $120,000 gross a day. Locies came down to the booming grounds at Royston from at least three different shows: Black Creek, Wolf Lake, and the Tsolum River.

Pride and Joy

Climax drive detail

With all that movement, safety became important. Dispatching had to be done with greater efficiency than in the past. Accidents in the industry were usually caused by just such a lack of planning. The engineer'd figure "Well, I guess that rig oughta be outa there by now" and he'd run smack into the other locie, or a speeder coming up. "There were always wrecks or something going wrong."

Waddy Weeks recalled a haywire sort of collision up at Elk River. There was a long dip on Diamond Hill and the locies used to freewheel down that and coast as far as they could up the long light grade on the other side. One night a fellow fell asleep on his way down the hill and before he reached the other crest the train started rolling back the way he'd come. Well, the hogger in the second engine figured he'd given enough time and headed down the line. The two trains met down in the dip, each roaring along in opposite directions. The second train was pushing a long string of maybe thirty or forty empties and that first train piled into them, splittin and smashin the cars, driving em apart "like a herd of buffalo."

Course, usually before things got too rough, the guys on the train'd have a chance to see what was goin down and bail out. Ken Halberg told of another hairy smashup out Caycuse Camp on Cowichan Lake. There was a long switchback there and the trains'd assemble at the summit for the four-mile trip below. It was about seven per cent grade all the way. The 100-ton Climax hauled out about twenty loads and the second train got ready to start out. Somebody'd forgot to set the retainers, which keep a sort of reserve air supply in the brake lines for just such grades. The train ran away and the crew bailed out with fifteen loads of logs freewheelin down the track. Some of them jumped the rails but the locie and the remainder made it all the way to camp smacking right into the back of the first train, raining logs all over the place. Course there's all sorts of those kind of stories. Like I said everyone's got em and together they puzzle together what this coast is built on.

A lot of the engines were moved around a lot, being traded or sold, or shifted to new shows. One of those was a 45-ton wood-burning Shay which started out at Powell River. It worked there at Myrtle Point for about seventeen years, then was moved to Menzies Bay in 1928. It went to Great Central Lake in 1953 and was barged to Vancouver in the early '60s, destined for the Phillipines. Customs people put an end to the deal and old Number One ended up at the Cowichan Valley Forest Museum, on the highway just north of Duncan.

Some of the other locies on the coast that made a name in one way or another were the Chemainus "6 Spot", a 50-ton Shay, Cathel & Sorenson's "One Spot" which ended up for a while on the mainline between Ladysmith and Nanaimo and now rests in peace in Ladysmith, a funny little 10-ton engine called the "Nanaimo" which was shipped around the Horn by sail in 1874, with a copper fire box and little side tanks. There was a locie which had originally operated on the New York Elevated Railway and ended up serving both mills and mines on the east coast of the island.

COWICHAN VALLEY
RAILWAY

Narrow gauge Rod Engine.
Saddle Tanks for Traction

There was a Climax which ran away from its Rat Portage hogger up Indian Arm on its first day of operation, hit a stump, jumped the track and took a swim, leaving only its stack up sucking for air. So many locies and so many stories: The smashup times and the quiet times: brewing coffee in the firebox, getting deer at night in the headlights when the camp meat was scarce, the smell of the warm cedar jam in June night air before fire season shut the woods down, or the sight of a doug fir giant silhouetted in moonlight on a frosty night at winter when the steam from the locie was pumped back into the crummy to keep the loggers from going numb.

But by 1950, those days were just about over. After about fifty years of being the center of operations the locies gave way to trucks, which had first shoved their unwanted and ugly (some would say) mugs onto the scene in the 1920's.

By the '30s only the largest shows kept trains running. Gyppo logging, with its cheaper family labour, shortcuts and trucks, contract logging cut into the train operations. Many things put the locies out of operation. The ad men talked about the versatility of the truck. They were the coming thing; speed was catching on; the style was changing. As the operations moved away from the accessible valleys and shore lands further up into the hills, trucks became more practical. They could take heavier grades faster, providing the conditions were good. Big trestles and the bridge crews were no longer needed.

·Rod·Engine·
—mainline—

If a locie was burning wood, you needed men to cut it and stack it and as the timber got more expensive you were burning up the profits as you steamed along. So they figured. Today only one full-time railroad operation remains, up at Englewood. Bob Swanson, one of the people most involved with logging trains over the years, being engineer and then licenser, figures it was a question of style. He points to the Copper Canyon operation where the railroad was hauling logs at $2.60 per thousand and the trucks' costs, spread out over fifteen years came to $15.00 per thousand board feet. Yet the big boys wanted the trucks. MacMillan said simply enough "It's my money. I'll do what I want to do with it." Today, Englewood runs its three 2400-horse diesels

twenty-four hours a day, hauling sixty or seventy cars at a time over its sixty-odd mile run. They haul for about $3.00 per thousand, a fantastically economical operation. It seems like the end of the logging locies was just as much a change of fashion as anything else. Of course, the fire hazard's cut down, and when and if the helicopters finally take over from the trucks there'll be all those roads eliminated, erosion problems eased and things move along, under the whip of that fellow called Progress.

But maybe there's some other kind of loss. Maybe some kind of gain. As the games all get more specialized, with the work done by fewer and fewer men, we've got more time, but life is more homogenized. Men get further from their roots

n the city, weddings vary little. Bride and groom going up the aisle, angelic flower girls, a bevy of cars sweeping through the city to a beflowered reception hall where the groom makes a particularly feeble speech, or again, he may launch out into a sentimental orgy about the lovely girl he has won as his life partner. I always feel anxious for the future of the dear things if he makes that kind of a speech.

There is more yet, as different persons recite laudatory remembrances, as the cake is cut and the bride and groom disappear.

You say to yourself, "I hope this is the last wedding I attend for a year. I'm completely broke. We whites are worse than the Indians with their potlatches. Come on, dear, let's go home."

As a seagoing minister whose parish for fifty-three years consisted of scattered camps and settlements along the upper B.C. coast, I was used to enduring inconveniences not imagined by my more comfortably situated colleagues, but monotony was never one. Let me describe a typically atypical wedding scene from the coast.

I arrived in my mission ship on the appointed afternoon and anchored in a lovely little cove ready to do my stuff. My first visitor was the groomsman, who came aboard with an armful of roses and decorated the ship's wee cabin. Crowded up against the forward bulkhead was the altar. To the port side was the ship's galley, which had been transformed as the pots and pans had been stored and the sink filled with roses.

Suddenly the groomsman saw the wedding party coming down a long, steep log chute and he rowed excitedly to shore in the ship's dinghy. The groom was carefully guiding the bride down the slippery logs, lest she fall and ruin the lovely white wedding dress she wore. They made the beach safely, with the help of two English friends who had recently arrived from India.

They all climbed into the tiny rowboat when, to my dismay, I saw it heave over as they pushed off. The groomsman leaped into the water up to his waist and steadied the little craft until they could all get out again, haul the boat up and empty it of the water that half-filled it.

On the upper deck of my ship I was sitting at the little organ, ready to play the wedding march, but I had to wait until they got under way again. Finally they came alongside.

"That was perfectly lovely," said the bride, "I never dreamed I would hear the wedding march today."

But the bride suddenly realized she still wore her pair of heavy, nail-studded boots. "Just a minute, please. Will you wait till I change into something a bit more suitable?" With that, as she sat down in the dinghy, she pulled off the big boots and put on a pair of satin slippers. She donned her wedding veil which she extracted from a small kit bag and then she was ready. Someone from the party hauled her up over the side of the ship and onto the afterdeck.

The groom and I were waiting inside at the tiny altar. The companionway down into the cabin was very steep, and the best man had to stand below and reach up to guide the bride down. She almost fell into his arms it was so steep. But finally she came forward a few feet on the arm of the friend from India and he stepped back, as there was very little space in the cabin for anybody at the altar save the bride and groom.

In the small cabin it all seemed so intimate and so sacred. There were only six of us. The ship lay gently at anchor in the peace and beauty of the little harbour, and we all felt in a world apart.

With the service over, I raised anchor and ran the ship around to another little cove, where we tied up to a float and wended our way up to a small dwelling where the kindly owner had arranged to hold a wedding breakfast. (We call them wedding breakfasts no matter what hour of the day they are held.)

Other neighbours were there ahead of us and quite a party welcomed the young people. It was a modest home, but utter kindliness greeted them as they came in and received the warm congratulations of their friends.

Someone had made a lovely wedding cake and when it came to the old custom of the bride and groom cutting their cake, someone shouted, putting a halt to the descending knife, "We don't use knives for that job out here. Just wait a minute."

He disappeared into the woodshed, picked up a very sharp double-bitted axe, wiped it off on his trousers and brought it in. "Here, my dear young lady, is the weapon we use out here."

So they laid aside the beribboned knife and pressed down on the long handle of the axe. It was so sharp and heavy that it went through all three layers of the cake, on through the plate and finally into the table, where it stuck fast.

Then they felt we must have a wedding dance and I went down and got Little Jimmie, the organ, and knocked off a few old tunes to which the party danced with faltering steps, as they swept down one side of the long room, walked across the uneven planks and made the return journey with the smoother grain of the floor. Our further gyrations to the music of the ancient gramophone were a bit gayer but equally erratic as the tempo changed frequently and the old machine came to a whining stop for want of winding.

Finally I took the wedding party back to the big log chute where they disembarked, rowed ashore and began the long climb up the skidway to the lake that lay beyond. From there they would row a mile or two to the little dwelling that lay on the shore of that mountain-girt lake.

The last I saw of the new bride she was back in her caulked boots, picking her way daintily up the slivered logs with the hems of the long dress gathered in her hands.

Naturally I've officiated at all sorts of funerals in my long ministry on the British Columbia coast. And now that I have "retired", I'm being called on quite often to bury old timers. One of these days they'll be burying *me*. But I'd like to tell you the story of the burial of a logger who had been drowned a few miles above Campbell River on Vancouver Island on his way back to his little cabin on the shore of Duncan Bay. He'd loaded masses of groceries in his crazy little lifeboat, but felt, as they say, that he needed "one for the road" before he got underway. That was his finish. A month later his body was found on the beach not far from his cabin. The rowboat had been caught in the powerful tides in Discovery Passage, and probably drifted out beyond Cape Mudge into the open gulf and disappeared.

I was just setting out in my ship for Rock Bay, hoping to make use of a strong ebb tide to get through Seymour Narrows, when the storekeeper at Quathiaski Cove called to me from the dock, "You're wanted on the phone." How often I've heard that!

It was the undertaker. "Hallo, Mr. Greene. Is there any way you can come over to Campbell River and take the funeral of poor old Tompkins. We've been held up by this confounded inquest, and I want to get it done today."

There was a note of desperation in his voice that worried me vaguely, but I did have a small margin for getting north through Seymour and said, "Well, I'll be glad to help you, but how soon can we start?"

"Oh, right away. Everything's ready."

"Very well, I'll be right over."

The undertaker met me on the wharf with his tiny little Ford. "We'll have to go up to the Hotel to get the boys who are helping."

"The boys" were a volunteer crew of loggers the undertaker had enlisted in some way to dig the grave, and who were "on call" if the funeral could be arranged. They had spent the morning digging the grave out in the woods up a side road where a logging operator had finished his "show" and set aside a few acres as a cemetery site. They had a tough job digging the grave, as they'd run into hardpan only a few feet down, and then given it up as a bad job.

They returned to the bar and waited for further orders. In the delay of finding a parson they had spent a bit too long in the bar and weren't in a very good humour. However, they were inveigled away with the assurance that the burial wouldn't take very long.

The undertaker, a man of even beamier proportions than myself, six loggers and I piled into the old Ford and headed down the road. On my knee sat the logger who seemed to be the "boss man". He nearly pushed me down through the seat.

"Where's the body?" he asked.

The undertaker hunched over his steering wheel and spoke without looking up. "Oh, just down the road a bit, in a boat house on the beach. We haven't got a mortuary here."

It was a very hot afternoon. And as we entered the boat house, we were almost driven back out of the place by the terrible stench. But we got the coffin outdoors, and I asked the undertaker, "How are we getting the body to the grave?"

"Oh yes. Yes... That's quite a problem."

Just then he spotted a man going by with an empty truck.

"Hey Carl! Stop a minute. Could you give us a hand to get this body down to the cemetery?"

"What cemetery?"

"Oh, the new one down the road where Higgins used to log. It'll only take a minute."

It was obviously the last thing in the world the truck driver wanted to do, but he was too good-natured to refuse.

"Okay. Put him aboard, I'm in a hurry."

We all piled into the undertaker's car again, but just as we started off, the truck-driver's big dog leaped up onto the coffin and laid his huge paws on his master's shoulders.

"Get that dog off that coffin," shouted the boss logger, his sense of dignity quickening. The procession came to a sudden stop, and the dog was hurled off onto the road.

"Where *is* this cemetery," I asked. "I've never buried anybody down here."

"Oh. Yes," said the undertaker. His broad face was now shining with perspiration. "It's about a mile down the road and up that side road to the old site where Higgins logged."

We drove up the side road till we came to a dead end.

"Where's the grave?" I asked.

The undertaker glanced nervously from one man to the other. "Well, it's not far—just over there a hundred yards or so. We'll have to carry the coffin the rest of the way."

There was nothing to do but go on and the six pallbearers took hold of the coffin, but soon came to a stop against an enormous windfall stretching across the trail a hundred feet in either direction. We couldn't fight our way around it carrying a coffin.

"Well, boys," I said, "It's up and over the top, I guess. Two of you get up on that log and we'll push the coffin up to you."

They weren't too steady on their feet, but they made it. Then they gave a mighty heave on the two handles nearest them and we pushed from down below. Suddenly the handles tore off the coffin, and the poor beggars disappeared over the far side of the log into a mass of devil's club. The language from that side became so hot that I thought they'd set the woods on fire. We heaved the coffin up onto the log, climbed up and carefully pushed it down to our two friends. From there on they had to put their arms in under the coffin. They never stopped swearing until we got alongside the far too shallow grave.

"Take it easy, boys," I said. "That grave looks treacherous to me. She may fall in. Just step easy." But the men were in no mood to take advice.

"We know what we're doing'. Come on."

Well, I suppose it was because they had to almost hug their end of the coffin that they walked along the edge of the grave, and suddenly it caved in at their end, dumping them with the coffin on their knees and about a ton of loose gravel following them.

There the two men sprawled in the grave, utterly helpless, waving their fists at us and cursing Tompkins, the undertaker, the parson, and their four comrades in language that threatened to melt the other handles of the coffin. It was terrible!

"Now boys, none of that, none of that," said the undertaker.

"Well, do something, you sloppy old----. Don't stand there gaping at us."

We dug them out and finally got the coffin onto an even keel.

I conducted a simple but fitting committal service, as I thought, but as I finished the boss man growled, "You ain't gointa leave it at that, are yuh parson?"

"Don't you figger we ought to sing something?"

"Sing? No, no, I don't think so. Nobody wants to sing. Let's go."

"Nope, we're going to sing a hymn."

"What sort of hymn do you have in mind?"

He looked around. "Lot's o' rocks round here. How about Rock of Ages?"

"I don't think so, Bill," I said. "We've really done the right thing by Tompkins. Let's go."

"Just hang on a sec. We gotta at least put up some kind of tombstone."

"That's impossible," I answered. "That can be done later."

"Later nothing. How about this?" He'd picked up an empty whisky bottle. "Have you got a piece of paper? Write old Tompkins' name on it. We don't know when he died, but you can put on the day we buried him."

I wrote as directed and the boss man stuck it down the neck of the bottle and rammed the flask neck down into the grave. "That'll do. That'll be there a long time."

I said, "Yes, it will" and thought what an amazingly fitting tombstone for poor Tompkins, whose end had come from what that bottle had once contained.

We drove back to Campbell River, and disgorged from the little car, very relieved to be done, although I was hopelessly late for my tide. The undertaker called the "boys" around him.

"Thank you boys, thank you," he began a little awkwardly, then hesitated. "I'd like to pay you something, but I'm afraid there's mighty little in Tompkins estate ..."

The big boss logger gripped him with one arm, and stuck his other fist up under the undertaker's nose. "Look here, governor. We don't want anything for burying our old partner. But if there's any rake-off on this show you better be damshur we get in on it."

With that, the party broke up. The undertaker drove southward, I hurried down to my ship, and the six stalwarts headed back for the bar.

Marry'n and Barry'n Logger Style

Canon Alan Greene was a missionary on the B.C. Coast for over 50 years. He died in Sechelt in November

Continued from page 121.

even than the hoggers were. To them, logging was more than a job. The locies were the very spirit of romance and glory. To a native like Charlie Jones who remembers that no white man'd go out on the floats in December the rain was so heavy, and who worked on the trains because it was a job and you had to get your $3.00 a day for grub somehow, there's not so much glory in it. Your life lay elsewhere. For people today, I guess it's something different again, but it's for sure that the white folk who ran them figured the trains in the woods were just about the most glorious place a man could be.

The sound of the whistle through the valleys was a siren call to a man's life-blood and a bit of the thrill has been captured in fiction by Roderick Haig-Brown and in poetry by Bob Swanson, who wrote these lines in "That Whistle in the Night" -

And to that end, Swanson himself designed an air chime to reproduce the individualist whistle sounds of the old steam locies, to conjure up the ghosts of men and machines shuffling through the woods before the city was dreamed.

Note - A great source book on the Shay locomotive is written by Michael Koch and called The Shay Locomotive, Titan of the Timber. *Bob Swanson has an excellent, but short B.C. government pamphlet on the history of logging railroads. If you want to see Shay locies and other geared engines in operation you can do so at Jerry Wellburn's Cowichan Valley Forest Museum, Duncan; at Fort Steele in the Kootenays; and at the Cass Scenic Railway in West Virginia. Once a year, around May 24 at Woss Camp, Englewood Logging fires up their old Baldwin steam engine for a nostalgic run.*

Silence forever - if you must -
The roar of steam and fire.
Let soulless men be satisfied
With the growl of a diesel flier.
The clanking rod and roaring stack
Forever fades from sight;
But diesel, diesel save for me
That whistle in the night...

My name is Henry George Pennier and if you want to be a friend of mine please will you call me Hank.

I am what the white man calls a half breed. Even Indians call me half breed and why not since I have been one all my life from the time I was born in 1904 at a very early age.

So begins *Chiefly Indian*, a book which disappointed me, having expected a lot more logging stories than I got. I don't know if Hank thinks much of his book either, but he made it clear that he doesn't really think of himself as a writer. That isn't where his values lie.

The story consists of a great many personal anecdotes. They have the flavour of the crummy after a day's work on the hill, smell of sweat, snoose, tobacco smoke, and the last cup of thermos coffee.

Then we took Mr. Fir and cut him up into 40 foot lengths and you would get only one length on a rail car. And a stumpy little Shay loci looking like a kindly old St. Bernard dog would hitch on to may be 50 of those cars and she would beeeep her whistle and waddle them down a twisty narrow gauge rail line through the deep forest to the salt chuck. Her monkey action gear on both sides would flash and her pistons would chug and steam would belch out both her ears and smoke would come out her head and boy that was sure a sight to make a man feel he was doing something big in the world.

Aside from one or two passages like that which are a flashpan of beauty and information, most of the stories move around the periphery of logging describing a long life beating about the south coast of B.C.

It is the naming of places and people that ties Hank so firmly to his subject and draws the reader into these places as his own . . . Chehalis, Harrison River, Hatzic Landing, Chilliwack, Bones the Snoose Eating Logger, Tin Lizzie, Ollie the Swede, Vedder River, and Sumas yard. The book is a collage of places and happenings, a man's life displayed as a series of single-frame shots. The interesting and redeeming aspect of Hank's book is his identification with "the boys", the gangs with whom he shared the common mythology of independence and a ribald togetherness, a mythology that appears to be disappearing from even its last stronghold, the woods.

This underlying mythology lurks beneath the lives of all who live on this coast; an unacknowledged force, it moves through the shadows of Vancouver office buildings and along darkened corridors in schools. The elegance and glitter of the city exists only a superstructure atop the language and lives of the Hanks of the province.

I was disappointed with the book because I wanted a mythical logger, a cross between Paul Bunyan and Ken Kesey, or an articulate half-indian writing of the dynamics of race prejudice in the logging industry. Most of all, I wanted a logger to tell me some details of his trade, his day to day life among the firs. I guess when a man lives very close to something, it becomes second nature to him, so Hank takes those things for granted and gives us the stories and small talk that power him through the day, the jokes that humanize the grind.

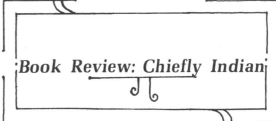

Book Review: Chiefly Indian

A lot of what you'll find in this book is the kind of thoughts that'll come along when your body's busy but your mind rolls on, thoughts while sawing timber, drilling auger holes in boom logs, the shared interior life of guys working jobs of hard labour. So you'll read about welfare handouts, lazy dirty hippies, facets of a philosophy shared by those who don't understand what's happened to their lives, who are on a merry-go-round of media searching for answers. The answer lies between the lines, but maybe Hank don't see it.

. . . but also I bet that the men who sit in those nice warmed glassed in cabs and move all those pedals and levers and throttles need engineers papers from some university to run them. Where's the fun? Where's the challenge? Where's the chance for a guy to get in there in to the jungle with just his muscle and his brains and slug it out with a tough opponent?

Hank feels he is a lucky man and is happy to have written this little book. It's this writing, and the telling of the same stories over a few beer that makes the difference, that makes his life shine. The book stands like an organic thing, made of what has passed into a life and been assimilated, as growth in a tree; "This I have been, this is what I remember, these concentric rings of growth which seem so similar to each other have been laid down through these many years. I stand here and you will tell me whether or not I am a strong tree or a useful tree."

What we end up with is not necessarily what we wanted to find, just as a stand of maple may appear in a forest of cedar. But the unexpected may yield up pleasures and knowledge all the more welcome for the surprise. In the memory of one tree comes the memory of the forest, so that we come to gain knowledge of our hidden roots.

Chiefly Indian, by Henry Pennier, Greydonald Press, Vancouver, 1972, $2.95.

HOW IT WAS WITH TRUCKS

There's a lot of jaws been broken over the question of where and when trucks first got into the woods - hell, they can't even settle on where the first railroad was, and trucks are a lot harder to keep track of than trains.

They can't say who made the first horseless carriage as far as that goes, but they can tell you who put the country on wheels - that's clear, Henry Ford. And as far as I know the man who showed the logging industry how to use trucks was Bill Schnare.

There were trucks in the woods before Schnare, lots of them, but they weren't getting all that far. Trucks were taking over every other hauling job there was by the mid-twenties so it didn't take any brains to try them on logs. Tretheweys had an old White around their mill, must have been 1922, out at Abbotsford, and you'd see it struggling by once in a while with some old stumprancher's logs chained on, but that was kind of a joke, like putting boxing gloves on a kangaroo.

Trucks couldn't be used the way they were operating in the woods those days, they were too rough. Those old brush apes were used to clubbing ox teams on the skidroad and crashing around in the woods with heavy steam equipment. They just didn't have the touch, their touch was too heavy - they'd wreck a truck just loading it.

Everything in the woods those days was made to be thumped around. If they hit a flatcar with a log, the worst that would happen would be it would jump off the track, and if that happened they'd just hook on a tong and yank it back.

I remember seeing them flip a truck loading with a duplex at Haney once. They set it back up real quick and kept on loading like Charlie Chaplin, just like it didn't happen. The truck drove away too, but as she took the turn out of the landing you could see the old wooden cab slouch off to one side like a stack of loose pancakes.

To those oldtime loggers trucks were just too frail and fussy, it threw them off to have one on the claim, like having a woman around. Gas engines made their heads spin. They could get along without 'em. It was the age of steam.

They were still logging the valleys, rolling out big train-loads of number one fir all day. When going got scratchy, they just pulled stakes for the next valley. Lay rails into the middle, set up the skidder and the skyline, and haul wood for all she's worth.

In '58 I was driving for Blondie Swanson up Desolation Sound and you could look down and see where Merrill, Ring and Moore logged in the twenties. There were big spoked wheels, a mile across, side by side the length of the valley. It was all back in second growth by this time and you didn't notice it at first but once you did you couldn't miss it, the old yarding patterns in the shading of the new growth. We were up 3200 feet in the last bit of timber on the mountain, which is the real change in logging between their time and ours. While there was that kind of going, it's no wonder they laughed at trucks.

Just the same there were some pretty fair trucks on the road by 1930. Federal, Fagel, Reo, Godfordson, Day-Elder, Fisher-Hayes, White, Leyland, Thornycroft, Diamond T, Packard. There were so many makes it was rare to pass two the same or even know of two exactly the same at first, like boats. A lot were built in machine shops on special order, and there was no standard rating.

There isn't much to making a truck, at least not the way they did it. Just brace up two pieces of eight-inch channel for a frame, Timken axle, Gryco transmission, Hercules motor. Any blacksmith could make the springs and driveshaft out of stock, and the radiator just hung in a cast iron frame. The radiator frame and the cab were about the only places they had any chance to use their imagination, and half of them just bolted an open seat across the frame.

Actually they were good trucks. You could throw a hell of a load on one of those old crocodiles. Just make sure you're on good ground. A touch of downhill helped too. Too much and they'd be scraping you up though. The goddamn brakes on those things weren't meant to be taken seriously.

You did have the emergency brake. Great big squeeze-handle emergency brake on the side of the cab. That was the true measure of the truck, the emergency brake. The bigger the truck, the bigger the handle. Some came right up to your chin.

I remember when the Detroit trucks first came out, they had a little handbrake inside with the button on top same as now, and guys'd be peering in the cab and saying what the hell kind of truck is this?

Those old emergency brakes would work alright, but one good stop was about all they had in 'em, and you damnwell saved it for an emergency.

Some had the gearshift on your left too but mostly it was where it is now, on the right. All the selector part of the gearbox was open - big sliding cast bars always full of mud and sticks. It'd take a twenty-pound pull to shift. Took just about the full reach of your arm. With sixty-five horsepower to work with you did a lot of reaching.

But those old Hercs, they had damn near a six-inch stroke and you could lug 'em down to where you could count the revs like cows going over the mountain. You'd wait till one wasn't going to make it, then pull er out and stomp the gas down for about two minutes to get the revs up to where you could get into the next gear.

The only way they could even those old four-bangers out was to hang huge cast iron flywheels on 'em, absolute top they could stand would be maybe 2000 revs. Any moren the flywheel would come right through the floorboards at you. Moren one man was killed that way, going down a hill with too big a load.

The steering wheels were great big wooden things about three feet across and flat. Had to be, because they had about as much reduction in the linkage as a bicycle, you were hangin on for all you were worth all day long. That was the main battle, to keep the front wheels going where you wanted to go and not where they wanted. You studied the road a long ways ahead. Under normal conditions you had the edge in brute force, but a rock or a rut could tie you right in a knot. The spokes would blur just like an airplane propeller, jesus, if anything was in the way, you could write it off for about three months. Next time you see an oldtimer driving, take a look how he holds his thumbs. Outside the wheel. It'll take three generations to wipe out that habit.

Once the flying saucers cleared out of your head, chances are you had a broken front wheel to deal with too - wooden spokes couldn't stand the least amount of sideways pressure. They were a real headache, wooden spoke wheels. In dry weather the spokes'd get loose in the felloe and clatter. If you didn't fix them quick the wheel'd collapse like an old wooden chair. They had special little halfround wedges and you'd see guys stopped on the side of the road banging them in.

Driving truck in the very early days was one of the real bullwork jobs, besides all the problems of being something new. Those first truckers, the men who brought trucking in, were a special breed. Half Edison and half Sasquatch.

They say the first truck show on the coast was Forbes Bay, just by the mouth of Toba Inlet, in 1926, and that may just have been the first big one. I never saw it myself, but I heard tell of some outfit where they used a truck to drag logs over a skidroad around 1920.

There was another outfit that tried to use trucks on pole rails with concave wheels. You can see how they were thinking - they were thinking here's a horse that doesn't get tired, here's a locie that only costs $800. They treated it like a locie too, they built a raised track out of timbers, fore and aft it was called because the logs were fore and aft instead of crossways like punching. It was two tracks, with squared saplings for guard rails, and open in the centre. At first they used sixteen-inch tracks, then the Compensation Board made them come up to thirty-two. Built on a gentle slope just like a railroad because of the no brakes, and no sharp turns because they couldn't figure how to make a truck so it would turn with a load of logs on it.

Come to any gully not real easy to fill and they built a timber trestle. Now let me tell you, coming down a plank road in one of them old hard-wheeled bastards, sittin out in the open on a board seat, a couple three thousand-foot logs jiggling around up behind your head, no bulkhead for protection, that steering wheel just like a bull's hind leg in your hands and mechanical brakes - you were earning your two dollars and eighty cents a day. Trestles rattling and jumping around, mud squeezing up between the planks? With mud or a touch of frost you could no more hold that thing on the track than you can hold a greasy pig with one hand. You sure tried, because to go off meant you went over, and not too many guys survived that. They nailed down everything they could find for rip-rap - branches, canvas, wrinkled tin. The best I guess was old stranded cable. It got better as it got whiskerier. But still they killed men like flies.

I can remember Dutch Parbury talking about driving up at Brown Bay - that was what Brown and Kirkland called one of their early truck camps - said you'd be looking through your floor-boards going over a trestle and seeing straight down through seventy feet of clear open space. Boards broke and jillpoked all the time - God! When he started out they asked him if he thought he could handle the "chute" and he'd said, oh yeah. One trip and that was it. He told the push, "I can see how you get a man to do that once, but I don't know how you get em to do it twice." In the depression it wasn't so hard.

It was a ridiculous thing to do with a loaded truck if you think about it, try and support it for miles on a wooden platform, but coming to it after years of skidroads and railroads, it must have looked like the only thing to do.

It took a fortune's worth of timber, and you couldn't use it again like rails, so it was something only the big camps could afford. On top of that they couldn't keep the trucks running. I remember hearing that truck logging had failed, something in the same way you hear balloon logging has failed.

But some outfits kept trying and got it working pretty slick. Jeremiason had a pretty good show up Vancouver Bay, and there was a bunch of Whites working at Holberg. The most famous I guess was Pioneer Timber at Beaver Cove. The setup at Pioneer was the work of the mechanic, Archie McCone. There was a real gyppo Edison, Archie McCone. Every camp he was at was full of gadgets and cute ways of doing things he invented. There were a lot of Gyro Gearloose types in the woods one time, I guess the problem attracted them: get those logs in the water without working so hard. I remember this Swede handlogger up Federic's Arm who worked an elaborate system of canals that somehow used the tide and moved logs for miles. The main improvement at Pioneer was the McCone pre-loader, which eliminated the delay and banging around of loading. The trucks had detachable bunks, and they'd build the load on spare bunks while the trucks were away, then when one came back, he'd just drop the bunks he had and back under the loaded ones. It was used for a long time. Everyone copied it.

McCone had a pretty slick way of turning trucks around at the dump too. At Beaver Cove it was a special problem because the bay is shallow and the road went away out on piles. They could have backed up, but McCone built this turntable at the end so that when you drove onto it you hooked a cable, and the cable pulled on a drum that turned the whole thing around as the truck moved ahead, and by the time you got to the end you were back where you started, pointing the other way.

They made the fore and aft system work, but look at the trouble and expense to build something like that. They still couldn't go up hills, and the timbered road was very inflexible. You left it where it was and brought logs to it same as a railroad. So it didn't cause any change. You still stuck to the valleys and used huge yarders to reach way far out for logs.

McCone was a master craftsman and famous in the woods. He built trucks himself, from scratch. It's funny, thinking about it, because Schnare wasn't anywhere near the man, he was just a little wizened-up old deaf mechanic from Abbotsford, and he never invented a damn thing, he didn't even bring anything into the woods, anything that other guys here and there hadn't tried already.

Schnare wasn't even a logger, he'd never been near the woods. But he was the guy, from his dirty little garage in Abbotsford, who saw where logging was heading before anybody else. He had something, but I still don't know what it was, to be truthful. It's not as if I haven't spent enough time thinking about it. It must have been some kind of insight that was so close to obvious common sense that you never saw it. The only real clue I have is that he died with several million dollars and I'll die broke, and we were both doing the same thing.

It really starts with the three-ton truck. Detroit started making three-tons I guess in 1932. They'd made some bigger trucks before that, and they'd made lots in the one-ton range but these were the first what you'd call modern trucks.

There hadn't been any real organized trucking around the Fraser Valley up until that time, but in 1927 the Cariboo Highway went in and when the three-tons came out a few years later, there were hauling outfits everywhere. Les McGarva and Irv Parbury started two rival milk hauling outfits in Abbotsford and ran them out of the beer parlour. They had tables in opposite corners and trucks would be pulling up and leaving outside all day. McGarva had four '34 Chevs and I started driving for him. Schnare did a lot of our work and he used to make Les mad as hell,

"You guys don't know how to use trucks," Schnare would say. "I could put twenty tons on those trucks." We'd go as high as eight tons on them sometimes, and they'd just be dragging their belly pans down the road. Schnare figured he knew everything because he'd run steam thrashing machines in Nebraska, and we thought the old coot was just talking silly. I know what he was thinking now, he was thinking he'd make em into six-wheelers - put tandem axles on the back - like he did on all his trucks. It wouldn't have worked for us though, we had to zip into town and back, we had to move hauling milk in cans.

Schnare's place was a kind of hangout. He was a pretty snarly old bugger, but there was always something going on. Things were always happening to him and he was always telling about it,

like the time he was in the York Hotel and the window stuck. Somehow the damn thing fell down on his arms and he had to shout down onto the street for someone to go in and tell the desk. He was close to sixty, I guess.

I was there when he got his first truck. He had a Ford dealership and he sold these two guys a 1934 three-ton truck for hauling into a tie-mill. They didn't make any payments and finally Schnare went out looking for em.

"Cakzickers took off on me but I got the goddam truck," he says. It was all battered and rigged up in some haywire way for hauling poles and he didn't know quite what to do with it.

"Mack, you tek that goddam truck," he says to Rendel Mackinnon. "You could mek money hauling logs."

We all figured he was trying to suck somebody in and he was I guess but what happened was his son Stan, I guess Stan was seveneen or eighteen then, he was listening to it all and afterwards he persuaded the old man to let him quit school and go hauling logs with this truck.

Well, by god if Stan didn't do alright, and the old man started to get interested. The next thing you know old Schnare was going around saying, "They don't know how to use trucks in the woods. I can haul ten times what they're hauling with the same trucks."

Still, nobody took him very seriously because all he ever had to do with trucks was working on em in the garage, he had never run em before.

Schnare, he had quite a few other trucks he'd sold to other guys, and everybody was behind on 'em, it was the depression and there was no money anywhere, so whenever he wanted one he just had to go out and get it.

So he took back two more trucks and sent 'em out hauling logs. Somewhere he found bogeys and made 'em into six-wheelers. They were the first six-wheelers in the woods that I know of and it was true it made them a far better machine.

Then he got the contract up on Vedder Mountain and he rigged up three more old Fords. That's when I went to work for him.

They were logging up behind Cultis Lake in a patch of timber right up on the mountain. B & K had logged out the whole valley all up around the mountain, but this patch had been left because it was too steep to get the railroad into it.

You couldn't see the fir in that forest. It was all cedar and maple, thick - you couldn't see the sky anywhere, and every once in a while there'd be a big black fir stump going up in the maple leaves. You honestly couldn't see any more than that, it was so thick in there. They smashed it all down, it was a different world. But god it was lovely wood. I've never seen fir like that again. They had to chop notches to get the tongs on the logs. For a month I averaged just over three logs to the load, and there were lots of one-log loads. The biggest I think was 8700 feet. And it was a buckskin — and only thirty-two feet long. Nine feet I think, nine feet at the butt, and straight. It sat in the landing for a long time and we kept wondering which one of us was going to get it. Finally they gave it to Les Bates on Number Three with the reason that he was the oldest. Also didn't have a family.

Top heavy! If that log rolled two inches to one side the truck would roll down the bank like a dog wrestling with a bear. Those one-log loads were cinched to the frame, that's what I hated - they would take you with em.

I had a hard time at first. I couldn't get used to Schnare's crazy way of doing things. Working with McGarva we'd had new trucks and we were pretty good to them. I couldn't believe the hammering they were giving these poor old Fords.

They were loading with a Skagit on a crotch line and you never knew what was going to happen next. Skagits were little donkeys made out of a Fordson tractor, and it could barely lift some of these logs. They went up very slow and came down very hard. Logs were dropping and banging around, and the tongs dancing and snapping every time you looked around. A crotch line can only pick a log straight up, they can't swing it, so you had to move the truck to get it placed right on the load. The loads they were packing on those trucks, you had to have it in perfect balance or you couldn't drive. But Roy, the guy who was head loading, he'd let you spot the truck, then hop out before they picked up the log. You couldn't stay in, the way they'd knock the truck around, it would buck you out, or else spear you on the gearshift. The goddamn old cab would crash and flap, I thought it would fly right off. Not that it would have been any loss - it didn't have any windows or doors as it was.

The goddamn things were so overloaded you could pop the rear end just starting out in the lan-

ding. You could twist off an axle any time you wanted. Hitting a pothole you didn't even see, the truck would heave like a schooner in a gale and creak and squawk. You would feel about the same as if you were about to walk down a rough trail with two sacks of spuds on your shoulders, it was bloody frightening with all that hill in front of you. And there was a lot I didn't know about driving with a trailer. If you hit the truck brakes before the trailer brakes and the cinches had worked a little loose, the logs would slip ahead and jam against the bulkhead. Then you couldn't steer, the front wheels would just skid across the corner into the bank. There was no way to move the logs and no power saws, so you got out the axe and chopped the ends of the logs back a foot or so. After I chopped twice through one six-foot butt I started catching on pretty fast.

They had planks laid down over the old railway grade and coming back from my first load a plank flipped up and jillpoked the trailer off into the ditch. Then coming down the second time I got too close to the edge to let some French fallers pass and the goddamn old single axle trailer pushed the shoulder out. I lost the load and they had to bring the cat nine miles to pull me out.

I was thinking good god, how do these guys do it, because I'd been driving for a while on the highway and I figured I knew how to handle a truck. But I just wasn't getting anywhere, and I was wondering if I should go quit or let Bill fire me.

So when he came to see the truck he grabs me by the shoulder and says, "Don't you worry Bud, I'm gonna get you a new trailer and you'll be hauling more logs than anybody here."

He could be good, but he was so hard most of the time you don't remember. Your time was always short, and any bill he ever paid he'd scribble "S & S Trucking, 1% off" and shave a couple bucks off. That was just the price of dealing with Bill Schnare. But men paid it, that was the thing about logging. Men would do things for a guy like Schnare they would never do for MacMillan or the companies because he was a character, a person. You could talk to him. You might be making the tight old bastard rich, but that gave you a feeling of satisfaction in itself.

Well, after I got the new trailer I was away. That's another thing. I didn't know the reason I couldn't stay on the road was because of the goddamn haywire single axle trailer I had. I thought it was something wrong with me, and so did the other guys. Schnare could see it was the trailer, but that was so obvious as soon as I made one trip, it was hard to even give him much credit for knowing it. The old fart had some kind of special insight that way.

Those trucks of his looked so goddamn awful you were afraid to get in em, in case they would fall down and you'd be trapped in the wreckage. They had no brakes at all worth talking about on the trucks, you were always fighting that. One time I got so tired of struggling and sweating I said enough of this damn nonsense and worked all weekend on my own time bushing up the linkage and putting in new linings. The first time I hit the brakes Monday the back wheels stopped so hard the whole goddamn truck stretched, and then I couldn't get the brakes off. The linkage was pulled so tight I couldn't even get a pin out to unhook it. Finally I chopped the rod with a chisel and just left it hanging. There was no way of keeping those mechanical brakes working.

Just a little while after that I was on my way up for a load and I met Les coming down in a long straight stretch. It wasn't steep, but his brakes were all used up from the hill and I didn't dare stop because I'd roll back all the way to Sardis, so we just sat there creeping towards each other with funny looks on our faces. We smashed together, steam was flying, jesus we laughed.

The reason Schnare could get by was, on the trailers, which is what really counts, he had real good brakes - five-inch drums and vacuum power, which was new then. Still, that wouldn't have been enough to hold those loads back without burning up, but he'd rigged up little water tanks on 'em, and you'd just stop at the top and open the taps. That was a helluvan improvement. With that, Schnare's trucks could handle the hills, and with the extra axles and big tires he could handle heavy loads on dirt roads.

Like I say, none of this was new or even new to the woods, except maybe the tandem idea. All these things were sitting around waiting for someone to put them all together on one truck. It was like coming up to a chess game, and suddenly realizing one side has his pieces set up so he can clean the board in three moves, but they don't see it because they're thinking some other plan. That was the way Bill saw logging in 1934. It had to be, or how else could some deaf old farmer with a dirty little garage out in Abbotsford walk in and take over like he did?

After I got the new trailer I had no more trouble staying on the road, but I still wasn't getting the loads. I couldn't get the goddamn old truck into high gear down on the flat. "I'll fix that," Bill says, "I got sumpnin will get thet truck moving." So one day he flags me down and he's got a supercharger. Well it was a little better, but I still couldn't get up there, she wouldn't hold on in high. So Bill says, "Here, I'm going to come with you. I know that goddamn truck'll go faster'n thet." It frosted you a little, because old Bill couldn't even drive himself.

So I get rolling and get into second and just about ready to go into third, and he shouts, "No, no, no!" He's signalling faster. So I keep my foot down on the gas and the poor little V/8 is hammering and screaming, I wouldn't have thought it could stand it. "Okay!" he says, and I drop it into third. Going into fourth I wait till my foot won't stay down any more, it's just shaking, but when I reach for the knob I can see him waving - it's so loud you can't hear - "No, no!" and I keep pressing until there's waves of heat pouring back over us and I'm watching for the pistons to fly up through the hood - "Now!" he says. Taking that extra bit all the way up, you could just get er to stick it in high if you kept er pinned right wide open, and that's how you'd go from Sardis right to the river, clear across the Fraser Valley.

I went through a motor every three months but that's what Schnare liked. He had a whole yard full of new blocks, and we'd change 'em in two hours on a Sunday. He spent half his time scrounging old parts, and whenever anything bust, he'd be right there and shove in a new one. Breakdowns didn't scare him - he was a mechanic. That's where he had it over the loggers, they were afraid of things going wrong because they didn't know what they'd do if they did.

I remember one time we were putting a new rear end in and there was no gasket. "Use string," he says. We didn't know what he was talking about, so he gets down and sets this string in grease so it'll stay put, winds it all around the bolts, "Now slap it on," he says. "We'll fix er better when we got time." It worked, just like everything else, and the truck got another load before quitting time.

We were getting paid five dollars a day and two dollars if we got over four loads and one week in August I was top driver with sixty-five dollars. I figured there was nothing but money working in the woods.

Goddammit, I liked it. It was a big job and I was good at it. We had those haywire old trucks working so you couldn't imagine how it could be done better. You got so you could hear the truck, you got tuned to its noises and the feel of it, so much you could tell how it was working, you'd had the whole thing together and apart so many times you were conscious of every goddamn bearing and how it was turning. You'd see a new grease spot on the ground in the morning and think that goddamn packing's getting loose again, and if you didn't fix it at least you'd make sure the thing didn't run short of oil. If anything started to go on the brakes you'd catch the slight change in the pedal or notice a wet spot on the wheel. When you get that sharp you get to the point nothing's an accident, it's always you missed something or ignored something, nothing really serious happens so long as you're on the job.

And if you did get into something, you knew how to get out of it. Say you lost your brakes - the water got plugged and the brakes started to burn up. A green driver wouldn't know what was happening until suddenly he was freewheeling down the hill, and there's nothing to do but jump and let the truck go. A guy who was on the bit would have seen the steam getting thin in the mirror five, ten minutes before. Even if the green guy did catch that he would have probably dynamited right there and pushed the drums all out of shape or he would have headed straight for the ditch and put the logs through the cab. The guy who knew what he was doing would wait for a good spot to go off, so he could get the trailer hung up first, before the truck.

You got so slick at everything you'd start taking shortcuts, like using the brakes to help get around a corner - if you touch the truck brakes you turn sharper, if you touch the trailer brakes you straighten out. Even a little thing like a mud puddle. A driver who knows his brakes are hot would go half off the road to get around a little puddle, but another guy will plough right through it and the cold splash would crack the drums. Then the truck would run away and they'd say, "the brakes failed."

There's a million things, but you get so goddamn smart after a while you get thinking nothing can happen to you. It was an art, it's gotta be. I don't see any difference between that and being a writer or raising pigeons, or whatever you want to name.

I'm sure if a historian were to write a book about truck logging he would start with some old farmer with a Model T and never mention Bill Schnare, except maybe in a list. But I remember people talking after that show on the mountain. There were claims like that all over the country, that the big association camps had left because they were considered inaccessible. Now Schnare and this little gyppo had gone in with an old 75 cat and a haywire little donkey, punched in a dirt road, laid planks in the soft spots, kept moving the road close to the timber so there was no yarding, and they made real money.

There were remnant patches all up and down the coast, every logger knew of a few, and all of a sudden here was a way they could be logged. Old trucks were suddenly at a premium, and anybody who could get together a Skagit and a truck were going logging on their own.

Schnare was picking up more old trucks wherever he could get them and taking jobs all over. He'd hear about some operator starting up or thinking of starting up. Then he'd go talk to 'em and the first thing he'd have them sign one of his "contracts". They were the damndest things - he'd write 'em in pencil in a battered old notebook he had, with all his own wording and they probably weren't legal or anything else but he figured it was the ark of the covenant. When we were finishing up at Vedder I remember he got all excited about measuring the distance we'd been hauling because he had it in the contract that if the haul got over twenty miles the price would go up. "I know it's over twenty miles goddammit, we gotta figger some way of measuring that road." What he finally did was, he painted a white spot on one of my back tires at the dump, then followed me all the way up in his car, counting the turns of the wheel. "Drive slow," he says. The way he figured it all out it came to just over twenty miles, and he made the logger pay a couple thousand bucks extra.

I moved with six trucks to Nanoose Bay where B & K was cleaning off a mountain patch much like the one on Vedder. The road wound back and forth up the hill, but coming down Schnare had

them put a run straight down the face of this hogback ridge. When you were coming up to the edge all you could see was the blue sky and the fishboats out on the gulf. Then you dove. One time I ran out of water near the bottom and the brake drums melted and welded right onto the linings. Had to cut it all up with a torch. Guys' tires were catching on fire all the time. You had your hand on the door handle a lot on that hill.

There was always a big argument about whether your brakes got hotter coming down slow or fast. Some guys claimed it was better to go fast because it meant the brakes were on for a shorter period of time. Other guys said the wheel still went around the same number of times but it was going around faster so that made it get hotter. The fast guys argued back that it got hotter going around slow because you were pressing harder and there was more friction. The way I figured it, you have to think of your brakes as a heat pump. Their job is to drain off the potential energy of the truck at the top of the hill by converting it into heat energy on the way down. The longer you give them to pump off that energy, the cooler they end up, but I could never make guys see that.

It was at Nanoose there was this little guy head loading, Corky his name was. Bouncy kind of a guy, quick you know. Natural clown. Whatever he was doing, it looked funny.

He was up on the load swinging a log as it came down. I think what happened was, there was a cat working there, and they snagged the line or something. Anyway, the log suddenly swung up and he jumped straight backwards for the browskid, the big log alongside the truck.

I was standing about fifty feet away watching. There was a piece of bark stuck in his corks, and he went right down on his ass onto the ground, his head went "crack" on the log. I remember

133

somebody saying jeez, you can hear the echo. He just sat there against the log, and we thought he was clowning. Then somebody says hey, you alright?

He was dead. Little knot size of a two-inch nail went right through his skull. Damnedest thing you ever saw. We couldn't believe it.

Quite a few other hauling contractors got going right after Bill and by the late thirties there was a real boom in small time operations going on all up the coast. Places like Texada Island and Jervis Inlet or up Johnstone Straits where the timber hadn't been extensive enough to interest the steam loggers or else had gotten too steep for railroads, men were swarming in with gas yarders and trucks. They'd yard a load into the tree, then to load they'd take a line rigged up with tongs, lead it through a block up the tree, and pinch the end of it in the windings of the mainline drum. The tree was rigged with a lean so the tongs hung out over the truck. They called it a pinchline and it was just one of the ways of getting by with one machine. Stuff like that really got going in 1940 when Archie McCone and Jimmy Lawrence brought out a cheap, light gas yarder called the 10-10 Lawrence. You could get 'em for $1200 minus the sleigh. It looked like the boom could go forever.

Just about the time everyone was starting to talk about what a wizard Schnare was with cheap old trucks he turned around and bought four brand new fifteen-ton Macks. They were the first trucks Mack sold in B.C., and Charlie Philp originally got set up as a distributor to deliver them. They had twelve-foot bunks and three-foot stakes and they cost twenty thousand each. It was the most anyone had ever thought of spending on logging trucks and a lot of people thought the old man had made an awful mistake. People said they were too big for logging, too heavy for the roads and the small operations would never pay for them.

They went hauling at Port Douglas up Harrison Lake and nobody'd ever seen anything like it. They had 502 cubic inch motors and air brakes and they would go up twice the hill and haul three times the logs of anything else around. You couldn't stop 'em. That was 1938. After they had been hauling two years truck logging wasn't a small time method any more. It was the modern way to move logs. People had been saying trucks would never touch railroads in railroad country, but after 1941 nobody was putting any new money into railroads, they were punching in road. Northwest Bay was one of the first big camps to go all trucks, and when MacMillan opened Franklin River in 1946 Schnare took in sixteen new Macks. They had mobile loaders to scoot from setting to setting and the trucks were radio dispatched and they never stopped. They had Swedish steel for drilling rock to ballast the roads, they had shovels to load it, trucks to haul it and cats to spread it and they've been building road at the rate of thirty miles a year ever since. Must be up over 500 miles now. The main spur is like the Trans-Canada Highway. Franklin River was designed around a new concept of logging, where you have small mobile yarding equipment like steel spars and trackloaders and you keep adding onto your road so you're always close to the timber. After Franklin River opened up locies started disappearing fast.

Schnare sold out in the fifties. I don't know how much he was worth but when Matsqui District put out a bond issue for their sewers Schnare bought the whole goddamn thing, and that was over a million bucks. I remember the first time I ever saw Schnare I was a kid selling raffle tickets and he grumbled and gave me a hard time, then bought the whole book of tickets. He died sometime in the early sixties.

After Nanoose Bay I quit Schnare and bought my own truck, a heavy duty Dodge, a beautiful truck. I don't think there were more than three ever brought to Canada. I figured that what an ignorant old man like Schnare could do a smart young guy like me could do twice as good.

At first I was hauling at Palmer Bay over the old railroad grade, which was supposed to have been the first railroad on the coast, then I moved to Garibaldi for North Shore Timber.

That was quite a show. It was owned by a little Hungarian Jew who'd been chased out by Hitler, and he'd scared up the most godawful ragtag bunch of alcoholics and old wrecks for a crew you ever saw. The war was on and men were scarce. The super was some toothless old coyote who'd been in the woods since they were using stone chisels, but he was so rummy half the time he didn't know where he was.

The first thing I saw him do when I got there, Les, the Hungarian, had some beautiful handknitted wool socks drying in the office and Zeke stole 'em. Naturally Les saw him wearing them, they had fancy zig-zags, and he just couldn't believe it, that his superintendent would steal his socks.

Another time we went in for breakfast in the morning and the cook was passed out on the floor with lemon extract all over his face. Zeke had it in for the cook anyway because he'd caught him sneaking a sandwich after hours and threatened him with a cleaver, so Zeke was grumbling to Les and I how you couldn't dare leave rubbing alcohol or shaving lotion sitting around or the cook would drink it on you. The camp boat had a big alcohol compass in it and I said how it was funny nobody'd got that yet. Les said after he left, "You shouldn't have said that in front of Zeke, he's worse than the cook." Sure enough, next day I checked and the compass was bone dry.

One day old Zeke was standing on a stump out in front of the tree, so bleary and shaky he didn't see that he was in the bight of the haulback and all that was holding it was a little sapling. The sapling sawed through, and the line picked ol' Zeke up right by the ass like a hundred-yard bowstring and flung him seventy feet. Joe Beef, who was another relic from Cordova Street - I never did know his right name - he was pulling rigging and Zeke came down right beside him. His ribs were sticking out and he was bleeding and screaming, and ol' Joe Beef says, "Ah, shuddup y'ol sonvubitch, that's just the shoe polish coming out so far." But they got him plugged up quick and shipped him out to Squamish.

That night in camp Joe Beef was telling us, "You know, ol' Zeke looked just like a leaf comin through those trees." He survived, and came back as bullcook, sweeping out the bunkhouses. Same camp where he'd been super.

This Les, it all must have been quite a shock for him because he was an aristocrat in Budapest, same as ol Koerner, his wife was in the opera and all that, but the funny thing was he seemed to really enjoy these guys. Not enjoy them, he admired them, he used to say there was no other men like them in the world. Everybody liked him too, he was a damn fine little man. He had no business to be running a camp though, the only reason he ever got any logs in the water was we put them in for him. That camp just ran itself, these old bastards were pretty slow until the sun got up, but nobody ever had to tell 'em what to do. It was the only camp I ever saw where they didn't give signals. They'd just glance at each other.

I was getting paid by the log, so every time I got over twelve logs I would pass out a pack of cigarettes for everybody on the loading crew. It didn't take them long to get saving all the small logs for me, and leaving all the big ones for the company truck. The only guy who didn't fit in was this little pissant named George on the company truck, and it didn't make a damn bit of difference to him but he was always meowing. "Look at all the money you're making." He's still up there, driving a schoolbus.

I got them to put Bob Hallgren head loading, he was just a kid then, I said you put the kid on loading and we'll take care of it for you. We did too, I even kept their old truck going for them. It was a good place and I was making money so I didn't mind. Later I moved the wife up and my eldest daughter was about three feet high then, I'd send her under the trucks to grease the throwout bearings. She could do it standing up and she loved it, but she had snow white hair and it would be black, jeez the wife would scream. One day she tripped on a cut open barrel and put about a three-inch gash in her leg. It didn't bleed, but this white baby-fat just bushed out like popcorn, like it was under pressure. I damn near fainted, but this doctor just shoved it back in and slapped on a bandage.

A friend of mine, Harry Bannerman, got to be super for MacMillan over at NorWest Bay and set me up with a contract for three trucks. I didn't like to leave Garibaldi, but it looked like a real step up so I sold the Dodge and got three trucks from Philp, the same Macks Schnare had first brought in.

I figured I damn near had er in the bag. It was a good haul and I was getting the wood but the big company situation was an altogether different world from what I'd been used to. You never knew what was going on. One day they would say, go to the west side, haul three loads. Then at noon they'd say, go to the east side and haul a load. The only people who had an idea what was happening were the bosses, and they just said, "We'll let you know in plenty of time what you're supposed to do." It was like being in school. Nobody was trusted to have any brains.

But at least Harry was in charge so I could feel safe. Then he got transferred. Turned out he'd been wrangling with the old guard group from Nanaimo, and they were too much for him.

As soon as Harry left they started putting the screws to me. There was a side that was so muddy my trucks were the only ones that could get into it and they told me if I would handle it they'd see I got looked after. I was losing an axle or rear end every day, and I would be up all night working. I'd have breakfast in camp and go back to work without seeing the wife for two or three days at a time. One time the cat had to push me and wrecked my trailer. "Use one of ours," they told me, "Go ahead, take it." Come the end of the sum-

mer my scale was so low I couldn't cover my parts bill. Not only was there no compensation for the rough going, I got a bill for $1200 for trailer rental. Anywhere there was bad going that's where I'd be sent. I didn't have radios, and the dispatcher would talk to the company trucks, then they would stop my trucks. George Robinson told me, "You can't stand this. You come back here and I'll have some good loads for you." He'd lay aside a few good loads, then one of my drivers would flag me down and say, "They want us over at the other side."

After a while they brought in a young kid with a haywire old Ford. He was from Nanaimo, and around Nanaimo they'd hated contractors from the mainland ever since Schnare came over. Besides that they were all Masons together. This kid couldn't do anything wrong. He was getting as much wood as all three of my trucks.

I can see now, I was trying to tell myself it wasn't happening. I'd seen men screwing each other around like that when I worked for Safeway, but the whole reason I liked the woods was nothing on the job was more important than how you treated the other guy. It just gave me a sick feeling to think it was changing.

I bitched to the dispatcher, but that was bitching to the drill sergeant. "You're getting the same as everybody else. Just go where we tell you and you'll do alright." Other places you'd make a guy like that come clean quick enough, but there they've got you by the short ones, they make sure of that. With me it was my contract, with the men it's seniority and the blacklist. The whole thing with the old style logger was, he was a journeyman, he was a pro for hire, and if he didn't like the way you said good morning he took out his time and caught the boat.

The story is told of Pete Ohlson, the Roughhouse Pete of the Swanson song, how one day they passed this new rule that anyone quitting had to turn his tools into the office before he got his time. Pete figured when they started playin around like that it was time to find another camp, but he didn't say anything and the next day he went out with his crew to move a side. They took down all the rigging and piled it up on the machine and then moved the machine over all the logs and stumps out to the track and loaded it on a car, which was about three days work ordinarily. Then after supper he goes into the office and asks for his time. "You can't have your time till you've turned in your tools," the timekeeper says.

So Pete goes to the bunkhouse and rounds up his crew and rounds up a locie and goes up and hooks onto the donkey and hauls it down to the shop, hooks a stump, skids this enormous machine with all its shackles and lines and blocks over in front of the office steps. "Okay," he says to the timekeeper, "Here's my tools y'little sonvubitch, now give me my time."

In the end I was ground right down to a frazzle and I had no choice but to bust the contract and pull out. That's when I began to see it was all over. When Schnare started, trucks were new and risky and the companies were willing to pay someone else to work out the wrinkles. Now trucks were proven and the companies were all getting their own. They'd put in a new tax law so trucks could be depreciated 30% a year and it worked like a tax dodge. Instead of declaring income as dividends they were piling it into big diesel fleets with fourteen-foot bunks, radio control and all the rest.

Now I could see why old Schnare had been in such a rush. He saw the door open, and he'd been around long enough to know how long it would get left that way. I turned my trucks back to Philp and went logging on my own.

There were still a few doors open in gyppo logging. Just before I turned in the trucks I did some hauling for two brothers in Parksville who had a little 10-10 Lawrence. Between them they were putting out four loads a day worth $500 a load. It was just a matter of doing the right thing in the right place, that was the theme of the gyppos, but I was still looking when the last of the timber got tied up by the companies and the door was closed on that too.

So now you work for the companies. If a taillight goes out you park and radio for the mechanic. He spends half his time driving and you spend half your time sleeping. Doesn't matter much because the machinery's gotten so good and the jobs been laid out so simple everybody can do the work half asleep.

You never think of your brakes, the drums are nine inches wide and it's all made out of miracle alloys that work white hot, half the guys don't even know what the pedal's hooked up to. There's just one guy to load you and it don't matter how he throws the logs on because you hardly notice they're there, they're all boomsticks anyway. The trucks never stop but the driving's so sloppy you don't get any more logs than we did before. It's like everything else. They've done away with the work but not the worker.

Four Poems by Peter Trower — Logger

From *Between the Sky and the Splinters*

THE BALLAD OF BOOTED BONDAGE

The waiting hill tipped ragged against the sky
in the press of the swelling sun. We shuffled our feet
and talked of booted bondage and days gone by
on a windless morning of heat.

'Back then', said the ancient hooker, shifting his snoose,
'she was rough and tough and they played it by hit or miss.
And I guess I've seen my share of shit and abuse
but never a show like this!'
'Its kinda funny but when I was young and quick
and my legs were good, they mostly logged on the flat.
But now I'm getting old' - and he rubbed his neck -
'we gotta work ground like that!'

And his eyes and ours crept up past the steel-spar -
that man-made symbol of modern efficiency.
We saw the claim with its rock-bluffs rugged and sheer
and we tasted the irony.

And then it was starting-time. Resigned to our lot,
we snuffed our smokes and began the weary ascent
as though we had sinned by living - God, it was hot!-
and this was our punishment.

We were damp with sweat when we reached the first of the logs.
We paused at last for a short but grateful break
and clung to the brush-furred incline panting like dogs
while the hooker puffed in our wake.

The whistle bansheed. Distant the rigging jerked
into metal motion. Chokers rattled and danced
up-mountain toward us. Hoarsely a raven croaked
and so the yarding commenced.

And we throttled logs with our kinky steel ropes -
logs that had stood as trees before we were born
and sent them shuddering truckwards down the slopes,
turn after headlong turn.

The day dragged on. The air was a scorching sheath.
The only moisture - sweat that daggered the eyes.
The snarling sun above and the fools beneath
who came to scrabble for trees.

The cables scraped a tune on the naked rocks.
We dreamed of beer in the air-cooled bars of town
and of sparks that might sow flame by the haulback blocks -
Much hotter they'd close us down.

In our groggy minds we nursed the greed for reprieve.
It would never come so what the hell was the use?
Then the hooker yelled and the sidehill came alive
as the roadline stump tore loose.

We dived for cover and held by horror, we stared
at the grizzled hooker whose legs were not fast enough
for the spinning uprooted stump that came like it cared
and swept him over a bluff.

There's little more. We packed him finally out,
dead as though he had never breathed or been
and they closed her down but I heard his words like a shout -
'It's the toughest show I've seen!'

And his grave lies elsewhere, carefully kept and unmarred
with a floral wreath and a plaque that bears his name
but his real stone is a cliff-face, pitted and scarred
on a logged-off logging claim.

SPAR-TREE RAISING.

The tree went up at last
and hung
like a symbol
across the sky
where we'd stuck it.

It had been a hard tree,
an unwilling tree
and had given us wooden battle
in the shaley landing
high above its growthplace.

It had refused us stubbornly
like a cornered
living thing
until we sweated in obscure contest
on the hill.

Three times we failed-.
the tree
lay laughing at us -
the hooktender
flung down his hardhat.

It was tired
end-of-the-week friday -
payday in fact
and the tree mocked us
on the high plateau.

We took a smoke-break
and considered that
it wasn't really the tree -
the tie-up lines were rotten -
but the sun crashed through the fog.

So we tried once more -
put a cat-blade
against the base of it
and under the throbbing mainline,
the reluctant spar came up.

Stood like a Gulliver
tethered by guylines
and I believe we sighed in relief,
had drinks from the water-bag
and perhaps joked.

LIKE A WAR.

No bombs explode, no khaki regiments tramp
to battle in a coastal logging-camp.
Yet blood can spill upon the forest floor
and logging can be very like a war.

We sat aboard a crummy, tension-creased.
The fog rose surely from the vanished east.
The hooker said - 'I've felt this way before
in Italy. It's something like a war.'

The hill was dark and filmed with icy slush.
We stumbled through the morning-clammy brush.
The sky was grey and vague. The air was raw
with winter and the game was like a war.

The savage cables rattled through the mist.
The boxing chokers cursed the men they missed.
We wrestled with their steel ropes and swore
and grumbled. It was very like a war.

Then far above us, shifting timber groaned.
The loader's lonely warning-whistle moaned.
Six logs came crashing down the foggy draw.
The guns had sounded. We were in a war.

Our names might well be written on the butts
of that blind downfall. Terror gripped our guts.
We shrank behind our stumps beneath the roar.
Like hapless soldiers, we were in a war.

And ever down the wooden missiles rushed,
an avalanche that battered, slammed and crushed
and passed us. And you couldn't ask for more
if you'd been spared by bullets in a war.

Foolhardy veterans, we resumed our work
and snared the timber in the swirling murk.
We'd tasted action now. We knew the score.
They paid us for engaging in a war.

The logging-slash rears weary in the sun.
No truce is called. No victory ever won.
We bear no weapons, yet the fact is sure
that what we wage is very like a war.

IN THE GULLY.

In the dripping gully
the spider-rooted windfall
sucks up under
the granite snout of the overhang
and stops.

Thumb the button
of the electric belt-whistle
I wear like a six-shooter,
confident the haul-back line
will jerk the jammed wood free -
but it doesn't.

Go ahead on the mainline again.
Cable grinds against stone
to no avail. The windfall
lies locked in the ravine.

Glance at my chokermen -
they gaze back blankly.
Not their problem.
Only and incontestably mine.

Nothing for it.
Go ahead once more.
The mainline
stretches to parting-point.
Imagine the mess if it breaks.
Hit the whistle again
at the last grinding moment.

Back slams the cedar
but this time
there is just enough slack
to unhook the choker.

Leave it there thankful, thinking -
Logging's a bit
like writing poetry.
Mind-cables wrench loose
the sluggish ideas,
sometimes to wedge them
in hopeless canyons
and knowing just when
to blow the whistle
and cut them off
is a knack
of no small importance.

A Fir Tree of the Mind

Four hundred and seventeen feet of living matter, of tree. The familiar Douglas fir suddenly looming unbelievable among its dwarfed brothers. The overwhelming *Ah-men* of utter mass. Imponderable ponderous mass. But live, delicately quick in rippling browns, fluttering greens, four hundred seventeen feet up. Up sheerly and as if forever slowly continuing to climb out of the stilled insubstantial forest floor dropping beneath that first man's feet, his Eden-stunned eyes being pulled birdlike into the green storm of its sky.

At four hundred seventeen feet in height it would have been as tall as the new Toronto Dominion Bank building at the corner of Georgia and Granville in downtown Vancouver. But the tree's forty stories would be growing and enriching, pitch authentic and pungent, to be shared among families instead of forty seized and seasonless ones of concrete and steel to be filled each morning by office workers.

The year would be 1895, not 1972. The man whose name is to be notched into the historical carcass of the tree is George Cary, one of the first logging settlers of B.C.'s coastal rainforests. The harbourer of this immense secret shout of a tree would be a lush fold on the North Shore of Vancouver known as Lynn Valley. This area had already afforded earlier loggers some very large, even huge firs, one thirteen feet across the butt.

Thirteen feet in diameter is huge, yet the Cary Fir would be nearly• double at twenty-five feet across the butt. Its circumference, seventy-seven feet. Walking around its base would be akin to circumnavigating some new world. Going around its ineffable girth it would come to you the power implicit in one of those tiny winged seeds the size of a hangnail; how sown on the wind and chance it could establish its ground and open out and probe down, plunge up and through its potential to finally become the heart of its promise, to be such towering praise.

The volume of the tree would certainly be respected by the fallers. Respected yes, or more likely, feared. The bark itself would be sixteen inches thick. Chewy absorbing insulation to the first axe bites. Just to begin to reach the actual wood would raise rivers of sweat in the muggy August underbrush. Try and stretch wide enough to grasp the awesome brute mechanics of falling such a tree with the equipment available in 1895. The undercut alone would take days. And what about the saw? Forged together from several blades, how awkward it would be.

Then as the tree neared falling to hear the terrible groans that would flow from its wound shaking the gut as the wedges were driven deeper and the cut widened. And when it slides to topple, taking half the forest with it in a delirium of flailing branches and a hail of cones, the cloud of dust and pollen billowing up from the forest floor to envelope ringing ears and thudding bodies. . . And when the cloud settles back down to reveal the fallen tree, its four hundred seventeen feet of life that keeps on going on under the boots: at two hundred seven feet the diameter still nine feet, to the first limb at three hundred feet. . . And when the cloud settles. . .

It is 1972 and the evidence seems indisputably weighed against the historical existence of the Cary Fir. Gone the forty green stories and now standing in its stead we have the monolithic fact of the T-D Bank building to bring to us what that tree's stature would have been if it were not a tall tale, a myth.

So the Cary Fir is cut down not by axes and saws but by the knowledge of the UBC forestry experts and it falls into the category of legend. Now it is a fiction invented to appease the need of B.C. people to have claim to a world's record. For the Cary Fir at four hundred seventeen feet would have easily topped even the redwoods. Still, for those interested, the Cary Fir is mentioned in the Guiness Book of Records, even though its measurements are reported as unverified.

And that word "unverified" is the problem. According to Professors Haddock and Smith of U.B.C.'s silvicultural department that word is one that gives far too much leeway to the imagination. Their examination of the photograph shown here, the one (the only one) that appeared to create and continue the tall tale as truth, reveals to them unequivocally, that the tree is not a Douglas fir at all but a coast redwood; and since no redwoods have grown naturally in B.C. since before the ice age, it couldn't have been cut in B.C. Their proof that the tree is a redwood and not a fir is:

1. There is a burl at the base of the trunk (to the left of Cary on the ladder) and that type of growth doesn't appear on Douglas firs but does on redwoods,

2. There are whiskery sprouts on the ragged chunk of its base the tree left when it was felled (to right of Cary on the ladder) and this again is a growth that can be attributed to redwoods but not to Douglas firs, and

3. The texture and shape of the bark is relatively smooth and free of deep crevices, and runs relatively straight up and down the trunk, all of which is characteristic of a redwood; whereas Douglas fir bark is very rough with numerous deep crevices and highly irregular longitudinal markings. They further point out that statistically speaking there is almost no chance of a tree that size being a Douglas fir, as it is one hundred feet taller and eleven feet larger in diameter than the largest Douglas firs reported in B.C. and elsewhere.

Professor Haddock summed up his case in a letter (part of the correspondence he has carried out over the past ten years in an effort to squelch the public's craving for a world's record) to one of the many publishers of the Cary Fir as a fact and not fiction story: "In brief, there is not a shred of evidence that any such tree existed. The photo is not faked, but was probably taken of a coast Redwood, doubtless in California, probably Humbolt County, many years ago."

The fact that George Cary cut the tree in 1895 or any year is nonsense according to the late J.F. Matthews who was a Vancouver city archivist and friend of Cary. Matthews writes to Professor Haddock: "Every word he (Cary) spoke to me has been recorded in writing. He said he never cut such a tree, that no such tree grew in Lynn Valley where he had done extensive logging." And explaining how the photo and the legend of the tree came about, Matthews had this to say. "About sixty years ago in the state of Washington I believe, the Hoo Hoo Club was formed by a group of lumbermen and occasionally they would have a banquet. One year it was held in Vancouver and as our lumbermen wanted 'to put one over' on their colleagues from the State of Washington, they invented the legend..." And Matthews concludes, "I don't know positively, but what I think the men did was use a photo of a Redwood and then concoct an inscription to go beneath it. I would not waste time on it..."

Adding to the evidence against the truth of the tree are the many comments of old time loggers who said no one in those days would have been foolish enough to cut such a tree even if it did exist. The skidroads and sawmill setups just weren't capable of handling a tree of such a size at that time in B.C.

Finally, there is no mention of the tree as either fact or local lore in the small historical booklet on the settlement and development of Lynn Valley written in the 1920's. There is a picture of a Douglas fir with the title "Largest Ever Cut" but the tree is the same huge fir mentioned earlier, thirteen feet across the butt.

Thus it would seem that the Cary Fir was a tale arrived at in later years, perhaps woven of many such tales, placed in the Lynn Valley area and granted to George Cary's name.

For some reason the history of the controversy over this tree's historical existence did not really begin until 1946. On October 24 of that year the Vancouver Sun printed a story on the battle between Canada and the United States for claiming the largest tree on record. The Sun gave these "facts": "John Palmer recalls that in 1895 George Cary felled a tree 77 feet in circumference, 25 feet in diameter, 417 feet tall, trunk 300 feet high to the first limb, 9 feet in diameter at 207 feet, bark 10 inches thick." The Sun also printed a reply from the U.S. Forest Service to the discovery of the tree in which they said they "think something was wrong with the measurement."

The next day the Sun published the (in)famous photo on the front page with a headline saying: "Lynn Valley Tree Largest". The paper assumed this proof would put B.C. in the world record books to stay.

Then on October 30 the Sun followed up this big scoop with a commentary by C.L. Armstrong, veteran Assistant Forester of the B.C. Forestry Service, who "positively identified the tree as a fir" and ascertained that "expert examination of the Lynn Valley giant's picture while not able to accurately substantiate full 25 feet diameter claimed, showed that the butt, discounting 'flair' or 'swelling' was apparently at least 18 feet."

Since this beginning in 1946 many publications have printed stories down through the years all tending to present the Cary Fir as fact and not fiction. And of course Professors Haddock and Smith of U.B.C. and the late Major Matthews of the Vancouver City Archives have all tried for the last ten years and more to put an end to the tree and label it for what they felt and feel it is, a nuisance legend in no way authenticated by any proof whatsoever.

Yet the tree still stands tall in many minds and I suppose it will continue to as even now it does in mine, swaying in the wind of a people's need for legend, for myth. For to me the public's desire for such a tree to exist in their memories and dwell in their dreams is deeper and much more than a provincial pride in waving a record at the world. It is more than a tall tale. It has its own truth that need not contend with the scientist's other. For the Cary Fir begins to grow into the ahistorical sky and ground of myth, an area where it does not so much ignore the evidence against its existence as subsume it, grow around it as an oyster orbits layer after layer of secretion around its found world of pain to produce a pearl, a larger world, one with a different beauty and quality. For the Cary Fir as myth seems to demonstrate man's reach to embody with the belief of his blood, the massively dense, the somehow gentle yet demonically intense sheer growth potential of such a rainforest as is found on B.C.'s west coast.

And who knows, perhaps there were a few redwoods that continued to grow in B.C. after the ice pulled back. Perhaps one grew in Lynn Valley. Perhaps waiting in some as yet undiscovered valley is tree as large as people wished the Cary Fir to be.

Yes, I hear you, Professor Haddock. The next one will be five hundred seventeen feet, no doubt.

It must have been one of the cranky war-surplus flying boxcars that took us north that spring, for we sat facing each other like paratroopers across the aisle, me and the three hypes. I can remember their faces with some clarity, for I knew them all by sight from the east end - Mousey Clinton, former gangleader, not much more than five feet tall with his dark, pinched, ghetto-child's face; Red Pell, once one of Mousey's lieutenants, deceptively gangling streetfighter in his pre-junk heyday, knife-featured, sallow-cheeked; even Bernie Grimes, older veteran of the first, wartime zootsuit gangs, gutter folk-hero with his sly-tough Irish hustler's mug and kinky red hair. All of them coming off heroin habits and sniffling or twitching periodically. All of them run out of Vancouver on floaters and heading for camp to kick and cool out for a while. Three scruffy legends on the lam who'd be damn little use the first few days until they rode out the crawling meemies of withdrawal.

A "floater" was a form of summary legal banishment, widely used at that time by the Vancouver courts to rid the streets, albeit temporarily, of bothersome rounders and junkies the police had been unable to nail on more serious charges. It was enforced by means of the all-inclusive Vagrancy Act. The neer-do-wells were playing gangchief.

The three of them had hired out to the same camp and we arrived there shortly. They disembarked, looking none too happy. I certainly didn't envy the cold turkey session that lay in store for them. As the plane took off again, I watched them walking up the dock with their packsacks, three woebegone underworld expatriates, off to pay their Hastings Street dues on a sullen sidehill.

The rackety plane roared away up Jervis Inlet, past Britain River where I had worked the previous year and on up that long, bending sound to almost the head. The country rose rugged and steep from chippy lime water to a zigzag of snowy scowling peaks and blackrock valleys. I knew little of the camp I was heading for but it was a foregone conclusion that we would not be logging flat ground.

The air, fortunately for my peace of mind, was quite calm that day; there was a minimum of the rattling and jolting that had marred most of the earlier coastal flights I'd taken. It was almost April and the world was warming up again after a severe winter that had kept all but the lowest level camps locked up tighter than drums till now. It had been a dour, depressing winter in more ways than one. Junk seemed to be spreading like an epidemic among the streetkids I'd moved with for

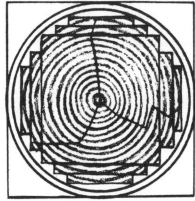

Sojourn
at Junkie Log

forbidden to return to the city for a specified period of time under threat of arrest. The period in the case of Mousey and Company was six months, but sometimes the exile was much longer. It was years before any sort of rehabilitation program would be established, and amounted to sweeping the drug problem under the rug and into the hinterlands. Out of sight, out of mind. This ostrich policy merely resulted in scattering hypes throughout the province to spread the gospel of stuff. They often hit the logging camps, which were eternally screaming for crews and where a man's past was his own business as long as he was willing and able to work.

"Hey man, you got a butt on you?" asked Mousey.

I tossed my package over to him. He took a cigarette, lit it shakily and flipped the pack back to me. Mousey, before he'd started sticking needles in his arm, had been a sort of pint-sized Al Capone, strutting at the head of his teenage mob like Evil Eye Fleagle in a black zootsuit, a stogie in his mouth. A couple of years before, he'd been one of the main subjects of a sensational article about hoodgangs in one of the local papers, under the pseudonym of "The Flea". Those days of dubious glory were behind him now. Hustling bread to support a habit left little time for

the past few years and the Belle Bar Cafe, our longtime hangout, was haunted with nodding hypes. There had always been users around in the shadowy backstreets of our world; now they were moving into the foreground, bringing narcotics squad heat and paranoia with them. Several guys and girls I knew quite well had become addicted in the preceding months. The sordid pincers of life were closing suddenly. Vancouver appeared to me at once more dark, inimical and dangerous than it ever had before. I even considered joining the Air Force to get away and actually wrote the tests but chickened out at the last minute. I decided to hire out to camp once again and consider things in perspective while I saved up a stake, but this time the streets, in the symbolic guise of Mousey and his friends, seemed to be following me right into the woods. At least they hadn't been going to the same outfit.

Derrick Point was the name of the place and it looked like a mighty small layout - two or three buildings on a sloping bank and a stiff-leg to walk ashore on from a small float. There was a booming area to the west of the camp but not much actual booming seemed to have been accomplished. A number of logs floated loose in a circular pocket. I couldn't figure out what sort of a highlead system they were using but the slash appeared to run a long way back up the mountain. I could see two spar trees, one only six hundred or so feet from the beach, the second far beyond and above it on a distant ridge. A skyline stretched between them.

A most unloggerly-looking man was waiting on the dock to greet me. He was short and slightly built with glasses and a rabbity, nervous face. I assumed he must be the timekeeper. It was hard to imagine what else he could be doing in the bush.

"Hi there" he said in a reedy voice. "I'm Bert Pringle. You must be our new chaser."

I confirmed the fact. I'd had enough of setting chokers and blowing whistles and had determined to advance myself to a better job come hell or high bloody water.

"We've got a pretty good little setup here," he informed me. "Nice bunch of fellers. Think you'll fit in fine."

"You keep the books, I guess?"

"Oh, I keep the books alright," he said, unoffended, "but I also work on the boom and sign the cheques. I'm the owner."

I felt as though I'd put my foot in it properly.

"Nobody takes me for the push," he went on, somewhat wistfully. "I suppose I don't look much like one. Actually, I used to own a hardware store but I inherited some money so I sold out and bought this place. I've always been interested in logging and I thought I'd have a crack at it, first hand, you know?"

I liked his honesty.

The next morning I woke to find my face covered with lumps and thought for a second I'd come down with some unnameable disease. It was only the work of industrious mosquitoes. The bunkhouse, for there was just one, held eight men, four to a room. There were only two other guys on my side, Ronnie Gannon, the rigging slinger, a tall, athletic guy with closecropped blonde hair, and a chokerman called Pat Brady whose dark Celtic features seemed vaguely familiar. I'd talked a bit with them the previous night but learned little except the fact that we all came from Vancouver. I hadn't been able to peg them much beyond that. They mentioned the skidroad a few times but most loggers did. That roaring slum was theirs by right of a million blown stakes and they fed it fresh money each trip, reeling among the cackling threadbare winos who had once been tame apes too. I was new in camp and they wanted words about broads and the Hastings Street dives so I gave them a few. They seemed like good guys and spoke well of the camp except "She's a whore of a hike to work in the morning!" as Pat Brady put it.

The vibrations I'd had from the place thus far had been reassuring. Pringle, who was evidently as much of a greenhorn as he looked but a likeable sort, had a partner called Gordon Crossley, a tall, grizzled, fortyish man who'd been in the game since the year One and upon whose savvy the venture depended. He was theoretically the woods foreman but doubled as engineer or hooktender whenever the need arose. His wife Angie, a plumpish, motherly woman of wan, fading beauty, took care of the cooking and, judging by my first sampling, did a competent job of it. There were three other crew members - Maurice DuBois, the hooktender, a wiry, ebullient Quebecker who'd taken his basic training in the eastern pulpcamps; Garth Evans, the whistlepunk,

emaciated, taciturn, of uncertain origin; and Gilles Benet, the second chokerman, another French-Canuck, fat, hooknosed, moustached, reputed to be lazy. It was a purely gyppo setup but that was fine with me. I much preferred small camps where it was easier to learn the business and had nearly hired back to the Minstrel Island country, my raftcamp stamping grounds of the previous fall.

We finished breakfast and headed up the hill. Crossley went with us as they were short an engineer and he was running the donkey. It was a whore of hike alright and I began almost immediately sweating out the sour winter poisons. We were heading for the farthest spar tree I'd seen from the water up a steep, rock and chunk-strewn slope that angled raggedly toward that distant ridge.

"Shit, am I ever out of shape!" I panted to Ronnie Gannon who was climbing easily beside me.

"You'll be okay in a few days," he laughed. "Hell, I goddam near died the first couple of mornings. This is the worst part anyhow. She's fairly flat on top."

We reached the spar at last. It stood in the mouth of a narrow gully that widened out as it went up and back across a gradually sloping plateau. About nine hundred feet distant was a third spar tree with a cold-deck pile jackstrawed around it. The rest of the crew, after a short breather, continued up the gully. Since I was the chaser, I stayed at the tree with Crossley. He started up the donkey which lay to the left of the spar on a rocky shelf. It chugged and purred idly in the morning air and we sat down on the sled runner for a smoke.

"You're swinging them quite aways out here," I remarked.

"You're not just whistling," he agreed, "but the way this bloody country's built, it's about all we could do. Have to handle the goddamn sticks four separate times before they hit the chuck. If it wasn't good wood it wouldn't be worth the headaches but there's a lot of number one fir back there."

The crew had reached the distant pile by now. Gordy glanced at his watch, took a pinch of snoose and blew a questioning "hi-hi" on the starting whistle. There was an answering blast from the whistlepunk. Gordy went ahead on the haulback and sent the butt rigging, with its two chokers lashing like lion tails, scooting off up the gully. A single whistle snapped it to a halt over the cold-decked logs. Ronnie was a good screamer. I could hear his yipping commands quite clearly before the punk transmitted them. There was really no need to holler much when you were swinging a pile, as the punk generally had a clear view of what was going on, but Ronnie just liked to yell. Howling signals effectively and clearly was a prerequisite for rigging slingers and hookers in those days and a matter of some pride. The screams of the best of them would have rivalled those of a soul singer in full cry. My brother Chris had developed a most singular shrieking style. My feeble roars weren't even in the running.

Ronnie and the chokermen got clear and he hollered the go-ahead, a single wail like the complaint of a wounded coyote. The mainline tightened and popped the choked logs free from the pile. They came slapping and writhing down the gully toward the tree. It was usual to hang a skyline between the two spar trees for lift when swinging out a pile, but they hadn't bothered in this instance. For one thing, both of the skylines the outfit possessed were already in use. For another, the gully was relatively free of stumps and there was considerable natural lift provided by the slope of the land. It was a way of cutting corners and saving on rigging-up time and it worked well enough.

There was a large fir stump topping a rocky knoll on the opposite side of the gully mouth from the donkey. It was well in the clear and Gordy could see me for hand signals, so I made it my base of operations. The choked logs came bucking and thudding in below me and I dropped them where I wanted with a downward hand motion. Slacking her down, I scrambled off my perch, undid the chokers and climbed back to safety. A circular wave of the hand sent the rigging skinning back up the gully again. That was the routine and it varied little. I was required to keep count of the logs that came in and did this by carving notches on a tally-stick like a gunslinger checking off victims. The logs were easy to stack in the flat floor of the draw and Gordy ran the machine well and with restraint as far as highballing went. By noon, I'd come to the happy conclusion that I'd hit a candy side - a relatively soft touch.

The panorama from my stump on the rim of that mountain shelf was wildly spectacular in the warm spring sun. The chewed ground spilled away, a crazy ramp of rock, stumps, log fragments, bushes and raw earth tipping down to the fool's gold glitter of the sea. The skyline ran like a dwindling silver thread through a jack in the top of the tree we were presently using to the brown crayon of the first tree far below, where a second donkey sat toy-tiny and silent. They were using a Tyler Gravity system on this section of the swing. It differed from others I'd worked on only in the fact that it was powered from the upper end by the machine with which we were now yarding.

Below the first tree, the ground levelled off considerably and ran at a gentler slant the remaining distance to the water. A second, shorter skyline extended from here to the end of a stiff-leg - several lashed together logs jutting out from the rocky shore and held stable by two horizontal guylines. This final lap of the process was, so Gordy had informed me, a tightline setup, ostensibly much the same as a Tyler except that it had no forward motive power whatsoever and depended totally on gravity and the pitch of the land.

The great snow-smeared mountains reared bluegreen huge in all directions around and beyond our little patch of havoc, primeval teeth grinding eternally the cud and porridge of the clouds. It was the first of my really high, grand hills where you could see forever across the wind and sense, like gazing at stars, how small you actually were in the whole tumbling scheme. Between turns, I forgot logging and let my eyes ride out like winged horses over that ocean of glittering peaks.

Closer to home and almost directly across the inlet, a much narrower channel, little more than the width of a good river, fingered away at a rough right angle among the mountain bottoms. There was some sort of settlement, a collection of neat brown buildings clustered on a grassy point to the east of the inlet arm. The place was certainly not another logging camp. I couldn't imagine what it could be and queried Gordy about it while we were eating lunch.

"That's the Malibu Resort. Supposed to be owned by some millionaire. Bing Crosby, Clark Gable, people like that come up in the summer. Cruise around in their fancy yachts and watch us bloody peasants busting our asses on the sidehills. Jesus! I'd sure like to shanghai a couple of 'em and put 'em setting snares!" He laughed hoarsely and took a swig of java straight from the thermos.

The day rolled on, smoothly and well. The logs trotted home like Little Bo Peep's sheep and laid themselves down obligingly on the growing stack. I was out of condition and sweated and panted a bit but it was a pretty easy go for all that. In a big camp they would have been swinging the logs out hot with a setup of this kind, running both machines at once - hooking the logs up for the second phase of their journey as soon as they had completed the first, skinning them directly to the lower tree and so on to the saltchuck. It would have meant several more men, a different rig-up for the donkeys and increased operating costs. They were doing her gyppo - step by step - and that was quite all right with me; my name was Simpson not Samson. Hooking the logs up again after unhooking them would have meant twice the work. The way things were I had plenty of daydreaming time.

I was a bit tired and sweaty by the quitting whistle but I felt fine nonetheless. We climbed back down the steep face of the mountain, joking and happy. We'd gotten a pretty good log count and Gordy was in a jubilant mood.

"By God! We'll have them bastards in the water and boomed up in no time!" he chuckled. "Keep little Pringle happy!"

I felt great. Only two days into this camp and quite at home already. I could see the smoke of the cookshack and taste the food Angie must have simmering for us. It was a good universe sometimes.

That night, after a gut busting supper of the kind you can only eat in the wilderness when you're young and fresh back from the gymnasium hills, Ronnie, Pat and I started talking about the city again. The other two began to open up a bit more, asking me if I knew certain Hastings Street characters. I recognized most of the names they mentioned - almost every one was a junkie. Although they didn't come right out and lay it on the line, Ronnie and Pat were undoubtedly dope fiends too. I'd never have taken them for users by their physical appearances but of course they'd both been in camp for several weeks and were in healthy shape. I tried to imagine what they must have looked like when they first arrived - a damnsight thinner and shakier for sure.

They seemed to have me figured for a fellow hype and I did nothing to dispel this illusion, probably for fear of sounding square. I fostered my silly tough guy facade for all it was worth in those foolish days when hoods were heroes and this time was no exception. It was mostly a dumb act that many of us played then among the authentic hardcases but it served as a protective camouflage and allowed a guy to travel in dangerous company with relative impunity. I'd been taken for a junkie before and even been questioned by the narcs on a couple of occasions. I wasn't aware at the time that I possessed a double who was a heroin addict. Perhaps they took me for him. In short order, they were telling me all their secrets.

"We brought a bit of shit in with us to taper off on," Ronnie told me. "It wasn't that rough of a comedown that way. Too bad she's all gone."

"Yeah," said Pat longingly, "I sure get yenny sometimes."

I thought of Mousey and the others on the plane. Judging by the number of addicts I'd met so far this trip, the camps must have been full of them. Actually, many were excellent loggers when they got straightened around. Ronnie and Pat themselves were damn fine rigging men. But the subject of junk never left their minds for long and was constantly coming up in the conversation. They clammed up when Gordy, Maurice or any of the others came in, however.

It didn't take many days of yarding to plug up that gully mouth. Soon there was no room left to stack the logs. There was still that amount and more left at the third tree but now it became necessary to clear the landing. I inherited a softer job yet, for I was put to chasing on the bottom tree and thus spared the chore of climbing the hill each morning. We had to switch the lines around first, which took a bit of bullcooking, but it was easy enough pulling strawline downhill and we soon had the Tyler in operation. It was a far cry from the odious A-frame at Carrington's where I'd had to struggle with chokerbells in the water and suffer the engineer's snickers at my clumsiness. This deal was a piece of cake. Since the Tyler was run from the top end, I was all alone in the landing. I had a whistle with which to slack the logs down and land them. All I had to do was run in, unhook the snares and skin the rigging back again. The rigging crew, mostly on account of the fat chokerman, Gilles, who was about as agile as an arthritic turtle, were none to speedy and I had a lot of time on my hands between turns. There was a good bit of old cable laying about and a couple of marlin spikes. I decided to try and learn how to put in an eye-splice. I'd helped out with splicing a number of times and had a vague idea of how it went. I messed up several perfectly good pieces of line before I figured out where all the strands should go. The botched-up eyes I tossed in the bushes where no one could see them. At last, I got it right, chopped off the excess strands and gazed at my finished product with awe and some pride. My first logger's eye! By Jesus! I was learning.

One day, Maurice, the hooktender came down the hill around mid-afternoon, in search of something or other. Probably he was just killing time. The logs were swinging out smoothly and since they rode well clear of the ground all the way there was no hang-ups for him to fight. I had just sent the rigging back and we sat talking on my splicing stump in the shadow of the tightline donkey. Although it was only the first week in May, the weather was unusually warm. The chokers were slacked into the pile over the ridge and below our line of vision. Ostensibly, the rigging crew was hooking up the next turn. We could hear Gordy's machine throbbing remotely above us.

Suddenly everything went dead - quiet the way it gets quite on swamp country evenings when all the bullfrogs stop in unison. Then the whistles began, first one extended moan, then another and

another. Long whistles in the bush generally denote trouble of some sort and several of them indicated a man had been hurt. Maurice was on his feet by the fifth blast.

"Sonofabitch!" he said. "A log must've rolled on one of those jokers. We'd better get the hell up there!"

He started urgently up the hill, moving sure-footed as a mountain goat. He had an edge on me in wind, being a non-smoker, but I wasn't far behind. My mind whirled with morbid apprehensions not untinged with a certain guilty excitement. What the hell had happened, and to whom?

I'd never climbed that formidable sidehill so rapidly before but I was bound to maintain the same flat-out pace as Maurice, who was literally spidering up the slope. I was in considerably better shape than when I first started but the effort of that frenzied ascent soon had me panting like a sick hound and sweating heavily. A dull sense of crisis drove me on. Maurice disappeared over the final ridge and I puffed after him, full of squeamish visions over what I might see.

The first thing I saw was fat Gilles sitting on the ground at the foot of the pile, rocking back and forth, groaning and clutching his ankle. Ronnie and Pat were standing around smoking and looking rather disgusted. Gordy was bringing the stretcher over from the donkey. It didn't exactly have the earmarks of a major calamity.

"What the hell happened?" Maurice asked Ronnie.

"Oh, Frenchy here fell off a log as we were coming out of the pile," he said. "Claims his ankle's busted but he won't let us take his boot off so we can have a look."

Maurice went over to the moaning chokerman and spoke to him soothingly in French. Finally, after a bit, he calmed down and consented to have his boot removed. The ankle was visibly swollen but certainly didn't look broken.

"Well, let's get him on the stretcher," said Gordy. "We'll have to pack him into camp."

I was reminded, as we struggled with our very vocal burden down that tricky and debris-strewn hill, of carrying my brother Chris out on the A-frame show the previous fall. But Chris was at least sixty pounds lighter than pudgy Gilles and the slope had been less extreme. This was a tougher proposition altogether.

If Gilles had weighed less, had been a better worker, been more seriously injured or at least kept his mouth shut, we might have borne him off that mountain in a little better grace. But Gilles was merely a heavy nuisance with an annoying cry-baby voice, who kept shifting his weight on the stretcher and making our task even more difficult. We nearly dropped him several times, and felt like doing so many more times than that. Undoubtedly he was in some pain but he didn't have to make such a federal case out of it. By the time we staggered into camp with him, any sympathy we might have felt had been completely negated. We rolled him groaning on to his bunk in exasperated relief and went to shower and change since it was too late to log further that day.

"Goddamn it!" said Ronnie, "I'm sure that lazy bastard's just goldbricking it so he can swing compensation."

We muttered disgruntled agreement to this notion. It was probably untrue but it suited our

147

mood at that moment to believe it. Slackers were not popular in a logging camp at the best of times. Gordy got on the radiophone with little Bert Pringle fussing around worriedly and ordered a plane. It arrived about an hour later and we were obliged to slide Gilles on the stretcher once more and lug him out along the stiff-leg to the float. He was still complaining vociferously. We were not sorry to see him go.

The next time the mail and supply boat made its twice weekly stop I had a letter from Chris, who had been out since February at Chamiss Bay on the west coast of the Island. I'd declined to accompany him, having had enough of that area in winter the year before at Tahsis. He was chasing on some incredibly high and treacherous cold-deck pile where they were swinging three smaller piles into a single tree - "Christ man, you should see this haywire set-up. The logs are stacked damn near to the bull-block. You wouldn't believe it!"

It sounded horrifically dangerous. I felt half-ashamed of the soft touch I'd landed myself with Pringle and hoped to hell Chris wouldn't get hurt.

We were getting a healthy stack of wood at the bottom tree and both Gordy and Pringle were anxious to see it in the water. It was unfeasible to use the tightline except at high tide; the logs simply collected on the beach in a mad jumble or "jackpot" that was difficult to deal with when it floated, especially for Pringle. It was decided to work in the evenings for a few days when the water was up. They weren't about to pay overtime to the whole crew so only Gordy, Ronnie, Maurice and myself went out. I hooked them up at the top and Ronnie unhooked them at the bottom while the hooker fought hang-ups in between. Ron and I had exchanged places for variety's sake. The angle of the land wasn't really sharp enough for a setup of this sort to work properly. Because of the lack of lift, it stuck halfway. Gordy and Maurice went out one Sunday and blew a bunch of stumps, which helped considerably. Ron and I would hit the sack at the end of twelve-hour days totally exhausted. But we were fairly coining money since the camp was already working a six-day week with time-and-a-half for Saturday. The boredom endemic to five-day camps was greatly minimized. Sunday was our true day of rest and we savoured the idleness like a treat.

Two new men arrived, a chokerman and an engineer. Pringle was getting nowhere fast with the booming up and Gordy had to be released from his machine running duties in order to give him a hand.

The donkey puncher was a sour looking character by the name of Curt Enberg. Except for his short-cropped black hair he was almost a Teutonic stereotype, with square-jawed, stubborn features. He was stockily built and of medium height but he held himself rigidly erect as though to appear taller. I remembered Chris once telling me of an engineer of this general description with whom he'd had a run-in. The name sounded right too. I hoped it wasn't the same guy.

The new chokerman was another hype I'd seen around the Belle Bar with Mousey on several occasions. He knew Ronnie and Pat well and immediately grabbed the spare bed on our side of the bunkhouse. His name was Jerry Prentiss, a gaunt-eyed hustler of about twenty-five with a bad complexion and shaggy brown hair. He had just gotten out of jail so he wasn't wired up, but he'd

brought a couple of caps with him. After supper he and the other two slipped off in the bushes to fix. They asked me along but I declined on the grounds that I didn't want to mess with smack any more. I still maintained the fiction of having been a junkie. It was a pointless deception but it afforded me a sort of artificial bond with the others and admitted me to their confidences. I did it, I suppose, for the same sort of murky reasons that I hung out with the zootsuit gangs. There was a perverse excitement in it. Years later Jack Kerouac in his novels would confess to a similar obsession with hoods and users. They were the existential hipsters of their day.

After a bit, the three of them returned and sat around the bunkshack, playing the nod and speaking in the blurred, extravagant way that guys spoke when they were insulated from the universe by heroin. Maurice came in and sat for a while to talk, rather ingenuously, about his woman who, in the way of most loggers' sweethearts, was running around with another guy while he was in camp. He talked mostly to me, with the others interjecting gowed-up comments every so often. He must have noticed their odd behaviour but he made no comment.

"Hell, man, you don't know what you're missing," said Ronnie, after the hooktender had left. "You should have cranked up with us."

"Yeah, maybe," I said, "but what's the percentage? I'm trying to stay clean."

My feelings about junk were extremely ambivalent in those days. It both fascinated and repelled me. I hadn't yet seen enough of its more evil aspects to completely prejudice me against its use. I didn't have much desire to sample it myself, being both needle-shy and a pretty thoroughgoing drunk, but that was only a personal preference. I had little objection to people shooting up per se. The sad end result of it all was still hidden in the future, both for them and myself. After a bit they stopped talking and fell back on their racks to coast. I lay down myself and slid into a science fiction tale, feeling, despite the fact that they were high and I was straight, a peculiar camaradie with them.

In a few more days all the logs were in the water and both landings cleaned out. It was time to move back up the mountain and swing out the rest of the pile from the farthest tree. The routine was the same as before except that the surly looking Enberg was running the donkey. I was dead certain by now from certain stray remarks he'd made that he was the same ornery bastard Chris had chased for at Harvey Log. I hoped he wasn't going to upset the applecart in some way. I liked Pringle's camp and was making better money than I ever had before.

We unhooked the lines from the Tyler system and strung them back up the gully once more. Soon a new crop of logs was socking into that rocky pocket for me to unchoke and tally. I sat on my fir stump throne between turns as before and dreamed out into the sprawling leagues of the summer universe. It was getting very hot and the snow had retreated, leaving vast tracts of greyblack barren rock exposed to the sun above the timberline on the incredible mountains. Ravens and gulls whirled crying through the shining gulfs below me and sometimes a majestic eagle plunged from its nest in some lofty far-off snag and glided like a predatory kite across the sky. A horde of gluttonous whiskey jacks appeared on cue each noon when the donkey went silent and hung about like small panhandlers, waiting for sandwich scraps and whatever other goodies we might see fit to throw them. It would have been another amiable session except for Enberg.

Curt Enberg was the sort of engineer generally described as "independent" along with epithets of a more trenchant sort. It meant simply that he'd often completely ignore the hand signals I gave him and drop the logs wherever he saw fit. It was part of my job to spot the logs and build the pile, and Enberg's presumption was annoying to say the least. He was arrogantly trying to run the whole operation from the sideboard of that goddamn machine. I resented it thoroughly but managed to maintain my cool for the first couple of days. Hell, we'd have the pile swung before long and I'd be back on my own again at the bottom tree. I resolved to swallow my anger and ride that high-handed bastard out.

But finally, Enberg got to be too much altogether. He had just landed a turn and I ran across the pile to unhook it. One of the chokerbells was fouled and I signalled the engineer to pull the log a little further ahead to clear it. He went ahead alright but when I signalled him to stop, that mean-assed ape went right on pulling. It was a large fir and he kept winding the bitch until, far ahead of the spot where I had intended it to sit it rolled right off the pile to the gully bottom, taking a couple of smaller logs with it. The choker was pulled tight again and there was no hope of getting slack where the log now lay. That was bad enough, but now Enberg, totally ignoring my arm waves and yells, went ahead on the fir again and nearly dislodged the log I was standing on. It was too much altogether and I headed for the machine in a blind rage.

"What's the idea, you man-killing sonofawhore?" I hollered at him. "Are you absolutely stone bloody blind?" I would have said a lot more but I was so incensed it was difficult to talk at all. I came within an inch of clobbering him. I was mad enough to punch him right off that mountain but some faint vestige of common sense held me back. It had nothing to do with fear - we were about an even match as far as size went - but fighting on the job was bad business and could get a man blacklisted. Enberg was quite aware of this too. We stood there glaring at each other for what seemed a very long time. Then his eyes dropped and he began to make grudging excuses.

"Couldn't see you too well there, I guess," he muttered weakly.

"Bullshit, you couldn't see me! You been deliberately ignoring my signals ever since we started. You could have killed me that last time. For Christs's sake, watch it from now on, eh?"

He didn't like it but he knew I was dead right. He muttered something about he would and I headed back to my stump, feeling much better.

Enberg deigned to heed my signals for the most part after that and the job became tolerable again. I continued to ponder on the mysterious Malibu Resort, wondering when Bing Crosby and Company were going to make their appearance. I'd learned a little more about the place. It had been built by a man called Hamilton, the inventor of the variable pitch propellor, shortly before World War Two. It was a case of unfortunate timing and

the venture was unable to get operational until 1946. It had not, despite wide advertising, proved the runaway success that Hamilton had hoped for, perhaps due to its isolated location. The moneyed and the famous had indeed patronized it for the first two or three years but celebrity attendance had dropped off sharply the past couple of summers and ordinary mortals could scarcely afford the steep prices. Nonetheless, the resort was supposed to be opening for business again in June. My chief interest in the place at the time centred around the fact that there was a bar on the premises. I hadn't had a drink for quite a spell.

One Sunday in late May after a fairly easy week we decided to take a spin across the inlet and check the joint over first hand. There were five of us - Ronnie, Pat, Jerry, Maurice and myself. There was no room for anyone else in the small outboard - the only boat the camp possessed. We set out in high spirits like a gang of boys embarking on some momentous adventure. We had vague plans of conning the caretaker into opening up the bar for us.

As we approached the place we could see the tidal rapids were running through the gap between Jervis and Princess Louisa Arm, the narrow tributary inlet.

"Hell, let's go for a roller coaster ride!" shouted Maurice, and headed the boat for the fast water. Just as the current took us, there was a loud thunk as we struck some underwater object. Suddenly the boat was yawing out of control.

"Can't steer the bloody thing," reported Maurice with some annoyance. "Whatever that was must have knocked the prop off!"

The small boat turned completely around and we were sucked through the rapids stern first. For some reason, we'd forgotten to bring the oars and had no control over our cockleshell craft whatsoever. Luckily, this was one of the shortest and least wild of west coast tiderips; there were no whirlpools or other spectacular hazards. We shot through it like a backwards bullet and the impetus carried us more than a quarter of a mile up that narrow fiord where we drifted foolishly to a halt.

"Guess this is what they mean by being up Shit Creek without a paddle, eh?" said Ronnie.

We began hollering at the caretaker, who had been standing on a rock bluff above the gap, watching the whole performance. Shortly he cranked his own boat alive and came foaming up the inlet to our rescue.

Soon we were ashore and walking through that eccentric white elephant of a place with its determinedly rustic buildings. There was a large central structure with a prominent notice board whose glass-enclosed photographs bore witness to the notables who had passed through. Grinning celebrities gawked forever from that plastic collage at yet another gimmick to pry them loose from their money. The individual log cabin units were priced at $50 a day. It was too rich for our blood.

Hey, any chance we can buy a drink?" asked Maurice. It stood to reason that there were several dozen gallons of hooch locked away somewhere inside that pretentious main building. There was even, among the outbuildings, a log cabin called cutely the "Malabar", through whose windows we could see tempting bottles gleaming from shelves.

But that old man must have been a paragon of sheer integrity. He denied our thirsts with a self-righteous vigour that would have gladdened the heart of Carrie Nation.

"Sorry boys," he whined. "I'm under strict instructions not to open them doors to anyone. It's regulations, you understand?"

We didn't understand. If he hadn't done us the service of towing the boat back to land we might well have strongarmed him and taken matters into our own hands. After all, we were loggers and had better business in this wilderness than he did. But the old coot had the law behind him and it wasn't worth the hassle. He made us coffee in his quarters and we drank it in disappointment. The bastard was incorruptible.

At last and at least he found, in his toolshed, a prop that fitted our engine and, mobile again, we bore back across the sound to Pringle's camp.

Bert Pringle was a strange enough person to be running a logging show with his prissy mannerisms, but then his father arrived to spend his vacation. He was a high-spirited old character in his seventies, who still ran a hardware store of his own and was terribly impressed by the fact that his son actually owned a logging outfit. He strode about in grey-haired innocence, saying "Yowser!" and "Nice day," and thinking that logs just came off some convenient counter someplace like nails or turpentine. He probably wasn't a bad old gent but it was difficult to relate to tourists after a hard day's work up the mountain. We suffered his bland ignorance with a certain philosophy. And we brought down the timber from the shelves of that land like a mob of storeclerks to please him.

The booming wasn't going too well and a tug had been contracted to haul the logs away at a specified date. That date was drawing close so they shut the yarding down and made us all boom men for a couple of days. It was ridiculous. None of us knew the first thing about dealing with logs in the water. The equipment was primitive in the extreme and they were using a hand winch to pull the swifters across that locked the logs in place. It was straight out of the dirty thirties when muscle was king. Two of us strained on that cranky winch. The logs popped ahead a couple of feet at a time as we sweated and reefed on that slavish crank. If you didn't pull it around a complete revolution and lock the gear safely into the logs, it could spin back violently under the stress and break your wrists. The rack was operated on the same principle.

For the rest of it, we stowed, pushing the logs into position with pike poles. Nobody knew too much what he was doing, for we hadn't hired out on this chore. We did it for Pringle, the Grace of God and the validity of our paychecks. Once I fell in with a peavey but didn't drop it and passed it to Ronnie as I surfaced. Bravo! someone cried.

Most of us fell in the drink at least once during that three day schmozzle. It was a regular Mack Sennet comedy of errors and half the time the tide was against us, but we persevered and finally got a four-section boom together. It was a sloppy-looking job but the log buyers weren't paying for appearances so it didn't much matter. A tug came in and towed it off down the inlet. Our wages were secure.

Since the arrival of Jerry the evening talk in our side of the bunkhouse was even more junk-oriented than before. If I closed my eyes I could imagine I was sitting in the Broadway Hotel, Milinas' Cafe or one of the other Hastings Street hype hangouts. Their conversation was relentlessly sordid and sadly fascinating.

"Sure had a close shave last winter," recalled Pat. "I was putting out and the narcs were hip to it. A couple of plainclothes bulls cornered me in the St. James Poolhall. I seen the bastards come through the door so I tried to swallow my stash but it was pretty big and I had trouble getting the mother down. I couldn't think what else to do so I dived under one of the tables. I'm laying under there trying to scoff the caps and one of the cops grabs my foot and tries to pull me out. It was a regular tug of war and I thought I'd had the course for a minute. She was nip and bloody tuck but I finally managed to get the shit down. When they finally yarded me out I was clean as a whistle. Should have seen the expression on their faces. They were madder than a bitch but there was nothing they could do about it. I laid low for a bit after that, let me tell you!" He rubbed his throat reflectively.

The bit of smack that Jerry had brought in had whetted Pat's appetite and he was getting itchy feet. One night he and Jerry decided to pack her in and head back to the city. A big dope deal of some sort was supposed to be happening and they wanted to get in on it. Ronnie, who seemed to have considerably more jam than the other two anyhow, hung tough but it left the rigging crew very short-handed and Maurice was obliged to set chokers.

It was getting extremely hot. The sun beat down mercilessly from a cloudless blue sky and baked that sidehill drier than a prairie dustbowl. The fire hazard was considerable and we went on early shift - starting at five in the morning and knocking off at one to escape the furnace fierce afternoons. I'd never worked this shift before and it was an odd experience climbing up the mountain in the spooky hush of dawn. It was refreshingly cool for the first couple of hours but the mosquitoes, noseeums and horseflies were astoundingly numerous and aggressive. We were compelled to smear ourselves with Skeeter Skatter to keep the carnivorous little bastards at bay. There was talk on the radio of putting a general woods closure into effect if the sizzling heat wave continued.

With the other two gone I got to know Ronnie better. He was from England originally, just as I was, and an orphan. He had come over on an evacuee ship during the war, with a group of other parentless kids. A good number of them had drifted into the Vancouver underworld and become junkies. It saddened me to hear about it. Ron was essentially a pretty decent guy, a good cut above Jerry and Pat, but heroin had him by the throat just as tenaciously.

"Hey, it's my birthday tomorrow!" he informed me enthusiastically one day. "My old lady promised she'd send me a present. Hope the broad comes through."

Sure enough when the mail arrived he received a small package.

He tore it open with considerable excitement like a kid on Christmas morning. It appeared to contain nothing but an automatic pencil in a tiny box. He unscrewed the pencil with trembling fingers and three caps of heroin fell out on the bed.

"Wow baby! I love you!" he enthused. "That chick's a natural winner. She always comes through! Hey man, are we going to get loaded tonight!"

It was a crucial point in my life. Despite my earlier refusal, Ron now assumed that I would crank up with him. I was sorely tempted. Hell, we were a million miles from nowhere! Who would ever know? I wrestled it back and forth in my mind. What the hell harm would one little fix do me anyhow? It all seemed very innocent and inconsequential out here in the wilderness. But then I thought of Hastings Street and the thin sickly phantoms with abscessing arms who haunted the booths in bad cafes, prisoners of their whining need. I thought of the desperate whores with their pitiful masks of lipstick and powder, laying twenty men a night to feed their habits. I thought of jail and sadistic cops and kicking cold turkey and dying of overdoses. I thought of being enslaved and getting queer for the very prick of the needle. And I psyched myself past the temptation.

Ron was more hurt than anything else by my decision. He tried every argument in the book to change my mind but I kept thinking those dark, down thoughts and shaking my head. I tried to explain my position and told him foolishly at length that I'd lied about being a user. "But hell, man, it's my birthday," he kept saying. He made me feel illogically like some kind of a mean sonofabitch but I managed to stick to my guns. Finally he gave up trying to persuade me and with a disappointed shrug sloped off to the can to toast his birthday alone.

Two days later the forestry slapped on a closure and shut down every camp on the coast. It was game over for logging until the rains came. Pringle signed the final cheques and they phoned for a couple of planes to fly us out.

"Looks like this might be a long one" said Gordy. "You guys should try getting some work off the spare board at the Beer Slinger's Union. That's what I usually do when I ain't in the weeds."

"Just might do that," I said.

Ronnie by this time had cranked up two-thirds of the junk at a half cap a hit but still had a cap left. He was paranoid for some reason about hitting the airport with dope on him so he shot the rest of the heroin in a single fix, just before the planes arrived. It must have been fairly pure smack. He got so incredibly loaded that he couldn't even walk the stiff-leg to the float and I had to row him.

"Takes dizzy spells sometimes," I explained to poor, naive, mystified Bert Pringle.

Then we were airborne and droning through perfect calm blue sky toward the voracious city. I was stakebound and thirsty. Drugged Ronnie slumped beside me muttering incoherently. Behind us Derrick Point and Malibu faded to dots in the distance and were gone.

NOTES & QUERIES

Re the picture and article on page 39 of the book with the sailboat on the cover.

This rock carving was found by Bruce Collison of Sullivan Bay quite a few years ago. He was cutting a trail and a sapling fell on the rock, knocking off the moss, and there was the carving. By the way, you have the picture upside down. According to books the cross is Spanish, as all Spanish crosses flare at the bottom. A friend showed us a book called *Signs and Symbols of Mu*. The people of Mu used these markings. The circle was the sun, the square the four corners of the earth and the triangle had something to do with the distance from point to point.

I see in another book you mention Joe Perry - we knew him well. He was born on Cape Verde Islands and stowed away on a ship.

> Mrs. J. Proctor
> Simoom Sound, B.C.

Could you please identify the vessel on the back cover of your second issue - we recently inherited the exact same photo and haven't got her name yet.

> Mrs. A. Zielinski
> R.R. No. 1
> Hornby Island, B.C.

The front cover shows the four-masted steel bark Pamir *casting off Cape Flattery in a storm after a visit to Vancouver in 1947. At that time she was a training ship owned by the New Zealand government but originally she had sailed between Germany and South America for the Flying P Line of Hamburg. She was lost in the North Atlantic in 1957. The back cover shows the* Pamir *entering the straits on a calm day.*

We have been trying to backtrack on the history of our boat, the *Swan*. We have her definite background from 1924 to 1972. We know she was purchased from Kelly Logging in 1924. We also know she was sunk at Kimsquit in 1922. We have been trying to find when Kelly Log bought her. They probably bought her from the Talkheo Cannery.

We have been told she was built in 1888, but have not been able to definitely confirm this. Can you tell us anything about her?

> Mrs. A. Talbot
> Box 1
> Matsqui, B.C.

There are too many Swans and you give us too few details for a definitive search of the record, but perhaps our readers can help.

They Don't Make 'Em Anymore:

Baker had the biggest hands of any man I ever saw. Probably the strongest too. They needed to be big and strong because Baker called on them to do some of the most difficult tasks. He handlogged for years in the Knight Inlet area. During that time he worked alone as did most handloggers, and if he didn't get wealthy he at least made a good living. His outlay was small. All one needed to go handlogging was a Gilchrist jack and a pail of grease.

If a handlogger got one log per day into the water, he would be doing fine. A section (portion of a boom of logs) would build up quickly that way. It was very hard work. To start with, a handloggers claim had to be overlooking the water and just as important, it had to be very steep. The falling of each tree called for careful consideration. They were felled with precision, so as to take up the most advantageous position on the ground. Sometimes on hitting the earth, the tree would slide off down hill for a distance. Skillful falling would have directed it so as to miss stumps close by and gain as much ground as possible in this first move. If necessary before falling, the logger would go so far as to build a mat of branches and brush, or even a bulwark of split timber to guide the tree on its first move.

Baker made some money at the business and then in the early fifties he bought the smallest logging yarder on the market and decided to go big time. With this came cables and chokers and gasoline drums and tools and no end of troubles. He planned on running a one man operation, but instead of getting easier, his life became one long round of confusion and really hard going. This type of logging was not his style at all. Every day something went wrong, and every day something had to be repaired. He fought a gallant battle against these odds and managed to rig a standing tree on his own. He topped it and hung five guy lines on it. To hang the lines he first had to climb the tree in belt and spurs, and hang a block on top. He then ran a length of rope through the block and climbed down with one end. He hooked a line from his drum onto the rope and manhandled it through the block and down. With this line he hoisted his guy lines. He would start his machine and haul up the guy line, shut off the machine and then put on belt and spurs and climb to the tree top to endeavour to wrap the guy line around it. As often as not he would arrive at the top and find he needed two or three inches of slack. This meant climbing all the way down again, starting up the machine to give slack, and climbing up again to the top. Baker figured he must have climbed the tree about 25 or 30 times in all. At that time he was 63 years old.

When ready to haul in logs to his spar tree, Baker would run his rigging out in the bush, stop the machine and walk out to the choker. As he hooked up a log, he would spot his next log to move so that when he went back to the machine he could figure out how far to run the rigging out next time. This was done by counting the wraps on the drum, and so he managed to run his one-man show. Unfortunately he did not seem to realise that there is a breaking point to every cable as well as to every machine. He was constantly in trouble. None of this I knew about him until I went to work for him.

I had been working in a camp at the head of Knight Inlet and we were due to close down about 12th December. A lot of snow had already fallen. Baker's claim was at Axe Point, about 15 miles down the Inlet. He was in desperation to get his logs from the spar tree into the water, and by now was hampered by the snow, and the prospect of lots more to come. He came up to our camp about a week before closing date, on a very cold day, in an open boat, and that night went from one bunkhouse to another trying to hire three men to go with him on 12th December and help him get his logs in. He was having little luck, as most of the men were eagerly looking forward to getting away from snow and logging and sidehills and inlets for the winter.

I felt sorry for the old fellow and volunteered to go with him and in a while two others decided to do likewise. Then we had more snow for a few days and by 12th December things looked grim and the weather forecast was anything but good.

Planes managed to come up the Inlet that morning, flying low underneath a solid cloudbank which concealed the mountain tops on either side of the Inlet. They commenced to ferry out the crew. The two men who volunteered to come with me lost no time in concluding that Vancouver might after all be more entertaining than Baker's camp. They packed their gear and put their names on the flight list. Old Baker had made an early morning trip in his open boat to pick us up, and I could see his disappointment. I felt I could not let him down, so I put my gear in his boat and we set off down the Inlet. It was a bitterly cold trip and the planes carrying out the men flew low over our heads. I began to have doubts about my own sanity.

At Baker's place the sidehill was steep and there was lots of snow. About fifty feet above the water sat three neat shacks. This was the camp. It was near noon as we entered what was a kitchen livingroom off which were two tiny bedrooms. The place was not too untidy. It was near noon and Baker suggested a bit of lunch. He put the kettle on a very old oil stove and found a saucepan to make soup. Then he turned to me as if it was of great importance to the economy of the whole business and asked,
"How big an appetite you got?"
"About normal," I assured him.

We had an adequate lunch and spent the afternoon splicing line, repairing equipment and hauling gasoline up the hill for the machine. That night as I was going to my bunk, he gave me a whole armful of Westerns to read. He had piles of paperback Westerns, and I found out later that he'd read each one several times. Stranger still I found out that although somewhere in his travels he'd learned to read, he still could not write. At one time he owned a small farm in Ontario but sold out when depression came. He then moved from camp to camp throughout Northern Ontario and by mid 'thirties had arrived in the Arctic. He lived one year with the Eskimos and spoke of them with great respect. The stories of his travels were fascinating and I looked forward to them at night.

Daytime was a different matter. We got up at 6 a.m. Baker would make breakfast while I washed the dishes from the previous night. He was a good cook. After breakfast we usually put some lunch together and then hurried to be at the spar tree by 8 a.m. A strange look would then come into his eyes, and he became a different man. Logs were supposed to be flying downhill at the stroke of eight. Even greasing the machine seemed a loss of valuable time. Baker operated the machine and I hooked up the logs. It was what is known as a tightline show. At the slightest hitch or delay Baker would be off his seat and out front of the machine, screaming, waving his arms and beating his hard hat on a stump. When I'd give him the signal he'd run back to the machine as if every split second counted, and tightline the log into the water far below us. Quite often on the way down, the open face choker would let go and the log would run free, off the road and into the bush. His quantity of logs was so limited he could not afford to lose one, no matter how small, so I'd go racing downhill and do a one man battle with the rigging to side block it back onto the road and toward the water again. Then again it frequently happened when a log reached the water, the open face choker would not release and it meant a trip all the way downhill and out to the boom to release it. Baker would then haul the rigging back up and stand at the top of the hill watching me climb. He would be furious with impatience and screaming that his grandmother, blindfolded and barefooted, could move faster in the bush.

Many times during the day we would have an argument, during which insulting words and general bad language flowed freely. In the heat of battle, I'd decide I'd had enough of this. I'd pick up my lunch bucket and telling Baker what to do with his whole outfit, I would head for camp. The old fellow would then come running after me, a completely changed man, and full of apologies would plead with me to stay. We'd sit and have a smoke and go back to work. Later in the day we would get into another battle. Baker would fire me and I would simply refuse to go telling him I had come here to see the last of his rotten logs floating down there and by God there's no way I'm leaving till then. He would then go back to the machine muttering and banging his hard hat on every stump.

During the Fall of that year Baker had lost a number of logs when a storm broke up his booming set up. He recovered a few of them, but was convinced that the remainder were still somewhere within the confines of the Inlet and were floating up and down as the tides and winds directed. Baker had a commanding view of about half a mile of the water from his perch on the machine, and every now and then he would switch it off and with great strides he would head downhill, start up his outboard motor and race out to retrieve a log that had been drifting with a new tide. When he first did this, and raced by me without a word, I felt sure he had gone beserk.

After we'd have dinner and coffee in his small kitchen, he became his normal self. He was very good company. Once a year he sent out a letter to his sister in Ontario. Shortly after I arrived at his place he came to me one night with a pen and a book of large size notepaper. He set it on the table and looked me straight in the eye for a moment. "Can you write?" he asked. I said I could.

"Good. Very good," he said. "You start writing and I'll tell you what to say."

I put down his address as Baker walked up and down the small kitchen floor. He was rubbing his great hands and acting like a senior executive. He dictated for about fifteen or twenty minutes and then came to the table and asked how much we had written. I showed him one page and almost half another. He seemed surprised at the progress and said,

"Good. Very good. What do you say we shove a full stop in there now and start off with a new sentence?"

Another night, Baker decided seeing as the water was calm, that we should go visiting his friend Carl and wife. They owned a small camp across the Inlet from us and were sitting out the winter there. He was a very experienced logger, and only after we'd had a few drinks there did I realise that Baker had a very definite reason for coming there. He would have to move his machine to a new claim in the Spring and asked many questions and sought advice on a variety of things. Carl was most helpful and most patient. Finally Baker jumped to his feet and striking the table with his closed fist said, "You run your own show

whatever way you want to, but don't think for a moment you're going to show me how to run mine" and with that he walked out and down to the boat. Both Carl and his wife smiled. They knew Baker and loved him for all his faults, and they knew he would be back again.

The night we got the last log into the water, there was no person more proud than Baker. There was a moon shining on the snow covered landscape and on the logboom. Each snow covered log was outlined against the black water of the inlet. Several times after dinner Baker would go out to the rock bluff above the boom and proudly gaze down on his log harvest. I was anxious now to get away, but Baker insisted I stay and help sorting out the logs, and make up the section. Every other job in the woods I had done, but never worked on the boom and I told him so. I insisted I couldn't walk on a log in the water. He insisted I stay. His booming ground was bad, and there was at least thirty feet of water underneath at low tide. It was wide open to winds. I decided to stay.

Next morning after breakfast, I made up lunch as usual. Baker came in the door from his outside freezer and gravely announced that we were out of meat. With that he reached into a corner of the kitchen stacked with saws, axes, shovels and rusty tools. In there he found an old rusty British Service rifle and a box of shells, and handing them to me he said "I must do my washing to-day. You go up the hill and get us a deer. There's fresh tracks in the snow this morning." He had no other means of getting meat as the steamboat had quit calling since all the camps had closed down, and would not come again until Spring. I took the rifle and lunchpail and went out. As I started to climb the hill I heard him shout from the door-way, "I'll pay you for the day, but don't come back without one."

I followed tracks all day, and at noon I cleared snow off a log and had lunch. In the afternoon I saw some deer and shot one. I hauled it downhill and into camp. Baker was anxiously awaiting my arrival as he had heard the shot and its echo. He dressed it efficiently and hung it up.

The booming of his logs did not take too long. One bitterly cold day about 2 p.m. while working on the boom, I was using a peavey to turn a log on which I was standing. I took a good pull on the peavey and the hook slipped. I went flying into the water of course and went down. It was cold. The log boom looked dark as I swam up. When I surfaced I reached for the nearest log and got my arms on it. Baker with a pike pole in his hand was there waiting for me. Then without either sympathy or assistance he just said "Where's the peavey?" I pointed down. He shook his head in disgust and walking away he said "That'll be the day when I fall in the water with a peavey in my hand and come up without it". I managed to pull myself up onto the log.

I got a plane out of there when the logs were boomed. As we circled I looked down and saw old Baker waving from outside his snow covered cabin. He would at least have some venison for Christmas.

About two years later I was again working in that area and heard that Baker had drowned off his boom. I felt sorry that another of the hardy independent old characters of the B.C. coast had gone for ever.

EDITORIAL

Like all places where man has spent any length of time, the B.C. coast is littered with the relics and leavings of earlier days: great, spectral cedar stumps with moss in the springboard notches; pilings like black fingers warty with barnacles in abandoned loggingcamp bays; sagging sentrybox outhouses beside crushed cabins; abortive mineshafts wormholed into cliff-faces, full of blind cave crickets; fallen totems facedown like drunk men in clammy alderchoked clearings by dead villages; forgotten fish-canneries and whaling-stations collapsing in the rain; slate quarries like huge flaking wounds where only weeds come now; a corroded Spanish anchor salvaged from two-hundred years of deep water; tombstones in the underbrush by sad Cape Scott. The lost, the given-up, the unwillingly-relinquished things and places of the westcoast wilderness exert a curious lure over anyone interested in the forces, foibles and failures that helped to shape the freewheeling identity that makes British Columbians unique. Despite the proliferation of high-rise buildings in its ever-burgeoning cities, this is still a frontier province. The blandness of the Eastern sophisticate is little in evidence here. We are not long from the log-cabins and the shoreline abounds with evidence of our pioneer roots - artifacts of other times - the bones of many a venture gone awry. Recently, the pulpmill town of Ocean Falls was saved from a similar fate when it was taken over by the B.C. Government but mostly the old things and places slip quietly into memory and decay as the influx of the new supplants them. In this issue we visit some outposts of the past in search of vanishing legacies, both Indian and white.

Peter Trower
April 22, 1973

* * *

Les Peterson chronicles the disappearance of over 30 of the upper coast's colourful waterfront communities, some barely big enough to deserve their own post office, others - like Anyox, Roy and Swanson Bay - surprisingly large. Peter Trower revisits the small camps, communities that weren't on the map at the best of times but made the coast a more hospitable place once than it is now. We have mentioned before the coast's impressive record of inspiring utopian settlements and here we look at two of the most intriguing: Scott Lawrance details the Finns' long struggle at Sointula, and in the first of two articles Howard White looks behind the scenes at the once-famous Indian mission of Metlakatla near Prince Rupert. Bella Coola-born Leslie Kopas shows a different way a unique seafront community can disappear - overcome not by rainforest vegetation but by the less resistable spread of modern day mass culture.

We hope all the oldtimers thinking about putting down their stories will be encouraged by the news that Frank White's freewheeling ramble on trucklogging last issue won the Canadian Media Club's award as B.C.'s best magazine feature of the year. Even if you're not up to an article you could make the job of reading subscription requests a lot more interesting by including a few lines about yourself or what you think of the magazine.

All is silent. Suddenly, a high, clear tone is heard, followed, at varying intervals, by echoes from surrounding crags and hills.

It is boat time. People, singly and in groups, gravitate to the landing - a piling pier thrust out from shore into a sheltered bay.

As the steamer's bow slides by the wharf, a deck-hand expertly heaves a throwing-line ashore. Someone catches it, pulls in the steel spring-line attached from amidships, and slips the spliced loop over a cast-iron bollard. The skipper rings for slow ahead, the ship is warped alongside, and bow and stern made fast.

A gangplank is eased from deck to the landing. A handful of human beings, clutching bags, packs and suitcases, feel their way down the cleated walkway.

The winch-man lifts the hatch clear, plunges his hook into the hold, and commences to bring out sling-loads of mail and freight.

The purser has candy-bars to sell, and fruit and newspapers not more than a few days old. Bits of conversation drift back and forth from dock to ship. A hopeful logger enquires about a job. He is told to try at a camp not far along the coast.

Finally, a manifest is produced to be signed. A few souls heading "outside" climb aboard. The gangplank is pulled in by its securing ropes, and the railing-gate closed. The ship's whistle gives a short, sharp toot. The stern-line is released. The skipper calls for slow ahead. The amidships deckhand pays out the spring-line as the ship's stern moves away from the wharf. The bow-line is released; then the spring-line. There are waves of farewell from ashore. Skipper and passengers return the courtesy. The ship backs silently out until there is clearance to turn, then heads into the channel and out of sight around the nearest point.

Year after year, this scene was enacted at regular intervals at literally hundreds of boat landings throughout the length of British Columbia's prodigious coastline. Such a scene is a rarity today both along the mainland coast between Vancouver and Prince Rupert and along the west coast of Vancouver Island between Victoria and Quatsino. Not only do ships such as this one literally not exist, but also the very ports of call themselves are disappearing.

With the advent of car-ferry service, communities served by road as far north as Lund do not need steamer service. But, between Lund and Prince Rupert, since loss of the general coastal steamer, hardly a mainland community remains.

The Northwest Coast of North America traditionally possessed five major tangible resources; fur-bearing animals, whales, fish, minerals, and timber. It had also its intangible resources - its prodigious peaks rising sheer from inlet waters; its miles of interspersed rocky shores and white sand beaches; its heaving, adventurous seas, and its quiet, grassy lagoons, breathing of solitude.

During the early years of the fur trade, sea otter, fur seal and beaver were almost exterminated. The building of the Hudson's Bay Company posts added very little new populations: they merely redistributed native peoples.

Maquinna

Chief Maquinna, who saw it all begin at Friendly Cove in 1786, by 1800 became so disillusioned with the fur trade's effects that he massacred the crew of the *Boston* in a futile attempt to put an end to the business.

Anthropologist Diamond Jenness estimated that the population of British Columbia's coastal native Indians, which stood at 15,000 in 1935, had numbered approximately 50,000 prior to the arrival of Europeans. Many of the tribes who suffered most by this wastage of 35,000 beings occupied territories where reduced native

Friendly Cove

population has never been replaced by white settlement. The Queen Charlotte Haidas, for instance, diminished from an estimated 8400 to 650; and the Bella Coolas from 2500 to 300. Many villages were wiped out so suddenly by smallpox epidemics that, although their sites remained marked by lodges and totem poles, their names have been lost forever.

Perhaps because the appalling obliteration of seventy percent of the Pacific Northwest aboriginal peoples involved unknown people, history books tend to give more space to Chief Maquinna's massacre. The great Chief, however, was probably quite aware of the enomity of the injustice his one token act sought to protest.

Coastal Steamer

Of the remaining four resources, all were renewable except the minerals. Up-coast mining towns, the most significant of which was Anyox on Observatory Inlet, lived on borrowed time. Built around a Granby Consolidated Mining and Smelting Company's huge mine, Anyox reached a population of 2500 in the mid-1920's, and its pyritic copper smelter was the largest in the world. Homes were supplied with electricity, hot and cold running water, and a sewer system. Cultural and recreational amenities included a hall that seated five hundred, a movie theatre, a

baseball diamond, a football field and a golf course. Yet by 1930 the mine was closed, and a fire in 1932 drove out the last remaining handful of inhabitants.

Surf Inlet, on the west coast of Princess Royal Island, ran a course parallel to that of Anyox. The Belmont gold, silver, and copper mine attracted 300 individuals to this remote site on British Columbia's raincoast - for a few years.

Many lesser mines also came and went, drawing their bits of humanity to form a succession of tidewater communities, then letting them go again. While no mines can be expected to endure indefinitely, those located along the northwest mainland coast and off-shore islands seemed doomed to become very brief candles indeed.

Whales, in the middle of the nineteenth century, constituted quite another matter. They roved the coast, singly and in great pods, seemingly as numberless as the stars. Throughout much of the coast, whalers went ashore only to flense their catch, creating nothing that could be called even a temporary community. The more remote places - Naden Harbor on Graham Island, Rose Harbor on Moresby, and Cachalot on the west coast of Vancouver Island - were representative of localities at which whaling stations were established. During the span of a few years, early in this century, ships from these ports set out to take advantage of the presumably inexhaustible supply of whales. Ashore, as many as two hundred workmen toiled to rend oil from carcasses towed into each of these three factories. As their predecessors had already done with the sea otter, however, these efficient whale hunters proved that their persistence could in fact exhaust the whale supply. Naden Harbor, Rose Harbor and Cachalot became ghost towns and the native Indians, having already lost an important source of clothing material, now also lost a valuable source of oil and food.

Of all the storied foods of the world, the Pacific Northwest salmon stands unique. Here was a food supply which not only required no planting or cultivation, but which also presented itself, voluntarily and in fantastic numbers, right at mankind's doorstep.

There is a tendency now to list the white man's canneries as the first fish processing plants along the British Columbia coast. Actually, at one time every native Indian village constituted a factory at which enormous numbers of salmon of all varieties were preserved by either a drying or a smoking process. These factories existed,

Nootka Sound

moreover, not only along the coast, but also as far up rivers and streams as the salmon penetrated on their spawning runs. Even beyond such natural runs, fish produce was carried inland along traditional "grease-trails". Best known of these is the one followed by Alexander MacKenzie to tidewater at the mouth of the Bella Coola River, but such trails once existed from the head of every inlet.

Nor was salmon the only salt-water fish that flourished along the Pacific Northwest coast. Infinitely more prolific, and sustaining some species of larger fish, schools of herring occupied every inlet, every patch of kelp, and every waterway among the off-shore islands. Whales plunged through their solid masses. Seals herded them into giant balls, to be devoured at their convenience. Dogfish harried their enormous schools from below until they rose to the surface to be further beset upon by seagulls and osprey. The native Indian took them in traps and sun-cured their fabulous catches for winter food.

Codfish once frequented every reef along the coast, all year round. Halibut were plentiful throughout the entire North-West. Anchovies swam in beautiful silver streams. Candlefish, better known on this coast as oolachan, produced an oil that could be used either as a food or as a fuel for lighting native lodges.

With the influx of Europeans, plants to process all of these fish but the oolachan were built at convenient locations near fishing grounds.

By the 1920's approximately 80 canneries were in simultaneous operation along British Columbia's coastline. Each cannery, requiring its quota of fishermen and its force of shore workers, comprised a village during its operating season.

To transport office staff and work crews to this string of canneries, to bring in supplies and to remove sometimes enormous packs of canned fish required the services of an impressive fleet of ships.

For more than fifty years the main fleet of such vessels were those that bore the familiar black and red colors of the Union Steamship Company of Vancouver. A typical Union Steamship vessel was the *Venture*. On a routine run from Vancouver, her skipper might make as many as sixty-five stops before his ship reached the canneries of Rivers Inlet.

Like a fisherman casting his line at various distances in rotation, the Union ships made a series of loops out of the port of Vancouver, all the way from Howe Sound to Prince Rupert. In the process, main stops might be visited by two or more vessels; even the tiniest stop received regular service.

I can recall, quite vividly still after many years, standing on the *Venture's* deck, deep into a mild, black summer night. Not a light showed anywhere. Suddenly, a bell rang. The ship's motion slowed. Then, a spotlight beam, startingly brilliant, pierced the solid darkness, moved slightly, to come to rest on a tiny logging float. In the circle of light stood one of the anonymous beings who invariably appeared, at any hour of the day or night, to officiate at the docking process. A sack of mail and a slingload or two of groceries later, the captain eased his ship back into a space intimately remembered, then, without whistle this time, nosed ahead, all but running lights extinguished, into the pitch-black night.

Although not every camp could be reached individually by steamer, each camp could find, within practicable distance, a center at which ships did call. Thus, ports of call such as Seaside, Longview, Vancouver Bay, St. Vincent Bay, Bliss Landing, Redonda Bay, Toba Inlet, Shoal Bay, Roy, Port Neville, O'Brian Bay, Forward Harbor, Blind Channel, Echo Bay, Allison's Harbor and many other stops came into being. Each of these localities, important and enduring enough to find its way onto maps of British Columbia, sustained a satellite of logging operations around it.

Also during the 1920's, at Swanson Bay on Tolmie Channel, a pulp mill and sawmill maintained a population of approximately 500. A pulp and newsprint operation at Ocean Falls supported a town of some 2000. These mills, provided with ample hydro-electric power potential, and located in regions of enormous timber resources, sent their endless flow of bales of pulp and rolls of newsprint into the holds of freighters for distribution to world markets.

In 1925, passenger and freight vessels served three large up-coast mining towns in addition to a scattering of small operations. They served some eighty fish canneries plus several whaling stations. They called at a necklet of scattered villages around the shores of Vancouver Island and a labyrinthine chain of stops along the inside passage.

Existence of this complex network of transportation routes, coupled with both the presence of fish and game and the availability of very cheap Crown land made practicable the establishment of homesites throughout most of the entire coast.

Some degree of farming and ranching was established at almost every one of the communities that have since disappeared.

Early in the century, the MacLennan family cleared land, planted apple trees and built a modern dairy barn at the head of Port Graves, Gambier Island. From Britain they imported a Jersey bull, for which they reputedly paid the amazing price of $25,000. Many Fraser Valley herds are still descended from this Gambier Island sire. For years, apples from this farm were shipped to Vancouver.

In 1925 Walter Wray was raising chickens at Vanguard Bay, Nelson Island and delivering eggs to Pender Harbor and Powell River.

Thomas Robinson managed to dig space for a garden in St. Vincent Bay, an indentation in the shores of Jervis Inlet. Today, a peach-plum tree that still bears fruit stands as a lone reminder of the former community there, large enough to support a school.

Thirty-eight householders listed their occupations as farming and ranching on Lasquiti Island at this same time - enough to support both an agricultural and stock breeders' association.

In 1925, Andrew Shuttler had lived nearly thirty years in Melanie Cove, an arm of Prideau Haven, Toba Inlet. By patiently terracing the steep slopes of his pre-emption, Shuttler had created room for apple trees, grape vines, and flowers. This warm-hearted pioneer befriended many coastal travellers, including Muriel Blanchet, who perpetuated his name in her reminiscent book, *The Curve of Time*.

At Roy, in the mid-1920's, George Byers kept some eighty bee-hives. Patches of fireweed from areas already logged provided nectar for the

Main Drag - Port Essington

Evening Winter Scene
Anyox B.C.

Watching the Start
B.C. Industries Canneries 1913

honey-bees, and the busy "capital" of Loughborough Inlet gave Byers a ready market for his honey.

At Port Neville, the Hansen family in 1891 had built the first general store north of Vancouver, to serve farming families. Although logging became the chief industry thirty years later, ten families still maintained some farming at the head of this unique inlet.

At the head of Kingcome Inlet, the Hallidays were already old-timers. The Halliday ranch welcomed - and played host to - any travellers who happened to appear during the amicable summer and fall seasons.

At Cape Scott, the northern tip of Vancouver Island, N.P. Jensen and his son-in-law, Theo Fredericksen, had brought cattle into the Danish-speaking colony founded there in 1897. Mrs. Fredericksen had learned the Danish method of making butter so pure that it could be kept canned indefinitely through hot summer days and still retain its original consistency and freshness. Butter and beef from the Jensen and Fredericksen dykeland at Cape Scott, and jam from Henry Ohlsen's tiny cannery at San Josef Bay supplied some of the diet of Quatsino Sound logging camps and mines, and of Rivers Inlet fishing grounds.

Refuge Bay, on Porcher Island at the Skeena River's mouth, and Port Clements, on the Queen Charlottes, proved to be not too far north for the raising of cattle and poultry or the growing of fruit.

Beef did travel up-coast from Vancouver packinghouses, but it was none too fresh even upon arrival at a logging camp or cannery, and very "high" indeed long before the next consignment arrived. Many colourful stories made their debuts into raincoast repertoire through the efforts of distraught camp cooks to provide their crews with edible meat.

Green vegetables travelled up-coast even more poorly than did meat, and fresh milk could not make the voyage at all. Near almost every logging, mining and fishing centre some settlers, to supply these needs, turned to gardening or ranching.

Perhaps most of these self-styled ranchers and farmers clinging to their patches of ground along British Columbia's coastline scarcely warranted their titles. Nevertheless, they did, from their wilderness clearings, contribute to a degree of self-sufficiency that vanished with the pioneers themselves.

If it could be predicted that the mines of Anyox, Alice Arm, and Surf Inlet would become depleted and the populations of these towns forced to move, it did seem in 1925 that fish canneries, based on self-renewing runs of salmon, herring, anchovies, and pilchards, were to be permanent features of this coast.

On the Skeena River Sunnyside, Claxton, British America, North Pacific, Inverness, Oceanic, and Balmoral became thriving villages during the fishing season, giving employment to native Indians, Orientals, and whites alike. Similarly, in Rivers Inlet McTavish, Kildala, Brunswick, Good Hope, Strathcona, Beaver, Provincial, Goose Bay, Wadhams, and Rivers Inlet Cannery kept many hundreds of shore workers usefully employed. Ecoole, Nootka, CeePeeCee, Kildonan, and Clayoquot, along the west coast of Vancouver Island, and Margaret Bay, Boswell, Namu, Butedale, Klemtu, and Kim-squit along the mainland coast were assigned to every child to be memorized as centres of the province's salmon-canning industry, permanently fixed in Nelson Atlases.

Perhaps the earnings of workers at these isolated canneries were marginal. Perhaps it was inevitable that improved technology would bring about the centralization of all canning at Steveston, at the mouth of the Fraser River and close to a large labour pool.

Earnings from summer cannery work were never meant to constitute sole annual income. These seasonal jobs did, however, sufficiently augment cash incomes of some families to such an extent that they could, in places of beauty and tranquility along the British Columbia coast, maintain homes which they could not have otherwise built or occupied.

Each cannery required - and therefore gave employment to - a manager, a bookkeeper, a millwright, a steam engineer, a maintenance man, a cook, and two or more net-men, in addition to its cannery crew. A total complement of somewhere between fifty and one hundred would not be an overly liberal average. With eighty canneries operating, a minimum estimate of 5500 cannery shore employees worked through each canning season.

Perhaps the majority of these thousands of workers came from the city of Vancouver. Many however, both Indian and non-Indian, made their way to fish canneries from small coastal communities or from isolated pre-emptions. Women from every native village on the coast found work at the rather specialist task of filling cans quickly and neatly. Non-Indian females from homes near many of the cannery sites were also made welcome when tens of thousands of salmon has to be canned at each one of these plants within a day after they were caught.

The closure of coastal canneries was followed by a consequent curtailment of transportation services. When the Union Steamships Company reeled their vessels back into port for a final time, they came filled with uprooted settlers, each with a one-way ticket to some urban center.

Despite their attachment to traditional homesites, native Indians, deprived of jobs essential to their economy, also upped sticks and attempted to follow their lost jobs to the cities. In this process, almost every coastal inlet lost its entire native population - even such well-known villages as Nootka, Nahwitti, Clo-oose and Takush disappeared. The Tsimshians have gravitated to Prince Rupert; the Northern Kwakiutls, to Kitimat; and the Southern Kwakiutls, to Alert Bay. All coastal tribes have lost to forces that have propelled the young to Victoria and Vancouver.

The closure of mines and the phasing out of sawmills and logging camps have compounded the mainland coast's population loss.

At the time of writing, the greatest single recent population loss is that brought about by the phasing out of the Crown-Zellerbach pulp and paper mill at Ocean Falls.

Here, since its construction early in the century, stood a community seemingly meant to endure. Throughout its existence, Ocean Falls housed between 2000 and 3000 people. Visibly, the town maintained church, school, hospital, hotel, apartment, cafe, merchandising, theatre, newspaper,

July 1st Tug-o-War
Ocean Falls B.C. 1919

sports, dairy, bakery, laundry and other facilities. It presented a significant stop for ships and planes. It offered a haven not only for boats owned by mill employees, but also for commercial fishing vessels. Without road access, the isolated inhabitants threw themselves whole-heartedly into community life.

Ironically, not only was Ocean Falls condemned to death, but its sentence was promulgated on newsprint created by workers whose jobs, whose homes, and whose even-tenored way of life were being doomed.

While deploring the near-loss to our coastline of the unique community of Ocean Falls, one should retain a sense of perspective in this matter of population loss. The shrinkage at Ocean Falls represents perhaps five percent of the shrinkage suffered by this coast during the past half century.

When Redonda Bay, Shushartie, Blind Channel, Echo Bay, Port Progress, Namu, Forward Harbor, Lockport, Waddington Station, and other coastal communities passed into oblivion, mention of their demise failed to reach beyond the surrounding hills. Yet they were pieces of humanity, both relieving and giving access - while they endured - to the wilderness surrounding them.

There can be no precise analysis made of either the exact extent or the exact degree of loss suffered by British Columbia's mid-mainland coast during the past fifty years.

With regard to the fishing industry, while the quantity of fish processed has not, on an average, dropped too badly, far-reaching changes in the fishing process itself have occurred. All mid-coast canneries, refrigeration operations and reduction plants have disappeared. At Charles Creek in Knight Inlet, the disappearance has become physical as well as economic. A slide has buried the two canneries which once operated there. Salmonberries now grow where salmon were once canned.

At some former cannery sites, floating camps are maintained, from where fish collected from individual boats are transferred to large packers

Port Neville Destroyed By Fire
June 25 1925

Native Habitations Nootka Sound B.C.

for shipment to Steveston or Prince Rupert. Since gillnetters, trollers and long-line fishermen still exist, and since some camps still operate, it cannot be said that the coast has by any means suffered a complete loss. Jervis, Toba, Loughborough, Knight, and Kingcome Inlets, however, once busy fishing grounds, have suffered almost total disappearance of commercial fishing in comparison to what they once knew.

Subtracting the number of existing fishermen and shore workers from the numbers involved in 1925 shows a loss of approximately 10,000. Most of this number was sustained by our mid-mainland coast, now almost barren because salmon destined for these waters are being caught far off shore and processed elsewhere.

During this same half century, the number of residents listed throught the west coast of Vancouver Island and the mainland between Lund and Kitimat has dwindled by about 7500. Ironically, the addition of these persons to a prodigiously-growing lower mainland urban population has contributed to overgrowth problems which are only now being realized.

The advent of power-saw, skidder, portable spar-tree, self-loading truck, boom-boat, and other labor-saving devices has made possible the production of vastly more timber per man-day now than before World War II. Rather than hundreds of small operations - often afloat on rafts - clearing off merely the immediate shoreline, today comparatively few camps, shore-based, reach far inland for timber.

In the change, the old public general stores which once lined the coast, serving some 5000 woodsmen, have been phased out; the men replaced by machines and the general stores by camp commissaries. About forty such stores, in existence in 1925, have disappeared from along the coast. So have some forty post offices.

A dozen sawmills and another dozen machine shops have also passed into oblivion since the mid-twenties.

Five hospitals have ceased to exist.

Early in this century, British Columbia threw open thousands of acres of coastline, in blocks of a quarter-section each, for pre-emption settlement. In order to obtain Crown Grant title, the land-seeker was required to complete certain basic improvements regarding home building and land clearing, and to pay the government one dollar an acre. Since the acquisition of title took up to five years, and since the pre-emptor was required to occupy his homesite for at least one-half of each year, neither the pioneer nor anyone else could speculate on this land to any serious extent.

Fish and clams from the water and wild berries from the woods, augmented by milk, butter, eggs and garden produce provided much of the settler's food requirements. Logging or fishing could yield enough cash during six months to enable the pre-emptor to spend the remaining six months of the year improving his property, prospecting for minerals, boat-building or pursuing any other activity in which he might be interested.

Today a single person or a family wishing to locate anywhere along British Columbia's depopulated coastline except at Ocean Falls would encounter incredible obstacles. Private property - holdings which did not revert to the Crown after the original occupants left - has become so inflated in value through speculative manipulation by absentee owners that the potential settler cannot compete with investors to acquire a homesite. The buying and selling of deeds to property along Canada's west coast is a more lucrative international game than the smuggling of gold into Macao - and it remains legal. Crown lands have long been frozen insofar as purchase is involved.

With the loss of scores of populated sites, lack of transportation access also faces the hopeful coastal settler. Union Steamship vessels - the *Cardena*, the *Chelohsin*, the *Catala*, the *Cheam*, the *Camosun*, the venerable old *Venture* - have long ago vanished. The *Tees*, the *Queen City*, the *Maquinna*, and their successors along Vancouver Island's west coast are no more. Some logging camps and all fish camps make use of company vessels to serve most of their needs.

Throughout much of the coast, fishing can be conducted now only by sports methods, and many waters once alive with schools of coho and spring salmon are virtually barren now.

Seasonal employment, except for a very few men at scattered logging camps, is literally a thing of the past.

One school of thought advances the argument that the wave of land-seekers and workers who once swarmed up our coast were of a different breed; that the present-day human being simply will not go north.

But many of the Ocean Falls workers, as the mill gradually limited its production, showed great reluctance to leave. Now that the British Columbia government has rid the path to Ocean Falls of obstacles, individual workers and families will make their way to this remote inlet again.

If Ocean Falls can be reactivated, why not Swanson Bay also?

If the government can see fit to sponsor a salmon cannery at Port Simpson, why not a plant at the mouth of Knight Inlet to process shrimps and prawns? A cannery removed from the Strait of Georgia to Winter Harbor, on Vancouver Island's northern coast, would diminish pollution problems and at the same time create a village near grounds where the fish are caught.

If high taxes in the lower mainland drive milk, berry and vegetable prices higher, and if overgrazed rangelands on Interior cattle ranches endanger ecology, what about regenerating farming and ranching on Lasqueti Island, at Port Neville, in Topaz Harbor, and at other spots along the coast? Such a reinstatement of agriculture to islands and inlets now remote would ease delta farmland pressures which have resulted in the controversial freeze on subdivision.

And finally, if the speculation-free pre-emption system enticed settlers to our coast sixty years ago, why not throw parts of the coast open to pre-emption again?

We must try to keep the phenomenon in perspective. While Ocean Falls is being revived, much of the coast is still dying day by day. Forces still at work will, unless reversed, force out more and more of our already nearly extinct coast

For instance, the Federal Department of Fisheries' attempts to rebuild salmon runs through reduction in the number of boats is resulting in the construction of a fleet of fishboats 100 feet and more in length. These vessels, with crews of ten to twelve men, invariably dock in city harbors. Meanwhile, small "inefficient" boats from the few remaining isolated communities are being relentlessly phased out.

Thus what was once a busy settlement buoyant with enthusiasm, becomes gradually another endangered place of habitation, and then a ghost town.

Captain George Vancouver named the southern entrance to Toba Inlet Desolation Sound in a fit of depression brought on by his immersion in an unpeopled coast. Seclusion, as Captain Vancouver realized, involves not complete removal from humanity, but removal only to a practicable distance from travelled routes.

Alex Rowley, at Foch, far up Powell Lake; Stanislaw Tillia, at the sand beaches of Nahwitti; and Cecil Ashby of the San Josef Valley could enjoy their measures of solitude and adventure only so long as the security of transportation endured. When the last boats called, they had to go. Andrew Shuttler, in landlocked Melanie Cove, need not feel desolate, for he knew that his fellows, though out of sight, were not far away. Today, the splendid isolation of our coast can be enjoyed only by those who can afford the luxury of yachts capable of comparatively long cruising ranges. These travellers find no Roy; no Port Progress; no Shoal Bay, no Kildonan; no Port Essington; no Butedale; no succession of land-logging shows; no A-frame floating camps; no apple orchards hidden in friendly harbours.

The re-establishment of Ocean Falls constitutes a desirable step, for it reveals a recognition by government that such a step is critically needed. Now, in order that this venture can succeed, in order to relieve population pressures from our lower mainland, one of the world's highest density areas, and in order to permit human beings to find a measure of independence, fulfillment, and seclusion they are being more and more denied, government, management and labor unions should discuss - and find - means whereby the equivalent of twenty Ocean Falls can be restored to our British Columbia coast.

Resolution and Discovery in Nootka Sound

SOINTULA
SALT FISH and SPUDS UTOPIA

If we lean our heads out far enough, there are many voices to be heard. Some wake in the light of dawn when the raucously chattering geese over from Nimpkish country are interrupted in their gabble by the eagle who swoops down and stalks along the tidal flats towards them like a wrestler. Some wake when the burnt-out root cellar sits in mid-day's silent rains and mutter about the lichen's weight in the limbs of the orchard's apple trees. Others arise and spread forth when sunlight beats upon the harbour and casts its nets into the shallows of the bay.

And sometimes, when night falls cold, dark, and cloudy on the island and the inhabitants huddle closer to the airtight, the cedars whisper the speeches of that Kurrika fellow, reliving in evergreen ceremonials the dreams of the Finnish utopians. "If the whole universe, such as we see it and conceive it to be, is one great being whose spirit visibly or invisibly appears in us; then, is it difficult for us to know what that love is which must be uppermost in us? Just as all the great celestial bodies of the universe form one harmonious unity, so nature in us, human beings, seeks harmony."

It was a long way from Finland to the lonely coasts of British Columbia. Men seeking an exodus from places of suffering and oppression, whether of the body or the mind, must frequently travel far to reach that place which brings peace. A dark night of wandering led a band of Finns from their native land, enslaved by Tzarist Russia, across Canada to the equally oppressive coalfields of Dunsmuir's empire in Nanaimo and Wellington. From there they moved north to Malcolm Island where only the primeval forces of Killer Whale, Raven and Eagle held their conferences of power.

So it was that when the settlers arrived, seemingly at great remove from the evils of the day, Kurrika, their mentor, named it "Sointula" - the Place of Harmony.

The miners labouring in the pits on the east coast of Vancouver Island were aware of this prophet Kurrika and his lonely exile in Queensland, Australia. They were sick of the conditions in the mines where almost 300 men had lost their lives in explosions and cave-ins since 1885. They were oppressed by racial discrimination and rampant intemperance. When James Dunsmuir, one of the province's earliest exploiters of people and resources, ordered a forced move of his miners to Ladysmith, they revolted.

They wrote to Kurrika in Australia offering him money for passage to Canada if he would come and lead them from bondage. Together they would work to establish a community free from the evils of church and state which Kurrika had attacked so vehemently in Finland, earning the displeasure of Tzarist and Finnish bourgeois alike.

"This world is lost unless its usurpers become aware of the ever nearing days of retribution. For too long has the priesthood pandered to the lower instincts of man and prevented the liberty of thought. Their destruction is near. There they are now, like the Tower of Babel falling into ruin in the midst of that iniquity." "That socialism which builds its future for a cataclysmic upheaval will not take mankind into a new and happy life. If the reason for misery is disintegration, hate and persecution, the road to a better life is co-operation, love and generosity." All that was needed was to leave the competitive and repressive cultural milieu and man's original balance would come into harmony with "the laws of Nature." He would prove that mutual aid was possible and then the surrounding disorder would heed and change.

Like other romantic reformists following Rousseau, such as Saint-Simon, Robert Owen, and Charles Fourier, Kurrika believed in the inherent goodness of man. He found Christianity thoroughly negative and anti-liberatory and sought other ways of relating to the divine in man. If a person was to love God with all their heart and spirit it would show in their love for their fellow. He invoked his followers to "worship God seven days a week instead of one" and heaped invective upon the Finnish church which opposed popular education, land reforms and trade unionism, all of which would increase man's love of his neighbour.

Kurrika is remembered as a dreamer and idealist by remaining colonists, most of whom were children at the time. "He was a real handsome man, tall. Guess he had a good personality. He was away a lot, did all the business for the colony but he mingled with the community same

as everyone else. He had long swept back hair trimmed at the back but I don't recall that he ever had a beard." Arvo Tynjala says he was "one of those flying types". Another remembers him having an open house for kids. "We used to go over there and read the funny papers. He had a subscription to the Daily World, about the only one who did. We used to real Happy Hooligan and all those."

It's not surprising that such a man would draw his opposite to complement his character. It fits well with the dynamics of climate and landscape and the sheer energy of the settlement that the other main figure in its development would be, as Aino Ahola says, "105 per cent materialist." Austin Makela came out direct from Finland to

handle legal affairs and organization. John Michaelson recalls, "to see him, he looked pretty serious, an ordinary sort of man, nothing special about him, but he had a good sense of humour in his writings. He had a good legal mind, good writer."

Makela arrived sometime after Kurrika landed in August, 1900. He was to help the prophet start the colony where "a high, cultural life of freedom would be built, away from priests who have defiled the high morals of Christianity, away from the churches that destroy peace, away from all the evils of the outside world."

Nowadays the settlers' children, armed with the wisdom of hindsight, side more with Makela's practical bent of mind. "They figured they could start a utopia, but you can't break away from the system, you can't go back to self-sufficiency any more, or even then." But others, people like John Michaelson, still don't claim to know why it didn't work. "I thought if they'd gone about it right, business would have succeeded - there was fine timber, good fishing, beaches full of clams, venison in the woods, why they didn't succeed I don't know."

Maybe they were beaten before they started by a hostile land that only the Kwakiutl and Nimpkish tribes had come to terms with before white man came and started changing things. Maybe the sheer distances and emptiness of scattered islands seemingly afloat in the ever-changing straits assailed them with a logic beyond their hopes and dreams. Nevertheless, the seeds had been sown, and from deep in the history of Europe, watered by circumstance, the plant began to grow.

Kurrika with them now, the men at Wellington founded the Kalevan Kansa Colonization Company whose purpose was to organize colonies and obtain land and machinery for Finns and other immigrants to B.C. The newly elected president of the company, Kurrika, accompanied by Matti Halminen, journeyed down island to Victoria where they hunted through many land brochures before deciding on Malcolm Island with its timber and agricultural "possibilities". It was the spring of 1901. Crocuses bloomed in the gardens of the Empress Hotel. On Malcolm Island the cedars met the waves on the shore. Though there had been an earlier attempt by an English and Irish religious sect to establish there, the island was deserted but for a lone Danish hermit and the occasional Kwakiutl clamming party.

In Namaimo the Finns started a newspaper - "Aika", the "Time". In it Kurrika broadcast advocation of the colony. He went on speaking tours through the northwest and into the midwest. Shares in the company were sold at $200 apiece, big money in those days. On November 27, 1901 contracts were signed with the government giving the settlers immediate control of Malcolm Island and promising ownership after seven years if the population increased and improvements kept up. The Finns were to become British subjects and teach their children English. Sointula became the third co-operative settlement of Scandanavians in the province, following the Norwegians at Bella Coola in 1894 and the Danes at Cape Scott in 1897. They were on their way to utopia.

On December 6, 1901 a sailboat pulled out of Nanaimo with five men on board headed for Malcolm Island to look things over and begin logging to provide timber for the buildings. The

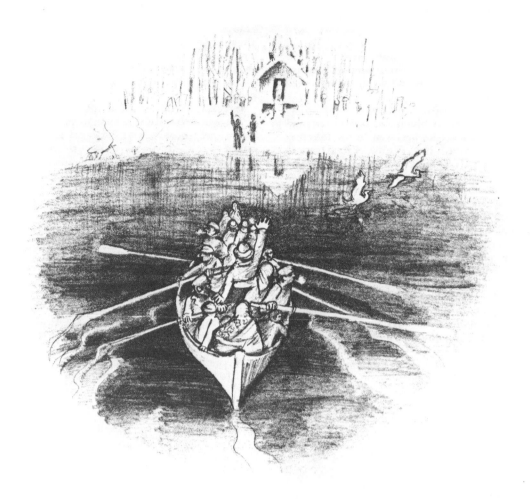

venture ended in near tragedy when a shotgun accidently discharged as the boat was passing through Seymour Narrows. Luckily, Johan Mikkelson was only wounded through the hand and the crew under command of Teodor Tanner got him to Alert Bay and safely aboard a steamer headed back to Nanaimo. After this ominous event the first four Finns anchored at Rough Bay on Malcolm Island on December 15. The new venture began at the darkest part of the year in a deep faith born of dreams and desperation.

By March, 1902 there were fourteen people on the island and from then on things began to move. Spring was here again with its promise of growth and hope. People came from the prairies and the plains; they came from Finland. They arrived to find a wet land, rich and ponderous, that shone in crystalline beauty with the sun and grew sullen and bitter with the dark scudding clouds. They found an island with virgin timber, great stands of cedar and spruce with here and there a rise of Douglas fir. The brows of the farmers darkened at the sight - their plows and harrows were useless for some time to come. They sold their animals at a loss on Vancouver Island. Many who came to the island were unsuited to this life and had never seen the like of it before. The dreamers, poets, writers, and lawyers, the doctors and farmers were all thrown together at the foot of nature's altar, on the beach at the base of these impenetrable forests.

Where were the fallers, buckers, sawyers and boat-builders that they needed? Nevertheless, there was hope and high spirits so they pitched in with what talents they could muster and started building. The sointulan experiment was unique in the area. It grew from nothing. The people came first. When places like Port Hardy and Port McNeill boomed it was around a single industry which preceded the people. From the start their inhabitants were serving the industrial machine, the centre. Sointula hoped to be its own centre. "The people went there first" says Arvo Tynjala, "and they started wondering what they were going to build. There was no industry or anything to draw them to live there. They went there on their own and started to build the community."

One of the first things they built was the sawmill. With the lumber produced there, they hastily put up shacks and more carefully put in the saunas, in many ways the centre of the early life, where people were born and people went to die. In April and May the settlers were at work on a guest house, excited by the numbers that were on their way. In June of 1902, the steamer *Capilano* was chartered from Nanaimo, bringing a load of supplies and settlers. By June 15, 1902 there were 127 shareholders in the Colonization Company.

Logging was under way at Mitchell Bay but it was fall before they realized they would not have housing for everyone in the winter. Living in tents in the summer was fine but they got mighty soggy and cool in December and January.

The Tynjalas, Urho and Arvo, then three-and-a-half and five years old, along with their several brothers and sisters remember a damp arrival on December 6, 1902. After traversing the float-walks from the boat to the shore they were placed in a tent until a house could be built or found. Urho's first memory of Sointula is the night rain slanted by the wind against the tent as puddles collected on the floor and rivulets trickled by outside.

It's Arvo who told us about the logging show at Mitchell Bay. "They had a horse back there that pulled the line out to the woods and then the donkey engine would pull the log in. The horse would take the line again because there was only one drum in that there machine. It was an old winch from a ship that was used and they'd got a boiler someplace."

Shortly after the Tynjalas arrived, with four other families from North Dakota outfitted with all their farm gear, there was the disastrous meeting house fire. The settlers had built a three-storey "apartment house" where single people and families without children could live. Like everything else it was thrown up in a hurry using fresh cut lumber from the mill.

"It was built out of rough, wet timber, straight green stuff that was newly from the woods and when the heat came in from the ovens it dried up - big cracks in the walls, an awful draught when it dried well enough. It was only a little over a month old when it burnt down - something wrong with the heating system, heated up too much and burst into a fire. There was a meeting going on at the same time on the third storey. Those were narrow stairways." In that conflagration the elements pressed hard against the foothold the settlers were trying to attain. Eleven people died. Some blamed Kurrika and some said it was Makela's boing. The inevitable rifts began to appear in the community built upon dreams.

They did what they could to hang in and make it work, but they were always plagued by one thing or another. Some years after the venture had folded Makela said "though we turned away from the world of capitalism, we were completely dependent upon it." It seemed that even Malcolm Island was inextricably bound to the web of the North American industrial complex.

The colony never managed to get out of debt. It was trying to make a go of industries that demanded large capital outlay. They sunk $2,800 into a new donkey, bought a drag seine and two tugs, the *Vinetta* and *Lottie*. In June 1902 the company owed $1300. In 1903 they floated a loan with Dominion Trust for $10,000 mortgaged on $20,000 worth of property.

The few products manufactured on the island, from the tailor and cobbler, farmer, logger, and smithy could not be transported to the trading centres at anything approaching a profit. The best pine sold for $5.00 per thousand board feet, cedar and spruce at $4.00, while hemlock was considered worthless. Towing costs cut into those figures sharply and left the colony about $3.00 per thousand on the average. That was the only industry to show any profit.

Fishing was a loss. The gear and waters were unfamiliar and Rivers Inlet salmon were selling for all of seven cents apiece, whether the fish was two pounds or twenty. Alert Bay held the cannery monopoly in that area and though the Finns held the rights to a cannery site in Knight Inlet, they couldn't afford to build it.

Still, in many ways the community was self-sufficient. Chimneys were formed of bricks made on the island. All the buildings were made from local lumber. The fires in the foundry and forge continued to rage, fuelled by charcoal produced on the island. The food cans which made the rounds from house to house from the common kitchen were made there as were milk cans and machine parts.

Food was scarce and simple but everyone got fed. The soil was poor everywhere but in the swamps on the far side of the island. There, some of the work groups went every day to dig drainage ditches and prepare them for fields. It was the same kind of land that Finnish farms prospered on, so there was hope for the future. So far, there weren't many vegetables besides potatoes and a few turnips and certainly no fruit trees but people worked the common gardens contentedly and got their daily share.

There was milk and a bit of butter from the cows, eggs from the hens, and game from the forest. The Finns didn't take too readily to fresh ocean fish though and usually had it salted, being used to fresh water types. A lot of the meals were a simple Mulligan made of beef, onions and potatoes. There was no tea for the sugar and prunes would be dessert fare for a month at a time. Still, nobody went hungry though the kids often attempted a raid on the kitchen and were justly repelled by a broom-wielding cook. Berries were a favourite of everyone. Salal especially occupied an important place. It was eaten dry like the Indians used it and its juice was poured on porridge in place of milk. Mothers sometimes complained about the lack of milk for the children but Aino Ahola doesn't remember being much affected. "It was the centre of the world to me and the world was revolving around it. I thought that's the way it was everywhere."

In November of 1903 a new building was erected to house the press and "Aika" reappeared after an absence of one-and-a-half years. It became a forum and a cultural focus for the community. A typical issue would carry articles by Kurrika on "Socialism and Social Philosophy", "Current Events", "The Question of Marriage", an article by a Mr. Ingersoll on Voltaire, and a humourous piece by Makela entitled "A Night in Alert Bay."

One of the pressing issues of the time which divided the community bitterly and spread abroad to fire rumours was the question of women, sex and free love. According to Kurrika, woman had been enslaved by man for generations, treated as private property and chattel, a position which was sanctified by the church. They had been removed from economic freedom by marriage and reduced to the status of non-person, blinded to their divine nature.

He wrote "Let us aid woman into a position of unconditional freedom and responsibility. Let us build marriages on foundations of ideal love. Let us dissolve those unstructured marriages, that as vestigal parts of the church still haunt us. Let us not acknowledge a marriage in which relationship is not centered on love, goodness and tenderness."

The actual incidence of divorce in the colony was next to nothing. There were virtually no single women around and the issue of free love remained largely an academic issue, but provided ammunition for those resentful of Kurrika. In the governing of the community, women had equal say with men, all issues coming to a vote before the assembled shareholders. "If there was something that was being discussed that they weren't interested in, then only the men would go, and vice-versa."

Women worked an equal amount to men. The work groups whether in the forest or the laundry elected their own leaders and were run with the

same principles of democratic centralism as the community as a whole. "There wasn't much to do at home but the women were as anxious to work as the men. They wanted to take part in the community work. They ran the kitchen and the bakeries and everything else that was suitable for women to work at. So the children's home was organized more for the smaller children." This would free the women to take part in the economic and political life of the community.

Arvo Tynjala goes on to talk about the children's home. "I was there myself, and I was an old man of six or seven years old then and I was there day and night. We had a kind of box, beds that were turned up against the wall for the day. When night came we shifted them down again and went to sleep. There was quite a bunch of them. We were there for days. That's where I got my first schooling, taught to read and write, in Finnish, of course."

Urho says Arvo didn't like the place all that much and one day when he was trying to sneak away he went to the teacher Mrs. Myrrti (young and not really Mrs. at all and blushing if she was called that) and told on the miscreant.

The kids became responsible pretty early and were thrown into the economic life of the place as soon as they could function. John Michaelson and a friend shared a whistlepunk job when they were only eight. Everybody's time was kept, man, woman and child. They were supposed to be paid a dollar an hour once the colony was stable. But that never happened.

In 1904, at Kurrika's prompting, the colony put in a bid on a contract to build a bridge across the Capilano River in North Vancouver. Kurrika tendered someone's estimate of $3,000. All the wood was to come from the forests of Malcolm Island. Camps were set up at the bridge site and work commenced but it wasn't long before they realized the calculations had been away off. Four months later, the colony had lost another $8,000 worth of free labour to say nothing of huge stands of first grade virgin timber.

The external world began to close in. Kurrika, with about half of the colony, left in an atmosphere of bitterness to try again at Webster's Corner near Haney. The prophet soon returned to Finland where the Russians were attempting to increase their cultural stranglehold on his country.

The labour power at Sointula was now halved. There was a huge load of debts. The newspaper

was discontinued and the press was sold at a loss. The last straw came when a boom of 150,000 board feet of timber valued at $3,000 was seized by creditors. The money was to have bought badly needed clothing and shoes. Dominion Trust moved in and took over the mill. At a special meeting on May 27, 1905, Austin Makela announced to the assembled shareholders that he had arranged with the government an exchange of all lands in return for a loan which would cover the colony's debts. Dominion Trust sold all property and forests that had come into its possession at $5 an acre.

Thus, paradise never materialized amongst the deer and bear, the eagle and the raven who made their homes in the sheltered islands of Johnstone Strait. A few remnants of the utopian ideals remained with the settlers who decided to stay and make of the land what they could, but no more would their vision be forced upon it. Rather, their wills were cast out upon the land itself and were balanced between the environment and the centres of civilization that demanded wood and fish from it.

The Sointulans still preferred to live without church and until 1972 the island had no policemen. The people took care of their own conflicts. If there was a dispute about a legal matter there would be a town meeting and Austin Makela, presiding as Justice of the Peace, would mediate and pacify. The occasional churchman dropped in to attempt to win at least the children to the faith, but without much luck. Aino Ahola remembers one such missionary coming to the school and showing slides. He chuckles and shakes his head - "No, we weren't convinced."

After the breakup of the colony the land was parcelled out in half-section pieces to the folks who stayed. "Everybody was working somehow or other and looking after themselves. There was no such thing as a community then - every family had its own living, raised its own milk and butter." The families began a pattern of employment which still continues. In the summer the men would head up to Rivers Inlet, at that time towed in their little skiffs, tents rigged up forward, by tugs and steamboats. There they'd fish for sockeye until August for the canneries and then head back home. In the fall and winter, everyone who was able would go logging.

When Kurrika left, his philosophies went with him. Times were changing. In 1905 in Russia was the first attempt at a Bolshevik revolution, thoroughly and brutally cut down. The labour market in B.C. into which the Sointulans were thrown was similarly oppressive. The utopian philosophy of Matti Kurrika - "a self conscious effort to discover the laws of Nature and of human progress" necessarily gave way to ideas of "class struggle", sentiments which prevail today amongst the old timers, a few of whom still look to the U.S.S.R. as the world's beacon.

It was hard times. "We used to go to Rivers Inlet not knowing what the price would be, but in the years when there was lots of fishermen around waiting to come and fish they didn't want to put the high prices on because if there was enough fishermen with the cheaper price, they'd take it of course. We'd get to Rivers Inlet and be already out and fishing when they'd announce the prices." Arvo Tynjala recalls that when he first went fishing with his dad in 1911 the price was ten cents a fish but that would drop to about six cents if there were a lot of boats out. And a lot of boats there were. Rivers Inlet in the old days was legally limited to 700 boats but there'd be up to 2,000 in the surrounding area. It was 1917 before the men were organized well enough to have a strike and then they succeeded in raising the price per fish from fifteen to twenty-two-and-a-half cents. It wasn't until the unions were formed that the fishermen succeeded in standardizing the price of fish per pound. That was around 1937.

The first attempt on the coast to start a fisherman's co-op was made in Sointula. The men were tired of contracting to the big canneries owned by people like MacMillan. They wanted to can their own fish and own their own operation start to finish. "They stepped on our toes you know, like usual. They're better businessmen than we are so I guess we got the dirty end of the stick in the end." The co-op was defeated in court by big business finance.

Things weren't much better in the mining industry either, which a lot of people were forced back to. John Michaelson was thirteen when he went to work in the pits. "I got paid $27 a month, a dollar a day." Laughing, "Tell that to these fellows who's starting to work for twenty and thirty dollars a day when they're fifteen years old."

Logging was another hard scene. The men from Sointula used to row a huge circuit of barren islands trying one camp after another. Of the two or three men in each 14 foot boat there'd be one who could speak enough English to ask about jobs and communicate with the foreman. "Conditions in the camps were really awful. Bedbugs there were aplenty. Loggers carried their blankets and bedrolls with them and if you wanted to wash anything you'd get some water from a creek in a can of some sort and build a fire and wash yourself and your gear in that. No showers or toilets. It wasn't till 1920 they started improving, trying to keep up with the changes in the States."

When organizing in the camps was begun by the Wobblies and others like them, the fishermen helped out by volunteering their boats to transport the loggers. They'd ship them from their camps to central meetings and smuggle in organizers. There was a virtual war going on there for many years.

On the island, the community had spread out, moving down the shore into Kaleva as far as the big conglomerate bluffs there. A few folks managed to get by with their farms. Teodor Tanner, Charlie Solo and Henry Lockti raised enough to sell but only Teodor and Charlie did it full time. They'd row their spuds, vegetables and apples over to Alert Bay and sell 'em door to door. Charlie achieved notoriety for refusing to get a motor boat for his trade til the end of his days. Tanner was known as the berry man and led happy gathering parties to the choicest patches of berries - salal, huck and blue - succulent bounty of the coastal forests.

In many ways life was easier in Sointula. Gone were the economic and ideological pressures, the need to "make it" on their own. There were a lot of dances and entertainments, nothing costing anything. Richard Jarvis, who'd tried to get a patent on his invention of the gill-net drum, in the '30's rigged up a generator so that movies could be shown. Later he held the power monopoly on the island and actually applied for a government contract but was beaten out by a mainland corporation.

Picnics were a standard part of island recreation. "Every weekend a whole flotilla of rowboats would head out for Mitchell Bay or Kalseevy, Haddington Island or the creek past the bluffs, I guess it's still there." Time passed leisurely and relaxed on the island, measured by tides and gull cries.

The co-op, another legacy of European social idealism, served the people well from 1909 on and prospered until the last few years when the shuttle service to Port McNeill made it easier for folks to do their shopping there. Things have changed a lot within the last ten years, very rapidly.

MacDonald Cedar is once more stripping the interior of the island of its forests. The abandoned farms are being bought up by the new utopians, many of them from California. The influx of Anglos finally culminated in a church which is also attended by the newly arrived Finns. The co-op store and fisherman's local are about all that remain, besides the Finnish language which sounds so musically from the docks and building sheds, of the social idealism of the settlers and their offspring. Still, it is a pretty and prosperous place as coastal communities go. The corrosive coast is always threatening and here and there, with its luxuriant growth and energy, has overpowered the primness of the Finnish aesthetic.

Had things gone differently, any number of things, there may yet have been a communistic co-operative society on the coast of B.C. The new attempts that are being made all the time by the disaffected young may well have much to learn from Sointula and her sisters, Cape Scott and Bella Coola. The dependency on outside capital, a lack of ideological or religious cohesion, a lack of selective membership that was prompted by the haste and desire to move - all these may serve as lessons.

The utopian ideal lives on, as poignant as memory. "Port McNeill was there then, but there was nobody there but the ducks and the geese....it's the most wonderful place. It's a big flat bay, you know, and the tide was low and there must have been thousands of geese and ducks the first time I saw that camp in 1905 or '6." Whispers. Promises.

Thanks to the many friendly and hardy Sointulans we talked to, to Lee and John for their hospitality, to the Sommers pursuing their own researches, and to Bill Langlois and the Oral History Project.

As though pushed inland by an aggressive arm of the Pacific Ocean, the Bella Coola Valley joins the sea and the interior of British Columbia by a short corridor through the Coast Mountains. Amid scenery that lifts the heart, the valley is generous with its wealth; salmon, timber, and rich soil. People live there: Indian people and white people. They are friends and strangers. They look at the world in different ways.

More than twenty years ago an Indian boy was chosen to help to accelerate the process by which Indians would look at the world as white people do. When he climbed onto the schoolbus with the white children in January, 1949, Dennis Snow was half way through an experiment. The provincial school administrators and the federal Indian Affairs officials wanted to know how an Indian child would cope with white classmates. They sent Dennis to Grade Five in the Lower Bella Coola Elementary School. It was an experiment in racial integration, they said.

All the other native school children went to the Bella Coola Indian Day School run by the Department of Indian Affairs. Their teacher was hired by the federal government in Ottawa. She was not a colleague of the other teachers in the Bella Coola Valley who were paid by the provincial government in Victoria. She and the Indian Agent were part of the Canadian colonial administration that looked after the Indians. (The Indians had no part in the election or appointment of officials in the Department of Indian Affairs, and they were not permitted to vote in provincial elections until 1949, nor in federal elections until 1960.) The Department of Indian Affairs had difficulty recruiting teachers. The Superintendent-General in Ottawa decided Indians should go to white schools. It would be good for them; they had to be integrated into white society. That was the policy in Ottawa.

There was a school on the Townsite too. The Indian village and the Townsite were separated only by a dirt road—"the line" some people called it. But only white pupils in the first three grades attended Mackenzie school. (Mackenzie was an important name in Bella Coola because the explorer Alexander Mackenzie had reached the Pacific Ocean at Bella Coola in 1793.) The other children in the valley went to the Lower Bella Coola Elementary School and the Hagensborg High School. Lower Bella Coola was up the valley from Bella Coola Townsite because white settlement had begun at Hagensborg, twelve miles from salt water. This made Lower Bella Coola lower than Hagensborg but higher than Bella Coola.

Dennis Snow went from the Bella Coola Indian Reserve into an alien culture at the Lower Bella Coola Elementary School. So did his teacher who was from Scotland, but she was not immediately aware of it because she believed that all white people were pretty much alike. Maybe that was why Dennis made it through the year and she didn't. He had five teachers in Grade Five, they came and went.

The teachers were city ladies. One by one they were defeated by the voracious wood-burning heater and the brats who threw .22 shells into it, the tempermental gasoline lamps that the children had to teach them how to operate, the hand-operated water pump in the schoolyard, the outdoor toilets, the community indifference to education, the lack of entertainment, the gossip,

the isolation and the east wind.

The teachers were outsiders. The entire world beyond Bella Coola was the outside, and unless born in Bella Coola, one was forever an outsider. Outsiders were the most heterogenous group in the Bella Coola Valley. They were not united by tradition like the other two groups, the Indians and the Norwegians.

The outsiders were school teachers, nurses, farmers, storekeepers, a telegrapher, a lineman, a fishery officer, an Indian Agent, a preacher, a

BELLA

doctor, and a policeman. Most of them had more formal education than the Indians and Norwegians. Some of them—the medical staff, the preacher, the Indian Agent—were part of the "Indian business" carried on by the church and government. The Indian Agent and the clergyman were the only white people with residences on the

Indian reserve. A few outsiders wanted economic and social change; they had no local traditions to cling to. Norwegian settlers said, "The outsiders are taking over everything."

The Indians, who were fishermen and hunters, believed they owned the land in the valley because their ancestors had lived on it for several thousand years. But in 1949 they lived on an Indian reservation, a small piece of land the government had returned to them after it had taken the rest. "The white men stole our land", the Indians

COOLA

declared. Indeed, they had never been paid for it and no treaty had been made. There were about 400 Bella Coola Indians. There once had been thousands but they had been decimated by disease.

The government had a policy: it took land from hunters and fishermen and gave it to farmers. In 1894 it had given some of the land to Norwegian settlers. The Norwegians intended to be farmers. But most of them turned out to be fishermen and loggers.

The Indians, of course, were the only ones with an indigenous cultural tradition. But their culture, tied to the land, sea and animals of Bella Coola, languished on the Indian reserve. Half convinced that their traditions were inferior to those of the Europeans because their technology was less advanced, the Indians performed their old ceremonies less and less. Suspicious of the unfamiliar, the Norwegians ignored what they could not understand. And many outsiders believed that imported values must supersede indigenous ones if local social conditions were to improve.

Dennis Snow learned Presbyterian hymns from the Scottish school teacher. But he did not learn the stories about Thunderbird, Raven, and Killerwhale. The stories were probably as valid as the hymns. More so, perhaps, for they were based on Bella Coola legends rather than Jewish and European ones. From their Indian neighbours, the white people could have learned about British Columbia music, British Columbia dance, British Columbia painting, British Columbia sculpture, and British Columbia oral literature. But they did not. They learned little about where they lived and who their neighbours were.

The Indians performed their traditional dances and songs, and displayed their masks and costumes on the reserve in Noohalk Hall during the winter. Men and women, dressed in button blankets and cedar bark regalia, sang the traditional songs while others danced to the music. On their heads the dancers carried the masks of Grizzly Bear, or Eagle, or Thunderbird, or Raven, or Wolf, or Moon, or Earthquake, or mythical creatures from tribal stories. Sometimes the dancer hopped from behind a curtain like a raven and cocked his head sideways to look at the spectators with a beady eye, and then as the singing changed in tempo, he put a blanket over his face and reappeared with the face of a bear and resumed his dance to a bear-like cadence. Other dancers wore masks holding white eagle down that drifted to the floor with the motion of the dance, symbolizing peace and friendship. Between serious dances, and even during them, clowns frolicked with absurd costumes and antics. After the dance, the masks were displayed for visitors to examine. White people had recently recognized the masks as important primitive art that was becoming commercially valuable in New York and Vancouver while its ceremonial value declined in Bella Coola.

Traditional Indian ceremonies were infrequent. During the winter Noohalk Hall reverberated most evenings to the thump of basketballs. The Indians were the best basketball players in the valley. They gave their top teams the names of their cultural heroes: the Eagles and the Thunderbirds. The Eagles were consistently the finest team in the valley. Friday night was basketball night in the Bella Coola Valley, and other community activities were scheduled for another time, except for the movie which ran both Friday and Saturday evenings. In a small community people are more scarce than time; people must be rationed.

At Easter, a basketball tournament brought seine boats and packers loaded with players from

Bella Bella, Klemtu, Ocean Falls and Namu. To Bella Coola kids, the new Indians were intimidating and the Ocean Falls visitors seemed sophisticated. The visiting players were billeted at homes: Indians with Indians and whites with whites.

Even the spectators at Noohalk Hall voluntarily segregated themselves. Generally the Indians chose the right side of the hall and the white chose the left side. But since many Indians and white were friends, there was much visiting. It amused the whites when the Indians shouted to the players, "S'oot! S'oot!" (Indians could not pronounce the "sh" sound. Example: "S'ucks, I sir wis I'd s'ot!") The whites could speak not a word of the Bella Coola language.

The community hall on the Townsite had been converted into the Belvale Theatre (50 cents for adults; 25 cents for children). Three columns of wooden seats filled the hall. Indians sat in the left column, white sat in the right column, and both races sat in the centre. White rarely sat on the Indian side. It was not disapproved of, but if done, it was noticed and commented on. But only new outsiders disrupted the pattern, usually through ignorance, but sometimes through perversity, like the staff from the missionary hospital.

Winter was the time for basketball, dances, visiting, card games, drinking, going to the boat, and enduring the east wind. When the arctic air slid off the interior plateau into the Bella Coola valley, it funnelled toward the ocean in a gale, howling through the trees, and twirling plumes of snow from the mountain tops. Slush pans hissed and bumped along the river until finally solid ice crept from shore to shore. At night, moonlight reflected from one snow-covered mountain to another. The valley was illuminated night and day. Little wonder that both sun and moon were important characters in the native myths. But direct sunlight failed to reach much of the valley bottom. At the Townsite the sun did not rise above the mountains in the winter. In January it peered through the Tatsquam gap for only fifteen minutes a day.

While the brutal wind prevailed, people stayed home to feed wood into heaters. On the Indian village and the Townsite, the only settlements with waterworks, the water pipes froze and the talk of the town was about who had water and who did not. Men dragged picks and shovels from property to property, dug through rigid soil, and set fires on frozen pipes.

During the winter, boat day was an important social occasion. Nearly everyone had time to drive to the wharf and exchange news. The Union Steamship Company sent the *Catala* or *Cardena* to Bella Coola once a week. The ships were Bella Coola's link with the outside. On them arrived mail, machinery, clothing, mail order catalogues, movies, four day old bread, two week old oranges, booze, travelling salesmen, medical supplies, cars, and people with special training. (Bella Coola exported fish, logs, lumber, and potatoes, most of which left by raft, barge, or packer rather than on the Union Steamship.)

A few people boarded the ship for a trip "down south" to Vancouver. They paid $35 for a ticket and then invited their friends to their stateroom. Everybody smoked and joked and drank rum until a blast of the whistle warned visitors to leave.

The elegance aboard ship overwhelmed the inexperienced traveller. First of all, how was he to cope with the dining room table, the menus with half the words in French, napkins in the form of Chinese puzzles, an arsenal of silverware, waiters hovering about like ravens, chairs that wouldn't slide up to the table, and do you tip at each meal or at the end of the trip, and how much? Later it was the linen sheets on the berth tucked in so tight a strong man couldn't push between them. There was solace in a deck of cards, a crib board, three other loggers, and a bottle of rum to ease the passage.

The weekly steamer was the easy way to leave Bella Coola. The hard way was overland. The traveller drove 50 miles west up the Bella Coola Valley to the end of the dirt road, then rode a horse 40 miles beneath the telegraph line to Anaheim Lake, then drove 200 miles of dust, mud and jackpine branches to Williams Lake, and then south on a gravel road that eventually reached pavement and the bright lights. Not many people left the valley by that route — and not with much baggage.

Because of the Indian population and the isolation, Bella Coola received medical and spiritual assistance from the Home Missions Board of the United Church of Canada. Most of the missionary nurses and the doctor at the United Church Hospital on the Townsite came from Ontario. The preacher came from British Columbia. He wasn't a missionary (although his predecessors had been) and perhaps that was why he seemed less religious than the medical staff.

Although situated side by side, both the Townsite and the Indian reserve had a United Church. This was not because the people of Bella Coola were devout worshippers (most weren't). The duplication of churches was the result of history and culture. Both the white village and the Indian village had been on the north side of the valley in the early years of white settlement. The Necleetsconnay River had swept down from the north and flooded out the white village in 1924. The whites moved to the south side of the Bella Coola River under the shadow of 6000 foot Mount Fougnor and built a town with a church. The Indians did not move until the Bella Coola river coursed through their settlement in 1936, tearing out the bridge that carried the water main from Tatsquam Creek on the south side of the river. With typhoid threatening, the Indians moved across the river beside the white village. Beneath the dirt road which separated the two villages ran the water main.

The Indians and whites easily shared the water main. But water mains are not symbolic; churches are. The church was an important symbol of the Indian community. The natives towed their church across the river at low water with two bulldozers. And that was why Bella Coola had two United Churches only four blocks apart.

Outsiders said, "This looks silly. Let's amalgamate the churches." But tradition cannot be abandoned easily. The Indians welcomed whites to their church as guests but not as members. The church, like Noohalk Hall, was a focus of the Indian community. It had a good choir, a large Sunday school, and active youth groups. The walls were lined with portraits of Methodist and United Church missionaries. To suggestions that only Emmanuel Church was needed at Bella Coola, the Indians replied, "It's our church".

Mackenzie Church on the Townsite and Augsberg Church in Hagensborg were not important centres for the white communities. Augsberg Church, which had been established as a Lutheran Church, was often without a minister. When it moved under the United Church banner in 1949, it had a tiny congregation. Religious activity at Mackenzie Church was supported largely by the hospital staff. Still, Mackenzie Church had been the scene of enough christenings, weddings, funerals, Christmas concerts and Thanksgiving displays to make amalgamation unattractive to many of its members.

The hospital staff were religious, well-educated outsiders. They had a style of life that created an enclave: Sunday School teaching and church attendance every Sunday, Bible study and youth group leadership during the week, frequent friendly association with Indians, a social and working life centred on hospital and church activities, and absolutely no booze.

They had a tradition that went beyond Bella Coola: the tradition of the Methodist medical missionaries on the British Columbia coast. They grew potatoes in front of the hospital and piled wood for the furnace and kitchen stove at the back; a single-cylinder diesel engine supplied electrical power. Unlike other whites, they visited Indian friends in their own homes. And Dr. Whiting adopted an Indian boy, a brother for his two blond daughters.

Possibly only the policeman felt the isolation of Bella Coola as much as the doctor. Both were always on call. To a large extent, law enforcement in Bella Coola meant arresting Indians for drinking alcohol. Although whites were permitted to drink alcohol, Indians were prohibited by law from doing so. (They were a different kind of people; the government in Ottawa made special laws for them). That's why, mainly, Indians got criminal records.

The United Church minister deplored drunkennessof course. But he put aside the Indian problem and attacked, instead, the white problem. He was invited to speak at a meeting of the local Loyal Order of Moose, a fraternal association based in the United States. He arose like a Jewish prophet and castigated the organization for rejecting Indians as members. The Moose Lodge officers were angry and confused; the constitution from the central office definitely stated that Indians were not permitted to join the organization. The Reverend Carmichael was a Vancouver boy just out of Union College, and because he was a city boy had never known the loneliness a city has for a small town stranger, but he soon learned what social isolation means in a small community.

In March westerly breezes replaced the east wind and the snow retreated into itself. The sun climbed higher in the Tatsquam gap, and under its warmth the dirt roads softened and boiled up. When the roads hardened again in April, the logging trucks began growling along them on yo-yo journeys between the bush and the salt chuck, occasionally running down one of the cows that grazed the roadsides. Fishermen spent the days beneath their gillnetters with caulking cotton, putty, and copper paint.

Early in April the oolachans entered the Bella Coola River to spawn. They blackened the clear water in great schools. The air filled with shrieking and plunging seagulls. Eagles perched in the cottonwood trees lining the banks and sea lions hunted at the mouth of the river. Indian men poled thirty foot cedar spoon canoes to the shallows near the Indian village. Standing in the canoes, they pounded heavy stakes into the gravel with wooden mallets and attached a long cone-shaped net to each pair of stakes. Each incoming tide brought a swarm of oolachans and each falling tide swept them back into the open mouths of the nets. The men opened the small end of each net and the oolachans slithered into the canoes filling them nearly to the gunwales.

After ripening for a week in bins, the oolachans were ready to release their oil. Men and women placed them in tanks of boiling water set on the river banks, and scooped out the oil that rose to the surface and put it in jars and tins. Throughout the year the Indians ate oolachan grease as a food, condiment and medicine. The whites did not eat oolachan grease.

In May the entire community was at work, loggers, fishermen, and farmers. But work stopped for Sports Day, the Twenty-fourth of May. Everyone in the valley gathered on the meadow beside the hospital on the Townsite. Ladies Aid societies from the Indian and white churches, the Hospital Auxiliary and the Parent-Teachers Association set up booths and sold hot dogs, soft drinks, cake, pie and coffee. The kids ran dashes, beginning with five year olds. Broad jump, high jump, pole vault, sack race, three-legged race, pie eating contest, bolster bar duel, and the mile race followed. Then fishermen from the Canadian Fishing Company and the British Columbia Packers Company sent their heavy weights into a tug of war and the valley echoed with "Heave, heave!" On the newly swollen Bella Coola River, Indian canoe races, log rolling, and greased pole walking completed the events. They had been planned on a time schedule but were performed on Indian time. That is, they began when everyone was ready.

Adults worked hard during the summer. Their children roamed the countryside like rogues, raiding orchards, stoning spawning salmon, "borrowing" rowboats, starting log cabins, swimming in the beaver pond, raiding crows' nests, watching fishermen pitch fish, learning a basic

vocabulary from loggers repairing equipment, helping farmers make hay, hunting terrified squirrels with sling shots, and fishing flounders from the wharf. Some days they visited Bob Grant, or more precisely, Bob Grant's cherry trees. Their host dropped his haying and went swimming in the slough with them before turning them loose on his cherry crop. When they were sated, he drove them home in a Model A Ford that he started with a crank and fed rolled oats for a leaky radiator. Later in the summer he warned the kids away from the bear traps with fanged jaws beneath the apple and pear trees. He showed them the swath through the salmon berry brush where a bear had dragged a trap. He had hunted it down at night with a flashlight and shot it while it growled and cried.

During the summer the Stick Indians rode their horses into the Bella Coola Valley from Ulgatcho and Anaheim Lake. (Anthropologists called them Carrier Indians). They came down the Canyon Trail, the Tweedsmuir Trail, the Bunchgrass Hills Trail, and the Canoe Crossing Trail. On the plateau above the valley the trails had been beaten deep into the dirt years before by pack trains carrying supplies into the interior. But in 1949 they were used by few people other than the Stick Indians who came to dry salmon along the Bella Coola River and to trade. The trail from Bella Coola to the plateau had been called a grease trail even before the white men arrived, for oolachan grease was valued by the interior as well as coast Indians.

The Stick Indians were taller and leaner than the Bella Coola Indians, proud and independent. They travelled with horses, camped in tents, smelled like wood smoke, and paid little heed to white men except to sell fine beaded moosehide and buckskin moccasins, gloves and jackets, and to buy the brightest clothes and flashiest jewellery.

The Stick Indians camped in the upper part of the Bella Coola Valley where the climate was hot and dry, ideal for drying salmon. When they had a good cache, they moved down the valley to camp beside Tatsquam Creek on the outskirts of the Townsite. They herded their pack horses onto the tide flats where the animals grazed on swamp grass among Martin Nygaard's cattle and learned the ways of the tides. The young men tethered their saddle horses near their camp, ready to rent them for 50 cents an hour to white youths. But they spent more money renting bicycles than they earned from their horses. They approached white boys with bicycles and asked, "You lent 'im?" Pipty cent one hour?" They had bought pocket watches and were very punctual. The white boys sat on the steps of the new Valley Cafe and ate their profits in ice cream and listened endlessly to Sioux City Sue on the Wurlitzer.

Then one day the pack horses were chased through town in a cloud of dust and dogs. Diamond hitches were thrown across packs, and the Stick Indians trailed up the valley to Canoe Crossing and Burnt Bridge. They took with them dried fish, new guns, and stories about Bella Coola. They left behind moccasins, gloves, odorous buckskin jackets and memories of tough, friendly individuals with names like Ulgatcho Johnny, Pretty Charlie, Jimmy John, Ollie Nicolays, Oggie Capoose, Laseese West, and Trout Lake Johnny.

A few years before, an outsider from eastern Canada had come to Bella Coola and married an Indian woman. She had moved to the Townsite with her husband. The government in Ottawa said she was not an Indian anymore. Just the same, the people in the Indian village said, "We always think of her as one of us."

The children were half-breeds, of course, but nobody in the valley called them that. The word seemed inappropriate somehow. But because of their origins the youngsters were not quite white

nor were they Indian. They were, nonetheless, part of the white Townsite.

In 1949 the pre-adolescent boys on the Townsite revealed the normally muted attitudes of their community. At the end of a day of play the white boys turned without apparent cause on a half-breed companion and chanted "Jimmy is a siwash. Jimmy is a siwash". The insulting name, insulting to an Indian, even more so to a mixed-blood, seared deep. Where did he belong now?

But adult attitudes seemed to be changing. Most

people in the Bella Coola Valley were pleased to be in the vanguard of racial integration in the schools of British Columbia. In September many Indian children joined the whites on the schoolbus. Dennis Snow was in Grade Six. He had been a successful experiment. "Indian children seem as intelligent as white children," white people said.

On October 31, 1949, the Sir Alexander Mackenzie Consolidated School was officially opened in Hagensborg. Sons of the Norwegian

pioneers gave speeches, the Indians performed a traditional dance, provincial government and Indian Affairs officials gave governmental blessings, and the United Church minister gave a prayer. A week later about 100 pupils in twelve grades filled the four classrooms. They left the one room schools and entered a building with fluorescent lights, flush toilets, steady heat from an oil furnace, a school library and a gymnasium. Primary schools on the Townsite and the Indian village were still used; the very young were still

protected from cultural shock. Whose culture and whose shock was in doubt since the Indian children outnumbered the whites.

In September new snow appeared on the spire of Mount Noosatsum, the 8500 foot mountain that reigned over the Bella Coola Valley. The snow highlighted the rope that ancestral Indians had used to moor their canoe during the Great Flood. For several weeks the snow moved down the mountains in gradual steps. It nearly reached the valley bottom.

Then a heavy warm rain arrived. The snow melted from every side valley and from every mountain from base to summit. The torrent ripped bridges from the roads and rolled across the farmland.

On the river flat in Lower Bella Coola, Bob Grant cooked supper just before the water reached the fire in his kitchen stove. He was a religious man. While his cows bellowed in their flooded barn, he sang hymns from his second storey window: *We Will Gather at the River* and *There is a Green Hill Far Away.* The river smelled like a newly ploughed field. The silt would lay an inch deep on Bob Grant's floors until his sister visited in the spring, but a little silt was a small price for the stories that could be told all winter.

Cold weather slapped the river into place again. Fishing season ended and the fishermen stored their gillnetters on the tide flats and began to cut firewood. The loggers quit work when the snow reached the felled and bucked logs on the sidehills. Basketball practice began at Noohalk Hall and at Lobelco Hall in lower Bella Coola and at the new school gymnasium in Hagensborg.

The Mackenzie Church congregation put on a "Christmas Tree" with carols, Bible reading, religious tableaus, Japanese oranges, and candies. Santa Claus distributed gifts lavishly. On Christmas Eve, while white families began to celebrate Christmas at home, the Indian community gathered at Noohalk Hall and distributed gifts and candies to their children and sang carols beneath their Christmas tree.

Between Christmas and New Years Eve hospitality reigned throughout the valley. On New Years Eve the white celebrated the end of the year at Lobelco Hall with a boisterous dance. The Indians did the same—with the same style of dancing—at Noohalk Hall. The next day the east wind roared off the interior plateau and through the valley and nothing moved.

When school resumed a teached asked the students to write an essay about Bella Coola. One boy wrote this: "What does the future hold for the Bella Coola Valley? There are many things which might happen. The road could be connected so we could drive to other towns and cities of Canada. The new road might bring people who will build bigger and better roads, bridges, houses, stores, and many other things. The communities might have electricity for everybody and pipelines to bring water instead of people getting water from wells and streams. All the Indian children might go to the same schools as the white children. A new school may be built in the Townsite. Bella Coola could become a tourist resort and an important shipping port. There are scores of other things that might happen to Bella Coola in the future."

Well, what a thing to say. The boy must have been the child of an outsider.

175

Metlakatla

—the name won't ring a bell for many people today, nor would a dingy cluster of shacks on the beach eight miles out of Prince Rupert by likely to rouse your interest if you happened to pass down that side of Venn Channel.

But there was a time, before Prince Rupert was thought of, or Vancouver a city, that this forgotten little Indian community was as well or better known around the world than the province it was part of.

"Metlakatla," the *Church Missionary Intelligencer* said exactly 100 years ago "is an out of the way place which would not be very easy to find on many maps, but still it is gradually becoming a household word in England, and multitudes who could perhaps be a good deal puzzled to define its exact location have gradually acquired familiarity with the interesting work carried on there."

Rich Victorians on safari always went to Metakatla, if they were anywhere near the Pacific Coast of America, and in those days they were never disappointed.

"The population is 1200. Its residents have a rifle company of 42 men, a brass band, a two-gun battery and a large co-operative store where almost anything obtainable in Victoria can be bought.

"We were received with displays of bunting from various points and a five gun salute from the battery, with Yankee Doodle and Dixie from the band. The Union Jack was flying. The church is architecturally pretentious and can seat 1200 persons. It has a belfry and spire, vestibule, gallery across the front end, groined arches and pulpit carved by hand, organ and choir, Brussels carpet in the aisles, stained glass windows, and all the appointments of a first class sanctuary; and it is wholly the local resident's handwork.

"This well-ordered community occupies shingled and clap-board dwelling houses of uniform size, 25 x 50 feet, with enclosed flower gardens and macadamized sidewalks, 10 feet wide, along the entire length of the street.

"These people have also a large town hall or assembly room of the same capacity as the church, used for councils, meetings and for a drill room. It is warmed by three great fires placed in the centre of the building, and lighted by side lamps. The people dress very tastefully and I am not sure but that they have the latest fashions. The women weave cloth for garments, and the pretty islets just offshore are virtual floating gardens which afford fruit and vegetables in abundance."

The lady misses a few things. There were oolachan oil street lamps on cross beams in front of each house, which were taken down Sunday evenings and hung in the church, the largest west of Chicago and north of San Francisco. There was a force of thirty uniformed policemen replete with boots, caps and brass buttons. There were two soccer fields and a playground with merry-go-round and bars. The flagpole rose from the centre of a three-storey octagonal hatbox which contained a fire hall, a jail and a dog pound, with a bandstand on top. And then below the church and the hall, on piles flush with the sea, was a cluster of long sheds. These contained the sawmill, the tannery, the soap and textile factories, printing presses, and cannery.

Metlakatla was built and occupied entirely by Tsimshian Indians. The only non-Tsimshian permanently living there was a stocky 5 ft. 4 in. Yorkshireman with a huge black beard, the Anglican missionary William Duncan. Duncan was not an ordained minister. Before arriving to save and civilize the Tsimshian of nearby Fort Simpson in 1857 he had been a leather salesman. He was 25 when he first came to the coast, and except for one brief trip back to Europe in 1871 to learn how to weave, tan leather, make rope, barrels, bricks, process photographs and play thirty musical instruments, he remained alone among the Indians.

To visitors he was genial and attentive, and loved to tell how Governor James Douglas had pleaded with him not to risk his life amongst the bloodthirsty Tsimshian when he first arrived in Victoria and how these same decorous industrious 'Ketlans perambulating up and down the street who hadn't indulged in so much as a fist fight for twenty years, in their younger days used to bludgeon slaves to death and rip flesh from bone with bare teeth for amusement.

When the Province of British Columbia was newly created in 1876 and Queen Victoria sent the Earl of Dufferin out to give it the royal tour, Metlakatla was his northern terminus. The visit gave him a whole new vision of Western Canada's potential. "What you want are not resources", he told the Victoria legislature on his return, "but human beings to develop and consume them. Raise your 30,000 Indians to the level Mr. Duncan has taught us they can be brought, and consider what an enormous amount of vital power you will have added to your present strength."

The example of Metlakatla was a major in-

threw me among a class of society which was above what I had been used to, and when seated in a beautiful room surrounded with the good things of this world, when all my wants were readily and eagerly supplied and I mixed among a class of men far my superiors in education, rank and abilities and treated respectfully by them, oh! I used to feel my heart overflow with gratitude for God's wonderful love in thus elevating me from the dunghill and raising my head thus in so little time and so graciously and greatly surpassing my every expectation."

It was at this point Duncan decided to leave business and become a missionary. A large London firm, hearing of his decision, offered a partnership and 5000 a year, apparently without tempting him to change his mind. Some people dream of becoming kings and others dream of becoming saints. Duncan, whose adult consciousness had been formed by the educated, evangelical Reverend Carr, dreamed ultimately of becoming a saint, and having achieved the status of a local celebrity twice by age 23 gave him the confidence to go for the dream. He entered Highbury Mission college in 1855.

Henry Venn, the guiding light of the Church Missionary Society through the middle 1900's, was no believer in the romantic 18th century notion of the "noble savage". "On more accurate inspection these pleasant imaginings shift into dark and horrible realities; and cruelty and cannibalism, and human sacrifice tell us too plainly that Heathenism is everywhere and always the same accursed thing."

But he insisted the Indian and the English gentleman were essentially the same animal, and the right sort of stimulus could bring primitive society to the European level in a matter of a generation or two. The main thing holding savages back was their unexamined faith in animal instinct, Venn taught. Once they were instilled with the value of restraint, the arts of civilization could be rapidly learned, and the day hastened when mankind would be united in one equal nation under God. The key was thus no more simple or difficult than making the natives conscious of original sin.

William Duncan found this philosophy congenial to the set of his own mind and mastered it to such a degree he was made a college monitor in his first year and was being considered for a teaching position when an urgent appeal came in for a mission at Fort Simpson on the Northwest Coast of America, and his training came to an abrupt end.

Duncan had little better notion of where it was he'd volunteered for than the Sunday School children who later read of his exploits. When he tried to buy life insurance, no company would have him. The area didn't even have a formal name, and was distinguished only by one thing: remoteness. It was the least populated and most isolated possession in the entire British Empire.

Captain James Prevost of the man o' war *Satellite,* who was the main instigator of the new mission, had promised accommodations in his own cabin, but Duncan found himself directed when he arrived to an upper hammock between decks, which repeatedly inverted and dumped him on the deck. He dined in the engineer's mess surrounded by uncouth tars who "could not speak ten words in sequence without ripping out an

fluence in the drafting of the Canadian Indian Act, and gave Duncan the authority to virtually dictate early B.C. Indian policy.

The anthropologist Philip Drucker says Duncan left a deeper mark than any other single person on North Pacific Indian history, a statement few would argue.

How this entire miracle was accomplished and how it was undone is a long story full of ambiguity and much warped by controversy, but there is no doubt that it begins in the unique person of William Duncan.

John Arctander, a Minneapolis lawyer who wrote the book *Apostle of Alaska* under Duncan's guidance in 1908, found the old missionary's "tendency to shrink from anything concerning his own personaltiy . . . so excessive", he could not even pry loose an exact date of birth, but the little information he did find indicates that Duncan was Duncan from the beginning.

Duncan was born in Stokes Burton in 1832 and grew up in Beverley, Yorkshire. His family was poor, and his mother widowed while he was still a baby. There were at least two sisters, they and his mother all, as he laments in his diary, "strangers to grace." After leaving home he had little to do with them, and his mother depended on the village parson for news. From early childhood Duncan had sought out the church on his own, and gained such notice as a chorister connoisseurs came all the way from France to hear him.

Two men in the village took special interest in the brilliant waif, A.T. Carr, the parson, and a choir patron named Cussons who made a place in his leather business when the lad came to the end of his free schooling at 13, saving him from the fatal drudgery of the mills.

Duncan probably took the advice of these high collared Victorian mentors more seriously than they could themselves, filling his diary with homilies like, *"Time of which we have so little, should always be fully employed. We should never let a moment pass without striving to squeeze something out of it,"* and squeezing his own life into a tortuous schedule: 57 hours a week business, 27 hours religion, 10 hours health, 27 hours education. In the course of four years he rose from errand boy to accountant to head sales, cleaning out Cusson's entire warehouse in a single road trip. Business colleagues turned their envy to unstopped praise crediting him with "one of the keenest business minds in England", and in the secrecy of his diary Duncan rejoiced, *"Travelling*

oath."

When he reported this outrage to the master he was transferred to the gunner's mess, which was even less to his taste, so when the ship docked at Rio he bought a sack of rusks, and moved to a dinghy hanging over the ship's stern, where he remained, reading his Bible and nibbling bread and water, for the major part of the voyage, emerging only to give evening lectures on self-improvement.

The mud-oozing scar in the forest that was Victoria in 1857 did little to make Duncan feel at home. The population was 200, 100 of whom wished nothing so muclas escape on the first boat south; the other 100 seemed to dull to care where they were. James Douglas manager of the company which owned Fort Simpson, was quite indignant when he discovered the Church had gone so far in plans to establish a mission there without consulting him, and at first refused to let Duncan proceed.

The whole of this "sterile and rockbound coast" as the British Home Office thought of B.C. in those days before the gold, had been handed over to the Hudson's Bay Company for the price of taking it. Fort Simpson where Duncan was headed, was the mainstay of the company's trade, owing to the carefully nurtured fealty of the Tsimshian Indians, who supplied fur, food, labour, sex, and once saved the Fort from fire by hauling water up the beach in canoes, all in exchange for a few high priced trade goods including whiskey. Relations with the Indians were so satisfactory, according to the early factor Amelius Simpson "that a half breed population is already growing up here."

Whether James Douglas, governor of Vancouver's Island and chief factor of the corporation, actually said "It is worth your life to go among those bloodthirsty savages", as Duncan later claimed, is hard to say, considering his own wife was one, but there's no doubt he wanted to keep the self-righteous young missionary away from the place. At first he tried to get Duncan to start his mission among the tribes camped around Victoria, then when Prevost, Duncan and the Anglican Church all insisted on Fort Simpson, made Duncan promise to confine himself to the fort, in exchange for free passage and board.

What Victoria and the long journey had done to bow Duncan's spirit the eerie voyage north completed. After Nanaimo all sign of civilization came to an end and a desolation more overpowering than the empty ocean began to settle over him. *The overwhelming solitiude and stillness of the shore, the monotony of the dark pines and cedars, of the channels and roaring cascades begat a longing for the sight of human habitation that swallowed admiration of the magnificent scenery.*

At Cape Mudge he saw his first totem pole. Passing close to an island just before Port Rupert, "Dismembered and disembowelled human bodies were seen strewn all over the beach," the remains of a small Haida trading party that had "committed some small breach of etiquette" passing through Kwakiutl territory.

Stopping every second day to wrench bark from the fir trees, the trip dragged on for two weeks of grey rainswept islets like visions of purgatory and rocky scraps of islands beyond counting. Once he looked up and a shout broke from his throat. The *Otter* was ploughing full speed for a dripping grey wall of granite a thousand times as massive as the largest building in London, but heeled over just as the nervous seagulls broke from the trees, and pointed into yet another inky looking flat expanse of inlet that opened on the starboard shore. The way they had come closed behind them and Duncan felt like he was being swallowed by a primeval age.

In Grenville Channel the land seemed finally about to seize the boat, crowding around and over, waterfalls splashing on deck and the shore in close magnified detail gaping with the enormous motionless spirit that possessed the country. And this was where his journey was to end. This place he was not passing through.

He was relieved to see the land relax into a low shore around the mouth of Portland Canal where Fort Simpson was located, and the place at first glance took his breath away. It was several times larger than Victoria. The fort, with its high peaked turrets and whitewashed palisades was more like a medieval castle than the squat bastions to the south, but the fort itself was upstaged by the mass of peak-roofed wooden buildings that crowded the tide line of the bay and smothered the slopes of the island out front like Birmingham row houses. Across the water it seemed a cheering picture of civilization, but closer, the beach scattered with dugouts, strange paraphenalia, and dark figures wrapped in blankets thrust him back into a strange world. The whole scene was swarming with masked and painted bodies like ants around a jarred log, and when the purser said to Duncan, "They must know you're comin", he realized with panic that it was his presence doing the jarring.

He pursed his lips tight without replying and pushed into the midst of the landing party. When the skiff was a hundred yards from the shore his eyes fastened on a naked girl defecating into the shin-deep water. At the same time he noticed a sulphurous odour hanging over the whole village, which was actually from the mud flats, but the thought never left him it was from sewage. Along the trail to the fort he clung closely to the factor, Captain McNeill, staring rigidly ahead. They were followed the whole way by a massive crowd of Indians, wildly dressed up, but silent. One young man with a smooth oriental face and elaborate wooden crown marched closely alongside in red striped bandleader's trousers, craning and peering into Duncan's face. Duncan felt a crushing pressure to speak or wave to somehow acknowledge the Indian's terrible attention, but only retracted harder into his shell. Passing one of the big houses by the fort he confronted a bony old woman bending over a hide with wrinkled breasts dangling like cockle necks around her waist and jerked his head away. His legs lost touch of the ground and he prayed for God's steadying hand to get him through the high gate.

In the security of his two small rooms he found himself thankful for the agreement that gave him reason not to go outside again. The shining vision of white collared aboriginals sitting up evenings in curtained bungalows reading aloud from the Bible that had been irresistibly piecing itself together since Highbury now seemed the fantasy of a child. The feeling of power that had let him dismiss mountains of difficulty was gone, and the mountains were back walling him in.

"I feel almost crushed with my sense of position,"

he confessed to the CMS. *"My loneliness, the greatness of the work, which seems ever increasing before me . . . together with deepening views of my utter weakness; these indeed at times seem ready to overwhelm me, but the Lord is my refuge."* It was several weeks before he even ventured up to the gallery where the company spent much time covertly sipping rum rations and watching the Indians. He couldn't sleep for the feeling all the wild mass outside, and the officers of the fort as

Neyastodoh understood that Duncan claimed to have brought the Tsimshians a paper from a source even higher than King George, the one whiteman called God.

Earlier, the Tsimshian had not been so concerned about white power, but things had happened. When the first white man had come and killed ducks with a hollow spear which had only to be pointed at its victim to make it fall, the Tsimshian "died". But their chief was great and when the

well, were all waiting for him to perform some miracle, like the messiah, and he couldn't think. His mind would not get up.

As he had always done, William Duncan filled his void with work. In utter extremity when the world and even God ceased to be dependable, he fell back on absolute work. "No work is ever done in vain", was his most cherished saying. So he became the first white man to learn the Tsimshian language. He began by copying a list of 1500 common words from his dictionary and forming 1500 essential sentences. Captain McNeill found him "an intelligent young Indian named Clah", and Duncan began pointing out objects, like his nose, and saying "nose", while Clah gave the Tsimshian. He soon realized Clah was learning English as fast as he was learning Tsimshian, so the work accelerated as it went. He added a series of self-improvement lectures for the men of the fort to his usual Sunday services and began a school for their halfbreed children. That steadied his mind somewhat and McNeill wrote Douglas, "He seems indefatigable to do good to all, both whites and Indians."

One morning an old and highly respected Kitlahn chief named Neyastodoh met him at his door and asked in Chinook if it was true that he had brought a paper from ohe white God.

The Tsimshian did not yet understand the workings of written language, and knew only that this extremely odd substance paper was some kind of medium for the white man's powers. When Lookinglass tore up a paper from King George, gunboats descended on Nawhitti and blew it into a heap of splinters. An Indian could get nowhere at all with whiteman unless he carried some good "teapots" (letters of recommendation) and the greater the man who gave the "teapot" the more power it gave its owner. From all he'd heard,

whiteman saw him coming at them in his paint, his eyes red with the blood of all his men, they "died", and when he began his dance they fled to their ship. More whitemen came with more guns, but the Tsimshian learned the trick of guns and were soon better shots than the sailors. Whitemen had frightening possessions, but out of their ships they were soft and helpless like hermit crabs out of their shells. They could not look in the face of a man with power and when they looked death in the face they whimpered and trembled like a child before it gets its spirit. Indians robbed them, made fun of them and shot them for their bracelets.

Whitemen saw how the Indians thought, and tried to change their minds. They brought pictures of warships in flocks like gulls at oolachan time and when the Indian put on his red paint, the whiteman put on his red coat and made thunder sounds on his drums. He brought the *Beaver*. The *Beaver* lost money but George Simpson told the governors, "Independently of physical advantages steam may be said to exert an almost superstitious influence over the savages; besides acting without intermission on their fears, it has, in a great measure, subdued their very love of robbery and violence. In a word, it has inspired the red man with a new opinion — not new in degree but in kind — of the superiority of his white brother."

Then in 1855 they shelled Nawhiti, and all the coast villages lived with a gun at their heads. Wise men like Neyastodoh knew the whiteman had a power that was changing their world, but it was not in men, like Indian power, it was in ways and things. Like later prophets of the ghost dance and cargo cult they saw this power as something that might be as easily captured by natives as whitemen.

It would have been harder for the Tsimshian to believe that a whiteman would come and hand them what they dreamed of, but a powerful Carrier medicine man named Bini had been in the village just two springs before prophesying just such an event, and left a deep impression. Duncan had been in the Fort three months now, and it was very clear he was there for none of the usual reasons. The Tsimshian were getting very interested.

When Duncan said he had indeed brought paper from God, the old man looked steadily at him for a long time and asked if he might see it. Duncan brought out the great Bible he hoped some day to use in a native church and the old man ran his finger along the gilt edging.

"Is this for the Tsimshian?" he asked.

Duncan assured him it was for all men. He looked it over minutely without opening it up, then thanked Duncan and wandered pensively away.

Sometimes Duncan would climb to the gallery in the blue black before dawn and gaze down upon the town. Across the bay were the housefronts of the island, and immediately below, the steaming rain-darkened rooftops of the nearest houses, dotted with boulders that held down the bevelled planks. If the air was still there would be a line of smokes in high rigid spires around the bay like ethereal totem poles. There was only one real totem pole, three houses to his left. Other times smoke would well up heavily in the holes and run down the housefronts like water, rippling the toothy designs. No matter how early, there were always a few figures working around the new houses, and often a bonking, splashing group of men beaching logs on the morning tide. There was great wealth in town and many housegroups were dividing and building. It pleased him to see them picking up European ideas. The new house on the island's peak had two glass windows, and so he'd heard, a wooden floor. It had gone up in less than two weeks.

As the light strengthened there would be more noises, interfering over the vague measured rumble of their singing. Everything in this strange country was performed in rhythm, and the most practical tool was bent into some design. When there was enough light to read, he would go down to his translating. Clah would come around ten and the children at noon. Usually you could tell by the clamour inside the fort and outside, if the Indians did anything interesting during the day, but he informed the sentry he was to be notified, for the sake of his studies, to make sure. The factor railed at the men for "gawking at the damn shenanegans outside while furs are rotting for lack of salt," but he was involved in the potlatching himself and no one paid him any particular attention. The rain and the black winter gloom would quickly drive you mad if you didn't find something strong in the way of diversion.

There was incessant potlatching. Twenty years before the 2300 Tsimshian of Port Simpson had been scattered all over the land between the Nass and Skeena rivers and down the coast. There were nine tribes. Possessing two major salmon runs and the great Nass oolachan run and controlling the access to the interior, they were the most mercantile and powerful nation on the coast. Their September "canoe market" on McLaughlin's Bay sometimes attracted 15,000 Indians from all parts

of the coast, and many thousands of dollars worth of furs, canoes, dried salmon and oolachan grease changed hands. This what made the site attractive to the HBC and, boasting of "the ease with which Indians can be brought into dependence by a Land Establishment", the company built Fort Simpson there in 1836.

The nine tribes were encouraged to move their houses nearby, and promptly did, surrounding the fort and intercepting all incoming trade. The company was thus deprived of its middleman's cut, but paying $12 for $400 sea otter pelts and selling soap at 50 mink per finger, managed to hold its own. And since the Indians had little in the way of expenses they also prospered, pouring most of their new wealth into potlatching.

"The other day a party of eight or ten females, dressed in their best, with their faces newly painted, came into the Fort yard, formed themselves into a semicircle, then the one in the centre, with a loud but clear and musical voice, delivered the invitation, declaring what would be given to the guests, and what they should enjoy. In this case the invitation was for three women in the Fort who are related to chiefs. On the following day a band of men came and delivered a similar message inviting the captain in charge.

". . . The person who sent the aforementioned invitation is a chief who has just completed building a house. After feasting, I heard he was to give away property to the amount of 480 blankets (worth as many pounds to him), of which 180 were his own property and the 300 were to be subscribed by his people. On the first day of the feast, as much as possible of the property to be given was exhibited in the camp. Hundreds of yards of cotton were flapping in the breeze, hung from house to house, or on lines put up for the occasion. Furs, too, were nailed up on the fronts of houses. Those who were going to give away blankets, or elk skins managed to get a bearer for every one, and exhibit them by making the persons walk in single file to the house of the chief. On the next day the cotton which had been hung out, was now brought on the beach, at a good distance from the chief's house, and then run out at full length, and a number of bearers, about three yards apart, bore it triumphantly away from the giver to the receiver. I suppose that about 600 to 800 yards were thus disposed of."

The potlatch involved everyone. Visitors or slaves gave play potlatches for good will. Men gave potlatches to erase the embarrasement of adultery. Suitors gave them to impress prospective fathers-in-law. Others gave them to move from 35th rank in the tribe to 17th. There were two women chiefs at Port Simpson, as a result of smart potlatching. If a man's parents were so obscure he could never be accepted as chief, he could potlatch his way to the special title of Eagle, which gave him the right to receive his gifts before chiefs at potlatches. One Eagle at Fort Simpson demanded his a whole day before, and was shot. The line between death and life was very sharp in the Tsimshian world—that was one thing that kept it so lively.

The man who managed to stay on top of this churning heap was the head chief of the Kishpokaloats, Legaic, the young man with oriental features who had stared at Duncan the day of his arrival. Other than his totem pole Legaic had no great distinguishing wealth in material possessions, but in his people's esteem he was worth millions. With his trade connections, his persuasiveness, his astuteness, his *power*, he could raise more wealth in shorter order than any man on the coast, probably including Sir James Douglas. Douglas had amassed a big private fortune, but if he once spent it, that would be his end. In the Tsimshian system of wealth a man was measured not by what he had but what he could do.

One day shortly after Duncan arrived, Legaic walked down on the beach with a party of chiefs and fired a shot at the factor's passing canoe, just to keep things in perspective.

Another time Legaic waited as a Haida trader tried to sneak past him into the fort, then shot him in the back just as the factor opened the door to hustle him in. It upset Duncan to see the whitemen granting Legaic the same fearful respect as his own potlatch rivals, honouring the heathen system. He saw himself as the official agent of civilization and took any sign of heathenism influencing civilized man as a personal affront. Whenever the gallery crowd seemed to be enjoying village antics without properly considering their implications, he felt compelled to provide critical commentary, which often gave him a hopeless sense of beating against the world with impotent words.

The other winter occupations of the Indians Duncan liked even less, although they weren't so wasteful of valuable property. The dancing and ceremonials were a different kind of evil, one that seemed to bare the very sould of savagery.

Just after he had given his first and rather shaky address to the Tsimshian Duncan was very alarmed to receive a delegation from a Kitselas chief inviting him to a dance in his honour. When he refused the chief himself came, insisting.

"Their performance and drum beating was to them what the Book was to us. I think they meant that as we met to hear the Book they met to hear the spirit speak through the dancers on these occasions. As I had no desire in the least to offend them, I thought I had better go. Upon entering I was with ceremonies, shown to a box, which had been placed for me, covered with expensive fur, on a sail doing service as a carpet. There were many people in the house. Over to one side sat a number of women who later on acted as a chorus. I looked just as glum as I knew how. I was not going to smile at their dancing anyhow, and felt half inclined to turn back, even after I had been seated."

The people on the platform around the edge of the firelight were gossiping and gobbling up handfuls of molasses and rice, which Duncan had *"upwards of a dozen occasions to refuse."* His heart stood still as the leaping orange light flashed him a cameo of the fierce Legaic, head together in close conversation with an older chief, mindlessly fondling the other's pudgy brown fingers.

When Duncan was seated the host held up his arms for silence and began speaking in a high singsong voice, ending with a bow towards Duncan while the people turned their hands palm upward and raised a chorus of hie-hie-hie sounds. There was some shouting outside and a loud rattling of feet over the loose roof boards, a lady put her hands over her face and the crowd made ooo's of anticipation, and a man with a bow ran in, chased by what Duncan thought in the uncertain light must be a tame bear, but was a very bear-like man in a bear's skin, beginning an absurd mime of

hunting that went on and one getting funnier and funnier until Duncan quite in spite of his earlier resolve found himself highly entertained. Other dances, with raven-men who dropped from holes in the roof and salmon-men who wiggled up from holes in the floor, followed. After several hours Duncan was very moved to see one of his half-breed students brought forward to read haltingly and without comprehension, amid much hooting and clapping, the opening paragraph of the *Franklin First Reader*.

Then began a more general sort of dance, a disorganized stamping and chanting to the sound of pounded fish boxes and wall planks, that went on for an hour, increasing in pace like a train leaving a station until the very roof and walls seemed to vibrate in furious unison with the jumping bodies and firelight. This Duncan did not enjoy, crisply refusing all entreaties to join. He saw one man off my himself depart abruptly into the air as if shot by a spring. Another started to hop about on his haunches like a frog, eerily croaking. Everyone seemed to be changing into animals, the uniform chant dissolving into a nightmare babble of yipping, yodling and wolf howling, each dancer abandoned to his own intensely passionate, half animal, half human noise.

Duncan couldn't bear to look and stared at the floor, clenching his hands to hide the trembling of his fingers. He felt as if his soul was being roasted on a spit, propped in his box smack at the focus of it all. He cursed his weakness. Why should this idiot savagery so affect him? A familiar mood of horror he recognized from nightmares he'd recently had overpowered his more deliberate thinking. He knew if he stood up to leave they would all stop and he would have to confront it, but finally he did, pushing like a robot towards the door as the host tagged behind begging him to stay.

The ceremonials often transpired during the day, involving mostly young men and women returning from spirit quests to be initiated into one of the secret societies. During the quest the youth would spend sometimes several months in isolation, fasting and ice-bathing until he had what we would probably call a nervous breakdown, when the depths of his subconscious mind heaved up and its most private contents came babbling out for all to see and hear.

This was said to be his spirit talking and he was led back to the village where the elders of his group shaped the main phrases and rhythms of his babble into a song, inciting him to an even more furious pitch and sending him through the town on wrecking sprees if were a grizzly bear or causing him to devour fresh killed dog meat if he were of the Naklam, the dog eaters. The ones whose souls were tempered by the highest heat were the Hamatsa dancers.

"Only the other day we were called upon to witness a terrible scene of this kind. An old chief, in cool blood, ordered a slave to be dragged to the beach, murdered, and thrown into the water. His orders were quickly obeyed.

"Immediately after, I saw crowds of people running out of those houses near to where the corpse was thrown, and forming themselves into groups at a good distance away. This I learnt was from fear of what was to follow. Presently two bands of furious wretches appeared, each headed by a man in a state of nudity. They gave vent to the most unearthly sounds, and the two naked men made themselves

183

look as unearthly as possible, proceeding in a creeping kind of stoop, and stepping like two proud horses, at the same time shooting forward each arm alternately, which they held out at full length for a little time in the most defiant manner. Besides this, the continual jerking their heads back, causing their long black hair to twist about, added much to their savage appearance.

"For some time they pretended to be seeking the body, and the instant they came where it lay they commenced screaming and rushing round it like so many angry wolves. Finally they seized it, dragged it out of the water, and laid it on the beach, where I was told the naked men would commence tearing it to pieces with their teeth. The two bands of men immediately surrounded them, and so hid their horrid work. In a few minutes the crowd broke again into two, when each of the naked cannibals appeared with half of the body in his hands. Separating a few yards, they commenced, amid horrid yells, their still more horrid feast. The sight was too terrible to behold. I left the gallery with a depressed heart. What a dreadful place is this! My only consolation I found to be in prayer and the blessed promises of God."

In *Patterns of Culture* Ruth Benedict says, "This cannibalism was at the farthest remove from the epicurean cannibalism of Oceania or the reliance upon human flesh in the diet of many tribes of Africa. The Tsimshian felt an unmitigated repugnance for the eating of human flesh," and in John Arctander's book Duncan himself lets it very unequivocally be stated that the Tsimshian never ate human flesh, but the story which appeared first in the *Intelligencer*, then in numerous books, became Duncan's trademark, carrying his name around the world and loosing a flood of donations. The Hamatsa ceremony was a ritual experience of evil, meant to chasten and purify initiate and audience alike in the most unforgettable way — like a hellfire and brimstone sermon in the Christian church.

In a more honest moment Duncan noted in his diary that violent noises, fighting and gunfire were taboo throughout the village during the ceremonials, leading him to speculate the activities were originally begun *"to keep peace during winter months while all tribes are together in camp."*

What Duncan disliked worst about the winter festivities was that it kept the Indian from achieving what Victorian and many modern whites see as the true goals of history — material progress and physical ease.

All the pleasure these poor Indians seem to have of their property is in hoarding it up for such occasions . . . They never think of appropriating what they gather to enhance their comforts."

They were not just indifferent to the concept of progress, they were consciously opposed to it. Aurel Krause, the only anthropologist to study north coast culture in its original form noted "chlakass" or change was "considered the cause for any mishap, like bad weather, illness or misfortune in hunting or war." External life was held still so the life of the mind could be pursued.

Duncan's favorite way of escaping from Fort Simpson was to write a long letter to the CMS. Then instead of a self-conscious little Englishman teetering over a heathen ocean he became the cool and highminded agent of a worldwide organization to whom the Tsimshian were just another case, to be cracked·

"There is hardly any prospect of our being able to change the pursuits of the people as far as getting their living is concerned," **he would write.** "The physical character of the country is such as to impel its occupants to be hunters and nothing else." **The CMS infused him with power through the mail. After finishing a letter he could go outside and face it all with a sense of detached superiority. It gave him a handle on the problem. His mind began to work a little. He sent Venn a picture of the wooden-soled Yorkshire clogs he'd designed for the Indians to keep their feet dry. They were greatly intrigued with his plan, he thought, though they continued to go barefoot.**

He even got up the nerve to write the Victoria Colonist on the city's Indian problem. "Treat unlawful Indians as you would unlawful whites," **he said.** "We are taught by our religion that all men are brethren of one blood, and if some possess greater advantages than others, those advantages are given to them to use for the common good of all. How then, are we discharging our duties to them when, after corrupting them with our vices, we drive them out of our sight?"

The Indians' savagery induced savage responses from the whites. To see God's work done, one must keep his head while all about him men were losing theirs. Duncan's old clarity was coming back, and with it the enthusiasm.

It was June, the air was buoyant as his spirit and Duncan decided to go out and face his people. He'd worked over his first public address until the words began losing their meaning to him. He would speak in the houses of the head chiefs so no one would have to enter under the roof of a rival to hear him. He asked permission from the friendliest chief first, and the rest eagerly followed. His thoughts were becoming hard and effective like wise hammer blows.

"June 13: Lord's-day — Bless the Lord, O my soul, and let all creation join in chorus to bless his holy name. 'He giveth power to the faint, and to them that have no might He increaseth strength.' I should have sunk, but He graciously helped me. Bless for ever His holy name!

"This morning I set off about 10:45, accompanied by the young Indian, whom I have had occasionally to assist me in the language. It rained very hard as we went, and, indeed, had been raining for a long times, which accounted for the news of my going not spreading as it would otherwise have done. In a few minutes we arrived at the first chief's house, which I found all prepared, but the people had not assembled. Very quickly, however, two or three men set off to stir the people up, and in about half an hour we mustered about 100 souls. My heart quailed greatly before the work, — Oh these moments! I began to think, that, after all, I should be obliged to get the Indian to speak to them, while I read to him from the paper in my hand. Blessed be God, this lame resolution was not carried out. My Indian was so unnerved at my proposal, that I quickly saw I must do the best I could by myself, or worse would come of it. I then told them to shut the door. I knelt down to crave God's blessing, and afterwards I gave them the address. They were all remarkably attentive. At the conclusion I desired them to kneel down. They immediately complied, and I offered up prayer for them in English. They preserved great stillness. All being done, I bade them good by. They all responded with seeming thankfulness."

It didn't quite fit the CMS letter, but he told Ar-

ctander how Quthray, a chief and head of the cannibal society, refused to kneel. *"The angry scowl and the ugly muttering of this chief showed that the medicine men recognized in the new teaching the death knell to their nefarious practices and disgusting deviltry."* Some wept and broke into their spirit songs when they saw Duncan talk to God. Others, Clah told him, were very alarmed by his talk against Indian ways. They had thought he was on their side. But they were still interested enough in white power that Legaic the next day asked Duncan to start a school in his house.

Duncan jumped at the chance. His sails were filling with wind after long becalment. The house had room only for 15 pupils, so he decided to invite only the children of leading chiefs. "Be wise in reference to the governing powers of the people," the CMS guidebook advised, "Convince the governors you do not wish to lower their authority."

It worked. The chiefs immediately offered to help him build his own school house. The only specific order he'd given to the Indians was to stop working on the Sabbath, realizing only later how faint an idea they had of the Christian calendar. He now took up a matter that had been annoying him since he came. He refused to give his Sunday service at the fort, informing the factor by letter he'd heard men cutting wood in the compound. If the fort was still on Sunday, the Indians would have something to go by. The factor stormed into his room, there was a burst of loud imperious voices and the factor stormed out, waving his arm to the men. "You can stop working. Someone else is going to run things around here now it seems." Duncan had always found strength in being unhesitatingly consistent. He remembered now.

At first many of the children came to class in face paint and spirit dancing dress, thinking the preparation for receiving white power would be like Indian power. Although some submerged part of his mind found *"the number of designs they have and the taste they display in putting them on is really surprising,"* he introduced a daily inspection to discourage it and was soon able to report, *"most have gotten in the way of washing hands and face . . ."*

Point number one in Duncan's course for the Tsimshian was "What God expects from us, being our maker." This was closely followed by drill and marching, which *"they went through very heartily but without a smile. They seemed instead astonished."*

To communicate the advantage of Christianity he would take a rotten stick representing the Tsimshian in his present state, and a green stick, representing the Christian Indian and bend them together showing which was stronger. When a child died unexpectedly in class, Duncan responded with an impromptu eulogy over the little body, *"impressing all present on the shortness of life and the finality of eternity."*

The hardest thing he had to deal with was their lacking of sense of duty. If some work didn't happen to appeal to them, they would walk out the door and throw stones at ducks. He recognized this as a deep rooted characteristic of Indian life. When they went off so vigourously picking salmonberries, it way only because the spring balm called them. Even training for their rituals, novices lounged about watching, never being asked to act unless they felt moved. They had been spoiled for generations beyond number, and he could not beat them for fear of the parents. Unballasted by any sense of original sin man was like a dry leaf in the wind, the victim of every whim that came by. To demonstrate how this defeated their progress was his greatest task.

He sent the kids home with diaries to keep watch on themselves. Shookuanahts' was the only one he ever saw again, but it gave him more hope than almost anything else that had happened, and he sent copies everywhere.

"I could not sleep last night. I must work hard last night. I could not be lazy last night. No good

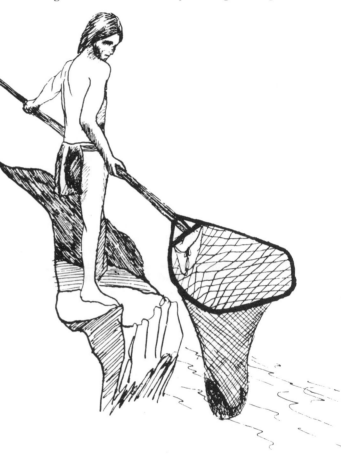

lazy — very bad. We must learn to make all things. When we no understand to read and write, then he will be very angry Mr. Duncan. If we understand about good people then he will be very happy."

Shooquanahts proved all of Duncan's work and theories at last correct. A tangible result. The Lord could not have felt much different when he turned the clay in His palm and saw Adam's features rise for the first time. Once the boy achieved this sense of shame and civilized purpose he became a brilliant student, shooting like a meteor beyond the others. He was the first Tsimshian baptized, under the Christian name of Samuel Marsden. His son Edward became the first Indian university student in the world, and led the Metlakatla choir when it toured the continent performing Handel's *Messiah*.

At first Duncan had instructed with blackboards, but later struck on the idea of assembling lessons in small booklets. *"This measure I have adopted more as a stimulant to the other Indians than anything else. When they see these little books* and hear their people read and explain them, I think a good effect will be produced."

The prospect of being able to look in on the whiteman's mysterious traffic in papers, for an Indian to be able to read — and write! — his own "teapots" seemed an unbelievable boon, the deliverance of what they had hoped from the white teacher. Chiefs were soon elbowing their own children for space in the classes and by September they wanted the new schoolhouse built worse than Duncan did.

"By about half past six we mustered seven or eight workers on the raft, though several more came out and sat on their doors, Indian fashion, as though they only wished to look on.

"This seemed greatly in contrast with their expressions to me yesterday, but such is the Indian. I knew it was no use to push, so I patiently waited. I proceeded up the beach to the building site but what was my surprise, when, on my return I met upwards of forty Indians carrying logs.

"They all seemed to have moved in an instant, and sprung to the work with one heart. The enthusiasm they manifested was almost alarming. Among the number were several old men, who were doing more with their spirited looks and words than with their muscles. The whole camp now seemed excited. Encouraging looks and words greeted me on every side, and the heavy beams moved up the hill with amazing rapidity. When the Fort bell rang for breakfast, they proposed to keep on — one old man said he would not eat till the work was done."

The framework was up in two days and the building finished within the week. He was going to make do with bark on the roof but Indians he barely knew brought him choice planks, as they emphasized, "without buying." In the fall of 1860 when L.S. Tugwell, an ordained minister, and his wife came out to help Duncan, the Indians built him a combination church and residence 76 feet by 36, with similar swiftness.

When the new schoolhouse opened Duncan found himself with classes of 200 and adult evening classes of 25. In addition he had Sunday services inside and outside the fort, daily baptismal meetings for the prospective converts, and spent much time going door to door expounding the evils of heathenism in individual conversations.

Readers of the Colonist were very impressed to learn Duncan had found 58 Tsimshian willing to renounce potlatching and the spirit dancing to follow the whiteman's God, but Duncan did not deceive himself on the point that none of his converts were ranking Tsimshian. They were the loose ends of the Tsmishian community, youngsters and halfbreeds, who had nothing to lose by dropping out. Of the 58 only 9 were over 30 years of age. The main block of Tsimshian society was solid as rock, as amorphous as mist. They would attend his school and church, pray until their faces shone with tears, they would agree with almost anything he said, then return to their dancing and potlatching without the slightest sense of contradiction. There were forces holding them together he could not imagine.

He began to resent the way they took advantage of his school without honouring his religion. "I shall always feel safe and happy in committing secular knowledge to those who seem in a fair way of making good use of it, but sowing it broadcast among heathen who having heard, reject the Gospel, will I believe result in much evil." He began to bear down harder on the real concern. "I said God had pitied their forefathers a long time, although they were bad and had not destroyed them because they knew not His way and nobody was there to tell them but now He had sent them His word and if they refused to hear He would soon cease to pity and they would certainly suffer for their sin."

If anything, by the fall of 1861 there was a resurgence of Tsimshian independence. Moffatt, the new factor, reported that he was becoming "exceedingly annoyed" with the Indians, who had fired upon him four times and were demanding "exorbitant" prices for their furs.

There were mutterings about that damn preacher getting the Indians' back up, but what had really jarred their universe was the gold rush. The Tsimshian had been dealing with whitemen for 70 years and most were ready to admit the whitemen had some great advantages, but there were still 60,000 Indians in B.C. and only 400 whites. The gold rush made that 35,400 whites and it was no more an Indian world. Two things happened to make the demoralizing effects of this change immeasurably harsher. With strength in numbers whites no longer maintained any pretext of respect and began to treat Indians like vermin. They robbed them, made fools of them and killed them for their bracelets. And the fantasy boom town of Victoria, with four-storey buildings, red fire wagons, negroes, easy money and plentiful booze, drew masses of Northern Indians away from their home territories and distracted them from their traditional concerns, like collecting food for the winter, for seasons on end. Indian leaders at Fort Simpson were so alarmed by the fall of 1862 that Legaic and eight other chiefs appealed to Duncan to help them with "strong talk" against prostitution and drinking. There was hunger in camp, along with a host of lesser physical and psychic disorders. Teenage girls were bursting with syphillis. Two tribes were constantly brawling.

One morning Duncan found Neyastodoh waiting beside the school door. The old man's eyes lifted heavily, and the slow voice took up as though continuing a long conversation. "If you want your people to be happy you must take them to Metlakatla." Metlakatla had been the winter home of most Tsimshian before Fort Simpson was built, about fifteen miles south. "It is better there. The old people built so many fires there the earth is soft and black and the water is fast and clear. The ground is dry there so floors never turn to mud in the fall, and the wind does not come through the walls in the winter. Fort Simpson is a place to trade, not a place to live. It is not the Tsimshian's choice. If you take your people home then maybe the old happiness will come back into them."

Duncan had fully revived his dream of founding an independent Christian community, and after one visit realized Metlakatla was the ideal site. His converts were anxious to make the move, especially as hazing had become intense, but they were but a handful of tag ends, and Duncan sensed the hard resistant core of regular Tsimshian society was starting to crumble. It wasn't the time to retreat, and he laid on his message. "Why is the Tsimshian so miserable? Don't you see what troubles your sinful ways bring? Why do you cling to your misery?"

As the Indians' predicament deepened, so did their hostility. The Kithrathla chief Seebassah burned a large pile of fur, a powerful gesture of scorn to the white world. The burnt fur smell lingered on the village for months; Moffat answered with a rice and molasses feast for everyone but the Kithrathlas and Duncan. Babies of white fathers disappeared. Moffat reported that 700 pickets had been stolen from the deer-fence around the garden.

One day two followers rushed to the fort where Duncan was rolling magnesia pills for an old woman with peritonitis and begged him to hide, saying Cushwaht was going to shoot him because the school dog had bitten him, but Duncan brushed them aside and went out to his patient. All the time he was at the old woman's side a younger woman who had followed him stared intensely into his face. It was Cushwaht's wife, gauging his spirit. If he appeared flustered, she would signal Cushwaht to come in and kill him. But if he did not feel threatened "his spirit was on top" and to harm him was to invite certain disaster.

Duncan now understood this and acted especially nonchalant; it occurred to him to return past Cushwaht's door but he refrained. *"God will protect you in the discharge of your duty but not when you run recklessly into danger."*

His followers were loud around thathe fire that night. Their man had outfaced Cushwaht, a chief and warrior, as he had outfaced the factor. This was surely proof he had the power of God. An old chief commented to Duncan later, "They are learning about God from you and you are the same as Him to them."

One very dark night Duncan was told there was going to be a moon on the beach. *"On going to see, there was an illuminated disc, with the figure of a man on it. The water was then very low, and one of the conjuring parties had lit up this disc at the water's edge. They had made it of wax, with great exactness, and presently it was at the full. It was an imposing sight. Nothing could be seen around it; but the Indians suppose that the medicine party are then holding converse with the man in the moon. Indeed there is no wonder in the poor creatures being deluded, for the peculiar noises that were made, while all around was perfectly still, and the good imitation of the moon while all around was enveloped in darkness, just seemed calculated to create wild and superstitious notions. After a short time the moon waned away, and the conjuring party returned whooping to their house."*

The next day, the first of December, Legaic visited Moffatt to say his young daughter had gone to the moon for her education, and until she returned there would be a period of stillness for the whole village. When Tsimshian girls reached their first menses they were trained at a secluded place for a month, and this season the coming out ceremony was getting special emphasis because of the perils of the gold rush. The tall girl with tilted wingshaped eyebrows unmistakably like his own was Legaic's only daughter, and he was very anxious to have Moffat close the schoolhouse because it disrupted the spell of the mysteries.

Moffat dutifully put the request to Duncan, who replied sharply, *"Not for a month, nor even a day will I stop. Satan has reigned here long enough."*

Legaic then begged for a recess of one week, then the girl's mother came to Duncan the morning of her return to beg for just one day's recess. Duncan would not grant an hour. She then asked him at least not to ring the bell, which disrupted the ceremony more than anything else.

"No, I cannot do that. If I did not ring the bell the scholars would think there was no school."

"Well, could you ring it softly, not so hard?"

"No, if I ring it at all, I will have to ring it as usual so it can be heard."

The woman left, weeping, Duncan watching with arms folded across his chest. "Mr. Duncan struck the steel," says Arctander, "and says he is inclined to think it was ringing a little more loudly that day, if anything. And no one who knows Mr. Duncan would doubt that for a minute."

About noon he saw them coming up the path single file, Legaic in the lead. He folded his arms and waited as the children fled. The door flew back and Legaic leapt towards him with a knife, snarling that he had killed men before and Duncan had to be punished.

"Kill him. Cut off his head and I'll kick it along the beach," yelled Cushwaht.

Legaic's eye locked with Duncan's, red with the blood of many men. Many, but not so many as it once seemed. In his uncle's eye the power of the Tsimshian had been the greatest force in the known world. That world had grown smaller and smaller, like a canoe on the back of a surfacing whale, but Legaic had not come up against the real implications of this fact until this instant.

Duncan glared back, his eye bright with the power of the Church Missionary Society, the Hudson's Bay Company, the Government of British Columbia, the North Pacific Squadron of Her Majesty's Royal Navy, and said, "Legaic, you are a bad man." The highest ranking Indian on the Pacific Coast "died". The knife hand sagged and his eye wandered to Clah, who was standing behind his whiteman concealing a pistol. The chief blustered awhile and backed out the door, followed by his painted crew. The world had just rolled over him, and he was a broken man.

He came back in half an hour, blubbering and showing Duncan his "teapots". Duncan took him by the elbow but he staggered away, staring crookedly ahead.

Duncan was light-headed at what was happening. It was as though he'd been trying for four years to push over an old building that was too solid, but now what seemed the main brace had buckled, and he pushed fiercely, the frame swaying madly back and forth. But still not breaking. He could still not break a single ranking Tsimshian loose from potlatch and spirit dance to commit himself to the new village, not even Clah. But he felt it was close — he could reach it, and all but grasp it. *"I can scarcely say now how many Indians will move with me; perhaps only a few at first . . ."* The medicine men were still holding hard.

Children came to school in the morning primed with loaded questions, like if the white God loves us why must we fear him? Whenever they said "White God" he knew the enemy had been busy. In turn Duncan sent Samuel Marsden to the displays of the medicine men. There was an old female shaman whose stock in trade was to ask volunteers to try floating a small green stone in a bowl, then herself carefully rest it on the surface of the water. Duncan's messenger would then pick up a small black stone from the floor and ask her to float that, which of course she couldn't do because she was palming a piece of green wood.

The preeminent shaman of the Tsimshian was a rail-thin man with a bouncy raven's-nest of never-combed hair named Loocoal. Loocoal had power in many fields. He was the best halibut fisherman and goat hunter in the village, though he didn't work steadily at either, and his advice and healing powers were sought in all situations. His curse, said Tugwell's replacement, the Reverend W.H. Collison, in his *Wake of the War Canoe*, was to the Indians "so fearful, that once under its spell they became defeated, lost all courage, and usually succumbed to the first attack of illness." Duncan had never spoken to Loocoal, but the shaman's words reached him on the tongues of friends and stuck in his mind like porcupine barbs, working deeper.

"It is not Tsimshian ways that are evil. It is the whiteman's way. The Tsimshian was not miserable until the whiteman brought misery. If the white god has powers over men, Mr. Duncan should ask him to cure the evil of his own people and there would be no need to cure the Tsimshian."

The Indians appeared to see inexhaustible wisdom in this simpleminded argument and Duncan could never find just the right line to counter it. *"Do not love bad ways, love God. Bad ways please us a little time then bring us misery . . ."*

Highmas, the head chief of the Kitseesh was ill and his brother Womankwot came for Duncan. When he arrived at the chief's house the people were all standing outside trying to keep everyone quiet. Duncan pushed through their restraining arms and barged in, catching Loocoal in the middle of an incantation over the sick chief. The medicine man, as Duncan said, "blew off steam", and stomped away. Highmas had a severe chill, and after Duncan placed him near the fire and gave him some medicine he recovered.

Duncan's friends were reservedly impressed, but terrified by Loocoal's anger. When you spit, don't spit on the ground, they told him. Spit up in the air. If he finds wet spit, he can make you sick and die. And when you cut your hair, be sure to burn it all up so there's none around for him to find. Duncan was sorry they still believed so strongly in the shaman's power, but he had an idea.

He immediately had his hair cut and sent a lock to every shaman in Fort Simpson. The whole of Fort Simpson was electrified. The white shaman had thrown down the gauntlet and the Indian shaman had to do their stuff, or admit their match, but none could find even the starting of a crack in that hard shell of Christian logic. Loocoal threw the hair away.

But he kept his eyes open, and one evening slinking past Duncan's residence he picked a piece of dirty paper out of the trash and straightened it out. It was a detachable white collar. Normally when a shaman prepares a voodoo he hides it in a place it can never be found, but this case called for a special approach. He flung the collar into the branches of a maple tree at the intersection of the village's two busiest paths. Whenever he passed that way he shook his raven rattle and made three circles around the tree.

Duncan was embarrassed and slightly angry about his dirty old collar thus appearing on public display, but it was so high in the thin switches of the maple it couldn't be retrieved without

causing notice, any time of day. He daren't show concern, lest it be taken as an acknowledgment of the shaman's power. All his work, all his career, now seemed to be turning on small hard decisions.

That Sunday in the middle of his sermon Duncan broke down in a long, hacking fit of coughing. It was not unusual; he'd had the cough since youth and in the extremely cold and wet and busy fall of 1861 it had grown much worse. But when he raised his head to continue, he saw every face in the congregation gaping at him, frozen masks of terror. It shook him, and he cut the service short.

No one would come out and say what they thought — just stared piteously on when the wild fit seized him. He too imagined it was turning suddenly chronic, but that was only because he had begun to dwell on it far more than he should. One day a foul-tasting lump coughed up under his tongue and he spat it out. It was blood. He had tuberculosis. He covered the spittle with his shoe.

At the evening Bible class Duncan explained how the cough had first seized him in England, and asked them to remember his having had it when he first came to Fort Simpson. He saw the eyes of his most devoted followers blacken with superstitious fear, and no one spoke.. Everyone at Fort Simpson was convinced that heathen charlatan was murdering him with a rattle and a piece of paper, and protesting only made it worse. Was the savage mind beyond redemption?

He couldn't stop coughing, and when his tongue felt the salty blood, waves of terror pounded at his temples and he choked it back down. If these sharks smelled blood his work was done. Sly heathen devils! If Christian reason were not so strong in him he would surely begin to imagine powers were at work on him, where his enemy was simply taking advantage of a natural weakness. When Arctander stumbled on the incident forty years later the old missionary was still full of anxious explanations. As the winter wore on, he realized what harm Loocoal had done. He could reason with a candidate all day, bringing him to the very teetering verge of declaring himself, then there would be a fit of coughing and the spell was broken. "I'll think some more," the candidate would say, suddenly distant. The work began to fall apart. Duncan couldn't sleep, and his health weakened. He thought of taking a trip to Victoria, or moving to Metlakatla, but if he left Fort Simpson in retreat there would be no need to ever return. His face grew haggard and behind his back they said yes, he is dying.

On March 18, 1862 the Victoria *Colonist* noted that an American miner had disembarked from a San Francisco passenger boat with an advanced case of varioloid smallpox.

"Imagine for a moment what a fearful calamity it would be," pleaded editor Amor de Cosmos, "were the hordes of Indians on the outskirts of town to take the disease." But to other Victorians the prospect of their colony's number one nuisance being somewhat reduced by natural causes wasn't so alarming. Since 1859 there had been a noisy citizens' lobby for driving the Indians north with gunboats, and the authorities were caught between this growing public indignation and the very real risk of starting an Indian war.

As isolated cases began to break out on the Victoria reserve, the paper's warnings became hysterical, but in spite of "the danger now posed to all classes," the authorities remained scrupulously inactive.

Duncan, who was in a better position to imagine the consequences of the news than any man, threw his moving plans into immediate action, at the same time renewing his attacks on the heathen. By May 14 the schoolhouse was down and made into a raft loaded with scrounged boards, furniture and 500 bushels of seed potatoes purchased from the fort. Men were already at Metlakatla preparing building sites. On May 25 the first canoe arrived from Victoria, several of whose paddlers had died of smallpox en route.

In a letter to the CMS published in the *Intelligencer* of September 1862 Duncan said, "It was evidently my duty to see and warn the Indians. I therefore spent the next few days in assembling and addressing each tribe."

But what sort of warning? The Tlingit shaman Kaka of Sitka had saved his village from the upper coast epidemic of 1832 by sending the people to their summer camps to hide. The memory of that nightmare was still strong among the Tsimshian and Duncan could easily have frightened them into evacuating. He might have explained some of the basics of prevention and quarantine, with the aid of his well thumbed medical text and his knowledge of Tsimshian, which no other man had. So small a sense of responsibility on the whiteman's part would have made Indian history so different.

Duncan's letter in the *Intelligencer* continues, "I had previously determined to make a farewell address to each tribe in Fort Simpson, but I now felt doubly pressed to call upon all to quickly surrender themselves to God." He had a list of rules which any who wanted to avail of this last chance to be saved must sign:

> To cease calling in conjurers when sick
> To cease giving away property for display
> To attend religious instruction
> To send their children to the mission school
> To give up Indan deviltry.

As Arctander says, he had no intention of making it easy for them. The pass things had come to that winter he knew few would sign, fewer than he could have persuaded in other ways, but he knew what he was doing, and left them with a promise of punishment ringing in their ears louder than any curse Loocoal had ever made.

By the time the Victoria Indian camp was stinking of disease like one great open pustule, the white citizens of the land were ready to act, and Douglas gave in to pressures to burn the shanties and drive the loathsome brutes out of sight. This action assured that every camp the length of the coast was infected the the week's end. When two whitemen stole blankets from Bella Coola corpses and sold them to a band of Chilcotins, the virus reached the interior and the epidemic ripped through the province like a forest fire. The closeness of Tsimshian society gave it an especially good hold. The disease blasted through the great open houses. Women ran to hug dying chiefs, and turned away, themselves stricken. Howling children ran to the sea to cool their flaming skin but the water burned too. The clouds flashed red and green, the earth tilted, whirled and slammed up.

"Those who had the fear of God in their eyes fled to me, while the heathen sought refuge in their charms and lying vanities. They dressed up their houses with feathers and rind of bark, stained red; they sang their heathen songs and kept the rattles of the conjurers perpetually going.

"One of the tribes which adopted heathenism to the full, went for a long time unscathed, and this filled their conjurers with pride and boasting words, and caused much perplexity in the minds of those who had partly shaken off heathen superstitions; but in the end this tribe suffered even more than any other, and their refuge was proven to be a refuge of lies."

Duncan's party, comprising some 50 persons in 5 canoes left Port Simpson before the disease started to spread and arrived in Metlakatla on May 28, to find the advance crew had cleared the village site, planted the potatoes, carried the schoolhouse up the hill, and had already built two houses. *"Every night we assembled, a happy family, for singing and prayer. I gave an address on each occasion from some portion of scriptural truth suggested to me by the events of the day."* His lectures, were still interrupted by coughing, but now it was just coughing.

On June 6 the first fugitives from Fort Simpson appeared, a fleet of 50 canoes followed by the sadly reduced family of Legaic.

"They desired me to undertake for them. They would not oppose my will. One of the chief speakers said — We have fallen down and have no breath to answer you — do your will."

Some of the newcomers Duncan sent back home. Others were made to sign his provisions and penned in a quarantine away from the village site. By the time it was all over Duncan had increased his following by almost eight times.

To Douglas the next year Duncan wrote, *"Your Excellency is aware of the dreadful plague of smallpox with which it pleased the Almighty God to visit the Indian of this coast last year, and by which thousands of them were swept away. While I am sorry indeed to inform your Excellency, that not fewer than 500 have fallen at Fort Simpson, I have gratefully to acknowledge God's sparing mercy to us as a village. We had only five fatal cases."*

Out of this good fortune Duncan planned, he said, to raise *"a model Christian village, reflecting light and radiating heat to all the spiritually dark and dead masses around us."* The Tsimshian were now like children, looking to him for everything, and already 35 frame houses had been built.

Bibliography

Duncan Papers. Vancouver, University of British Columbia Library.

Usher, Jean. *William Duncan of Metlakatla.* Thesis, Vancouver, University of British Columbia Library.

Church Missionary Intelligencer 1858-62. Victoria, The Provincial Archives.

Duff, Wilson. *The Indian History of B.C. Volume 1 The Impact of the White Man. Anthropology in British Columbia, Memoir No. 5, 1964.* Provincial Museum of British Columbia, Victoria, 1964.

Arctander, J.W. *The Apostle of Alaska: the Story of William Duncan of Metlakatla.* New York, 1909.

GHOST CAMPS of Howe Sound

by Peter Trower

When my brother Chris and I were very young, he used to have a recurrent dream about somewhere he called the North Forest. Since we were living in England at that time, were forests of any sort had been at a premium for centuries, his visions were ascribed to childish fantasizing. But it must have been more than that. The War came and changed the direction of our lives; we crossed the Atlantic in a dangerous year and jeopardy so extreme it was ungraspable; crossed, by rail, a continent so wide and myth-strewn it frightened us more than the sea, to arrive at last in what could only be the mighty North Forest land of Chris's dream - mountains, ocean and foggygreen trees as far as the mind could stagger. We had reached the vision.

Trees enter your mind in British Columbia and stay with you even in cities, marching down the valleys of the brain, watching you with ancient emerald eyes. They were here before man and are the true inhabitants. You feel their presence always. They claimed Chris and I from the start and took us over totally when our widowed mother remarried and we moved to the isolated pulpmilltown of Port Mellon in Howe Sound. Here we were hemmed in by forest on all sides but the sea; it became our playground, the best part of our world. We learned to run the trails quick as the Indian boy who was our friend and whose grandfather made us yewwood bows. The trees watched over us and even school was fun in the one big room by Rainy River. And the mill stank and stewed the trees to pulp.

The first logging camp we ever saw was abandoned, and its echoing empty buildings became the mansions and castles of boyhood play for Chris, myself and our grimy chums. The loggers had finished the claim and moved on, leaving us a legacy of shacks to rejoice in or ruin. The camp lay little more than a mile from the mill on the eastern slope of the Rainy River valley and was easily reached on foot. It was our grand gathering place and headquarters for adventure when the desk lids slammed and set us free from the pleasant rigours of learning. Comic books could

still be found in attics where forgetful loggerkids had hidden them, and mislaid toy guns glinted among the salal bushes.

The camp straddled a riprap road that perched on pilings the better part of its length to compensate for the undulations of the land. It ran more than eleven miles up the valley into some of the ruggedest and most ravaged country I can ever remember seeing. They'd raised merry hell on those hills with their crosscut saws and whip-cracking steampots, left a sprawl of flattened acreage where only ferns and fireweed grew among the stumps and shattered slabs. Down this dangerous course had come skidding the archaic trucks with their teetering logloads, clinging desperately to the wirewebbed planks as they careened over dizzy narrow bridges, whined and grunted and suicided down steep grades, snorted and shuddered and breaknecked down that one lane dangerway to the ultimate dump. As the twisted wreckage of such a truck broken-backed in the brush at the foot of a steep slope attested, they didn't always make it. But now the dump had been dismantled and only gasoline ghosts at midnight drove that road.

We were vaguely aware, from the overheard conversation of grownups, that numerous men had been maimed and killed up that splintered valley in the ruthless Depression days, but to our naive minds it was a Saturday staircase to incredible romance. It was the bandit-ridden badlands of every Western we'd ever seen and a Martian footpath beyond the drab company town of tarpaper shacks with flyash snowing blackly through the trees and the rotten egg smell that pickled your soul.

There was an abandoned Japanese shingle mill at the very end of the road where once we camped quivering overnight in a windy darkness full of dead donkey punchers. They had had telephone connection with the beach from this point to monitor the trucks and a receiver still hung on the wall in one of the shacks. We often picked it up and shouted obscene nonsense over the line, half daring someone to answer. One spring we ran halfway to the beach in terror after spotting simultaneously three mother bears, belligerent and protective with their cubs. The shingle mill buildings collapsed under a particularly heavy snowfall the following winter and in 1945 the valley caught fire in a summer lightning storm and went up like a tinderbox, consuming the better part of that remarkable road with its pilings and giddy trestles. Many years after, Chris and I logged in the same valley on a number of occasions and I tried to recall my youthful perspectives. But they were gone down forever into some deep canyon of memory as I snarled and scrabbled and moneygrubbed with the rest.

The Rainy River camp and road were our first kickoff points to high adventure in those enchanted years, but they were not the only ones. There were rumoured to be at least two other ghost-camps in the area of considerably older vintage, and inevitably we found our way to both of them.

The first of these lay several miles further up the Sound in the mouth of the McNab Creek valley. Apparently the government had tried to interest homesteaders in this location back in the Twenties but the scheme had, like many another projected west coast settlement, fizzled out quickly. Soon the loggers came and claimed the rich timber for themselves. They had been gone for some years now and new vegetation burgeoned about the not yet sagging buildings that remained. The log dump jutting out into the small bay was still in good shape and one day we tied up there excitedly and hurried ashore to explore the place. There were a good number of us, as it was part of a school excursion, a sort of directionless field trip, designed more to get us out of the classroom to burn off some energy than anything else.

We poked around the visible buildings finding rusty cables, blocks and other bits of wornout equipment they hadn't deemed worth taking with them. Fishermen, beachcombers and tourists had long since picked the place clean of anything valuable or useful. Then one of us discovered a partially obscured trail leading off among the brush-choked alders. Four of us slipped away from the main group and ventured along it, hopeful but not really expecting to find anything much. The trail disgorged on a small clearing and a hidden log cabin that seemed almost miraculously intact. There was still a padlock on the door and the windows were unbroken. It must have sat untouched for years, exactly as its owner had left it.

It was a mystery and like all Mark Twain-approved boys we thrived on mysteries. No Injun Joe cave or Mississippi swamp shanty could have held greater lure. We pushed our way through the ferns and tangled undergrowth to peer through the rain-stained glass.

Nothing could have prepared us for the exquisite and unlikely sight that greeted our eyes. The place was sparsely furnished - little more than a rickety table, a couple of bargain basement chairs and a narrow cot in one corner - but stacked on the table and on a couple of rough shelves was the most incredible collection of ancient science-fiction magazines I'd ever seen outside of a secondhand bookstore. There were no dishes, bedclothes or other signs of recent occupancy, simply that treasure trove of lurid books, beckoning us with pulpy, irresistable fingers. I was an avid science-fiction fan and communicated my enthusiasm to the others. Whether we broke the window or the lock I can't recall, but in very short order we were inside that magical shack.

From the musty smell of the place it had been unoccupied for some time but the cabin was soundly built and the cedar shake roof apparently didn't leak. Apart from a slight mildewy odour, the books were all in excellent shape. It was an unbelievable haul. They were mostly rare large-size Amazing and Science Wonder Stories from the Twenties and early Thirties with hypnotic Frank R. Paul covers. We pored over them wide-eyed. Most of them had been published before we were born. Finally and with some slight argument we divided up the spoils. It was like ransacking a mirage.

Soon we were staggering back down the trail, each with a chin-high armload of glorious blood and thunder. Miss Steeves, our teacher and the ostensible leader of the expedition, was amazed and slightly apprehensive. "Where in heaven's name," she inquired, "did you find all those?"

We told her roughly the truth, omitting the part about breaking into the cabin and she allowed, after a bit of hesitation, that she supposed it would be all right. She was a very small woman and always rather ill-equipped to cope with such country louts as we were in those days.

It took me at least a year of persistent inveigling and bartering to relieve my partners in crime of their shares of that heady loot, but I finally did. And what singular logger left such a wealth of collectors items behind him in the first place and walked away with the whimsical key in his pocket I have never to this day been able to imagine. Whoever he was, he solved our reading problems for a considerable time to come.

The third camp was a good deal more remote. It was perched on one of the higher ridges of Gambier Island and attainable only after an arduous climb up roads that were half washed out. The occasion for our going there was another school outing about a year later. Perhaps myself or one of my fellow bookfinders suggested the destination in vain hope of hitting the jackpot twice. On a warm May morning about forty of us set out for that mysterious mountaintop goal.

The way was steep but we were full of young energy, and expectation drew us like a magnet. We came over a rise at last, all the oldest and wildest boys far ahead of the teachers and girls. There it stood, a lost settlement of split cedar buildings like a misplaced movie set, forlorn among second-growth timber on the hillcrest. Here the long gone woodsmen had lived, headquartering in the heart of the brush country rather than commuting from the beach in the customary fashion. It was a lonely memorial to nameless loggers who had plundered these slopes and gone.

There were ten or twelve buildings in all - one fairly large structure that must have been the cookhouse, the rest small, three or four man shacks as opposed to the bigger, roomier units we'd seen in the earlier camps and around the millsite. We stood for a second gazing awedly in the silence at this rough outpost we'd heard about for so long. Then with excited whoops we scattered in all directions to explore the place. Disappointingly the shacks, though still in reasonably intact condition, were devoid of any sort of booty whatsoever. Either the vanished lumberjacks had been exceedingly frugal men or the place had been gone over with a finetooth comb by previous scavengers. After the fabulous find at McNab, it was a palpable letdown.

What happened next is difficult to explain in any rational terms. The initial feeling of wonderment and discovery were abruptly replaced by something quite different. Perhaps it was the war news hammering at us daily with reports of violence. Perhaps it was the fact that the place was miles from anywhere and belonged to on one. And perhaps it was simply that those hollow buildings had yielded up no prizes. In any event something mad and destructive took hold of us all.

"Let's play commandos!" hollered somebody and we charged on those flimsy ancient buildings like hordes of berserk savages.

Grabbing up any sort of club or bludgeon we could lay hands on we battered the thin cedar walls, sending the weathered shakes flying. Doors were torn from their hinges and the windows went out one after another with tinkling splashes of glass that gleamed explosive in the sun. A couple of the strongest and most ambitious boys managed to level one small cabin completely, and the walls and roof came down with a ruinous crash. What rain, wind and snow had failed to accomplish over the years we managed to effect in fifteen or twenty minutes of senseless hooting vandalism. By the time the laggard teachers came into view and with shouts of outrage, commanded us to stop, we had the place half demolished.

We stood sheepishly in the shambles we'd created while they read us the riot act in no uncertain terms. Demands for some explanation went unanswered. None of us really had any. Dire retribution was promised in the form of adverse reports to our parents and we quivered in our guilty boots for a bit. But by the time we got back to the milltown that evening the incident had lost much of its enormity and was gradually forgotten.

Amazingly enough after our delinquent behavior on Gambier, they took us some months later on a further excursion to Potlatch Creek, about twice as far up-sound as McNab. Perhaps there was method in their madness, however. There had obviously been some kind of camp or settlement there long before, but the buildings had either been towed away or levelled. Nothing remained but piles of ancient bottles and cans and a few rotting moss-covered boards. It was most discouraging and we deemed the trip a complete washout.

Up to this point we had seen no live logging or loggers, only the deserted and half-healed traces of their passing. This situation was shortly to be remedied. Rumours began to spread that a brand new camp was to open, just east of the mill.

We rushed over to the area after school nearly every day for a while to watch raptly as the bunkhouses and other buildings floated in on barges like Noah's Arks to be hauled up above the tideline. A couple of busy cats had bladed out a campsite for them to sit upon. A pair of donkey engines disembarked and pulled themselves up the beach with their own mainlines like spiders spinning in reverse gear. Two spanking new yellow logging trucks roared importantly ashore with their bunks jutting out and up from either side of each cab like demon horns when you squinted your eyes at them. Several miles of new road had been cut back into the valley and the fallers had been at work for several weeks. It was shortly before the advent of practical powersaws, but on clear days when the wind was right you could hear the great trees going down with distant thunderous impact. It was all noisy, surprising

and quite magnificent. The loggers had returned!

The purpose of the camp was to provide logs for the ramshackle sawmill that operated in conjunction with the Kraft plant, producing lumber for export and slabs for the boiler room furnaces. Our stepfather was superintendent of the mill at that time and a good friend of the logging camp boss. Being an old brush ape himself and pleased with our evident interest in the business, he arranged one day for Chris and myself to ride up with one of the logging trucks and see how the yarding was done with strict instructions that we stay well in the clear.

It was a goliath bedlam of thundering engines, shouting men and imponderable cables, pencilled ominously against the hills and sky. The groaning monolith of the spartree shook to an earthquake of power and strain as the wood was wrenched from the brush. The logs kicked and wriggled through the intervening distance and hit the muddy landing with a splattering thwack. A wiry bearded man unhooked the chokers and the rigging clattered back up the slope to the toy-small figures who stood waiting resignedly in the wan afternoon light. I was disillusioned. It seemed to my twelve-year-old eyes very confusing, frightening and more than a little dangerous. I made up my mind then and there that if there was one thing I wasn't going to be when I grew up it was a logger. I liked the deserted camps much better.

Shortly after this our stepfather was drowned on a timber cruise and we left the Port Mellon area, not to return for many years. And of course, despite my childhood misgivings, Chris and I both became loggers in the end.

The ghostcamps of my youth are thirty years gone now, reduced to overwhelmed wreckage or bulldozed to oblivion. Some years back while surveying in the McNab Creek valley I discovered the smashed-flat ruin of that miraculous cabin where we found the books. And more recently, when I logged the same valley with a brand new crop of loggers, even those sad traces had been swept away. The once new camp we saw open beside the mill is itself less than a memory. All that remains is a derelict log dump with grass growing between the planks, pointing toward Gambier Island where the hilltop camp we punished long ago lies like a pack of decaying cards among the creepers.

NOTES & QUERIES

Readers of Raincoast Chronicles, who include the participants as well as the scholars of B.C. coast history, make up the most expert and complete pool of coastal information in existence. If you have a question the books can't answer, an unidentified photograph or simply a fact you'd like to share, write Notes & Queries, Box 119, Madeira Park, B.C.

In your last issue Mrs. A. Talbot of Matsqui wrote saying she was unable to trace the history of her boat the *Swan* prior to 1924. The *Swan* is a narrow converted steam tug of about 45' built in 1891 by Bob Drainey at the head of Rivers Inlet. Drainey was at that time manager of Rivers Inlet Cannery but later set up his own business at Namu, taking the *Swan* with him. The next time I ran across the *Swan* she was owned by Kelly Logging on the east coast of Moresby Island. In 1923 she was lying in Coal Harbour, still owned by Kelly Log, and I chartered her for a short period that year, after which she was operated in general towing by Billy Bennock of Pitt Lake. It was he who installed the diesel engines.

Captain D.W.Peck
Cowichan Station, B.C.

My family and I were most interested in your No. 3 issue of Raincoast Chronicles, as the photograph of the Diesel Engineer, on page 16, is my father, Allan Rae, from Beaver Cove, B.C.

Your magazine is an extremely interesting gathering of material.

Arlene Matkoski
Woss Lake
Beaver Cove, B.C.

I was brought up at Soames Point on Howe Sound. I remember there was a superstition: if you picked a certain kind of seaweed off the beach, took it home and dried it over your fireplace, it would bring you good luck. I have found out since that this type of seaweed is *Sargassum*. Since I left Soames Point eight years ago, I haven't met anyone else on the coast who has heard of this superstition, or how it got started. Any ideas?

Gina Bennett
Kamloops, B.C.

I refer to the letter from Mr. Lillard about the rock carving in MacKenzie Sound.

I was first shown this three or four years ago by some friends from Gig Harbour, Washington. They had found it by chance a year or so previously when they knocked off the moss which then covered the rock.

I gave a slide showing the carving to Dr. Ireland of the B.C. Provincial Archives, who in turn showed it to several people, including the Surveyor-General. No one came up with any explanation.

J.R. Genge
Sidney, B.C.

We are truly impressed by the number of Chronicle readers wandering around in obscure, deserted MacKenzie Sound knocking the moss off that particular rock. Your friends are the fourth party to claim discovery since Mr. Zablosky's photograph appeared in our second issue. The only person to offer a positive opinion as to the carving's meaning and origin so far is Tom Hudson of Campbell River, who states:

These signs are to be found all over the world, where they were spread by the wise men of each age, as a reminder of the basic principles essential to every form of life including man. The circle is infinite around the invisible centre which creates it, used as the symbol for what many people call God. It contains all things but is itself nothing — zero. The line symbolizes the individual, also direction and polarity, since it must have two opposite ends. The 3 or $\triangle$ represents balanced strength, in construction or in thought. The 4 $\square$ or $\top$ (right angle) represents truth, reflected in such phrases as "square shooter" or "on the level". All creations in the universe are based on these true principles.

THE BLUFF

Men among ghostbone black
alders on the silent ridge
move
distantly in a shadow play -
their business is toil.

They are putting the coup de grace
to my childhood bluff
where once as foolish boys
we crawled across dangerous ledges
testing out for life.

After the good ground is gone
they must desecrate the rocks
burn sticks
bulldoze casually
all the dreams to dust.

I bear them no malice -
I am them
but early in the morning
no men move among the alders
birds and quiet make love on the faraway hill.

THE ALDERS

The alders are the reoccupiers —
they come easily
and quick into skinned land
rising like an ambush
on raked ridges
jabbing like whiskers up through the washedout
faces of neverused roads.

The alders are the forestfixers
bandaging brown wounds
with applegreen sashes —
filling in for the fallen
firs —
jostling up by the stumps
of grandfather cedars —
leaning slim to the wind
by logjammed
loggerleft streams.

The alders are the encroachers
seizing ground the greater trees owned
once
but no more.

It is the time of the alders
they come
like a bright upstart army
crowding the deadwood spaces
reaching
at last for the hand of the whole
unshadowed sun.

Peter Trower

The GREAT PACIFIC SEALHUNT

In 1867, while John A. MacDonald is trading drinks with his cronies in Kingston to celebrate Canada's confederation, the land westward from Winnipeg to Victoria the domain of buffalo, Indians, fur traders, Metis and mountains, a sailing schooner, *Surprise*, mastered by Captain William Spring, moves slowly up Johnstone Strait.

Lookouts watch the kelp beds and rolling water for a sign of the migrating seals travelling north to the Pribilof Islands in the Bering Sea to breed. At the cry, "Boats out!" four sailing skiffs drop off the side of the schooner and move out on the open sea. In each there are four Indians from Ucluelet — one to steer under the small sail, one to row, and two hunters armed with rifles and clubs. They move in a U-shape, two to three hundred feet of water between them.

The seals are sighted; the boats form a square around them. The seals quickly disappear underwater, but, being mammals, they are forced to surface for air periodically. Each time they do, a bullet drives them back beneath the water. The men try not to hit the seal as even a small hole in such a valuable pelt will sharply reduce its price on the Victoria market. The seals in desperation stay underwater longer and longer, until they either drown or are so weakened they can be killed with clubs.

The skiffs, often so far from the mother ship that her masts are only tiny black sticks on the horizon, are quickly lashed together and the men begin to skin the animals, some of which are seven feet long and weigh over eight hundred pounds. Many that have been killed sink too fast for the boats to get to them and are lost; at times they

lose three for every one they get. The skins are quickly stretched and the bodies are dropped back into the sea.

The hunt will continue all day, until darkness or a sudden squall drives them back to the *Surprise*. The oarsman gets fifty cents a skin, the hunters two dollars. The season is wide open for both male and female fur seals.

It is called pelagic sealing and it will last from 1867 to 1911 when the great herds will be so decimated that treaties and empty boats will drive the schooners into bankruptcy. But for almost fifty years, Victoria will depend almost exclusively on the fur seal industry. At its height it will employ 1400 whites and 1700 Indians in 122 schooners. Fifteen thousand people will depend on the industry, which will earn one-and-a-half million dollars a year for Victoria and establish it as the major port of its time.

It was estimated in 1860 that there were more than five million fur seals in the North Pacific. By 1911 there were only 150,000. But that is far ahead of the story of the seal and man. It involves Spain, Russia, Japan, England, the United States and Canada; it will almost start a war when the US seizes Canadian ships on the high seas; it will leave Canadian sailors languishing in Russian jails in Siberia and will leave Indian hunters stranded without weapons one thousand miles from home; it will be the reason Alaska is purchased from Russia; it will cause a fashion sensation in all the major world centres; and it will firmly establish British Columbia as a firm member of the Dominion of Canada at a time when America was seriously thinking of annexing the west completely, to cut off both Canada and England from the Pacific.

The first seals were discovered in the South Pacific by Sir Francis Drake when he bravely and ruthlessly decided to raid every Spanish set-

tlement from Lima to San Francisco. In the waters of the south he came upon great herds of seals, some of which he killed to provide his ship with food and oil. He went on to pillage the Spanish colonies, but eventually arrived home in England with a few vials of oil and fabulous stories of the limitless herds of seal.

There was a ready demand for any type of pure oil at the time, which increased as industrialization gradually became a part of European life. Drake's oil came to be known as train-oil, and commanded a high price. Before long English ships were sailing for the south. The furs were dumped overboard, along with the meat. All that was wanted was the thick fat between the skin and the muscle. This "blubber" was melted down in tanks and guarded carefully during the long sail back to England.

The slaughter was parallelled only by that of the buffalo during America's railroad heyday some hundred years later. By 1800 one British ship reported a kill of 57,000; another, 65,000. By 1811 over sixteen million seals had been killed and the South Pacific was once more empty of British ships - but also of seals.

The seal fur was considered of little value at the time, although under the coarse outer hairs was one of the most beautiful furs in the world. It was an unknown Chinese who in 1800 discovered a process for removing the outer hair, and he kept it a secret until 1843. The Chinese were the market for Pacific furs and the Russians were their biggest suppliers. Hundreds of thousands of fox, marten and other land furs were traded each year for spices, tea, opium and silk. The sea mammal whose fur the Chinese valued most was the sea otter. Within a few years it was almost extinct, but the fur seal was ignored or the fur was shaved off and the skin used to make bags and luggage, until the unknown man in China discovered how to reveal the fur.

Suddenly China was voraciously demanding more and more fur seal skins. Peter the Great of Russia was very interested in this trade with China, as he could make a great deal of money by selling their goods to Europe, bypassing the Near East, traditional caravan route for Chinese commodities. In 1789 he issued a warrant of discovery to Captain Bering to explore the northern ocean and see if Siberia and North America were joined by land. Bering crossed Siberia on foot and built two ships on the Pacific. He discovered the Bering Sea and the great ice cap of the north but he sent back a young man with 2,000 otter skins and 6,000 blue fox skins. This young man, Gerassim Pribilof, also carried a story with him, half-legend, half myth, of islands in the northern sea covered with millions of seals. He returned and named them for himself: Pribilof. St. Paul and St. George were the principal rookeries for the North Pacific fur seals. There were other islands between Japan and the Pribilofs but they were not as abundant in seals as these other two. Czar Peter quickly took over control of them and when it was learned that the markets in Canton were paying high prices for seals the Russians began the killing and exporting of the skins.

In 1843 the Americans discovered a dye formula which destroyed the Chinese markets and ruined Russia's fur trade. The Russians were going broke with their wars and the excesses of the Czar's courts and in 1867 an American named Seward purchased what was then called "Seward's Folly" - now called Alaska - all for seven million dollars, including the Pribilof Islands and the great seal rookeries.

In a few years the secret of the fur seal pelt was known in Britain and America. A Professor Henry Wood, after the visiting of the Pribilofs, estimated the seal population in 1870 at five million plus.

He stated that they were so numerous man could never deplete them. In 1874 crews were sent from San Francisco to the rookeries. The kill was 400,000.

Although the Pribilof Islands were then under tight control of the Americans, the fur seal spent only the breeding season there. The remainder of the year they travelled in a great circle over the north Pacific, following the coast of North America and California north to Alaska, branching through the Aleutians into the Bering Sea. If America would not allow sealing on the Pribilofs, then Captain William Spring and Captain James Christianson were determined to hunt them on the high seas. The schooner *Surprise* hunted the migration routes with eight canoes manned by natives from Ucluelet and Nitinat. The take that year was one thousand pelts, and soon vessels were hunting them out of San Francisco, Port Townsend, Seattle and Victoria. Pelagic sealing was a lucrative business and by 1879 there were sixteen schooners outfitting at Victoria. The United States had made it against the law for its own citizens to hunt seals on the high seas and their ports were closed to sealers. The schooners shifted their registry to Victoria and continued to hunt.

The problem with their hunting methods was that most of the seals killed on the ocean sank before they could be caught and skinned. It was also very difficult to distinguish males from females. On the breeding grounds one bull fur seal could breed with a harem of up to fifty females. If only the young males were killed then the seal rookeries could be maintained. But the prices were high and the men anxious to get as large a catch as possible. There was no way to tell if a pelt was male or female after it was skinned and salted.

It was estimated that in 1882 there were one hundred thousand fur seal killed to obtain the fifteen thousand that were sent to England. The United States, seeing the danger to the rookeries and to their own lucrative business if the pelagic sealing continued, declared that the seals were American property whether on land or sea, and despatched swift gunboats to the North Pacific to control the sealers. Any schooner found with spears or rifles was seized and the crew arrested - at least the white men. Any Indians found on board were marooned on the nearest land, sometimes a thousand miles from home. Left without weapons or proper clothing, many a crew of hunters perished in the wild north.

But in the years following 1867 Captains Spring and Christianson had added new ships to their fleet. In 1870 the converted sloop *Reserve* under the command of Niles Moos and the schooner *Wanderer* with Captain Sebastian of Nanaimo sailed out of Barclay Sound with a crew of Ohiat hunters. J.D. Warren, a Prince Edward Islander, put out in the schooner *Thornton* as owner and master. They were followed quickly by other ships and crews, all of them damning the Americans for their high-handed actions on the high seas.

But the seizures continued and soon began to cut into the fleet. At any time, a schooner could be boarded by an American gunboat and if found with guns or spears aboard was impounded and left to rot in an American port. Many a Canadian found himself in prison. Soon the Russians and Japanese were impounding Victoria sealers and the Indians refused to sail on them. Captains greedy for the seal furs were soon impressing Indian crews by force. They either worked or starved and in the north the Kwakiutls almost went to war over the kidnapping of their people.

To be taken by an American was bad enough, but the Russians and Japanese were not so kind to their captured crews. Many men were left adrift in

small boats in the Bering Sea. In the early 1890's the Russian cruiser *Zabiaka* seized the *Maria, Carmelite, Rosie Olsen,* and the *Vancouver Belle* in the vicinity of the Copper Islands, which were seal rookeries still in Russia's possession on the east coast of Siberia. The sailors were imprisoned in Vladivostok and were finally rescued by an American who, upon finding they were incarcerated there, bought their release. He was Captain George Dewey, who later became an admiral in the United States Navy and won the battle of Manila Bay.

The conflicting claims over seizures and the depletion of the seal herds continued. In the 1850's the seals were said to be so thick you could almost walk on their backs from shore until you were out of sight of land. But in 1894 the slaughter was 500,000 seals, and a treaty signed in Paris allowed hunting on the high seas except for a sixty-mile radius around Pribilofs. By 1910 the herds were decimated to a mere 150,000 and in 1911 the Sealing Convention was signed by the United States, Great Britain, Canada, Russia and Japan. Pelagic sealing was outlawed by all signatories and the seal were to be carefully controlled by the companies working on the Pribilof Islands. A share in the annual revenues went to each signatory under the treaty and the great sealing fleet was doomed. In 1911 it was auctioned off to whoever had the money to bid. Steam had replaced sails and many of the schooners went for a song or were left to time and teredoes on the wharves.

But the romance of the great seal hunts left many stories behind. Of men set adrift on the ice, of Indians left to die on the Alaska coastline, of ships such as the *Carlotta G. Cox,* under its Captain Byer who left for the grounds 200 miles off the Japanese coast in 1894. On April 7 the boats were launched and were soon caught in a tidal rip

followed by gales and were quickly driven off from the mother ship. Days later they drifted ashore in Japan after suffering from lack of water and food, sharks and an attack by a sea monster that reared up out of the ocean and almost capsized them all. As it passed them by it bit off a three-quarter inch painter as casually as if it were a thread.

In that same year the *Agnes MacDonald* out of Victoria lost a crew to a gale and the men were never found, although their boat was discovered still outfitted with hardtack and fresh water, her guns lashed to her seats. The *May Belle* that year lost three boats to storm and fog with all crews, and the schooners *Matthew Turner* and *Rosie Sparks* were wrecked in storms. The great novelist Jack London wrote stories of the year he shipped out of Victoria and Rudyard Kipling wrote poems about Lukannon, a long rookery beach on St. George Island in the Pribilof group. Millionaires' yachts were used to catch seal, alongside splintery, patched old boats. Men died in the freezing waters of the Bering Sea, and men made fortunes, including several Indians who after a time owned their own schooners and set record catches. Many an old salt told his stories in the saloons on Johnson Street in Victoria, a miniature Barbary Coast full of sailors and gamblers, whores and drunks. The Occidental and Jubilee saloons took many a man's pay of the season in a quick night of gambling and drinking from demijohns of imported Scotch whiskey. The men were wild and free and the women just as mad.

The great sealing fleet of Victoria is no more but many a tale is locked away in the city archives and in the minds of the few men left who remember those great and terrible days when they hunted the fur seal out of Victoria and damned the cruisers and gunboats as they took their toll of the disappearing herds.

Non-European Iron Among the Haida: New Evidence

It has been generally postulated, even concluded by some, that the culmination of North West Coast Indian woodwork and totem carving came with the fur trade. This period, with its associated tools, wealth and leisure time, is supposed to have produced work which far surpassed any of these people's earlier efforts. 1840 to 1880 has been cited as the "golden age" of totem carving in the Queen Charlotte Islands, for example.

Putting the social implications of the fur trade aside, and examining its physical implications, it is obvious it gave access to iron tools. However, it is evident that iron tools were available to the Indians before the coming of the White Man, therefore taking away much of the previous importance put on the White Man's influence. The metal was worked and set into the tools so important in the now famous art of totem carving.

When Perez traded with the Haidas off Langara Island in 1774, "It was perceived they had a great fondness for articles made of iron for cutting, but they did not want small pieces. We were interested also to see that the women wear rings on their fingers and bracelets of iron and copper, and the great value they set on them. Of these metals some were seen, though very little." The copper could possibly have come from trading with the Tlingit Indians or the Russians.

In 1884, J.G. Swan bought, "fine images, three inches long, made of pure native copper by swedging and cutting." The old Indian woman who he procured them from said that according to legend, they were traded from the Copper River Indians. Native copper is known to be fairly abundant in the Chilkat country of the Tlingit.

The iron perhaps came from the wreckage of Japanese junks that were swept onto the northwest coast. There are at least eleven records of Japanese junks being found off or wrecked on the northwest coast. Four of these occurred on the B.C. or Washington coast.

One of these was on the west coast of the Charlottes in 1831. There were apparently two survivors from this wreck who were enslaved by the Haidas. Later in 1833, these Japanese were bought by the Hudson's Bay Company at Fort Simpson and given their freedom. In 1833 a junk was wrecked near Cape Flattery.

"Many of her crew had perished and several dead bodies were found headed up in firkins, in the customary Japanese style, ready for burial. Out of seventeen persons, only two men and a boy had survived." They were rescued by the Indians and eventually taken to England on the H.B.C. vessel *Lama* in 1837 and later to Japan.

Another junk was wrecked at Nootka Sound in 1875, of which we have no further information.

In 1927 a Japanese fishing boat was found adrift off Cape Flattery, encrusted with barnacles and seaweed. Ten bodies were found aboard, some in a dismembered condition indicating they had been used for food. The boat had been adrift for eleven months.

These and other unchronicled wrecks contained much iron. A wreck of a junk found on an island off Southern California was described thus: "The planks were fastened together on the edges with spikes or bolts of a flat shape with the heads all on side." These junks have probably been drifting onto the coast from at least as far back as 1639. At that time, under the Shogun Igemitsu, an edict was issued commanding all junks to be built with open sterns and large square rudders. This rendered them unfit for long sea voyages and confined them mostly to their own country as the Shogun wished. When these vessels were caught in storms and pushed out to sea, the rudders often broke. Falling helplessly in the troughs of the waves, the masts too were smashed about and eventually broken.

These vessels were carried across to the northwest coast by the Kuro Shiwo, or black stream, that travels at an average speed of ten miles a day. Japanese material continues to come across to the coast today; during a year I spent roaming the Queen Charlotte Islands by kayak, I found every kind of Japanese trash, glass balls, bamboo poles and other somewhat less popular items - underarm deodorant cans, plastic bottles, and even a marine mine from World War II with Japanese characters on it.

Dr. John Swanton in 1970 recorded a most interesting legend concerning a wreck of what was probably a Japanese junk. His informant was a Mr. Abraham of Skidegate, who had originally learned the tale from an old man of Ninstints village at Anthony Island. The story was said to

boat nail

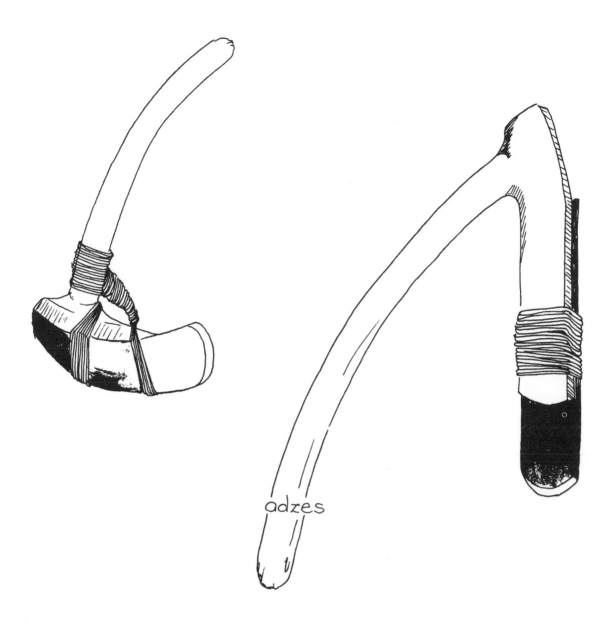

adzes

chisels

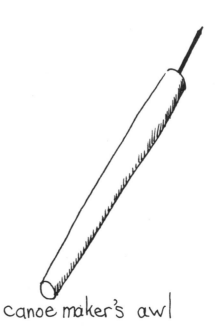

canoe maker's awl

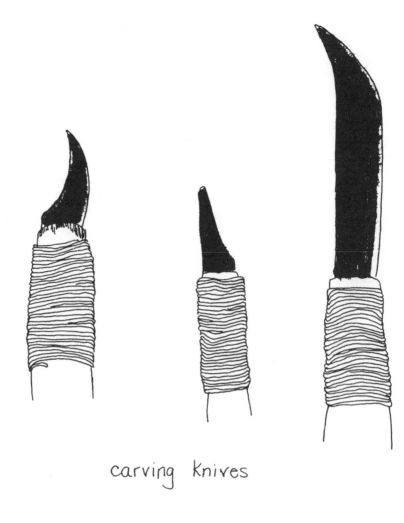

carving knives

halibut hooks

have taken place at Yaku Lanas or Middle-town. This village was on Gowgaia Bay, in a very rough part of the west coast of Moresby Island. The legend is reproduced in full; I have added several foot notes of my own, besides Mr. Swanton's.

The Story of Him Through Whom La'gua Spoke

At Middle-town La'gua spoke thgugh a certain one. After he had acted as shaman for a time, while they sang for him, he began to whip something. At once he began to fast. All that time he whipped it. The town people wanted to see it. They wanted to see the thing he spoke about.[1]

After a while he sang that he held his supernatural power, La'gua, in his teeth at the end of the town. His supernatural power also made the water smooth for some time.[2] *All that time they fished for black cod. Every time they came in from fishing those who handled the lines gave him two black cod. His wife had a great quantity.*

By and by La'gua told him to go out fishing with them. He went with them at once. After they had fished for black cod for a while and had started away, they came to a point of iron sticking out of the water. Then the shaman sat upon it.[3] *And he gave them directions. "Go in, and then come out to meet me," he said to him.*

As soon as they had unloaded their black cod, they went out to meet him. It was evening. They called out to one another. Then they approached each other. When they called out after it had become dark he answered them. At once they went to him. Immediately all the canoes began to tow it ashore. They used a black-cod fish-line for the purpose.

After they had paddled for a while, it become broad daylight, and they towed it in at the end of the town. It was only for Those-born-at-Sa'ki.

After they were through eating they began to split off iron wedges. When they got through with that they began to hammer out the iron. They made spears and knives of it. The news of this iron passed over the island. At once people started to come for the iron. They exchanged a slave for one piece of iron. They kept selling it. They worked this into war spears throughout all of the villages.

This story is quite probably based on a real event in Haida history. The great value of iron is obvious, yet is certainly not an unknown thing to the inlet people if they were so eager to procure it. They undoubtedly would use it for woodworking tools as well as for their weapons. This story, presumably, takes place before the coming of the White Man.

Notes to Legend.

1. It was his supernatural helper. The people fasted and drank sea water for ten days with him. Fasting and drinking warmed sea water till one vomited was a common habit of the Haidas when they desired success in one facet of their lives.
2. Calm water was one of the most prayed for things on the West Coast.
3. The Shaman treats this "point of iron", or most probably the remains of a Japanese junk, as if it were a whale. He claimed to have caught it with the help of his supernatural powers.

Bibliography

Barbeau, Marius. *Totem poles, a by product of the fur trade.* Scientific Monthly, Dec. 1942, Lancaster, Penn.

Bolton, H.E. *Fray Juan Crespi, Missionary Explorer on the Pacific Coast. 1769 - 1774.* Berkeley, 1927.

Brooks, C.W. *Japanese wrecks stranded and picked up adrift in the North Pacific Ocean.* San Francisco, 1876.

Swan, J.G. *Report on the Queen Charlotte Islands.* Smithsonian report for 1884.

Swanton, J.R. *Contributions to the Ethnology of the Haida.* Vol. 5, Part 1, Jesup North Pacific Expedition, New York, 1905.

Swanton, J.R. *Haida Texts and Myths.* Wash. 1909.

Carved knife handle

The Tale of the Snot Boy

God created woman on the island of Yuquatl. She was entirely alone in the rain forest; her only companions were dogs without tails, deer without antlers and ravens without wings. She was so lonely she cried; morning, noon and night she wept. And Quautz hearing her bawling took pity on the young woman.

One morning when the woman was out digging clams with a sharp root, a copper canoe appeared in her cove. The canoe was full of young men paddling with copper paddles. She was so stunned by the sight that she couldn't run and hide. When the canoe touched the beach, the handsome young man standing in the bow stepped ashore.

This man was the God Quautz. And he'd come to this island beach, so he told the woman, to give her a companion. When she heard this she once again burst into tears: she cried so hard that her nose began to drip. Suddenly she sneezed the snot onto the gravel at the God's feet.

The young man ordered her to pick up the yellow discharge. To her amazement she found a tiny man, perfectly formed, struggling free of her snot. She was so amazed that she barely heard Quautz telling her to keep the man in progressively larger clam shells until he grew to man size.

When the young woman finally began to thank
Quautz, his canoe was only a glint far off-shore.
Hearing a strange noise she looked up: a raven
was flying from tree to tree, deer crossing the tidal
flats tossed their antlers at a pup chasing them,
wagging his tail.

Captain Herbert Clifton, a Tsimshian Indian, was born in the village of Metlakatla, a few miles to the west of the city of Prince Rupert, in the late 1870's or early 1880's. It is very difficult for me to determine, with any accuracy, his exact age as I saw no change in his appearance in the fifteen years we were closely associated.

My first meeting with him was in 1906 when I was going to school at the Inverness Cannery on the Skeena River. He was then Master of the steam tug *Florence* owned by the J.H. Todd interests of Victoria and used as a tender for Inverness. I have been unable to trace her builder but think it safe to assume that it was Orvig at Port Essington. She very much resembled the design that he was known for.

A couple of years after this the North Coast Towing Company associated with Georgetown Sawmills at Georgetown, which is 17 miles north of Prince Rupert and 9 miles south of Port Simpson, bought the steam twin screw steel tug *Topaz* in Vancouver and brought her north to take care of the expanding delivery of lumber to the new city of Prince Rupert as well as the canneries along the coast. Captain Clifton was hired to take command.

Captain Clifton's certificate was an unusual one in that it was a certificate of Service rather than a certificate of Competency which was usually granted. Certificates such as this were granted in those days by the Department of Marine and Fisheries and it would seem that they had bent their rules to some extent to accommodate Captain Clifton on the advice of the Anglican Church.

Much of my time served at sea before getting my Master's Certificate was served under Herb and I can say, without doubt, I learned more of handling a tug from him than from any other source. He was also a sterling example of a man.

As a young man growing up in Metlakatla Herb married an Indian girl and, being restless to get away from the village where there was no employment except in the fishing season, he and his bride went to Hazelton and signed on with the Hudson's Bay Company to pack on the Babine Trail.

They were a husky pair. Herb stood well over six feet, while his wife was a well built woman taller and huskier than the average of her people. He told me that he carried on his back as a regular load, three fifty-pound sacks of flour while his wife carried a regular load of seventy-five pounds. This, for a distance of nearly eighty miles.

When the packing season closed the couple returned to Metlakatla where they built one of the nicest homes in the village overlooking the sea. Later Herb joined Bishop Ridley's mission boat and finally got command. In addition to his duties in connection with navigation he was also called upon to play the organ. Herb was the cleverest musician I have ever had the good fortune to meet. His favorite instrument was the violin but he could get music out of any instrument placed in his hands. I remember his first experience with a saxophone. A "wise guy", thinking that at last he had come up with an instrument that would stump Herb, handed him the sax and sat back with a smug grin, waiting for Herb to fall flat on his face. But after doodling around a bit he came out with some of the hits of the day.

Herb was always a welcome guest at our home in Georgetown and often when he was held over waiting for a tide he would stroll into our living room and sit down at the piano and play enchanting music for hours on end. These visits were greatly enjoyed by my mother because although she played she also enjoyed hearing someone else. There was not much opportunity for Mother to enjoy someone else's playing as we lived in a very isolated area.

When the first pipe organ in northern British Columbia was installed in the Anglican Church in Metlakatla, Herb took over as organist. On one memorable occasion when I had called him to Vancouver to take one of the tugs north after refit I learned that one of the world's renowned violinists was conducting a show at the old arena building. I bought two tickets for the recital and took Herb to his first such entertainment. When I glanced over to see his reaction to the violin solo I was not surprised to see the tears rolling down his cheeks. He was that kind of person.

One of Herb's more astonishing accomplishments was the ability to write "calling cards" freehand in old English script. His ability got to be well known with the result that he did the cards for a good many of the fashionable ladies of the time.

Although his hands were large and he was as strong as a bull he could, after making a few samples, go on and write fifty or a hundred cards which could not be distinguished from the original. His log books were also written in this beautiful manner and were a sight to behold. How I regret not keeping one!

Herb was not without wit. One time he was assisting a surveyor who was mapping several islands in Venn Passage not far from the boundaries of Metlakatla. He and the surveyor had taken time out to eat their lunch and before they resumed work the surveyor heard a call from nature and went into the bush. Shortly after, he asked Herb for the Indian name of the island as he was anxious to preserve the native names as much as possible. Herb answered "Clianchi", which sounded alright and was carefully noted on the map. It turned out that the word meant "The island that was s--- on." The name still appears on charts of the area.

As I moved away from the north in 1919 and did not return until the Second World War days, after Herb had gone to the happy hunting ground, I was robbed of the opportunity to continue my association with this fine friend and superb gentleman.

BOOK REVIEW:
MIST ON THE RIVER

To start with, this is a biased review, so much so that I suppose you could call it an advertisement. Being a latter-day academic drop-out, I don't have to get into the vagaries and niceties of whether or not Hubert Evans is a major or minor novelist, a proponent of regionalism in Canadian literature or any other time/space/or culture slot I could fit him into.

Let's flash first to a scene along the beach at Roberts Creek, where the salmon are crowding forward in their autumnal trip home. The stream in front of Hubert's had been dammed by some high seas the winter before and Mister and Missus Salmon were having a hard time making it past the jam. Hubert, though pressing on in years, when he found the creek was blocked, hauled out his pick and shovel and cleared the way, a matter of course.

Hubert's also written a number of novels, as well as trucked, sailed, hiked, rowed, and swam over most of the coast and a good chunk of the interior. One of his books sprang from some years teaching with his wife up in the Hazelton area. The Gitkasan people there became their close friends - the warmth and understanding that flowed between them becomes evident in the book Mist on the River.

Just reissued as a number in McClelland and Stewart's New Canadian Library, the novel brings a neglected but central problem of B.C.'s history to light. Life in a country will change with technology and communication but some of the old ways and patterns are inevitably imprinted onto the new. When two races meet, or collide, the waves of impact will travel wide and echo far.

The young native protagonist is caught in a unique web, spun by the racial intrigue, but whose patterns have been felt in all our lives. The family and tribe with the old, time-honoured ways, the dreams of the ancestors on the starless nights, pull in one direction. In the other pull the voices of the New, the Unknown, the promise of better things ahead, Progress, which for the native of this coast from roughly 1800 on has worn a white mask.

The voice of the old is Paul, hereditary chief, who is the craftsman, canoe-maker for his people and keeper of those ways, and for the whites at the cannery, the boss in the boat shed. He tests the allegiances of young Matt who must struggle with the self-contempt arising from being a member of such a "backward" race. The people from upriver go to the coast seasonly each summer, to work in the canneries around Prince Rupert and Rivers Inlet. The novel contains some fine descriptions of that migrant existence at both ends, coastal and headwater, from the tar paper shacks on pilings where the fresh and salt water mingle, to the fine stands of maple in the sun-lit valleys.

Where once the economic life of the people was tied to barter with the coastal tribes and the great run of oolachan, now it is hinged not to a natural pulse but to the economics of the market. No longer is the take-home pay measured in fish oil for food and fuel but rather in dollars to be spent in company stores and white supermarkets.

But there are the good whites too. The school teachers and the truly humanitarian doctors whose modern ways, though distrusted, save lives. Moral questions are held in abeyance, in half-light, riddled with the contradictions that reality entails. The company, the doctors, the teachers, the old natives and the young all striving as best they can to make sense out of the whirling currents of the mingling of the racial streams, all make the mistakes compounded by the nature of their desires.

A review of this book fits into this magazine in a very crucial way, pinpointing as it does one of the underlying dynamics of any story of the coast. This coast, in which we face these ghosts.

EDITORIAL

You can spot a fisherman anywhere. There is a roll to his walk. There is a certain mournful whine in his voice, sharpened by years of complaining about bad catches.

There's a sadness, a slowness, as if too deep knowledge of the darkness below life's surfaces had taken the hurry out of him. A patience borne of waiting — waiting for openings, waiting for weather and tide, waiting for fish. No one learns more of waiting than fishermen.

In their eyes is none of the animal spark you find in the loggers' eyes, the scent of male animal, twitching tail. Fishing is not so dumbly masculine a species of work as logging; women take well to its slow but complicated rhythm.

The logger is up in the pub bothering her maids and starting fights; the fisherman is down on the float, sitting on a fishbox mending gear and jawing politics. The logger has a new tinsel shirt he will tell you how grandly he paid for, but it will probably be on his hotel room floor once used, and ruined when he stumbles back to camp. The fisherman has on wool and tweeds bagged to his shape, and he prefers to drink on the boat among his own.

There is a diffuse deepness in the fisherman's eye, like the cloudy gulf he lets his gear into, and lets his mind into. The logger's work is fast and dangerous; he must keep his eyes open. The fisherman works blind, feeling his familiar but never-known world with the sightless, superstitious part of the mind.

The logger is strong like the land but the fisherman is stronger, like the sea.

THEY'VE GOT THE DIRTY THIRTY BLUES, Tom and Jack, drifting around the inlet mouth by Salmon Rock in leaky skiffs, trying to scratch a living, and a damn meagre living at the best of times. They only pay seven cents a pound for dressed coho and if the boys hustle five bucks a day they're doing pretty fair.

Tom and Jack are hometown boys from the nearby village but many of the others have come from Vancouver or elsewhere. They live, these transients, in tents and makeshift shacks on the beach, just within the protective hook of the bay where the village lies. They are proud men, choosing to maintain some vestige of dignity in preference to panhandling, stealing or taking relief. It's a marginal existence. Maybe if they're lucky they can save enough in five or six years to put a down payment on a gas-boat. Then they can head upcoast, get in on the big runs and make some halfway decent money. Meanwhile she's a hand-to-mouth proposition.

It's Sunday but a workday nonetheless. Can't afford any time off at this racket. Their equipment is rockbottom minimal — crude bamboo poles and gut lines — all they can afford. Some of them also carry herring-rakes in hope of striking a school of "stinkies" for bait. The rakes are used to scoop the thickly-clustered fish into the stern of the boat like so many wriggling leaves.

But the salmon are the money fish. They hook them laboriously, one at a time, whenever the stubborn buggers condescend to bite. There are maybe twenty boats in all, working fairly close together. Tom and Jack are no more than fifteen feet apart. The salmon ain't biting worth a damn.

Lost, lean years when the village is young and the world a simpler place of one-to-one relationships and fixed beliefs. The school science books still hold the atom to be indivisible, and television's an expensive gimmick you've heard the odd rumour about but sure don't ever expect to see. The moon's just a thing in the sky that pulls the tides around — too damn far away to even worry about. Inconceivable war that will end the Depression forever in North America and unleash horror and deprivation of a much more drastic sort elsewhere, waits scant years off. They are holding a bloody dress rehearsal in Spain and someone you know knows someone in the Mackenzie-Papineau Battalion but it is all very remote and doesn't have much bearing on the price of fish.

The price of fish is traditionally as little as the canneries can get away with paying you — two cents a pound for spring salmon, three-quarters of a cent for humpback, ten cents apiece for dogs. A fledgling union — the P.F.C.U. — is attempting to organize and negotiate a better shake for the fishermen but it's a tough struggle. Partly it's the inflexible attitude of the operators but another major source of difficulty is the large Japanese fleet whose complacency toward low prices tends to maintain the niggardly status quo.

The skiff fishermen are the worst off of all, making little more than bare grub money on the best of days. There are maybe five hundred rowboats actively working the lower Gulf. Salmon Rock at the mouth of Howe Sound is only one of the spots they frequent. They gather at numerous points —

SKIFFS, GILLNETS

AND   POVERTY-STICKS

Lasqueti Island, Poor Man's Rock — praying for strikes with considerably more fervour than any Sunday wonder from Shaughnessey Heights with his expensive tackle. They work in as close proximity as possible to the fish buyers, who advance them food and tobacco. Day after day, as long as the weather's even half feasible, they row seaward to woo the elusive quarry — to bob for salty hours and dream of palmier possibilities.

Most of them graduate to gas-boats in time. They are unprepossessing craft with plodding Easthope or Vivian engines, but they beat rowing all to hell. By God, they're mobile at last!

As they head upcoast that first, independent time, they pass their former comrades in their cockleshells, still hauling them in the hard way. They wave in an offhand, superior manner, bound for Smith's Inlet, Rivers Inlet, the Nass, the Skeena — brawling northern waters and big summer runs. The canneries are booming — there are eighteen in Rivers Inlet alone — and they'll process all the fish you can feed them but the money is still a long way from good. If a man can clear six hundred dollars after food and expenses it's a good season. Still, it is a definite step up the ladder, for all that.

The game of gillnetting, while safer than some, is not without its hazards. The obvious one of course is simply falling overboard and drowning. In rough water or when a guy has taken on too much booze this possibility is always present. Crazily enough, in common with other sailors, many fishermen have never learned to swim, but even a good swimmer would have little chance in a coal black blowing sea with no lifejacket and his unconcerned boat thudding farther away from him every second. Another way a man can get it is by asphyxiation from carbon monoxide fumes. Boats are sometimes found circling aimlessly with their occupants unconscious or dead.

In one such incident, slightly more gruesome than most, the man had collapsed against the very engine whose gases had undone him and the flywheel, by the time he was found, had worn half his head away.

Then there is always the chance of being wrecked, for the coastal waters can be a maze of circuitous treachery, especially in fog, mined with deadheads, hidden reefs and whirlpooling rapids. Many stretches of the jagged shoreline are desolate as the dawn of time, devoid of humanity for miles in any direction. A man cast up in such an area, perhaps shivering in some blind cul-de-sac of a cove walled round with

unclimbable cliffs, might wait for days before being found — sometimes forever. Savage storms can boil up without warning in the open waters and high winds charge down the inlets from snowy channelling valleys. There are certainly dangers, but the men face them with philosophy.

Gillnetting by hand is rough, exhausting work. The nets vary in depth and mesh size according to the variety of salmon being fished, but they all share one factor in common — they're heavy as hell to wrestle back aboard with any kind of catch in them. Really gets you in the arms and back. Sometimes you get so goddamn tired, you feel like chucking the whole business and going back to the skiffs but some old tenacity keeps you going, the same tenacity that has sustained fishermen in all the waters of the world for centuries. Their ghosts pull with you.

When the season is finished, the men head home with wallets, if not bulging, at least comfortably lined. In the off months many of them will put up the poverty-sticks, as trolling poles are wryly called, and, weather permitting, cruise the sheltered sounds in search of spring salmon. Trolling is simply a more elaborate form of skiff fishing. The poverty-sticks are in essence giant fishing rods, jutting out from either side of the boat like wooden antennae. From these hang the trolling lines with hooked steel flashers attached at regular intervals. When the fish are really biting, as many as twelve lines may be used but they are seldom biting with any such gusto, particularly in the sparse winter months. It's slim pickings for the most part, which accounts for the nickname.

Now the war, long threatening, explodes across Europe. It's still a distant thing, however terrible — a misfortune involving a lot of very faraway people who should know better — but the repercussions are not long in being felt, no matter what your leanings or allegiances.

The fishing industry is of course affected along with everything else. Many drop the trade and head overseas, if not to save some great aunt, then for plain, damn adventure. As for the rest, people still have to eat. Fishing, along with logging, pulp milling, mining, farming and other key trades, is soon classified as essential work. Its practitioners are largely made draft exempt and frozen to their jobs. Fish prices at last make a significant jump and the lid comes off generally as far as quota regulations are concerned. It's a mad scramble for wealth. Men who were walking around with holes in their shoes a few months before are suddenly flush.

A whole new branch of fishing evolves during the war and a lot of money is made at it. This is the catching of dogfish — a primitive and highly prolific relative of the sturgeon, hitherto of no commercial value due to the long standing belief among fishermen that its flesh is inedible — fit only for fertilizer — despite considerable proof to the contrary. Now however, diet research burgeons and vitamins become increasingly important. The liver of the dogfish is rich in Vitamin D and it is hunted for this sole organ. The rest is thrown away. They're paying a pretty buck for a chunk of the guts, and the gulls can have what's left.

Apart from the introduction there is no radical change in the general pattern of things for the first two years of the war. The fish still make their coastal migrations on mysterious cue, the men still sail to waylay them — except that there's a lot more money around now and the skiff fleet dwindles noticeably as more and more of its members graduate to gasboats.

Then comes Pearl Harbour. The hostilities spread like a brushfire around the globe. All at once, they're uncomfortably close to your own backyard. Suddenly those energetic little guys you've been fishing alongside for years are no longer simply your rivals but sinister enemy aliens. And then they're gone, the lot of them, in one fell, Defence Department swoop. The internment of the Japanese will become a subject of much hindsight controversy in the relaxed atmosphere of later years, and will generally be conceded to be somewhat of an over-reaction, although it seemed a reasonable idea at the time.

The hapless Japanese, most of them no more loyal or disloyal than any other citizen, are forced to sell their boats and then shipped to Interior camps to wait out the war under surveillance. Their disappearance leaves many empty gillnetters and a huge gap in the fishing fleet, soon filled by an influx of eager newcomers to the game, many undoubtedly bent on staying out of uniform.

It is a free-booting period of outright plunder. Overfishing reaches scandalous proportions with no thought for tomorrow. Hell, the way they're burning up the world, there may be no tomorrow! This shortsighted don't-give-a-damn attitude results in the near-depletion of some stocks and dangerous thinning of others. It will lead to skimpy runs, impoverished years, but no one considers this. Live for now!

In any coastal town in those war years it is impossible to be unaware of the fishermen. The very tempo and flavour of village life is geared to their comings and goings. Years are judged good or bad according to the salmon runs; the economy waxes and wanes to the vagrant rhythms of the fish. In a good year, there are smiles on the most taciturn faces, new clothes for the wife and kids, money for beer and updated equipment like radiophones and power drums. In a bad year, wry faces predominate, belts are tightened, credit extensions awkwardly requested from local merchants. Often the younger men go logging as necessity demands, helping to foul some of the very spawning streams that beckon the salmon shoreward in the first place. The oldtimers put up the poverty-sticks and troll for whatever meagre bounty they can get. They don't believe in mixing trades.

To Rivers Inlet and the other northern meccas all such boats as are able set out in the late spring to hopefully reap their share of the yearly harvest. Often the younger wives go along with their men to work the canneries that still flourish in the upcoast inlets. Most of the sons go too, as soon as they are old enough to be useful.

The fishermen are Scots and Finns for the most part, proud, weatherpummelled men, left wing to the extreme in their political leanings, fond enough of their drink but able to carry it well and given to consuming it in the privacy of their homes. They dress, except for weddings, funerals and other formal occasions, in a similar rough-and-ready fashion — heavy brown woollen pants, police suspenders, thick work shirts with longjohns showing underneath even in summer, mackinaws of various patterns and colours but frequently simple grey, elasticsided fishermen's slippers. For headgear they favour toques or cotton caps. The younger men often add a few colourful variations of their own but the oldtimers are as conservative in their dress as they are radical in their politics. They tend to be close-spoken, a trait learned over many years of lonely, rocking sea hours.

But if most of the fishermen prefer to keep their own counsel, there are always a few who do not. These are the out-and-out reprobates, bachelors for the most part, who scrape only a fringe living from fishing when they bother to go out at all. They spend most of their waking hours sitting, in one state of inebriation or another, around the decks and holds of their invariably ill-kept boats. These unsanitary characters have names like Dirty Alec or Old Swen and thirsts of an extremely catholic nature, but they are never unwilling to pass on their own version of fishing lore — lurid accounts of knife-fights in netlofts, groggy trysts with Indian girls from the production lines, record runs when the fish swam thick as fleas on a dog's back, ghostships, gambling and buddies who came to bad ends.

As the war comes to an end, the fishing business slowly rolls into another phase. The short-lived dog-fishing industry dies with the development of synthetic vitamins, cutting off a valuable source of revenue for many and relegating that much-maligned creature to the status of a nuisance fish again.

Equipment is becoming increasingly more sophisticated. Nylon nets are now coming into general use but they are much more expensive than the old type. Radar and sonar devices are being installed by many boats and some sort of radiophone is becoming almost mandatory. There are holdouts of course among some of the more recalcitrant oldtimers and one such, a grizzled Scot by the name of Kenny Campbell, suffers a rather unnerving experience as a result.

Campbell, an elderly man and semi-retired, has been fishing the coastal waters the better part of his life. On this particular occasion he is on his way home from Rivers Inlet after the summer run. His boat, the *Betty*, is a battered thirty-footer and its 10-14 Easthope, which has been running on sheer nerve for a long time, is on its last legs. When the old engine splutters and dies a few hours out of harbour it's no surprise to its owner, who's dealt with the same situation many times, but this time it appears that no amount of monkeywrenching, coaxing or cursing is going to revive the old girl. Scantily-provisioned and radioless, Campbell watches the coastline gradually fade from sight as he is swept oceanward by a southeaster, the *Betty* tossed upward and heaved back into giant swells, water rushing in and out of the cabin.

After six days the storm finally abates enough that Campbell can tackle the old Easthope again. After several hours he gets her going again and for two days heads east, but no sooner does the coastline come into sight once more than the engine gives up the ghost again. No gas.

But the waves push him relentlessly toward the jagged coast and Campbell is helpless as they crash the *Betty* against a giant reef just off shore. Several hours later he finds himself on the beach, exhausted and half-starved, disoriented, talking to himself. Somehow a benevolent fate leads him to a hunters' cabin in the nearby woods, where, at the end of his rope, he lies down to die. For another week he keeps himself alive there, until he is miraculously spotted by a small plane and the Coast Guard comes to the rescue, forty miles south of Cape Flattery in Washington State. After a period of recuperation in hospital, he returns to Vancouver, leaving his unsalvageable boat behind him. He leaves his fishing days behind him too, for after this harrowing ordeal Kenny Campbell has had more than enough of the sea. Later, he will discuss his inadvertent odyssey with a certain dry humour. "Missed my pipe a hell of a lot more than the grub."

altogether and re-sold for other purposes. This effectively limits the number of boats working the coast in any given year.

The cost of maintaining a complex of upcoast canneries close to the fishing grounds begins to loom prohibitive. It becomes infinitely more practical to load the fish aboard huge packers and haul them, stored in brine, to modern processing plants in Vancouver and Prince Rupert. Here they are close to shipping facilities and retail outlets. One by one, like snuffed out candles, these rackety old salmon factories with their piling perched shades, their moribund belts, rancid stinks and Iron Chinks — begin to die. One by one, they are abandoned like wornout toys along the sopping shores of Rivers Inlet and the Nass.

Today things are pretty much mechanized and orderly in the B.C. fishing business. Expensive too. Hell, in the old days you could outfit as fine a boat as you could want for $5,000. Now it costs anywhere from $40,000 on up. Those damn licences keep going up every year too. There's lots of guys around whose licences are worth more than their gillnetters.

The main trouble now is with the offshore fishing. Japanese and sometimes Russian ships with ultramodern equipment, cutting into the runs beyond the twelve-mile limit. There'll be a good many International Courts of Inquiry before they sort this one out. Meantime, there'll be Cod Wars off Iceland and maybe Salmon Wars here — who can tell?

The game goes on, and for the most part it's all

Few oldtimers make their exits from the business in such dramatic fashion. Most depart the game without fanfare as a concession to advancing years and ebbing energies. There is no shortage of younger men waiting to fill their boots and the number of boats working the B.C. waters remains constant.

Indeed, without the rigorous controls exercised by the Department of Fisheries, many men would enter the trade. But important lessons are learned during the unregulated war years, the chief of these being that fish are by no means an inexhaustible resource. Through development of hatchery programs, the stocks are gradually brought back to an approximation of their former strength and quota regualtions are strictly enforced. A system of licensing is instituted whereby individual boats are only allowed to work the salmon runs for a ten-year period. They are then purchased by the government through a buyback fund, phased out of the industry

pretty routine. Gillnetting's not half the bullwork it used to be since power drums although these can be dangerous. A guy got caught in his net, wound round the drum and killed a while back. Still, as a general rule, they're pretty safe. Sure beats hand-hauling. Yeah, they're getting her down to a science.

Sunrise at the Fraser's Mouth

Orange peel, apple cores and beer bottles
bobbing among the nets,
everyone half asleep or fully,
the sun lost in mist.

Waiting always waiting for something
at the beginning of time we wait
for the miraculous babe to be born
or the price of fish to rise.

The burned mist lifts and melts and goes;
under the sea are rainbows.
We are cupped in watery chaos.
Milleniums swim in their womb.

Orange peel, apple cores, bottles
the packer trudges toward us.
There is no peace or content in this waiting
but we stir and move into wonder.

THE QAGAIS BROTHERS travel through Howe Sound in a canoe which is the youngest brother. The people at Squamish are glad to see them because they have no salmon. The Squamish think that maybe these heroes can get the Salmon People to visit. The Qagais agree, but only Snookum, the sun, knows where the Salmon People live.

They change youngest brother into a salmon and attach him to the shore by a stout line. Snookum likes salmon but he is a wily sort, not about to fall into a trap. He puts all the brothers into a trance and flies down upon the salmon as an eagle, his bald head flashing like whitecaps. He pounces on the salmon, breaks the line and flashes back to the heavens. The third brother is changed into a whale and attached by a stouter cord to the shore. Snookum throws the brothers into a trance and flashes down on the whale, sinking sharp talons into its back. Though he pulls and heaves, he cannot break the line and soon the two brothers wake up.

"Don't struggle, Snookum," they call. "You can't get away unless we help you and we won't do that until you help us." Trapped, he agrees, telling the Qagais that the Salmon People are to be found a long way west, out beyond what is now Vancouver Island. "To visit them, you must prepare strong medicine, great power." As Snookum flies away, the brothers disperse to gather herbs and medicine. Next morning, Qagais and the Squamish sail for the west.

They paddle many days and finally arrive at an island surrounded by great floating chunks of charcoal. A foolhardy Squamish youth tries to skip his way across this barrier but slips and drowns. On the island's lee shore is found a safe beach, where smoke of rainbow hues arises from a beautiful village.

The Squamish approach the village, marvelling at its wonders, and are met by Chief Kos (Spring Salmon) who greets them and accepts their gifts of herbs. Two boys and two girls of the village enter the sea and become salmon; then are caught in a trap behind the village, are roasted and served to the travellers. The guests are warned to return all the bones back into the sea, careful not to destroy or lose any. The bones are thrown to the sea and soon the boys and girls are again seen playing with their friends. After several days of feasting, one of the Squamish, curious, withholds a bone and one of the children bursts into the lodge in tears, covering a gaping hole where his nose used to be. The missing bone is returned to the sea and his nose is whole again.

The corpse of the youth who had drowned washes up and is brought back to life by the Qagais. Each kind of salmon offers him their eyes, since his were lost in the sea. Those of the dog salmon fit.

Kos promises the Squamish that he and his people will visit them so long as they treat the bones as they were shown, so that the people will be able to return home healthy. The Squamish are satisfied. Now the people will have enough to eat. They return home and bid goodbye to the Qagais.

The·Welc

SUCH MYTHS AND ASSOCIATED CEREMONIALS are found from the Tsimshian in the north on the Skeena as far south as North Central California with the Northern Maidu, and east as far as the Lemhi Shoshone in Idaho and the Paviotso of Pyramid Lake in Nevada. Salmon was the staple of life on the north coast and far inland, occupying the place of the buffalo to the plainsmen or corn to the southwesterners.

"We believe that everything happens in cycles — life moves from birth to death to birth again. If anything happens to interrupt that cycle, it is destroyed."

the fish would instantly smell it and abandon him, so that he, his friends and relations, must starve." British ships cruising the coast found that the Indians would not part with raw fish but would only give away fish that had been cooked.

The native people understood clearly their dependence on the salmon and had no wish to offend it. Deer and salmon were never eaten together. They were taken in different seasons and to eat them at the same time would be to muddle the cycle and offend one of the animals. The Indian was woven into this pattern of life as preserver — not even as one link in a great chain of being, but rather as warp in a tapestry of flux. Nature was not a playground for the drama of Christian salvation, where matter and spirit struggled for man's soul.

In the First Salmon Ceremony, the Coast Indian revealed his relationship with the salmon, and by extension, with his entire environment. The ritual followed with the first salmon was followed likewise with other animals, notably bear and deer, and in some areas, the first berry crops were greeted similarily.

The First Salmon Ceremony was one of the few that was not connected with clan or familial privileges but was a source of cohesion and renewal for the whole tribe. In this way it was a throwback to a more egalitarian society which existed before a changing technology, with a resulting concentration of power, had fully developed. With the arrival of white trade goods, which could so readily and visibly concentrate wealth, such features were bound to be submerged.

The ceremony of the First Salmon varied from tribe to tribe but everywhere the same elements are discerned. The normal handling of the salmon — the catch, its transport, cleaning, cooking, and consumption — was elaborated and lifted above the normal and everyday.

On the Skeena, the first Salmon was welcomed by all the shamans. Four of them carried it to the chief's house. They wore bird's down and red ochre, shook rattles and fanned the air with fan of eagle tail, carrying the salmon as they would a visiting chief, on a new mat of cedar bark. The young, ritually impure, left the lodge and the shamans entered, dancing a greeting to this honoured guest and singing songs of welcome. With great dignity, the fish was cut with mussel shell knives by two women shamans. They chanted to the salmon its honouring names — Chief Spring Salmon, Quartz Nose, Two Gills on Back, Lightning Following One Another, Three Jumps — cut its lower side, took out the stomach. Everyone present had some of the cooked fish. The remains were given to be consumed by the fire.

The fish was everywhere treated as befits a most welcome noble guest. Bird's down was scattered upon it and before it. The Kwakiutl had a different song for each variety, the fisherman and his wife performing the ceremony with simplicity. "O Supernatural One, O Swimmers, I thank you that you are willing to come to us."

me·Guests

The ritual of the First Salmon Ceremony, injunctions, and taboos were all oriented to maintaining the basic cycles of life, to preserving a balance between living and unliving and keeping an abundance of food for the people. Alexander MacKenzie, following a grease trail to the coast at Bella Coola in 1873, discovered that the natives there objected to his iron kettle and took it away from him because its smell might drive the salmon from the river.

The party of explorers nearly came to blows when they were about to break another taboo and ship venison in their canoe. "His only objection was to the embarking venison in a canoe on their river, as

Among some people, the first salmon was eaten only by the owner of the stream in which it was caught. Such was the case with the Nitinat tribes. "The first fish came in January. There was always a male and a female together in the stream. The chief would get those fish, the first that were caught. Later when he had caught enough, when he could put no more in his smokehouse, he would give the fish to the other people. There was always enough fish for everyone. He always gave away the fish from his stream."

Chief Charley Jones on the Renfrew Reserve explained the relation between the chief who owned the stream and fishing gear and the tribespeople. The owner had a great responsibility to his people and it seems the distribution was much more equitable than that imagined by MacKenzie when he came across the same arrangmeent on the Bella Coola. "One man appears to have an exclusive and hereditary right to what was necessary to the existence of those who are associated with him. I refer to the salmon wier or fishing place, the sole right of which confers on the chief an arbitrary power."

One of MacKenzie's concerns was the fact that such a massive wier as he saw could not have been constructed by one man alone, but would require the concerted effort of the entire tribe. Charley Jones' fish traps on the other hand, which he still uses, would be built by one or two men and would catch five to six hundred fish at a time.

MacKenzie describes the trap that he had seen. "It was nearly four feet above the level of the water at the time I saw it, and nearly the height of the bank on which I stood to examine it. The stream (50 yards wide) is stopped nearly two thirds by it. It is constructed by fixing small trees in the bed of the river in a slanting position (which could only be practicable when the level of the river is much lower than when I saw it) with the thick part downwards; over these there is laid a bed of gravel, on which is placed a range of lesser trees, and so on alternately until the work is brought to its proper height. Beneath it the machines are placed, into which the salmon fall when they attempt to leap over."

Wiers and traps were the most efficient and widespread means of fishing. They were never overly destructive of the run, as once enough salmon were caught to supply the tribe through the winter, the rest of the run was permitted to proceed. The traps were fitted with moveable doors which permitted the fish to pass upstream.

Wiers were used if the stream was shallow, narrow and relatively slow. On larger streams, they were placed on the sides. Commonly constructed from a series of tripods, against which was laid poles and lattice work, they would be used in conjunction with dipnets or spears. The framework was permanent but the lattice which was held in place by the current could be removed and replaced when damaged. The salmon, congested on the downstream side of the obstruction, were easily taken.

Great quantities of salmon were needed to tide the tribe over the winter. In 1904, a fisheries inspector on the Babine river found sixteen houses, about thirty feet square and eight feet high, filled with tiers of salmon. Acres of racks covered the shore. It was estimated that one family would use about 1,000 sockeye salmon during a winter. Such quantities could only be caught with a very efficient technology and an abundance of fish.

To aid the catching of salmon at wiers, various techniques were adopted by different tribes. Some built runways along the top of the wier, while others fished from canoe. Many hunted at night when the salmon were less wary, stabbing with submerged harpoons on contact. Some tribes favoured dark, rainy days and a muddy swirling river, but others, such as the Nanaimo tribe, laid white rocks on the bottom against which the fish appeared in sharp silhouette. Below the dams, fish were harpooned from rocks in mid-stream and along the shore.

The basket traps, primarily used on the east coast of Vancouver Island and the lower mainland, could also catch large numbers of fish with minimal effort. A salmon is unable to seek out a small opening when it is being swept downstream by the current, whereas it can find the entrance to a trap when forging ahead upstream. The traps were made of lattice and were usually curved into a cylindrical shape. A set of stakes or pickets was frequently used to guide the fish to the trap and also to keep the fish from leaping over it.

Another type of trap was a rectangular cage measuring about six feet by ten to twenty feet, open

on top and downstream, with side dams to guide the fish into the box where they were speared or netted from above. Another trap had its entrance on the upstream side and used slanted grids up which the salmon floundered. Where it was possible, grids were suspended under falls to catch the salmon whose leap faltered. In all the traps and wiers of this nature, the Indians made use of a process of natural selection, as it was the strongest salmon who would get upstream to spawn.

In tidal flat areas, such as those around Courtenay and Bella Bella, large rock constructions were built near river mouths to trap fish and seals when the tide fell. Remains of these rock walls can be seen at Powell River, Pender Harbour, and Comox among other places.

The spears which were used in conjunction with these constructions have been in evidence since the earliest times, showing an evolution in the types of harpoon used since the beginnings of salmon fishing perhaps 9,000 years ago. Commonly, these spears would be made of a light shaft of cedar up to twenty feet long, fitted with one or two socketed foreshafts, each nine or ten inches long. Heads were detachable and fitted with lines. Frequently the butt end would be splayed for greater speed and accuracy. The heads themselves were made of either two pieces of barbed bone, or wood armed with bone points, attached with sinew or cherry bark and spruce pitch. Flaring barbs of bone, horn, or hardwood made sure the fish was secure. When the fish was struck, the foreshaft came away from both shaft and spearhead. The spearhead, imbedded in the fish, was hauled in on a length of cord made of plaited sinew, kelp fiber, or Indian hemp. When not in use the spear tip was sheathed in spruce or cedar root. Spears were infrequently used alone, but almost always in conjunction with wiers.

In some places salmon were netted. Tsimshian myths describe the first use of a bag net dipped through an ice hole. Near Victoria and in the Gulf Island area, salmon were seined with a nettle fiber net hung from canoes, anchored to the bottom with stones. In a similar technique, two twenty-foot logs would be anchored at right angles to the shore. They were parallel and wide apart as the net, twenty to thirty feet, which was suspended from two canoes, lashed to the logs. Cedar rope lines were attached to each corner of the net, weighted at the seaward corners. The middle section bagged and caught the fish which were sometimes guided by streamers of kelp suspended on a line which was buoyed by a bladder or cedar float anchored in place with a rock. When a sufficient number of fish entered the net it was hauled in between the two canoes.

MacKenzie mentioned the use of dragnets in the Bella Coola country: "The men were fishing in the river with dragnets between two canoes. These nets are forced by poles to the bottom, the current driving them before it; by which means the salmon coming up the river are intercepted, and give notice of their being taken by the struggles they make in the bag or sleeve of the net." Similar nets were reported on the Fraser.

To make these nets, the dried stems and roots of nettles were rolled between the palm and the thigh, then joined with quick backward motions. Red cedar bark and willow bark were also sometimes used. The Sechelt and Squamish bands used Indian Hemp (apocynum cannibanum). In the southern part of the coast, women made the cordage and men wove the net.

The salmon thus caught would be taken and prepared for winter use – being salted, or smoked or dried – or would be consumed fresh, by boiling or roasting. The tribe would be in good spirits, for another year's run had been successful. The Salmon People were still pleased with the treatment they were receiving from the Indians. Once more they could return to their own homes.

"O Swimmers, this is the dream given by you, to be the way of my late grandfathers when they first caught you at play. I do not club you twice, for I do not wish to club to death your souls so that you may go home to the place where you come from. Supernatural Ones, you, Givers of Heavy Weight, I mean this, Swimmers, why should I not go to the end of the dream given by you? Now I shall wear you as a neckring going to my house, Supernatural Ones, you Swimmers."

Day of the Hand Troller

HAND TROLLING, sometimes called rowboating, was for generations a recognized method of commercial salmon fishing on inshore waters along the British Columbia coast. It increased toward the end of the First World War and reached its peak in the thirties.

In the worst of those depression years, an officer of the old Fishermen's and Cannery Workers' Industrial Union estimated that for most of the blueback and coho season from 500 to 700 rowboaters, some of them women, spinner, rod and herring line fished the grounds from Cape Mudge to Gabriola Pass and across to the entrance of west Howe Sound.

Now they have gone the way of the boat pullers and the dorymen. Some found work in less precarious fields. Others, then in their youth, put their hard won knowledge of the ways of salmon to good use and are now among the highliners of the offshore trolling fleet.

The driftwood shacks under the rock bluffs and strung out along narrow beaches have fallen in. Teredos have eaten away the skids — at the Cape several skidways were from 300 to 400 feet long — over which, morning and evening, they hauled their double-enders, dugouts, skiffs and a variety of other small craft.

Where did they come from? What were their backgrounds? How did they live, afloat and ashore, for five months each season and for longer than this if they fished springs?

They came from every province of Canada and judged by present day standards, their way of life was primitive.

Some came from coastal logging camps, recovering from or permanently handicapped by injury, or to be their own men and free of the push.

Some were "escapees" from the notorious work camps of that equally notorious decade; youths and men from all parts of the country and a scattering from other countries as well. Many were R. B. Bennett's "derelicts."

Others came from stump ranches and coastal settlements. A few brought the wife and kids along.

Among the regulars was a core of the old style rugged individualists, those who refused to knuckle under and take orders from any man. Some were well educated but preferred the free life to the rut.

They were open-handed, generous with their help. They were a rugged breed of men and women. They had to be.

Those who had catches to sell to scow or packer after a day at the oars, ate.

Those who had not, shared another's meal. Failing that, they made do with rock cod or headed for the nearest clam bed hoping that tomorrow would be their lucky day.

FOR THOSE PHYSICALLY OR TEMPERAMENTALLY UNEQUAL to the life, that lucky day seldom came. In fact, with blueback and coho prices what they were even after the lengthy 1936 strike, the most experienced and persistent hand trollers seldom ended a season with more than a few hundred dollars. These were the men able to buy or, more frequently, build themselves smooth pulling seaworthy boats.

Carvel planked double-enders of 15 feet or so were popular. Such boats were capable of carrying a sprit sail for travelling from ground to ground.

A fast, streamlined herring rake was essential. A five gallon water can, grub box, handshaped dipnet, blanket, possibly a tarp or ground sheet, a few cooking utensils pretty well completed the outfit. Not all possessed slicker or gumboots and a change of clothing was something of a luxury.

Gear was of the simplest. A hank of green cotton line; a lead or two, half or one pound; hooks, bought by the dozen, rarely by the box — Harrison light sevens usually; a few fathoms of cuddyhunk, swivels, split rings.

And if you were an old hand, your own spoon hammer and a 24 gauge sheet of your favorite spoon metal — you made your own spinner "blades." For until herring were of a size to be raked and threaded on a rod hook, usually by mid-July, spinners were used almost exclusively.

Most hand trollers used single spinners, the blades sometimes adapted from the once popular wide spinning "Cowichan" type but shorter and with more "dish" and hence easier to pull.

Other men, a minority, claimed to have better success with "tandems" — two much smaller blades which with skill or luck could be made to turn in opposite directions.

Herring dodgers had not yet come into use by rowboat men. For bait "chunk," an inch long strip of skin and flesh cut from the isthmus or gill opening of a freshly caught salmon, was used, at least until mid-season. Impaled on the hook, it fluttered approximately the width of two fingers back of the end of the spinner.

IN THE MATTER OF SPINNERS, design apart, two conflicting schools prevailed.

The first maintained that brass was the only metal required, whereas the second school was convinced that salmon reacted to color, though don't ask them why. They therefore made themselves sets of spinners of the shape they favored, ranging from brass, bronze (light, dark and "gold") with often a brass and silver "fifty-fifty."

During one heated debate between members of these opposing schools, the brass man asserted that his metal was all that was needed and that "if the fish don't like it they can so-and-so leave it."

They did just that and before the month was out the many metal man had the questionable satisfaction of seeing the other head for Vancouver to try to get his name put back on the relief rolls.

But did the failure lie with the man and not the metal? Seemingly it did, for at the Cape, Hornby and the north end of Lasqueti some top spinner men used brass exclusively.

On one point however there was complete agreement — spinners should be "worked" slow or fast turning, smooth running or erratically as indicated by how the fish were hitting — or not hitting — and by a variety of conditions, the light, state of the sea, feed and so on. For this the spinner was found to be more versatile than a spoon.

Speed could be varied within a boat length, a pull on one oar then the other made it swerve or lift and fall to excite cohos and blueback and thus get them "off balance." If the fish were coming short or not hooking properly, the spin of the blade could be altered within seconds, wider or narrower, by holding it edgewise on the gunwale and giving it a few taps with the fish club.

The rowboat man fished one line only, with his spinner seldom more than five fathoms astern — sometimes closer than this if the fish were really hitting — and his line slip-knotted around his thigh. He could vary his depth somewhat by sliding his lead either up or down where it hung directly overside. But until commercial rod fishing was introduced in 1932 the hand troller's range of depth was limited.

OPENING DATE FOR BLUEBACK FISHING in the Gulf in the early thirties and before was May 15.

At that date the runs were mainly concentrated

Quathiaski Cove, around the Cape to Dogfish Bay facing Cortez Island.

On the Cape proper there were some 40 to 50 shacks, some occupied by two or more persons. Dogfish Bay had a number of shacks and there was the odd one wherever there was a beach.

The Native Indian fishermen were camped in Discovery Pass just inside the lighthouse.

Recently one oldtimer who fished the Cape — and they are hard to find nowadays — estimated the total of "genuine" Cape fishermen at 150, though this figure may well have been higher. Part timers — loggers, farmers, and others who came when the fishing was good — increased this estimate considerably.

Most of the fishing was on the Cape proper, so except for the Indian village, the Cape had the largest group.

There were four or five separate groups or villages, with its own social life, friends, enemies, gossip and spats as in any community.

Each reportedly had its own distiller with his distillery against the days when bad weather kept the fleet ashore.

The principal cooperative effort was on the beach, helping one another haul their boats up and down the lengthy skidways.

The Cape was undoubtedly the most hazardous area of the Gulf. It faces southeast and is a dirty piece of water in any wind, most of all in a southeaster. To hang tight on the grounds with a blow

around Nanaimo, Grey Rocks and Ballenas. Soon they spread over to Lasqueti (Sangster Island, Squitty Bay, Poor Man's Rock) then to that island's upper end ("Bare Rocks" and the "Flat Tops" as they were called locally). Olson Point and Jenkins on the west side of Lasqueti were usually fished later.

As a rule, as the season progressed, the fishing fell off in the south and improved in northern areas.

A sizeable number of rowboat men wintered around Nanaimo, the Gulf Islands and Victoria. These usually began fishing at Grey Rocks, moving north to their favorite grounds as summer approached.

On the eastern side of the Strait others wintered at Pender Harbor, Egmont, Roberts Creek, Gibsons, Vancouver. These usually started the season at Sangster and Squitty.

Cape Mudge was undoubtedly the largest hand trolling area in the Gulf of Georgia. While most of the fishing was concentrated on the Cape proper, the area ran all the way from Poverty Point past

coming was asking for trouble, especially when the wide tide flat was exposed.

Fishing grounds on the Cape were known as the Outer Kelp, Inner Kelp, Bell Buoy, and others. The beds comprising the Inner Kelp lay a quarter mile or so offshore, while the Outer Kelp were a mile or more out. A complete tour meant a row of several miles.

The rowboat man's routine was, up at dawn, a quick breakfast and out to his favorite kelp bed by daylight. There he would be on the oars more or less until dark. Then back to the shack for supper and bed.

When fishing was slack, several miles must be covered prospecting other kelp beds.

Fishermen on the Cape were serviced by collecting boats which usually made two trips daily, bringing any groceries and supplies needed. Few if any collecting boats carried fresh water to grounds where none existed until this service was won as a concession by the strike.

The other large camp was made up of Native Indian hand trollers. They fished with dugouts and all men and women and children able to row took part.

It was a never to be forgotten sight to watch 40 or 50 dugouts in Discovery Pass soon after dawn on a clear morning.

Two or three scows were anchored in the bay where the Natives camped. They dealt mainly with the scows.

Along exposed stretches of the Cape gales destroyed the skidways every winter. For many seasons they had to be renewed by the fishermen themselves. However, in 1936 or 1937, through the efforts of the Fishermen's and Cannery Workers' Industrial Union and its local at the Cape, the federal government was prevailed upon to instal cement runways.

Many hand trollers remained in one area throughout the season. Others followed the fish from ground to ground, though it is debatable if they did any better than those who stayed put. Certainly they worked harder for their fish.

Some men hand trolled springs during the winter, one group going as far as Princess Louise Inlet and icing their catches with icicles from overhanging rocks. Winter springs could also be rowboated close to the herring pond in Nanoose Bay.

THE FIRST ROD FISHERMAN in the Gulf, commercially, was Tom Rogers. Mooring his boat to the spar buoy out from Hornby wharf, he started casting with straight herring for bait, much to the amusement of fishermen onlookers. This was in 1928 or 1929. His immediate success convinced the sceptics.

So began what is currently known as mooching

In shallow water, Tribune Bay at Hornby for instance, two ounce leads were used, whereas in deeper rod fishing places, four ounces proved more effective. The hooks, of a size but lighter and with a somewhat longer shank than an Atlantic salmon "low water" hook, were baited in two ways.

The first, used to good effect when the herring were not closely schooled, was to insert the point of the hook up through the lips at a slight angle, give it a partial twist then imbed it in the body through or immediately back of the gill covers. This gave the bait a measured, side to side motion and resulted in the occasional spring being taken while working on the coho.

The second method was to enter the point through the mouth, back through most of the body cavity then bring the point – point only, not the barb – through the skin close to the dorsal fin. This method caused the herring to spin as if stunned or crippled as herring appear to be when tightly schooled and charged into by feeding coho.

A variation of these two methods was to start with the first, thread the herring up the shank of the hook and enter the point a second time at the dorsal. At times the first worked best; at other times the second. But experience proved that they should not be switched haphazardly for best results. Coho, when not avidly feeding, can be "set in their ways."

WITH THE ADVENT OF COMMERCIAL ROD FISHING, the rowboat man was able to take coho down to 12 or even 13 fathoms consistently. No longer need he row continuously. Instead, he need only hold his position against tide and/or wind and sea.

With the butt of his rod tucked under one thigh,

by sport fishermen. By 1930 a man was not considered a real commercial rowboater unless he owned a rod outfit.

This consisted of a bamboo rod (two bits at the scow) a walnut reel ($4 and up), a large mouth dipnet and a well made herring rake. These rods came from China – tropical bamboo was useless.

Herring rakes, shaped from straight edge grain fir, had teeth from a strand of stiff wire cable cut in pin lengths and inserted one third to one half an inch apart on the rake's leading edge. Later, "Staybrite" leader wire was used. Rakes ranged in length from 10 to 14 feet.

he kept one eye on his rod tip, the other on the watch for herring.

The instant he sighted any, provided he was an expert at raking overside, his rake would be lifted from the forked stick in which it was cocked up over the bow, swung out and down, reversed and brought up hand over hand, its teeth up. He would then shake the impaled herring into the boat forward of where he sat.

Time and again, the slashing rake as it scattered the herring, attracted a salmon which hooked itself before he had time to drop the rake back into place.

This overside raking was a skill not all rod fishermen acquired. Instead, they secured their rod, knelt or stood in the bow and raked from that position. However, what they did acquire were revealing glimpses of coho behaviour which few fishermen, commercial or otherwise, have had.

They would see a column of jack herring, a yard or so wide and several times that in length, swimming leisurely under or alongside his boat, with coho, equally unhurried, riding herd on them, spaced at regular intervals, five or six on either flank.

As they watched, they would see a single herring break from the herd, a coho swing toward it, take it and with a heave of its gill covers, expel it, sending it spinning end for end.

Thus was demonstrated the coho salmon's exasperating trait of "skinning tails."

Herring are wary and difficult to rake. Eventually you run down a few, thread one on your hook and reel it down to the depth at which you were fishing when you were cleaned of bait.

You finger your line, feel the slightest of taps, reel it in and find the after end of your hard won herring skinned as smoothly as a banana is peeled. No teeth marks as when a trout or grilse worry it.

Yet another coho quirk: Six or eight of you are fishing together, your boats scarcely oar length apart, all of you merely holding against the tide.

One man feels action, then a second, then others. Lines are stripped in all from the same depth. Every bait herring has its head crushed. At other times, a tiny nip is taken from behind the herring's dorsal fins, yet the herring is not mauled or marred.

ROD GEAR IN THE THIRTIES was much inferior to the monofilament available today. Main line and leaders were of "Japanese gut" — strands of raw silk which soon became limp and soggy. Some men replaced their leaders every 10 fish and retied their hooks every third one.

In commercial rod fishing the boats were often bunched, at times only a length or two apart. As soon as the best depth was found, reels were locked.

Depth was of the utmost importance; cohos in late season change depth less readily than earlier and for a man to be off the depth by as little as a couple of feet

It was during these slack periods that the skillful rod fisherman stood out. Taking coho while they were really hitting was easy enough. Taking them while they were not was a skill which came only with experience.

A man might finger his line in inch by inch and thus trick the salmon into seizing his bait right at the surface. At other times he would let it sink quickly and hook one as it followed the bait down. A skinned tail told him that salmon were still there.

A net of tiny bubbles signalled the presence of a herring school and when pea size salmon bubbles wavered to the surface he often held position for hours in expectation of another feeding flurry. On shallow grounds the salmon behavior varied, but there also knowledge and experience helped.

THE SAME COULD BE SAID for "herring line" fishing. For this, gear was of the simplest: a four ounce sliding lead, several fathoms of 30 test cuddyhunk, one swivel, one Harrison light seven hook.

The raked herring had to be large enough to spin the hook and was trailed three fathoms astern, seldom more. With the lead slid up, the tail of the bait could be made to ripple the surface; slid lower a depth of several feet could be obtained.

Here also the bait was worked, with eye and hand alert for salmon making passes at it. Some men taped thumb and forefinger to prevent line burns, for if the fighting salmon was allowed to get its head, something had to give. Not many rod men, even among those most proficient, mastered the herring line.

It is said that Barclay, a Flower Island regular, devised this method of rowboating. Certainly it was used by him with outstanding success.

Accounts of record catches are difficult to verify after this length of time. Catches of 85 and 87 by rod men in a single day are known to have been made. With spinner and chunk a Vancouver Island fisherman took 120 July fish in a day, and another at Bare Rocks took 142.

One September a rod man took 500 heavier coho in 20 days' fishing. Over the years, and especially in the twenties, it is likely that even bigger catches were tallied.

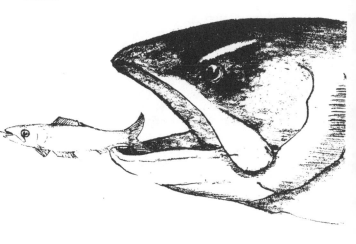

meant fewer solidly hooked fish. And with boats so close to one another, to let a fish run means fouled lines — and on occasion foul language!

The instant the rod man felt the weight of the fish, he rapidly stripped in line so that it struggled head up at the surface only to be skittered into his waiting dipnet before it had really begun to fight. With the heavier late season fish this speedy boating was not always possible. However, it was always attempted.

The fish often actively fed no more than once or twice on a tide. For perhaps 20 minutes every boat was taking fish, then as abruptly as it began the flurry was over.

Today, the vast schools of bluebacks and coho which made such catches possible have vanished from the Gulf of Georgia as completely as the way of life of the rowboat men who followed them.

IN THE NORTH COAST COUNTRY this smelt-like fish was as important as the salmon. Its arrival in the spring was crucial to coast and interior tribes alike. A week of dancing would precede the trek over grease trails from Kispiox and Kitwancool up on the Skeena. People along the snowy trails and icy rivers, loaded with skin of rabbit and marmot, bear grease, cariboo meat, dried berries. The trade for grease, fishing places, shelter for the short, still bitter cold season. People too, down from coastal Alaska, hungry for the *Alumandkum*, the "salvation" fish.

People and fish would arrive at the mouth of the Nass and Skeena Rivers about the middle of March. *Nass*, whose very name means "stomach." The forests still hung with winter's quiet, snow and ice. The roar of the oolachon run still muffled by the blue-green

surf would smash into the frigid inertia of winter with a flurry of activity and announce another spring.

When the fish was late and the winter had been hard, people lay in their drift shacks, freezing and going blind from opthalamia brought on by the sting of icy wind, smoke, and sun-glare. Late or early, the commotion with the arrival of the fish was equal.

Preyed upon by man, fish, bird and sea-mammal alike, the tiny fish brought chaos and profusion to winter's singular emptiness. "They are followed into the mouth of the river by hundreds of seals, porpoises, sea-lions and fin-back whales, feasting both on oolachons and on one another. So eager were they in its pursuit that the largest mammals almost grounded in the shallows and when they discovered their position they struggled furiously, fought and

224

bellowed in such a manner that they might have been heard for over two miles distant. None of our hunters would venture out in their canoes to attack them, so fierce was the fray.

"With the arrival of the fish the scene changes. First there are the Indians in their boats or canoes with their dogs hauling their sleds along the ice to the various caps. Then the sea-gulls begin to arrive, first in flights of hundreds or more, but soon increase to thousands and myriads, until they appear like snowflakes filling the air."

The fishermen with their various gear, moving about on the ice, lanterns at night and shouting, laughing in the dark, chopping two holes through which the net is hung. Nettle nets, purse shaped, scooping the silvery fish like small change. The front opening is a ring of cedar withes, help from the forest. They lift the nets out and open the roped-together closed end, spilling the fish, flopping and flailing onto the ice. Dog sleds, yappings, the runner's songs on ice, cries of direction, mush. The fish are speeded to the shore where the bins wait, hungry, three to four feet deep of wooden mouth.

By run's end, each family has bagged five to ten tons of fish! They are each about ten inches long, prized for their oil. Candle fish they called them, so rich, a wick stuck in the mouth would turn the fish to a torch. Red glow, shadows on the ice, cedar dim lit shapes, sputtering oily fish, fire from the sea. Garnish for dry fish and berries.

Fishing on the ice is best. Later, drift ice in the springing river threatens nets, rips them, carries the prize away. Then, it's better to use the rakes, long poles of cedar, planed flat and fitted with sharp needles of iron or hardwood, maybe spruce, flesh piercers an inch apart. Some canoes hold four or five men, two raking from the bow, the rest midships and stern paddling. Others solo, in small canoes, paddling with the rake and each stroke jerking the impaled oolachon into the boat.

On shore, the women prepare the harvest. Many are eaten immediately, the calories rapidly consumed by the starved winter flesh, the heavy work of the fisheries, the taste of smoked salmon for a while becomes a memory. Many are salted, smoked, or dried on racks in the sun. The smell of the oily fish wafts into the forest, exciting nose of wolf and sleepy-eyed bear. Several tribes, offering prayers to fish and birds for the coming of spring, celebrate first fish ceremonies, sprinkling eagle down upon their saviours.

The officiant may be a middle aged woman, eyes imperious to folly, wearing Haida hat and mitts. She places the first fifty oolachon on a special fire of spruce bark. No one blows on it to aid the flames. This would bring north wind down the Nass with ice flows to rip the nets. All brown on one side the fish are turned onto a new cedar mat beside the fire. "Lowaa, lowaa, lowaa" deep and sonorous chanting "Great honour to the oolachon, great thanks." Browned on the other side, the fish is served. Chew slowly with the thoughts of thanks, may many more seasons be as gracious. Hold flat in the hand, eat as

hot as you can, don't blow to cool it down. Storms will come and if anyone drinks water, rain is sure to come and ruin the oileries. When the fish burst in the fire, skin crackling deliciously, yell "more oolachon are coming up, hey."

When all the fish that's wanted whole, dried or smoked, is put away, the oil extracting begins. Originally in cedar boxes, drop the rocks in, quick hot from the fire, red hot soon starts the boil and the oil rising to the surface. Later, after the white man came, the vats have sheet iron boxes and sit atop the fires: quicker, less fuel, labour, less fire.

Once gathered the oil is carried back to the villages across the grease trails, so named for the drippings that sank to mix with needle of evergreen, mould of oak. Carried by relay in boxes of 150 to 200 pounds, held in place by a cedar band around the forehead. Some of the women were the greatest packers. It was one of these grease trails that opened the coast to Alexander MacKenzie's overland trip, a latecomer to the well-travelled trails.

Further south, the Kwakiutl of the Alert Bay-Kingcome Inlet area welcomed the oolachon somewhat later in the year. The fish don't arrive at the Fraser until April or May.

Fishing with dipnet, the Kwakiutl pray – *"Go on friend, act the way you're supposed to, according to the place of our Chief Above, who placed you in my ancestor's hands. Go, gather up that fish, be full when you return. Now, friend, go into the water where you may stay."*

These nets were triangular or rounded. They could be found here and there the length of the coast, used for smelt and herring, some places to dip salmon from out of traps, rapids, or night-time eddies. Again, made of nettle, the stems and roots pounded and combed, then woven, they were hung on frames three to six feet around and fitted to a ten foot handle.

Prepared for eating, this prized fish still adds needed food supplement to the diet. Used once on salmon, halibut, herring spawn, seaweed, on berries, crabapples, and cranberries for dessert, in some homes it now occupies an honoured place on the kitchen table beside the ketchup bottle and radio of weather reports and pop tunes.

Around Alert Bay, where the oolachon run into Knight and Kingcome Inlets, the Kwakiutl still recognize the traditional fishing grounds. The owners don't guard them like they used to though. Some people still go to net the oily fish in the spring. They are placed in the ground and start to break down. For ten days, they decompose, then are placed in a vat. Boiling water's poured on. Rising oil is scooped and bottled, no longer in kelp gourds but in gallon jugs. In the early sixties they sold for $5 a gallon; nowadays the price is $25.

The price has gone up. In 1877, one Henry E. Croasdaile, of Victoria, broke into the Nass trade, buying fish from the Indians who were paid about $1.25 a day. He shipped a small quantity to England. The rest he sold for a dollar a gallon. He shut down after a few seasons. Oolachon didn't show a profit.

IT WAS HUGE, sprawling across a great patch of shore and out over the water of its protective bay. Technologically it was no doubt inefficient. But as a total process, probably no industrial operation received such high tuning as the Pacific Northwest salmon cannery.

In 1867 the salmon canning industry reached the Fraser River. From there it spread up north until almost one hundred canneries had been built throughout British Columbia's coastal waters. By 1957 almost all canneries beyond the Fraser delta had closed or disappeared.

During the years they operated, these canneries brought a unique way of life to the northwest coast.

These canneries came about through an unusual series of circumstances, typical of this part of the world. First of these was the canning process itself. Fraser River sockeye salmon had been shipped, salted in barrels, from Fort Langley, established in 1827 by James MacMillan for the Hudson's Bay Company. But salted fish appealed to a limited palate, and sometimes arrived at its destination in no palatable state whatever. Canned sockeye became immediately popular and retained its taste indefinitely in the can.

Establishments such as Fort Langley, Fort McLaughlin, and Fort Rupert, which had been built to receive furs but which had grown into the fish processing business, thereby set a mode of operation for salmon canneries to follow. Some canneries were, in fact, built literally within a stone's throw of trading posts, which were being phased out at about the time that the canneries began to appear on the scene. The cannery manager would have much the same powers as his prototype, the post factor, excepting the enforcement of criminal law. Much as furs had been brought to the trading post, so would fish be brought to the cannery. As the trapper had received tokens or script for his purchases rather than currency, so would the fisherman draw books of coupons with which to buy his needs.

A further circumstance joined with these phenomena to provide an additional ply to the thread; namely, a work force. Twenty years after Confederation, when the placer fields that had drawn a tremendous stream of miners were exhausted, the whole of British Columbia could count hardly fifteen thousand inhabitants. The need for fishermen could be met in part by providing gear to local native Indian men. And Indian women could provide the important task of filling the can neatly and exactly with sliced salmon.

But a great gap in manpower still existed at both ends of this packing process. The whole fish must be cleaned and its head and tail severed; packed cans must be cooked, cooled, and nailed into wooden cases.

To make up a labour force which the white population could not furnish the Canadian Pacific Railway, during the early 1880's, imported some fifteen

FISHING RIVERS INLE

thousand Chinese laborers. For a time, as prodigious amounts of rock and earth had to be moved all along this phenomenal route, all of these human machines were needed. Within a very few years though, as the two ends of rail neared each other, camp after camp closed, releasing their work forces to search for other jobs. Just as the Canadian Pacific no longer needed this pool of human labour — huge for that time in British Columbia's history — prospective cannery builders needed it desperately. It could be said without too much danger of contradiction that the majority of the Canadian west coast's canneries which came and disappeared again could not have been put into operation without borrowing from this army of Oriental workers.

The very early salmon cannery existed almost entirely on manpower. The salmon was caught by hand labour, cleaned and sliced by hand labour, and

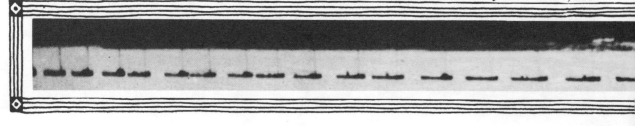

BY SAIL AND OAR

Nevertheless, despite all problems, Robert Draney and Thomas Shotbolt managed to bring Rivers Inlet Cannery into being in 1882.

While the Owikeeno people of Rivers Inlet remained numerous, native fishermen could man a large proportion of gillnet skiffs. These people had fished the inlet — their hereditary tribal waters — from time immemorial. In addition to the trap, the hook, and the spear, they were already accustomed, by the time Europeans arrived, to the use of a fibre salmon net. Any further deficiency in white fishermen was made up by transporting north numbers of Japanese boatmen, who quickly adapted to whatever conditions existed in their new surroundings.

During the 1890's, the ethnic composition of upcoast fishing fleets began to alter. Norwegian colonists settled in the Bella Coola Valley, and Danish-speaking immigrants established a colony at Cape Scott. From the beginning, men from both of these settlements sought cash incomes from work "outside". As they were already north, Rivers and Smith Inlets did not seem remote.

When, early in the twentieth century, families of Finlanders, rebelling against what they felt to be enslavement of the working class in their homeland, established the community of Sointula on Malcolm Island, the ethnic balance that was to persist at canneries in these two inlets began to take shape.

Since the cannery required both a large level space and docking for steamers, it invariably involved a structure on pilings. Projecting from some part of this wharf, and attached to it by a ramp, narrow lines of floats projected, like thin fingers from a hand, more or less parallel to the shore. Pilings and floats, it might be said here, have formed an indispensable foundation of almost every enterprise along the northwest coast right up to the present time.

Against the shore side of this wharf the cannery was built, leaving broad planked surfaces out to the sheer drop into deep water. Near the cannery, and usually on firm land, stood the boiler room. This all-important plant was called upon not only to power all canning machinery and to cook the canned fish, but also to keep the entire community ablaze with light.

Nearby also stood the equally important company store, office and cook-house and dining-room for manager and staff. Here a cook — generally Chinese — performed miracles between weekly steamer-calls with meats and vegetables already not fresh upon their arrival.

Somewhere, on flat ground or hillside near the cannery, stood the manager's home. From its location, it seemed to dominate the cannery area. Actually, while salmon were being canned, or while fishermen were in from the grounds on week-ends, the manager had little time to view his domain from his front window.

Few industrial operations have been so influenced

packed by hand labour into cans which were themselves produced by hand labour on the spot — cut from tin plate and soldered into shape. Even when E. A. Smith's "Iron Chink", just after the turn of the century, eliminated the cleaning and slicing processes, and when the American Can Company introduced ready-made containers, the fish cannery still demanded, throughout its days, a great input of human exertion, both at sea and on shore.

All of British Columbia's inlets possessed tremendous runs of salmon. Only Smith Inlet and Rivers Inlet, though, were home to the spawning sockeye, the only variety canned during early years of the industry. Located two hundred miles upcoast from the Fraser River, these northern waters seemed very remote and forbidding to an immigrant who might, in any case, find an opportunity to harvest boatloads of the world's prime sockeye from the great river.

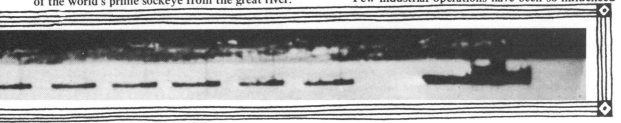

by one individual as was the upcoast salmon cannery by its manager. The plant belonged to a company, but the success or failure of its operation depended on the acumen, the tact, and the personality of the man in charge. Until the radio-telephone made its advent after World War II, the ten or so canneries operating in Rivers Inlet shared one telegraph set. Except for the most urgent of communications, the manager drew on his own resources when decisions had to be made.

Even at the best of times, keeping his varied racial groups working in harmony to keep his production line running smoothly took a person of rare quality. Somehow, even during the periods of critical international ructions, with more diplomacy and less power than surface appearances would indicate, he held all together. While, for instance, Japan was making war against China during the 1930's, Chinese shore-workers processed without incident salmon caught by Japanese fishermen.

generation ago.

Strangely enough, the strikers' solidarity resulted in part from the multifoliate personalities of their cannery managers. While paid to represent cannery operators, the qualities that made them less accustomed to ask than to command rendered each, in varying degrees, unsuited to act as followers rather than leaders. As men among men, while they could not speak out, many inherently sympathized with the beleagured, desperate strikers. In all of the bitter recriminations that invariably accompany an issue so momentous as a strike in times of want, the cannery manager, in general, suffered little as a result of the role he had played during very critical days. Seemingly born rather than made, the ethos and the modus of British Columbia's salmon cannery manager represents a mine for almost unlimited study.

Somewhere, also, at one end of the complex, stood the China House. Here, during off hours, the all-male gang of shoreworkers made their own way of

·Arrival·of·the·Workers·

One phenomenon, the price paid the gillnetter for his fish, the manager could not control. The lowering of this price below what fishermen felt to be a subsistence level led to a two-week strike in 1932, and to the Great Strike of 1936, which cost the entire season. Despite pressure put on Chinese, Japanese and native Indian fishermen and workers by canning operators and by federal government agents, all of these groups chose to suffer loss of an entire season's income rather than break faith, even with national enemies. In each of these instances salmon prices were higher for the year following. But many fishermen during these pre-welfare-state times, knowing of the miseries strike action would bring to their families, still chose the ultimate weapon at their command in hopes of making a better way. From a vantage point of today's instant strike and exorbitant fish prices, it is difficult to comprehend the enormity of the action taken by workers of more than a

life, eating, sleeping and playing Fan-Tan with ivory or pig-bone markers. The fishermen knew nothing of these, to them, nameless individuals. Washing most fastidiously at cold-water taps outside their plain wood building or sitting on a sunny evening, they conversed incessantly in a tongue of which the non-Oriental learned never a tone.

Many stories of so-called "Tong wars" became entangled into northwest coast fishing lore. Investigation into the bases for such bloody episodes reveal but a few actual incidents. There were far fewer cases of knife-play among Orientals than of gun-play among non-Orientals along British Columbia's coast. Rivers Inlet canneries did produce gun-play, during the Great Strike, but they saw precious little wielding of hatchet or knife.

In the area of the store and office, living accommodations were provided for a bookkeeper and whatever clerks the canning operation required. The

·Chinese·Women·Canning·

bookkeeper — usually, a permanent company employee assigned to a cannery during the fishing season — kept records of all fish delivered and of expenses incurred by each fisherman. He also kept account of times worked by canning crews.

The millwright, because he enjoyed the dubious privilege of living at the cannery site year round, was provided with a home much like that of the manager. When the last can was packed away, the millwright began his winter-long chore of dismantling, repairing, and re-assembling the entire mechanical plant. If two or more millwrights were needed for this job, they enjoyed at least a minimum of human company. Even

so, they — and their families, if they were married — led their lives during the rainfilled off season almost entirely removed from direct contact with other members of humanity. Separated by waters that could become stormy enough even with summer winds, they could visit but little from one cannery to another during the short, grey days of winter. Somehow these men contrived to complete their appalling tasks in time so that, as the next season rolled around, when the first salmon presented itself to the great long line of machinery every piece of metal was ready to do its job.

Cottages or apartments housed the net-men during

·The 'IRON·CHINK'·

Weighing · Cans ·

their months at the cannery. These men made their way upcoast sometime in early spring. In the vast loft above the cannery, with a steady rhythm of rain on the sloping roofs above their heads, they fought against time to make nets ready for the sockeye season. New nets, in pre-World War II days made of Irish linen by Barbour, who held a patent on the only practicable knot, were ready to be "hung" with cork-line and lead-line. A small rope, fed through a mold which stamped the cannery name to bits of lead and affixed them to it, acted as a long sinker, holding one edge of the net down. A larger line, to which wooden "corks" were threaded at intervals, kept the other edge at the surface. Nets two years old were retired, to be made into float-ropes. Those from the season before were mended, stripped and re-hung for another season's use.

Native Indian families from up and down the coast migrated to Rivers and Smith Inlets each summer for the winter's "stake" to be made there. Each cannery provided a quarter of cabins for these people.

Sociologically-minded writers have, over the years, expended a considerable garland of words on the deplorable conditions which Chinese and native Indian peoples were forced to endure during the fishing season. Such criticisms however, neglect some essential considerations.

While cannery housing for these peoples was unquestionably primitive, it was equally primitive for any white fishermen who wished to spend weekends ashore. The cannery provided a plain living space with beds, stove, table and chairs, and storage shelves. But during the days when gillnet skiffs were powered only by oar and sail many fishermen, white as well as Indian, came from homes that lacked running water, oil-fired stoves or electricity, one amenity with which all cannery buildings were supplied. This sort of housing, then, did not seem too inadequate to tenants of years gone by.

Furthermore, the Rivers Inlet sockeye run arrived in the very middle of summer. Today well-to-do outdoor types leave fully automated homes, by choice, to spend much of this same season in summer camps just as primitive as were the cannery cabins of fifty years ago.

Prior to the early 1920's propeller-driven boats were not allowed to carry nets. Regardless of how a fisherman might arrive at the cannery, he must perforce fish from a skiff equipped with only the power of his own two hands. Some arrived by steamer from Vancouver or Victoria; others, by means of vessels from Bella Bella, Sointula, Alert Bay, Cape Scott, and other localities. Some of these boats would see duty as tow-boats and as fish collectors.

The fisherman, having received word earlier in the year that a net and skiff would be reserved for him, appeared at the cannery about a week before the season's opening in order to assemble his necessities. His skiff, tarred inside and painted outside in the cannery colors, had already been launched, and must be bailed of its rainwater. A cotton tent or a hinged "dog-house" had to be attached to this 25-foot craft, forward from the main bulkhead.

Into this little space — "home" for the days on the fishing grounds — he stowed a week's groceries, Primus stove, and bedding, without mattress. To a piece of old line provided him he tied a rock gathered from the sheer beach for a crude anchor. When all else was ready he pulled his net aboard.

During opening day, usually the third Sunday in June, the manager despatched tows of skiffs to various fishing grounds. Like a general deploying his troops he sought to cover all fronts. No one knew just where the best schools of sockeye would appear. It was the manager's responsibility to ensure that boats from his cannery were stationed at every likely passage.

Fishermen rowed out from the cannery float to where a tow-boat waited. As each skiff arrived, more tow-line was paid out. In Rivers Inlet, skiffs were not linked one to another, as was done in other places along the coast. Here, each tow-boat was equipped with a heavy line. At skiff-length intervals, smaller lines, about four feet in length, and with hardwood eyes set in the loose ends, branched out alternately from either side of the main line. Each fisherman received one of these branch lines. He fed his painter rope through the eye and tied the end in a bow-knot amidships.

With the latest arrival nearest its stern, the tow-boat set out toward its destination, pulling as many as forty skiffs.

A fisherman had no contact with the tow-boat, sometimes far ahead of him. When he wanted to drop off, he was obliged to follow a very exact and very strenuous procedure. First, seated, well braced, he pulled undone his painter, and held it by the end. Then, with the other hand, he grasped the tow-line, which lay, rigid from the pull on it, alongside his skiff. Holding to this, and travelling full speed, he gradually let out his painter, through the eye of his branch line, allowing the bow of his skiff to veer away from the tow-line. Selecting his own "moment of truth", he released, first painter, then tow-line, at the same time beseeching his private gods to keep him clear of the double column of vessels charging at him from astern.

Once clear, he was on his own, far from another human being, on a sea not necessarily calm. In a ceremony dating from days when fishermen carried no timepieces, canneries fired a gun at six o'clock each Sunday, the commencement of legal fishing for the week. Far beyond the range of this sound, the individual fisherman had to depend on his own reckoning.

When six o'clock — or its near approximation — arrived, the fisherman rowed a few strokes, then threw over the stern a buoy attached to his net's cork-line. A flag on this buoy displayed his cannery's particular colors. Letting out a bit of net to catch in the water, he then commenced to row, at right angles to the channel and, if he was beyond the inlet in Fitzhugh Sound, far from shore.

With the trailing end of the cork-line tied to the skiff's stern, and the sun still high in the northern June heavens, there was nothing to be done now for an hour or two. Now was the time to consider the world's woes. With neither radio nor reading matter, the fisherman, as much as any other follower of a lone pursuit, was forced to turn inward for mental stimulation. Mingled with rational contemplation of his net, totally unrelated minutae linked in strange trains of thought. Accompanying images, equally unrelated to a factual world, flickered in a weird kaleidoscope across some vast abyss of the mind.

Nothing much is recorded as having come from these unnumbered bouts of intertwined reason and fantasy. No monumental story; no cosmic-conscious philosophy; no great work of art seems to have been produced on the gillnet fishing grounds of Rivers Inlet. Perhaps the subconsciously realized comedy-relief aspect of the phenomenon; of a time of peace interspersed between times of uttermost elemental strife, smothered any chance of the fisherman's bringing his imaginative musings to fruition. Very often, when wind and rain prevailed, there was little occasion for anything but practical thought and action.

At night, with wind screaming and sky blackened by clouds, body and mind, during waking hours,

· on the Boardwalk ·

·Loading·Gillnets·

·Towing·to·the·Grounds·

became absorbed in a brooding evaluation of the general Scheme of Things. At such times, the bobbing lantern at the net's far end — set there to replace the flag before dusk — might assume overwhelming proportions. Sometimes the only light in view, it seemed like a living, friendly being, the only spark with which he maintained any contact whatsoever. If the storm were to overthrow it, the night would become dark indeed.

Soon after dawn, after having dozed in fragments, the fisherman must "pick up" his net. For this operation he dons hipboots, oilskin apron and, if rain is falling, rubber coat and sou'wester hat. If he has managed to procure one, he pulls in the net over a roller attached to his skiff's stern. To facilitate setting it out again he "splits" the lines, throwing cork-line forward and letting lead-line fall just behind his boots. Salmon caught in the net he forces out backwards

The collector — tow-boat of the day before, if the fisherman has not travelled too far — pulls up alongside his skiff sometime during the morning. He pitches his sockeye aboard, passes his tally book to the skipper for a record of his catch, and asks about fishing elsewhere. Somewhere, far off, there has been a big catch — but the collector is heading in the opposite direction. He stays put for at least another day.

On Friday he waits, net aboard and covered, to be towed back to the cannery. Here he learns the ritual of precious days spent at a calm moorage. He must pull his net up into one of the "bluestone" tanks lined along a portion of the wharf-edge, leaving damaged portions hanging out. The copper sulphate solution in the tank dissolves destructive algae from the immersed part of the web; and a net-man, his mending needle flashing faster than the eye can

· Picking · up · the · Net ·

from the mesh that holds it behind the gills.

With net and fish aboard, he must pump or bail his craft. Then, as tides have probably swept him miles from his chosen grounds, he must row or sail back. Round-bottomed skiffs are almost impossible to row against wind and tide, but their keels permit a certain amount of tacking. Flat-bottomed skiffs, even though they were provided with centreboards, gain no way in a tack into the wind, but can, with an expenditure of almost superhuman energy, be rowed into it. Finding a "drift" clear of other nets, he now "sets out" again.

With one eye on the watch for his collector, he can now take time for a rudimentary breakfast. The adept cook could produce, in wind and wave, morsels of rare delight from the tiny Primus; the culinary duffer used the contrivance sparingly, and frequently ate his food cold.

follow, miraculously sews new mesh into the gaping holes.

If he has a cabin ashore the fisherman carries bedroll and other essentials to it. If not, he remains aboard his skiff, as the majority choose to do. Surprisingly, although he has been bone tired through most of the week at sea, he whiles away the long evening. He walks along to the cannery to see his fish canned. He moves from one knot of fellow fishermen to another, picking up bits and pieces of the jumble of lore that he must somehow classify and remember. Without benefit of chart, he learns to piece together such terms as Fish-Egg, Addenbrooke Light, Swan Rock, the "Jap Drift", Rouse Point, the Haystack, Charcoal Bay, Long Point and others into some semblance of their relative locations. He hears of whales, that might sink his boat; of reefs; of seals, that pilfer during the day; and of human fish-thieves,

Delivering to the Collector

who steal from nets in the dead of night.

All that he hears is real. The human thieves steal silently, with the amount of their theft never known. The seal is also silent, and maddengly elusive. The fisherman can gain respite from this intelligent creature only by pulling in his net, complete with sockeye fish-heads left by the marauder, and removing to some other spot.

Whales are not so silent. The sperm whale — as much as eighty feet in length — occasionally visits the fishing grounds. Here, rising above the surface now and again to blow, it cavorts about the net, plucking out salmon with the delicacy of a human hand. The fisherman whose net this enormous beast of the sea is treating as a smorgasbord sits at the stern of his craft, knife in hand, ready to cut his cork-line should the whale become entangled. At night the sound of a whale blowing enters the very soul. But it never loses its finesse, and finally goes on its way.

Killer whales pass by in pods, two or three at a time always at the surface, blowing and arcing their high black dorsal fins. Although they literally never pause to pluck fish from nets, their grim-looking, seemingly purposeful movements make them appear even more foreboding than their larger relatives.

In his wanderings to the limits of cedar planking, he gathers impressions that will remain with him through years to come. Every glance of a stranger face; every syllable of an unfamiliar tongue merges with the composite mist of memory. A gestalt of buildings and boats set against hemlock and cedar forest imprints on some inner eye. Sounds of machinery record on an inner ear. Half a lifetime later, all might be recalled with amazing clarity.

As the season advances, tow-boats that had headed out toward the open sea now turn their prows up-inlet. Here, the fisherman encounters physically sites which had been only names. Toward the head, the inlet is a pallid green, whitened by milky waters from Mt. Silverthrone and from Klinaklina Glacier. Whereas at Fitzhugh Sound foothills rolled slowly back, at Shotbolt Bay mountains rise abruptly from the inlet's floor to nearly five thousand feet. So sheer are some of the totally bare slopes that a fisherman in bright sunshine may see clouds form around these peaks, and watch rivulets of fresh water stream down the smooth rocky slopes at the prow of his skiff.

As the salmon ready for the last phase of their

cycle, their journey up the Wannock River, boats from all canneries gather near the inlet's head. Gone now is the limitless space of the open Pacific. By day the familiar dots of cork-line floats can be seen in all directions as fishermen struggle for room. By night lantern lights twinkle from shore to shore, giving to the waters the appearance of some immense troop encampment of bygone days.

Now, as the season nears its end, ships that call at the cannery with supplies take aboard cases of canned salmon. If the pack is large, a freighter will appear, pitting its sedate progression against the clock to clear the fishing grounds with its valuable cargo before nets are strewn across its way.

Just as suddenly as the sockeye had increased, they diminish in number. As July turns to August, the talk turns to next year's prospects. Charles Lord, Fisheries Officer, has usually made his predictions known by this time. Based on spawning conditions, hazards of flooding and slides, and on whatever other phenomena might have affected fingerling escapement three years before Lord's calculations, for weal or for woe, are respected as the word of doom.

There is talk of future plans. Some will continue to fish the fall season on seine-boats. Some will turn to logging. A few will return to "stump-ranches",

where they will spin out their stakes with odd jobs and winter trap-lines; perhaps, at the same time, enjoying a bit of pie-in-the-sky prospecting. While together all are boys, and the whole world a series of heroic episodes. There will be time enough later, in solitude, to contemplate the slim roll of bills that must somehow endure through lean Depression days ahead.

The last Friday arrives. The last tow to the cannery. The inlet is as bare as at the dawn of Creation, with never a scar to show where a million salmon have been removed. The net is pulled into a bluestone tank for a final time. Personal belongings come out of the skiff; it has done its job, and will soon be stored for the winter in the cannery loft. Accounts are settled with the bookkeeper. The manager shakes hands in farewell. As he leaves the wharf, the fisherman finds his being torn a thousand ways in emotional contemplation. The season has ended.

Gillnet fishermen still make their way, in their high-speed boats, to Rivers Inlet. Their monofilament nylon nets catch the sockeye salmon. There are fish camps here and there where supplies can be bought — for cash. But of the canneries that gave a unique flavor to the inlet for a lifetime, hardly a sign remains.

·FRIDAY·NIGHT·AT·WADHAM'S·

THERE WAS A GREAT LACK OF VEGETABLE FOOD in the native diet. The coast continues to thwart would-be farmers with its ceaseless luxury of growth. Still, there are to be found the same items that supplemented the Indian diet of sea fare. Nettles, water lilies, bullrush, seaweeds, numerous potherbs such as chickweed, sorrel, and plantain are still plentiful, ready food for the forager.

But the majority of the nutritional vitamins and minerals had to come from the sea. Up to ninety percent of dried fish by weight is protein. The minerals calcium, potassium, phosphorus and iodine were plentiful. Fish liver is a good source of vitamins A, D, Thiamine B1, and Riboflavin B2. Vitamin C, the lack of which was the scourge of so many early seafarers, was available in small quantities in the much sought after herring roe.

The roe of several types of fish was used but herring in particular was relished. It is still eaten, but with dubious legality. Japanese fishermen eagerly seek out this prized contraband. The method of gathering has not changed from aboriginal times. Branches of spruce or hemlock are weighted down in bays known to be herring spawning areas. The herring lays its eggs upon the branches which are hauled to shore when the eggs have reached sufficient size. They are eaten either fresh or dried.

O. M. Salisbury in *Quoth the Raven* describes a Tlingit village in the midst of roe gathering: "The village is literally hung with fish eggs. The big branches are split up into smaller ones, and on the porches of some of the houses, clothes lines have been strung and the branches hang from them, swinging in the wind. In other cases spawn-laden kelp is suspended from lines in the doorways. At another place a different variety of seaweed, laden with eggs, fills all available space, while the fish-net fence at another is hung with hemlock boughs, first being dipped with warm water to soften them, and then are compacted into cakes and are packed in containers for preservation. Those deposited on seaweed are

treated the same way, except that they are dried and packed together and later covered with herring or seal oil. They are cooked and greatly relished."

Some tribes mixed salmon eggs, berries, oil and seaweed, all fresh from the sea, and cooked them in a basket woven from spruce rootlets. Herring themselves were used as food by many northern tribes, ranking in importance with oolachon among the Tlingit. They were taken in various ways – on rakes, with dipnets, drag nets, or in closely woven baskets dipped into the sea.

Cod was another important source of vitamins, especially from the liver. They were always available as a food but because they were singular creatures and relatively small, they never achieved the importance of either salmon or halibut.

An interesting feature in cod fishing was the use of a spinning lure, first reported by the Spaniards at Nootka in 1792. Made of three curved wooden tail pieces bound into a socket, they would be thrust underwater on the end of a long pole. They spun rapidly back to the surface, glinting like small fish. They were used when the cod were spawning in shallow water. Lured to the surface, the fish would be gaffed or speared.

One of the spears for cod fishing featured a three pronged head. The outer two prongs were fitted with barbs on the inside edges. When the spear struck home, these would spring out from a fitting and hold the fish firm, the prongs on either side of the body.

Gaffs were made with detachable heads, with points of steamed and fire hardened wood. Some were armed with barbs of bone. Once the fish had been gaffed, it could be played until it was exhausted and then hauled in. There is some controversy as to whether this gaff was used before white contact. Sometimes, fishermen trolled for cod using halibut hooks, or towed another lure, a tomcod filled with small pebbles toward which the cod would swim until within range of the spear.

Spears were also used in the rivers, particularly near the mouth of the Fraser and up as far as the Pitt River-Harrison Lake area. Paul Kane describes the same technique being used by Indians on the Columbia River. The shafts of the spears were huge, up to seventy feet long. The point was detachable, retrieved with a line of cedar rope. These spears would be propelled to the depths of the river upon contact with the sturgeon. Smaller spears were used in conjunction with torches at night to take the big, curious fish.

"We had a different way of fishing for every fish" says Charley Jones, taking pride in that fact, suggesting a particular reverence for each type of fish, unique beings deserving to be regarded as such. It was such honoured varieties and copious quantities that supported almost exclusively for hundreds of years the first settlers of these coasts. Now, various areas are shut down due to danger of mercury poisoning and there are threats of "over-spawning," something no Indian ever dreamed of. And so, the white civilization continues to continue, still believing that it sets the status quo reality for the rest of the planet, and any other way is an oddity, an aberration, something done before the facts were in, while other ways, other visions, other worlds whisper in the roar of the waves.

GARDEN · VARIETY

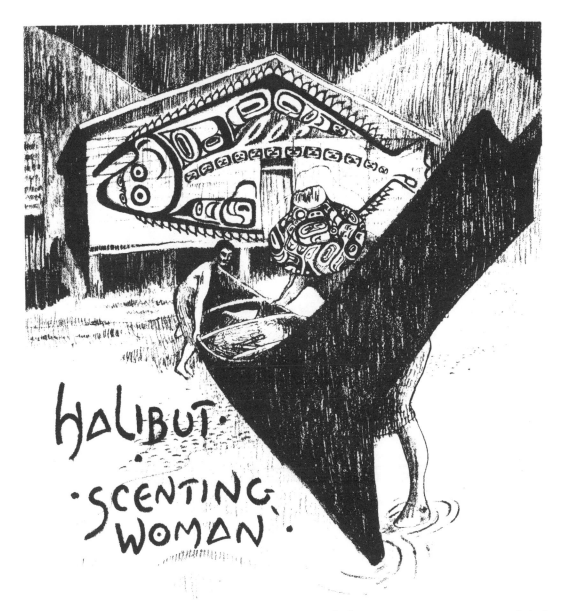

HALIBUT·

·SCENTING·
WOMAN·

"THERE'S DIFFERENT WAYS TO CATCH EVERY FISH," he told me. Halibut, trolling with a line from a canoe. Up and down the coast, abundant and favorite — Sproat saw the Nootka fill a hundred canoes to the gunwhales in half a day. Collison in the Queen Charlottes watched as an old man and his wife filled their canoe in less than two hours, with fish weighing eighty to a hundred pounds.

Judging from what is left of the halibut population, such accounts are hard to believe. White fishermen, who took over the halibut fisheries as early as 1888, soon depleted the population greatly, so much so that in the early 1900's conservationists had to scramble to save the big flatfish from extinction. Gone are the halibut that were caught in Howe Sound and off Point Grey to be sold by Indians to the early inhabitants of what was to become Vancouver.

The native fisherman generally had a power to help him when he fished for halibut. A bigger and more difficult catch than salmon, halibut called for a song, a spirit helper. The best fishermen possessed songs which they received from these beings — simple formulas which concentrated the mind, inspiring confidence and perserverence in the fisherman. For things like carving and weaving, or catching salmon or oolachon, no great power was needed, but to catch bigger game, whales, cod, or halibut, a supernatural helper was essential.

One Nanaimo man had a dream about catching something fierce. He hauled in a fish-shaped stone the next day and took it home. He dreamed again. When his luck was poor, he should rub this stone with his hook. For many years, with the stone wrapped up in a cedar chest, he obeyed this dream and prospered, becoming great and wealthy. When old, a special way to paint the stone came in a dream. He was to put it back where it came from. Flashing like lightning, the stone disappeared into the depths.

There is little doubt that such a receptivity to "supernatural" forces, increasingly validated by science, would have a great effect on not only the maintenance of tribal society, but also, through attunement to natural signals and events, the preservation of the ecological balance.

The myths and rituals of the native Indian enhanced and developed the sense of cyclic rhythm in nature and the interdependence of all beings. Their technology was highly developed, so much so that in 1887 A. P. Niblack of the Fisheries Department said, "the most modern appliances could not compete with the methods familiar to the natives."

Fully dependent on their immediate environment, the Indian did all in his power to preserve and protect his resources, minimizing destruction where he could and elsewhere enhancing natural productivity.

In this Kwakiutl ritual, one discerns the close relationship between the natural world in which man lives and the language and thought which structure that world. Patterns are developed to place man firmly in the rich tapestry of being — ritual emphasizes his oneness with all life.

The fisherman steams his knot of spruce or yew into a U-shaped curve. To this he attaches a point of bone or stone, wrapping it with twine of cherry bark. Onto this hook he places a piece of cuttlefish, as he will in the fishing. As he does so, he sings —

"O Younger Brother, pay attention. Now, Younger Brother, your dress has been put on. You will go to the village of Scenting Woman, Born To Be Giver Of The House, Old Woman, Flabby Skin In The Mouth. Now, clean and purify yourself, Younger Brother. Do not let go of Old Woman, Flabby Skin In The Mouth, Born To Be Giver Of The House when she takes hold of you, good Younger Brother. I shall blacken you, Younger Brother, with these spruce branches, that you may smell good, that you may be smelled by Scenting Woman when I first put you in the water."

He beats the hooks in his spruce fire, blackening and hardening the wood. He hangs them up and goes to the forest, searching for pieces of spruce, small and straight, for cross pieces. With spruce root he binds these to the hooks. Sometimes he carves the shank.

"O Friend, come, for you yourself called me to you, that you with your uncommon supernatural power might hold together the cross pieces, our friends. Do not break apart when my Younger Brothers are taken hold of by Scenting Woman."

The hook is ready now. Attaching it to his line of cedar or willow bark, made from the twisted middle layers of the tree, he is ready to fish. Around Victoria, the fisherman ties the hook to a line of kelp.

"Now, go for it, Scenting Woman. Do not play looking at your sweet-tasting meat. Take it at once, Born To Be Giver. Go ahead Old Woman, take your sweet-tasting food. Do not let me wait long on the water. Go ahead, come on, my Younger Brothers are dressed with your sweet-tasting food, O Flabby Skin In The Mouth."

Drawn down by heavy stone sinkers and sometimes marked by floats, carved like gulls perhaps, the line sinks to the depths where it is grabbed by the halibut. The float dips, up comes line and fish, where it is dispatched with a carved wood or stone killing club. Then, the fisherman takes the hook from the mouth and stabs it into the fish four times, in quick succession.

"Now Old Woman, look well at this sweet-tasting dress of our Younger Brother. Tell your tribe how good it is. Go down again, Younger Brother. Find Old Woman, Flabby Skin In The Mouth, Born To Be Giver Of The House."

Back goes line, hook, and sinker, drifting past the kelp. Waves pound the shingle beach in front of the village. Sun hangs around fog bank.

The sight of an eighty-pound halibut rising beside a twenty-foot canoe is awe-full. Dark brown hulk, totally unlike the swift gun metal silver flashing of the salmon in the river. One Haida song captures the power of the fish, the dark meaty presence.

"The Chief has it in mind to bite —
Old Coming Across Around Island thinks he's
going to bite.
Shadows increase in Rising Steeply, Hasten Chief.
Great One Coming Up Against the Current
Starts to think of biting.

Big One Who Comes Taking Pebbles Into Mouth
Thinks of biting.
Hey, look at the bait,
White Stone Eyes.
Great Eater
Thinking of the bait."

A tale of the Supernatural Halibut from Big Island, west of Yan on Masset Inlet, Queen Charlottes. Two brothers went out fishing together every day. Only the elder ever caught any. He'd get up early and put on shaman robes and mask, go sing at water's edge to supernatural devilfish. The devilfish would bite his hook and end up as the day's bait. One morning, it finally happens. Younger brother gets curious. He follows his brother and watches the proceedings. Next morning, rising early and peeking at his older brother still snoring in bed, he goes down to the beach, tries on the robes and mask. Sure enough, the devilfish rises to the song and is caught. Back to bed, Elder brother was somewhat amazed not to catch anything. They go out fishing. Soon Younger brother hooks a gigantic halibut.

This halibut tows them around the entire North Island, around Cape Saint James, and tows them finally back to where they started. There on the shore all the people of the village are in mourning, thinking for sure they were drowned, because it was several days ago that they disappeared. The canoe is stopped, so they pull in the line, heavy with the weight of the halibut called Never Appearing, Going Round The Island. When the fish surfaces, the waters around them are filled with halibut, which they load triumphantly into the canoe and paddle to shore. They told the people "a big halibut bit one of our hooks and swam around the whole island with us." Never again did the younger brother attempt to get the day's bait.

Animals of power swimming the seas, hidden since the white man's iron tools, his forgotten dreams. We believe we know a lot about the world, but do we? Do we really? We have only seen the acts of people. We know nothing about this mysterious unknown world.

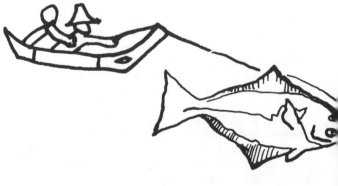

Tides

THINK OF THE TOWBOATS out on the straits, stretching a distant even thread of motor noise through the night. They work the tide shift. Think of the weary gillnetter rolling in his bunk, setting the alarm for the change of tide. Think of the Haida clamdigger hunched over a cloudy hole in the glassy plain of a Queen Charlotte Island sandflat, breakers roaring in the distance and a briny wind cutting through neoprene layers right to the numb core of her bones. As winter progresses she will hunch in the blue dawn, then the bright noon, then the moonlight again, as the tides command. They work in the tides' time.

Tide. The word has been in steady use since the Saxons. They said tid, and it meant time as well. Tide was time to them. They too lived with their backs to the land and their eyes to the sea.

"Time and tide wait for no man." King Canute. Scylla and Charybdis. The image of the whirlpool, or maelstrom, or vortex, recurring over and over as a symbol of the extremity of experience.

Out there in the corner of the third eye, the tides have influenced our culture more than we know.

Here on this coast the Indians knew, with a thoroughness only a people whose lives had pulsed in the tides' time for ten thousand years could know. The perpetual dependable shifting of the water was one of the groundswell rhythms of coast mythology and in the most basic stories of creation and transformation the tide is always present, changing the scene, moving the plot along. In a typical Salish flood myth it's not the rain that drives the native Noah to the dry peak of Anchor Mountain, but the wrathful flood tide.

Most coast oldtimers, approached cold for some comment on the tides will say something like, "Tides! You want to know about tides! Well, she comes in and she goes out. That's about all I can tell you. She comes in and she goes out."

But just at the mention of the word you will probably detect a faraway look in the corner of his eye, the sort of transfixed look you find in the eye of a troller whose boat and bodily form have just come into dock but whose mind remains hooked into some deep mystery back in the gulf. The tides of this coast, upon which fishing of all things depends, is an inexhaustible study, drawing the thoughts of many different shades of men to a same transparent fineness.

Most people, faced with making some sense of the tidal mystery, will invoke the hidden astronomical machinery of the sun and moon. Admittedly this is where it starts, although finally it's only a minor part of the explanation.

The sun and moon pull on the earth and it swells a little on both sides. Not the sea only; air and land also. It has been estimated that Vancouver rises and falls 20 inches each time the moon goes by. The sky tide is estimated in miles, and jostles the atmosphere in ways that are well known to farmers and fishermen and recently to scientists as well.

The sea tide is comparatively slight, averaging perhaps two feet in the open ocean, a very faint two-headed bulge held fixed by the sun and moon as the earth slides around underneath it so that generally we have two tides a day, two rises and falls. During the equinox when the sun and moon are straight out off the equator these tides are equal in size, but as sun and moon range north or south of the equator, most extreme during the solstice, they pull the bulges askew so we pass through the thick middle of one and only the thin edge of the other. This is when you hear fishermen speak of the "big tide" and the "little tide".

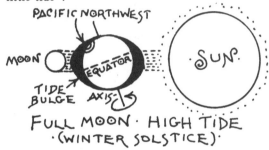

FULL MOON · HIGH TIDE · (WINTER SOLSTICE) ·

Since the moon is on an elliptical orbit it varies in distance from the earth, and this causes long term variations in the range of the tides. Another thing that causes long term variations is the relation of the sun and moon to each other. During the new and full phases they pull in line creating "spring tides", and during the quarters they pull against each other, producing "neap tides".

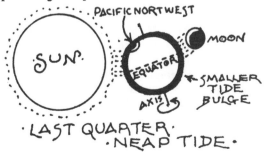

· LAST QUARTER · · NEAP TIDE ·

These astronomical motions are extremely regular. If that's all there was to it the whole world would read its tides from the *Farmers Almanac*, which in fact started out as a primitive sort of tide book in the 16th Century.

Hydrographers have a saying: all tides are local. There are so many local factors that affect tidal behaviour the neat graph rhythms of sun and moon become lost in a scribble; if it has final order there hasn't been a computer made that can begin to crack it.

There's wind. In 1943 the Masset clamdiggers' co-op almost went broke because a hard onshore wind kept the surf from baring North Beach all winter, and in 1953 North Sea gales boosted Dutch tides 30 feet, breaking miles of dyke and drowning 2000 people. Tides are continually delayed and hastened, increased and diminished by strong winds. On this coast it can be generally stated that a hard southeaster will push the tide up and hold it up, and a hard westerly will have the opposite effect.

But mostly there's land. Theoretically tidal range decreases with latitude, but Frobisher Bay in the Canadian Arctic has ranges of 35 feet, second highest in the world, owing to its scoop-like shape, and the world's largest tidal whirlpool is off Lofoten Island in the Norwegian Arctic. Fundy and Nantucket are less than 200 miles apart but the one has 50-foot tides and the other 2-foot, all effects of local geography. There are parts of the world like Chile and Western Africa where the coast is so straight and rational tides can almost be calculated from the calendar, but they are the antithesis of B.C. The northwest coast is the most intricate in the world, as involuted and inscrutable almost as the brain itself. Even water has a difficult time finding all its crevices, and ends up in a continual frothing confusion. West coast tides abandon the most fundamental laws of tidal action, devoid of any logic but their own.

Oceanographers have built contour models acres in size, pumped water in and out for months on end, and produced armfuls of theories but in Georgia Strait tides make and break up to a week out of phase with the moon; in an area that is supposed to be semi-diurnal Victoria has diurnal tides 20 days of the month, and no one knows why.

The tide tables are offered as simple observations, compiled through years of watching by such notably un-theoretical folk as the Bill Logans of Clo-oose, who took readings that were used to establish the current tables for Nitinat Bar in the late twenties. "We'd walk over to the bar with a stopwatch and time high and low slack, all hours of the day and night, all kinds of weather. It was a couple miles I guess. We were pretty spry then."

The B.C. coast is basically in two parts, with huge islands on either hand, Vancouver south and the Queen Charlottes north. Stormy exposed Cape Caution, with its cold blue beach sand ground fine as flour, marks the mid-point. In the lee of the islands are the vast protected waters of Hecate Straits above and Georgia-Johnstone-Queen Charlotte Straits below. Then there are the inlets, basically 13 major systems, and four further series of inlets on the outsides of the islands, the great lagoon of Masset Inlet in the centre of Graham Island like the hole in a doughnut, and a multitude of lesser inlets, arms, bays, channels and islands any direction you turn.

As the 1.5-foot ocean tide, moving in from the southwest, strikes the Vancouver Island shore simultaneously from Nitinat to Cape Scott, it slops up to an average height of ten feet. At Port Alberni, at the

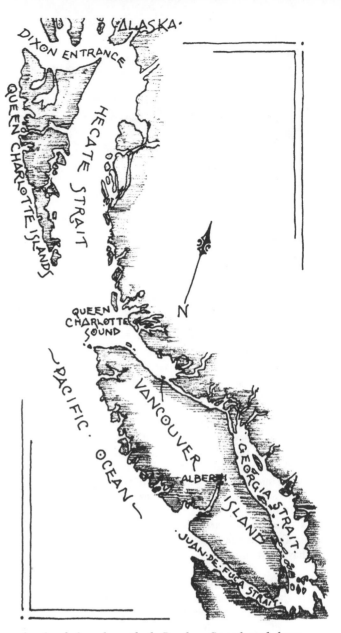

head of broadmouthed Barclay Sound and long-stemmed Alberni Canal, it's twelve feet. This funnel effect was particularly evident during the Alaskan tidal wave of 1962, which passed with little notice at Tofino on the outer coast but caused severe flooding at Port Alberni.

The tidal swell actually jars Vancouver Island on its base. The earthquate seismograph at Beacon Hill each day records the slightest backward movement of the shore as the tide comes in, and the slightest outward movement as it retreats.

The tide enters the Strait of Georgia by curling around Cape Flattery and running southeast down Juan de Fuca Strait. This reverse turn is not easily accomplished and those prone to think of severe tidal turbulence as a property of constricted inland channels might be surprised to find fierce rips and overfalls out here miles into the open ocean from Cape Flattery. The same thing happens where the tide enters around the north end of the Island, off Cape Scott. And nearly out of sight of Cape Knox at the top end of the Queen Charlottes, where the stream is turned down Dixon Entrance, there are overfalls steep enough to capsize large boats. Moving oceans don't change course very gracefully.

On the west coast of the Charlottes the tide is also

in the ten-foot range, but arrives a half-hour later than at Vancouver Island.

The tide progresses very slowly down the 60-mile length of Juan de Fuca Strait, filtering tediously through the narrow passes of the Gulf Islands, and arrives in Georgia Strait delayed a full six hours. But once the tidal swell reaches this regular, open basin it covers the full 130-mile length in 30 minutes without great variation in range or current; Powell River, Nanaimo and Pender Harbour can all use the Point Atkinson table in the tide book. In Vancouver Harbour however, less than two miles east of Point Atkinson, a separate table is required. Vancouver is inside the narrow neck of Burrard Inlet, and any inlet with a constriction at its mouth has tides distinctly its own. The floods tend to be later and smaller. At Holberg at the end of constricted Quatsino Inlet the tide comes 45 minutes later than at Clayoquot just outside, and at Porpoise Bay below Sechelt Inlet's notorious Skookumchuck Rapids high tide is two hours and 13 minutes later and 6.4 feet smaller than at Sechelt a few thousand feet of low isthmus away on Georgia Strait.

There are all degrees of landlocked inlets on the coast, from Burrard, Princess Louisa, Sechelt, Drury and Draney Inlets with their increasingly small necks, to Nitinat Lake on the west coast of the Island where the seas of the open Pacific have pushed up a gravel bar that dries at low tide, to big lagoons like Von Donop's on Cortes Island or Bradley lagoon in Blunden Harbour with its reversing salt water waterfall, to Powell Lake at Powell River which hasn't had a tide since the ice age but still holds salt water.

The most outrageous bottleneck on the coast is probably Nakwakto Narrows near Cape Caution which drains a system of four inlets — 700 miles of shoreline all told — through a passage barely 1000 feet wide. There is a small streamlined island in the middle of the narrows called Tremble Island, that is reputed to shake so perceptibly the trees dance in a big tide. It may be the swiftest tidal rapids in the world, achieving velocities of 24 knots, but for all its thunder and whirling spume it never manages to get the water in Seymour Inlet down more than four feet before the outside tide, which has a 14-foot range, meets it on the return and sets it roaring back in again.

At the heads of deep-mouthed inlets tides have greater than normal range and occur almost simultaneously with outside tides. Whaletown on Cortes Island is 52 miles from the head of Bute Inlet but the time difference for high water is only three minutes and for low nine minutes. The range, following the tendency of the tidal swell to surge up as it runs inland, increases by 2% to 12%. In the big northern inlets much the same picture holds true.

As the coast divides basically into two regions, so in turn does the south region itself. Vancouver Island is shaped like a Haida longhouse, gable on, with its roof peak pressing the mainland shore near the top of Georgia Strait. This gives the inland waters very generally the shape of an hourglass, with the broad expanses of Georgia and Queen Charlotte Straits at either end narrowing into Johnstone Strait, then nearly pinching right off as the roof peak jams Quadra and Sonora Islands against the mouth of Bute Inlet. The tidal stream which enters around the north end of the Island flushes down Queen Charlotte and Johnstone Straits with relatively little impediment until it crashes into Sonora and Quadra Islands here at the pinch in the hourglass. By the time it has boiled through the great rapids of Seymour Narrows, the Hole-in-the-Wall and the Yacultas, this northern tide is almost the same "age" as the south stream, which it meets about seven miles farther down.

Savary Island, a wispy crescent of sand with brown

soft beaches and fir trees that arc out over the waters tufted like palms, rests here in the calm eye of the tides and Bill (the Beak) Ashworth of the old Royal Savary Arms, a long Ichabod Crane sort of guy with a lopsided grin, never tires of eulogizing the unnaturally gentle climate this favoured position endows, advertising year round swimming and periodically greeting visitors in leis and hula skirt. More precisely in the middle of the two streams is rocky Mittlenatch Island towards the Island side, and it too breathes a kind of halcyon air, serving as the night roost and nesting ground for thousands of the gulf's seagulls.

It's a different story just up the way at Cape Mudge. There the wide swift river of Discovery Pass piles into the Gulf in a mass of rips that constitutes one of the most un-serene pieces of water on the inside passage, particularly in a southeast blow. A lump hardly big enough to slop your coffee on the ebb tide, when the tide turns will rear up in a short high sea that has been the end of more than one unwary vessel. Still, those blessed with local knowledge can sometimes skirt over towards Wilby Shoal and ride the big back eddy all the way into Quathiaski Cove for a level coffee and another serious look at the tide book before heading into Seymour Narrows.

North of the pinch in Johnstone Strait is another bad place for mixing wind and tide. A big flood may run south at four knots, and a southeast wind coming up the strait will brush up a short high chop that can make your small boat skipper wish he was back in the Dust Bowl.

But anyone who heads up there in a southeaster pretty well deserves what he gets; the more innocent predicament is to be caught in Johnstone Strait with an ebb running up against a westerly, which is just as wicked. "Westerlies bring clear weather of course, so in the morning you'll think ah, what a lovely day, and set out on the flood tide, then by noon it changes and suddenly you're in trouble. In Johnstone Strait there's not many places to hide either, except on the bottom, and there's lots of company down there."

North of Cape Caution the tides work in different ways. The ocean tidal swell washing in through Queen Charlotte Sound fills the deep inlets like Smiths and Rivers, Dean and Burke in the same way as the deep inlets to the south, but the open-ended channels tend to fill from both ends with tidal streams meeting in the middle. Tides in Grenville Channel for instance, that straight-walled, 60-mile alleyway approaching Prince Rupert from the south, meet either at Morning Point or Evening Point depending on season and weather. What is considered very smart is to reach Evening Point at high water slack so that you have the flood pushing you in and the ebb pulling you out.

The main factor that shapes tidal behaviour on the north coast is Hecate Strait. Because at the lower end it's 80 miles wide and 200 fathoms deep and at the top end 40 miles wide and 10 fathoms deep — the classic scoop shape of Fundy or Frobisher, the tidal swell surges from about 15 feet at Bella Bella up to 26 feet at Prince Rupert.

"You get the lowest low tides, minus tides, in the middle of the day during the summer, which works out to be just the time we're up there packing gear and grub up and down those ramps. It's climbing a ladder, not walking a ramp."

Water is such nervous twitchy stuff. How much so

you don't always realize because it's clear and you can't see what it's doing but mark it with something, look at a mud puddle with a little trickle entering it and see the fantastic ceremony and brown filigree that attends the slightest movement, and the histrionic way moving water reacts to the slightest irregularity in its path, enacting all implications, so many swirls and counterswirls it would take a week to catalogue just what happens in one mud puddle.

Then think of this coast, as intricate as life itself, 17,000 miles compressed to 500, and the water swirling back and forth multiplying complexity by complexity . . . of course no one understands the tides, not in the way you could write about anyway.

To the people who live and work on the seafalls the task of knowing the entire spectrum of tidal motions, currents and eddies and rips that are as significant to fishermen and towboaters as the qualities of soils and contours of land to the farmer, though perhaps it's felt more than known. This obscure and subjective science is often referred to in official circles with certain grudging respect as "local knowledge."

"There is a condition near Prospect Point," says second-generation Vancouver towboater Bill Cates, "that I think I ought to call attention to. This is the meeting of the back eddy with the ebb stream. As a big ebb pours out under the Lions Gate Bridge, a strong back eddy is formed which runs along the shore from Siwash Rock towards Prospect Point.

"It is customary for boats entering Vancouver Harbour to take advantage of this eddy and get as close to Prospect Point as possible before entering the ebb stream.

"The danger lies in the fact that the vessel is approaching the Point with about a two-knot current in her favour, when suddenly she is struck on the starboard bow by an adverse stream of about six knots and thrown half-way across the narrows directly into the path of outgoing traffic.

"When a tug has scows or a car barge this ebb stream is doubly dangerous, as the tug enters the stream first and is swept westward while the tow continues east. The towline will come slack at first then tighten with a snap. Several tugs have been capsized by this happening.

"On coming in the Harbour the south shore of course is favoured. There is not much eddy until the Harris house is passed, 500 yards east of the bridge. After the house is passed an eddy forms in by Lumberman's Arch and extends in to Brockton Point but care must be taken as there are large boulders in the area.

"When leaving Vancouver Harbour, especially with a tow, it is good to buck out against the last of the flood. The first of the ebb then sweeps close along the south shore to Siwash Rock and in no time you are at Ferguson Point where the guns were placed during the war. This condition, unless the ebb is very small, only lasts a short while and is much more pronounced when it is raining and the Capilano River is high. As soon as the ebb stream reaches any strength, the eddy I was talking about forms and then it would be impossible to tow a boom southwest from Prospect Point.

"My father used to tell me how the steamer *Beaver*, the first steamer on the coast, was wrecked just south of Prospect Bluff. She was a side wheeler, with her rudder placed in the same position as on an ordinary vessel. With her speed of four knots it meant the rudder had very little effect. My father also said that on this trip the crew were sober and therefore not normal. However she came slowly out of the narrows and to dodge the tiderip the captain swung her bow to the south. As soon as the back eddy struck her bow she swung around and ran ashore just west of Prospect Point. I don't think any attempt was made to salvage her.

"The tide will change from a strong ebb to full slack in a matter of about 20 minutes. Right after low water slack by the tide book a line will form across the channel. There will be a rippling foamy edge appear along this line and all water in this area will start eastward. This is the first of the flood."

And on it goes, a clockwork universe of eddies within eddies, a study not of one lifetime but many, always changing but as the wise realize, forever doing the same things.

"It is a strange fact that after a tide[1] peaks although it still has a large range, it will not develop the same fierce currents as a tide that is making. My father showed me this when I was a small boy . . ."

'Bonanza' on 2nd Narrows Bridge ~ Burrard Inlet ·

THE YACULTA RAPIDS (pronounced Yooclataw) run between Sonora Island and Stuart Island off the mouth of Bute Inlet. They are longer and rougher and twistier than Seymour Narrows on the Vancouver Island side but they have the great advantage of better protection at the south end, which makes them the choice of anyone who has reason to avoid the volatile seas off Cape Mudge.

There are two parts to the Yacultas, the rapids between the Dent Islands and the rapids between the Gillard Islands. Boats travel due north up Calm Channel, then enter Gillard pass by making a hard left turn heading due west between the Islands. The Dent Islands are passed either by turning 90 degrees right up Tugboat Pass, between the Islands, or by heading straight into Dent Rapids along the Sonora shore. Tugboat Pass is about 700 feet wide and the other slightly more. The stream runs 8-9 knots in the passes and breaks up in huge rips and 40-foot whirl-

[1]Coast people have almost as many meanings for tide as Eskimos have for snow. A man may say he is waiting for a clam digging tide and mean the simple going down of the water, or he may say there's a lot of tide in Alert Bay and mean a lot of current. In this case Captain Cates means a tidal cycle, building up to a peak height and then falling off over a period of many days.

pools on the downstreams side.

The waters between the two rapids are further confused by the fact that Bute Inlet dumps a lot of boiling water in through Arran Rapids on the east side which runs 9-10 knots and has a decided reputation for man-eating.

The people who get the most ulcers out of these rapids are undoubtedly the towboat men, who face the regular problem of herding frail and ponderous log booms from the northern logging camps down to the mills in the south. Barges and the practice of bundling logs have taken much of the pain out of it today but until the late 50's it was all flatbooms. Dozens of small tugboat companies were competing with each other for myriads of little gyppoes that blighted the hills around Minstrel Island and up Knight Inlet like a great scrofulous plague. There was a steady stream of booms making south and the Yacultas were like a revolving door on $1.49 day.

Captain Hec Fisher, who put in a half century or so on that route, says the classic approach was to arrive off Henry Point a mile above Little Dent an hour and 20 minutes before low slack. That way the tide was running against you but not too hard and as it eased off you could sneak up so when slack came you'd be as close in to the pass as you could get.

Still there was no chance of making both rapids in one jump, unless it was a miniscule tide. You'd tie up at Mermaid Bay on the south side of Big Dent and wait for the next low slack 12 hours later. There would be a high slack within six hours but you couldn't move on that because you couldn't get through before it turned and started hauling you back.

Day after day there would be four and five boats waiting over in Mermaid Bay.

"Well it's a dangerous situation you see because everybody's trying to make slack water, but you can't all be there at the same time. Somebody's going to be late.

"Whoever's got the most power to buck up, he's going to get out first. But the next guy he's got to think pretty careful what he's doing, because you always overtake the guy ahead of you, the tide's always stronger behind, and if you get too close you can't keep out of each other's way. But if you wait too long you're going to end up in white water."

Why skippers get grey. Do you let the other guy get a tide up on you, and get back up north before you so he can poach on your carefully hoarded camps, or do you head in late and risk a $40,000 boom?

"I went through there with the *Active* one time," says Captain Jack Ryall, another half-century man, "and hell, I took a whole side of the damn boom out and just about took the winch off. Right at Gillard Island light."

There were many options, depending on your power, the size of your tow, and whether it's half-sunk pulp from some ass-out-of-his-pants barefoot gyppo who doesn't believe in boomchains or nice peelers put together just like the Kon-Tiki, but mostly it was a matter of time and tide, and as you churned down Cordero Channel you'd be phoning ahead and watching the water and putting all these things together in your head trying to find the easy combination. Sometimes instead of bucking into Mermaid Bay you could slip in on the last of the flood and save six hours right there. To really frost the poker players in at Mermaid you could smoke-stack 'er right across their noses and over through Arran Rapids.

"Say you're coming through on the last of the flood. Well by the time you get to Mermaid Bay you only need another twenty minutes tide and bang, you're through Arran Rapids. Mind you've got that long pull around the backside of Stuart Island but then you're twelve hours ahead of the guy that stopped at Mermaid.

"Now not everybody could *do* that. It's a straight shot but there's a bad rip, it breaks up very bad on the flood, on the other end, on the Bute side, there's some bad holes there."

If you made it it was a real notch on your pole but if you missed and had to call the other guys in to help you back to Mermaid they would keep you hanging your head a long time. Still, the man who would gamble on the tides like that would be thought more of than the mother gooses who always took two days to get through.

There were a few like Ryall who used the Hole-in-the-Wall a lot. If they could see a traffic jam shaping up at Mermaid they'd turn off into Nodales Channel, go down Discovery Passage, cut back through Okisollo Channel and duck out through the Hole in a 20-mile U-shaped bypass. The hitch was running the Hole, a narrow rock-studded alley with sheer 1700-foot walls and 12-knot rapids. It was four miles long and a boom three sections wide would just fit.

"What you'd generally do was take the last of the flood, just enough tide to get through. That way it would be slack when you got down to the lower rapids and you could buck the rest of the way out."

"You could tell by the rocks how you were doing. You'd know the rocks — one would always look like a snag but it was always a rock. Another would look someone's face you knew, lying down. Well if the tip of the nose is just braiding the surface of the water, you're okay, but if it's out down to the oysters you better give'er everything she's got otherwise you're never going to make it.

"You hit it wrong sometimes, you're too early, and suddenly it's all white water and there's nothing to do but try and steer it through. There are places you know you gotta stay away from, other places it can't hit no way cause there's back eddies and you're flyin' around like mad trying to stay out of trouble because once that boom hits the beach, why everything's crackin and flyin, chains are pullin out of the ends of sticks and you got logs all over the place, it's not a very happy situation.

"Taking chances. It's always from taking a chance. You're late on the tide. You should of stopped. You say, oh I'll make, I'll make it."

A lot of skippers wouldn't go near the Hole but Ryall says it's one of those things that looked bad but once you got to know it was all in a day's work.

Hec Fisher towed through Nakwakto for 15 years and felt the same way about it.

"There's no worst places really. It's more what you know best is easiest."

SALMON DON'T LIKE TO BUCK THE TIDE. The only time they will do this is when they're late returning to the spawning ground, pushed to it by that terrific instinct. Once at the river of course they will not only buck heavy currents, they will swim up waterfalls. But in the sea they move with the tide, favouring back eddies around points and in rapids to make the easiest headway. When the tide turns against them often they'll lay up in a bay till it changes. They follow the contour of the land. That's why you always see the net boats hounding the beaches, sometimes stringing a gillnet parallel to the shore to catch the fish weaving in and out.

No one watches the swirls and counterswirls of coastal waters with a keener eye than the trollers. They spend their days searching out rips, psyching out unseen bottoms, watching for signs of feed. What is feed? No one but the troller knows. He spends his days hunting it, talking of it incessantly but the normal eye sees nothing. It's what the salmon eat evidently, a fine mysterious substance that flows with the water.

"Feed goes where the tide goes. If you're bucking the tide your lure's bucking the tide and that looks artificial. Salmon won't bite that, salmon aren't stupid."

So if you can figure out where currents are meeting and bunching the feed all up like they bunch the scattered drift up sometimes on the surface, you'll find the fish because they know how to find it too. Trollers hardly notice what the part of the coast looks like that's sticking out of the water, except when they want to take a fix on a good new hole. They spend all their time piecing together this dream of the part that's underneath, plotting it all out in their little black books.

Generally they hunt for upwellings or rips. Anywhere there's a lot of tide generally there's a lot of sea life, a lot of feed and a lot of herring hanging around the feed and a lot of spring and coho hanging around the herring. Places like Seymour Narrows and the Skookumchuck have a lot of ling and grey and rock cod too. The best time for the Chuck, say the cod men, is two hours before and two hours after slack.

The best fishing is often two to three days after the highest or lowest tides. You set a gillnet an hour-and-a-half before slack at least.

"There is a breeze always comes up at the change of tide. With a flood you'll get a southeast and a northwest with an ebb. We call it the tide wind. You look over at the treetops and it's dead calm, but there's a little breeze on the water."

Then there's the wind tide. A good wind will build up a surface current of two or three knots. It's a bugger when you're trolling, you can't slow the boat down. Makes you go too fast.

You catch more fish on a flood tide. Humpies swim ahead of a rip. Dogs follow. Cohoes swim in a rip.

An old Swede told us wherever there's a rip, there's coho. They swim in the back eddies that form along each side of the rip.

"I remember one time I vas op in Camano Sound. I vasn't catching a ting! It vas getting late in de day and I figured I'd about had it but I saw one fish yump so I tot vell I make one more set den I have a good rest. So I set de net and go below. It vas dead calm and I vas cooking someting and I remember I heard, blip, blip, blip . . . blip, blip, blip, and I vondered now vat de hell is dat. So I goes op on deck and oh my yumpin yeesus, here's a grrreat big rip yust strrreaming out of Surf Inlet. Vas de change of tide you see. Vell, *yunk!* you should haf seen de yunk dat rip was full of — vood and sticks and kelp and bark yust sticking out of it. I couldn't see my net for de yunk. Well I figure I lost my net for sure. I vas so mad I say to hell vit it and go back below. I stay dere awhile, trying to read, trying to sleep, till finally I figured, maybe I'll pull it in for de cork line.

"So I go back on de deck. I could only see a few corks, dey were dese old plastic kind yust shrunk op like prunes. The net vas pulled out so much, I tell you dat net must haf gone halfway to China. I pull on her and man is she *heavy*. Vell dat net was yust *full* of northern coho. Dey vas in dat rip."

"I NEVER DID KNOW too much about navigation," says Jimmy Sewid, one of the most successful fishermen in B.C., "but I was very familiar with the tides. You have to be very careful with the tides. Most of the time I just looked at the water to tell the direction it was going to change. All the tides were different and I knew them all. They were all in my head."

Jack Ryall says, "You get to know a place, you'd just know it, that's all." Jimmy Sewid says, "It's all in my head." At a certain stage words can do no more than point in the direction of what is unsayable. It's like when you've been some place in the city, not long enough for your waking mind to absorb the location but long enough for this other part of your mind to get an impression so you say, "I don't know where it is but if I see it I'll recognize it." Or sometimes you'll be walking in the woods and you'll think hey, this looks familiar, I've been here before, there should be a little hollow stump right over there. So you go over and there it is, but when you were there before or for what, you have no idea.

If someone came up and asked you how you knew, what would you say? I just know. It comes in from that foggy accurate part of the mind too rational people don't use because they can't prove it's there but good fishermen, towboat skippers, nuclear physicists and poker players rely on it for all the important things. It's a kind of consciousness this coast of endless intricacy enforces upon those who come to bargain with it for their livelihoods, and marks them with a deepness.

"When the tide is ebbing," says Captain Cates, "all the creatures of the sea become listless. The crabs which you may catch in 40 to 50 feet of water and which have been coming constantly to bait during the flood tide will cease to feed during the ebb. It seems queer that they would know the difference in that depth of water but such is the case. Even although the tide is still high and the flats are well covered, all the crabs and small fish will disappear as soon as the ebb starts.

"Along the edge of the receding sea the ducks and gulls feed and the herons wade out quietly on their long legs to catch the small retreating fish with a lightning dart of their long pointed beaks.

"Now as a big ebb reaches near its extreme low, a tension seems to come into the air. I have asked many sailors and they say they can feel it. Certainly the fish and birds and crabs know the flood is coming. A little before low water all these creatures reappear and become very active. Any fisherman will tell you that low slack is the time to catch salmon as they race around in the little eddies and snap up smaller fish. All along the shore gulls swoop and dive for there is renewed life in the sea. The old Indians smile and say *kwa-'kwatts*, the tide is rising.

"As the tide reaches its crest, the tension eases and peace seems to come to the shore of the inlet. In the summer this is usually in the evening and an old Indian friend of mine used to say, "Take your white man's pleasures and give me a nice *snaaquaylsh* (dugout) and let me paddle far up the sloughs where the smell of the salt grass fills the air and I can see the flounders scooting away in the clear water and hear the birds in the trees along the shore singing their sleepy eveining song. There is no peace like the peace of *Kwahaluis*, the full of the tide."

•Skookumchuck Running•

The Bank Trollers

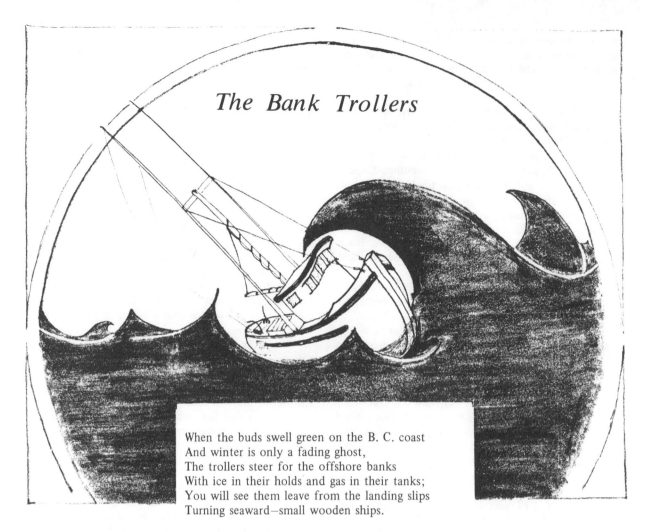

When the buds swell green on the B. C. coast
And winter is only a fading ghost,
The trollers steer for the offshore banks
With ice in their holds and gas in their tanks;
You will see them leave from the landing slips
Turning seaward—small wooden ships.

From Port of Vancouver, from snug James Bay,
From Rupert Harbour at break of day,
From tide-swept Juan de Fuca Strait,
From the narrow gut of the Lions Gate.
Or out from the mouth of Queen Charlotte Sound,
You will see them roll to the salmon ground.

They go to plow in Hell's Half-acre
On the breast of the old grey widow-maker.
With hook-scarred fingers they ply their trade
In the place where the ocean storms are made;
From dawn till a bloodshot sun goes down
To feed hungry folk in some distant town.

From Umatilla to Icy Strait
From gaunt Cape Beale to Skidegate,
The troller's poles go waving by
Etched sharp against a bleared grey sky.
From Dixon's Entrance to Puget Sound,
On the Virgins, the Goslings, the Steamboat Ground,
Where a myriad herring and needlefish breed
And kings and silvers upon them feed;
(Springs and cohoes to you and me)
Silver torpedoes that swim deepsea.

They ride the groundswell where grim Cape Cook
Thrusts to the west like a giant thumb,
They wallow abreast of Cape St. James
Past which the screaming nor'westers come.
The Horseshoe, Tow Hill, or far to the south
In the troubled waters of Nitinat's mouth.
Late in September they fish awhile

By foggy Swiftsure or Forty Mile,
'Till the fall southeasters drive them home
Chased by combers all white with foam;
Or over in Nawhitti where the strong tides flow—
All these are the places the trollers know.

Rose, Aladdin, Baltic, Norn,
Bear Island, Luard, Early Dawn,
Norfish, Ube, B.C. Queen,
Mary Ann W., Williameen,
The *Galley Bay* and the *Micmac Chief,*
Angler, Seafarer, Frontier, Rage Reef,
Nipantuck, Juju, Caroline B.,
Gilboa, Master, Madelon C.,
More Kelp, Highdiver, Morien II,
Saturnina, R. W.,
Ten Grand, Four Forty, Never Again,
Dual, Kalmor, El Alamain,
North Cap, the *Rhona,* the *Wendy Ghael,*
And one with an owl on her riding sail.

These are but a few, a thousand more
Steer out from the British Columbia shore;
Hundreds of little wooden boats
Wide in the belly, deep in the keel,
Able as any craft that floats
On the Seven Seas. Thin lines of steel
Cut through the depths with a humming sound
When they shoot their gear on the salmon ground.
Shark and dog-fish hang on their flanks
As they pitch and toss on those offshore banks.

And those who man them are men who have come
Without blare of trumpet or beat of drum,
From the Labrador, the coast of Maine,
From Lunenberg, Trumso, the Shetlands, from Spain,
From the shallow Baltic, the old North Sea,
From the heel of the Boot of Italy.
Finns and Norskys, Canucks and Yanks
Drag trolling gear on the salmon banks.

No weekly paycheck, no eight hour day,
Not so many hours for so much pay.
Out there beyond pierhead or harbour docks
They take no orders, they punch no clocks.
They own their boats (if not always clear),
Their souls are their own and so is their gear;
They can sit when they choose on the booby hatch
And view (when they get it) a good day's catch.

Rain, fog, sunshine, in calm or blow,
Loaded or empty they come and go;
By chart and compass, by reckoning dead,
Sometimes by guess and a sounding lead.

Not always safely. Swirling fog,
Five degrees error, a half-sunk log,
An offshore breaker—such are the chances
A troller takes at these deepsea dances;
In a watery ballroom far from land
Where the step is a devilish saraband.
Where flung spray spatters like showers of hail
On a taut, triangular steadying sail.

Driving shoreward in the dark of night
To drop his hood in some sheltered bight,
A lone wolf troller strains eyes and ears
For hazards that every seaman fears.
(No holy abbot of Aberthbrock
Has placed a bell on Bonilla Rock).

A freshening wind and a rising sea
Hammers the coastline under his lee.
Sudden he lifts on a great dark mound
That turns to white with a roaring sound.
A smash. Impaled on a sunken rock.
A second roller, a second shock.
Midships she bursts like an egg let fall
On a concrete walk. Her timbers all
Are riven, splintered, torn apart,
Stilled is the beat of her iron heart.

And the man that helmed her to her death
Dies with her. One last gurgling breath
And his struggle ceases. Slowly down
His body sinks to a sea-mat brown
Where mermaids sit combing theri weedy locks
On jagged, barnacle-crusted rocks.
There the crabs will pick till his polished bones
Lie white in the locker of Davey Jones.

No bells will toll for his passing. He
Will be mourned by no crepe-clad company.
No graveside eulogy will be read.
Only above his heedless head
The surf will boom and the seagulls cry
Will be faint, far-off in a windy sky.

In some distant anchorage, some safe bay,
When he writes his log at the close of day
Another troller will make this note:
"Lost, up Hecate, the fishing boat *Carioca*.
Seven ton. West coast troller. Crew of one."
Then he'll go below and put on the pot
And sip his coffee when it is hot,
Turn into his blankets and go to sleep,
Thinking of others still riding the deep.
Small wonder if now and then to him
The facts of life are a trifle grim.

Wind, fog, rain, on those offshore banks,
High-peaked groundswell or steep tide-rips,
While there's grub in the lockers and gas in the tanks,
The salmon trollers must make their trips.

Is there ease or glamour in this their life?
Ask any salmon troller's wife.

Why do they plow in Hell's Half-acre
On the breast of the old grey widow-maker?

Why do they follow this chancey trade
In the place where the ocean storms are made?

The answer is simple. I do not lie.
They fish for a living. As you and I
Must work for a living
Until we die.

Book Reviews

The Cape Scott Story

Lester R. Petersen, writer-historian and frequent contributor to *Raincoast Chronicles*, has just published his *Cape Scott Story*, a very human and fascinating account of settlers struggling to survive both adverse elements and crippling isolation at Vancouver Island's northernmost tip.

Petersen's interest is more than academic. He spent his earliest years in the community — by then almost abandoned, has revisited the area on numerous occasions and can draw on memory for his moving descriptive passages. In a thought provoking opening chapter, he advances some intriguing theories about prehistoric racial drift and the early coast Indian cultures. He moves easily from the macrocosm to the microcosm in succeeding chapters, telling how the first short-lived Danish colony was established just before the turn of the century and of subsequent communities that sprang up in such places as San Josef Valley and Sushartie in the wake of the initial failure.

He tells of simple pleasures in lamplit cabins, of packboard feats over slippery trails and the pure joy of infrequent boat days. He captures the pathos of deserted farms and the eerie emptiness of Indian-haunted beaches. The book is embellished by some excellent photographs.

The Cape Scott Story, by Lester R. Petersen, Mitchell Press, Vancouver, 1974, $3.95.

No Foreign Land

NO FOREIGN LAND, by Ted Poole and Wilfred Pelletier, is a graphic account of one Indian's search for identity and meaning through the blind alleys, strewn with false values, of white society. The story is told in Mr. Pelletier's voice. It describes the warm sense of community of his Reserve upbringing, a sense that is all but lost when he leaves his people to enter the whiteman's city. He enjoys considerable success in business and ends up owning several profitable ventures, but something is wrong. Throwing it all over, he returns to the Reserve where he spends a couple of years in minimal circumstances rediscovering his roots. When he enters the white man's world again, it is with an entirely different attitude. He becomes an active public speaker for Indian causes and a co-director of the Nishnawabe Institute, an Indian educational and cultural project for which he still works in a continuing search for self-realization, the furtherance of ecological sanity and dignity for all men regardless of race.

That the book works so well is due in large part to the yeoman job done by Pelletier's friend Ted Poole in coordinating, editing and embellishing the material. Poole's sure hand and poet's eye are evident throughout, although never intrusively. It is a happy collaboration, for the men share a common philosophy. Poole was for twenty-five years a resident of Grantham's Landing on B.C.'s Sunshine Coast where he developed his sensibilities as a writer and his long-time interest in the problems of the native people. *Raincoast Chronicles* hopes to publish a new story by him in the near future.

No Foreign Land, by Wilfred Pelletier and Ted Poole, Pantheon Books, New York, 1973.

Drunk on Wood

Canadians, according to some obscure survey published recently, buy more poetry per capita than any other country in the world. Perhaps it has something to do with the climate. In any event, it is hoped that they will see fit to buy *Drunk on Wood*, an excellent collection by Charles Lillard. In a spare, virile style enlivened by predominantly natural imagery, Lillard draws on his experiences in the logging camps and back country of B.C. and Alaska to produce some memorable verse, comparable in many ways to the work of the very fine Interior poet Patrick Lane. Both pluck their images primarily from the outdoors, are adept at capturing the awesome presence of raw wilderness, the movement of man and animal against its enormity, the sad slow anger of dispossessed Indians:

GRETE LISTENS TO BOBBY-JACK

That's it. Sit on the dunnage bags,
how about a cup of tea?
It's almost too late, I'm old
and hear more voices than I see.
Where are the caribou this year?
There are no caribou, no caribou this year.

We always had caribou — like trees
on that mountain or spring geese
they are past counting, too many.
Now whitemen pepper this land
with cattle, their hides will jail you —
They aren't caribou.

The lost caribou, the caribou . . .
and if I say the Old Ones are talking,
their wrath growing like sourdough in a pot
and their mercy . . . well . . .
it'll tree your Jesus again.
But who'll listen? There are no caribou today.

This is great stuff, well worth the attention of anyone who enjoys finely wrought poetry of the robust sort.

Drunk on Wood, by Charles Lillard, Sono Nis Press, Vancouver, 1973, $7.95.

CHILKAT CHIEF · DEW · KAMOOP · B.C. GIRL · ALERT

·ZEPHYR II·
BELLA BELLA

NAMU· JULY 1973·

251

WILLOW POINT

Unloading a Dragger at Campbell Avenue

(October 1971)

The TOR II sitting with stern half underwater

rasping winch breaking down
every ten minutes
still dark
the north shore lights winking
thru the drizzle
sometime around dawn
the sea gulls are just there
perched on the tin rooftops

standing up to my ass
in Skidigate soles
pitching them into the bucket
hoisted overhead
the slime / sticky shit
dripping on my head
hose and scrub the penboards
stack them astern
dumping tons of rotten yellow ice
over the side
& pumping the bilge
a grey cloud around the boat
soaked right through
oilskins and indian sweater
by 9 o'clock
and the bums are lined-up
on the wharf
to beg or steal a fish

Stikine

boys head
in the river
slick as a seal
fell backward
out of the boat
into the current
came up
screaming
a look of terror

this time
last year
two little girls
and the guy
trying to save them
drowned
in a rain storm

he came back
a day later
wrapped in a net
& the fisherman
pulling his set
by lantern
went religious

BOOK REVIEW

Between the Sky and the
Splinters

Peter Trower, the logging poet, needs no introduction to readers of *Raincoast Chronicles*. His axe-hewn ballads and lyrics about alder-filled clearings, stubborn spar trees, sad sawdust hulks and ancient hookers who shift their snoose before they speak, prompted a clamour of requests for this first major collection even before it was announced.

Peter Trower is no dust jacket lumberjack. Born in 1930, he grew up in the pulp mill town of Port Mellon on Howe Sound, left school early and has spent most of his adult life on the upcoast bunkhouse circuit. He is a natural writer who has made little effort to publish, although his work has appeared in some of the most respected literary publications on the continent, notably *Poetry (Chicago)*, and has won the support of such established writers as Al Purdy, Irving Layton and Earle Birney.

He is not an innovator in form, choosing to write in language that is familiar to him, and this is partly because he has had to be innovative in content, reporting in from slash ruined hillsides not previously known to Canadian literature and proving new bodies of rapture and despair, pockets of perfect consciousness not commonly thought to occur in such places.

As Patrick Lane writes in the introduction, this is surely the kind of thing Dorothy Livesay had in mind when she wrote, "the real poems are being written in outports/ on backwoods farms . . . men with snow in their mouths . . . resonant/ indubitable." No one who loves the west coast should miss this book.

Between the Sky and the Splinters, by **Peter Trower**, **Harbour Publishing, Madeira Park, B.C. 1974, $3.50.**

They Don't Make 'Em Anymore: Peck Easthope

Easthope! Just say the word, even now, a full decade later, and grins go up all around the room. Lasthope you mean, someone will say. Jesus Light of the World, someone else. Then without further provocation the stories will start: "First Easthope I ever owned was in '32 when I bought the old Sheila B *off Gordie Dewar. Had a little 8-12 in it. Beautiful little motor. Best motor Easthope ever made if you ask me. But it had the hell scared outta me ..."*

Horses were never much help to settlers here. The only access was by water, but water that was so sheltered from wind and cranky with tide as to make sail a useless tool. It was for this reason the region became the scene of some of the earliest experiments in steam navigation and why that first of motorized vessels the Beaver *became so central to its history.*

They are relatives, Beaver *and* Easthope, *not simply in purpose – the one originating access to the coast, the other democratizing that access – but also in that blockish primitive character that gave them their place in people's affections. Both were early ventures into unknown technologies that long outstayed their times. The Easthope was truly one of the first commercially produced internal combustion engines, slow and massive and deliberately simple, the dream of a 19th century inventor that had become an anachronism by the time Detroit engineers finally persuaded fishermen to abandon it for the high speed age a half-century later.*

Both came to be cherished as peculiarities, and there's nothing B.C. cherishes more than its peculiarities, in its Beavers *and* Easthopes *and* P.G.E.s *as in its* DeCosmos's *and* Gagliardis *and* Ma Murrays. *It's to do with being a longstanding place of refuge for the world's individualists and oddballs, a category that by no means excludes the remarkable company of Easthope fathers and sons that continues to offer a full maintenance and parts service from their Steveston machine shop. (The last Easthope motor was made in 1968.)*

Percy (Peck) Easthope worked in the family machine shop from the beginning and with his late brother George managed the business from 1914 through 1953, its busiest years. With the help of his fellow Vancouver pioneer Joe Simson we were able to get his story down on tape in two sessions last April and apart from some minimal rearranging in the interests of chronological order we offer it as it was spoken.

My dad had no desire or likin' for business or anything else, his mind was right on inventin'. Experimentin'! *All* the time. It was in our family. It was a relative of ours invented the safety pin, and Pop, he developed the first ball bearing, for a bicycle.

He used to race on those high wheels, you know, the big wheels? He had a medal for it. And when those first came out they had a plain bearing, you see? And Pop and his friend knew that was a lot of friction on those main bearings you see, so he thought well, we put a roller bearing or a ball bearing on that see, and they did. And they were the first ones that did it. Put the ball bearing on the bicycle. That's the first time it was used in the world. That's where it was invented, right there.

One of Pop's main projects in England, just before we left, was an aeroplane. He was in there in 1880 some odd, trying to build a flyin' machine, him and his brother. It had two fans, one vertical and one horizontal, y'see, somethin' like a helicopter and they had 'er hung from an A-frame affair – pedal powered y'see – and they'd climb up there and pump away like blazes and cut 'er loose y'see. Heh heh. Didn't work of course. This was what, twenty years before the Wright brothers. After that they tried makin' a motor for it – ran on gun cotton! No gas in those days, no fuel. Otherwise they might've made a go of it.

That was Wolverhampton. Staffordshire. We were all born in Wolverhampton, Staffordshire. Six boys and three girls. Well, two girls then. One came after. So Dad, he thought he'd like to come to a new country to bring up the boys in, you see?

That was '89, we came out in 1889. Settled in Burnaby. Kingsway and Edmonds. We built Edmonds Street – had to, to get to the place. My dad, someone down in Westminster sold him the lot – there was a little boom on you see – and great big fir and alder stumps you know, ten feet in diameter, right in the middle of that! The Gilley Brothers were loggin' all around our house – *with oxen*. Not even horses yet. That's when we came out y'see.

Coming out, what switched him to Westminster, some people on the train, they got talking to Pop you know, and they said whatayou been used to doin', what's your line, and oh, he said, "I'm mechanically minded," and this that n'other, you see? He was going to the O'Kannigan Valley! Hah! The O'Kannigan Valley. Going to take up farming, you see. And they asked Pop if he had any experience and well he said, "I had a window box one time!" That's all he knew about farming. So they persuaded him, they said well with your line, you know, we think you better continue on to New Westminster. Just a small city starting up there and they'll need people there in your line of business. You see? Mechanicin' line of business. So he decided to keep on to the end of the line.

That was 1889. I was born in 1885, I was four years old, you see.

And oh, it was just wonderful, there was an Indian on the other side of every tree. And Pop, when he came out, he'd heard about that, and he equipped them all with Bowie knives and guns and everything else – they had guns when they landed up 'cause they thought they'd have to fight the Indians and bears.

But as far as the kids were concerned, oh it was close to heaven you know, hunting around. We all had muzzle loaders, you could get muzzle loaders for three dollars then. There were other guns around, but Dad bein' experimental minded, he used all the money he could get hold of on his experiments. He tried all sortsa things when he come to this country, experimentin', and we didn't have any cash. So all we had was muzzle loaders. We shot grouse and ducks, you see? Burnaby Lake was great on ducks. And grouse, on both sides of the road, all the time. Willow grouse.

At first Dad worked down in Westminster for Armstrong-Morrison — they built the first wagon bridge across the Fraser, at Westminster. Then he got into the bicycle business. Down on Hastings, right in the middle of the block Barr and Anderson had a plumbin' business, between Abbott and Cambie. Right across from Woodward's. Barr and Anderson had a plumbin' shop there and it got a little too small for 'em and Dad rented their shop and they built another one in the same block about twice as big.

and they always joked 'im, they said well about every half-hour he'd have to take a little dustpan and a little broom and he'd sweep it all together again and get it goin' again. Ha ha. But it worked. That was the real start, right there.

That was the first gasboat in Vancouver. Ran on petrol. Petrol was out then, you see. That was in 1900.

I remember seein' it many times. It had a cylinder about as big as a quart jar, had a little wee bit of flywheel on it and, it worked ennaway. Pop gave him the principle of it you see – all you need was a crankshaft and a connectin' rod and a piston and so on you see. Two-cycle – it had the valves in the cylinder, side of the cylinder. And he told him you see, every time it went down it sucked in the charge

(L.) Vincent : Ernest

Well my dad, bein' the inventive type, said well, I'm not goin' to buy bicycles from C.C.M. and these, I'm gonna make one. So he started in and he did make a few. Bought tubes and parts and braised them together there in the shop, made a few there. The Easthope bicycle. Ha ha.

My brother Vince, he was about 18 those days I guess, he worked with my dad in the bicycle shop. And he got lookin' through some American magazines, and down there you know, there was a motor called Roberts, two-cycle engine came out, around 1900.

And, my brother Vince said, well I think I'd like to make a little gas engine, Dad. Well Dad in the old country had a planing plant and the power in it was a great big natural gas two-cycle engine. Single cylinder stationary engine. And he knew the principle it worked on, see? And he told Vince, he made a little drawing of it you know, how it worked, said I think we can make that. They got a little lathe in there in the shop, and a drill press, and made a little engine, about a half horsepower. Hah!

He made a little engine and he put it in a Peterborough canoe. And it worked. Put it there, and the darn thing, his friends he'd take 'em out for a ride

and when it came up it compressed it, at the top of the compression stroke you had to fire it you see, and down she went again and that's all there was to it. See? Well that was the start.

Then they made a little three horsepower, cast iron, he got the patterns made, got them done at the foundry you see, and *Dan Martin* was one of the first boatbuilders in Vancouver, they got him to build a little 18-foot boat. They got him to build a little boat for that and they put it in and called it the *Swan*.

That was the second motor. And, my it was a wonderful little boat and a wonderful little engine. Designed that himself with a timer and that – you couldn't buy a timer in those days, and they had a mixin' valve on it, no carburettor.

That started things movin', right there. Then our friends wanted them, we had some friends named Hodder, they were fishermen and they lived on Barnston Island up in the Fraser River and they had a 25-foot dugout Indian canoe and they said how about making an engine big enough to go into that canoe. So we made one five horsepower, stepped it up to five. They bought one, put it in that canoe and all the fishermen, when they saw them going up the

river instead of sailing and rowing, y'see, ha ha, oh! we gotta have an engine! Well that started the thing goin' in the fishin' industry. That was the first gas fishboat. An old dugout.

Well we could see what we had ahold of then, and the rest of us started to get behind this new business. There's a picture somewhere I wish I could find, of the gillnet fleet in those days, all these Columbia River sailing boats they had in those days, settin' out for the start of fishin' oh my goodness there must have been two thousand, all with their sails up fannin' out over the river just like a great big flock of gulls. The sun glowing the sails — it was a beautiful sight. A beautiful sight. All them boats to put motors in, you see.

Of course the fishermen didn't all go for motors right off. It was slow to catch on but it came about right, just about as we were able to fill orders they would come in. We moved down to Coal Harbour, the lot where Western Machine is now is where we went to first, and as more orders came in we'd put on a few more men, get another piece of machinery, you see.

Be about nineteen five when we moved. It wasn't long you see, before we needed a bigger place. We went down nights and put in a ways and we'd bring these fishboats in sometimes five at a time, to convert them over.

Most of the boats belonged to the fishermen but they stored them at the canneries. All the same type of boat. All about 24-foot, you see? by 7-foot-6 you see. They called them the Columbia River type. Round bottom, double ender. Good model. Good boat. Wallace, you see, when he first started in he built an awful lotta those. For the canneries. The Burrard Drydock Wallace. That's how he got started. Right down on False Creek he did that. He used to build 'em 25 at a time. He was one of the first ones you see, to build those boats.

I think he built 'em for 75 bucks each. Good boats. A centreboard and sail and oars y'see. Well when we converted 'em we took out the centreboard, put the engine where the centreboard was, and bored a hole down through the skeg in the back, put the p'pellor on, we used to do 'em *five at a time.*

So at first it was just the men who owned their own boats who got power. It was only these late years when canneries started financin' fishermen. And they would give us an order for 15, 20 engines! B.C. Packers and Canadian Fish and that.

What sorta guys were the fishermen then? Oh . . . drunks. The only time they would work is when they

· Ernest Sr. (L)· Bill Menchions (4 from L.)   · Peck (3 from R) ·

were fishing you see? They'd stay on their boats, a lot of 'em, and all the time they weren't out they'd be drinkin' their money up.

They would be pretty excited when they came to buy their first gas motor. After rowin' and tryin' to sail you know? Against the current all the time? They'd be puttin' all that behind them, you see, when they came to get a motor.

Pretty snappy little motor that two-cycle, power every stroke you see. They were a little bit not so economical *quite*, as the four-cycle. You couldn't get the same *scavenging*, you see. The four-cycle uses the in-between stroke as a *scavenge* you see, to scavenge out the cylinder. Two-cycle there was always a little bit left in, after the exhaust went out, there was a little bit exhaust in, that mixed in with the incomin' charge y'see, and took away the efficiency of it. You see?

Also they were touchy as to slowin' down. You couldn't control 'em like a four-cycle. They would miss you know – putput . . . put . . . putput . . . They'd backfire, you see, and one thing another.

That was before reverse gears too. They ran 'em backwards for reverse. You just pulled the switch. You cut the ignition just as it's coming up on compression, and *just* before it goes over, you throw it in again and it's sposed to start back the other way, start running backwards you see. But if you were a thousandth of a second late, she'd jump forward you see.

I remember we sold one to some Japs. It was a great big boat they had. A bunch of Japs out at Steveston. Well they came in to our wharf, there was four or five of 'em on the boat – ennaway, they headed 'er right into the wharf, straight into the wharf – you should never do that with a two-cycle you see, ha ha, well the fella on the bow, he's giving the orders. Go stern, go stern Easthope! Go stern! Hahaha. And he kept hollering and yelling and waving go stern, go stern, go stern Easthope! But then, instead of stoppin' she speeds up and crash, omigosh, these fellas on the bow fly through the air right onto the wharf. Oh damn Easthope, damn Easthope, damn Easthope! Hahaha. It was quite a tricky business y'see.

The fishermen weren't too good of mechanics in those days y'see, that was the thing. They had no idea how it worked. It worked, that's all they knew. If it didn't work, they didn't know anything. Funny story there. You know we used to sell 'em to these Swedes? One of 'em on Rivers Inlet, he had a five horsepower. Well, something went wrong with it and he couldn't start it, he was out fishing, way up the inlet, y'see, way from home? And so he got the oars out, after he'd played himself out turning the flywheel, hahaha, he got the oars out, and he says that son of a son of a thing, it was sittin' there laughin' at me and I was pullin' and rowin' he says, I could see the damn thing laughin' at me you know, heh, you know the engine sittin' there doin' nothing' . . .

He unscrewed it and dumped it overboard. Threw it over. He says I couldn't stand it. Heh heh heh. It's a fact. You see he didn't know what was wrong or anything with it.

Oh, they were temperamental alright. You could flood the base, that was one of the chief things.

We had an oil cup on the front, for lubricating the connecting rod and piston, and it went into the cylinder just at the bottom of the stroke, y'see? Went in and then it went down into the base. At the bottom of the stroke about halfway up the piston, the oil would go right into the piston pin. Lubricate the piston pin. If they forgot to fill the cup she'd let out an awful squeal. That was the piston pin. They had to quick slow 'er right down then pour the oil to 'er for a few minutes, then everythin'd be alright.

Ignition worked off an eccentric. There was an eccentric on the crankshaft with a rod comin' up to drive the waterpump, you see. Well we used this motion for our timin'. We put a finger on the end of that rod and against this we had a brass plate, attached to the cylinder, so the finger was drawing a circle on the brass plate like. Well now at the top of this arc we had an insulated contact with a wire goin' to the plug. And we had this finger hooked up to a buzzer coil and a 6-volt dry cell. So every time the finger went over the contact it shot a little shot of juice through to the plug, fired the charge in the cylinder. The brass plate was on a clicker so you could rotate it to advance the spark. It was simple as

we could make it. That was our idea. Always to find something simple so the fishermen could work it. They thought gas engines were too complicated and mysterious you see, they didn't want to trust them. This is what we had to overcome.

We made two-cycles in quite a few different sizes. Started in with the small one, then the five, and then we built a heavy duty ten. It was a six-inch cylinder. Then we made that engine into a three-cylinder. Six by six – we called it 30-horse.

That was quite a motor. We had Dan Martin build us a yellow cedar, forty feet long, five foot beam – a real narrow boat. So we put a thirty-horse in it and we could go out there and beat the old C.P.R. . . . whatzis name . . . *Princess Victoria*. We were going around twenty mile an hour.

I was in the shop pretty well from the start, no not right from the start — it was this brother Vincent and my dad to start with. It wasn't Easthope Brothers then on the nameplate, it was Easthope and Son. That was that brother y'see, Vince. Then he had an accident, he had an operation, had to go in, he had a lump on his neck. Took him, had a bad doctor and he killed him. He never came out of the operation. Later we found out this doctor had done the same thing to three other people. But we didn't go to doctors much, y'see, we didn't know.

Oh my, that knocked us flat. We never did recover from that, we had a lot of trouble. Another brother came into the picture then, brother Ernie. You see? Had to be somebody to run the outfit y'see. And this other brother he was good on gas engines and that, but he was just like my father. He had this strong inventive part of his nature. That's Ernie in this picture here. That's the first hundred mile an hour boat.

Brother Ernie, he built it. Got an Italian Hispano airplane engine and he souped it up and put it on that boat — *Black Arrow* he called it, made his own reduction gear — and he clocked it a hundred mile an hour. The first in the world. This was around 1930 or before.

Well, this inventin' and experimentin' didn't fit in too well with business. He was workin' away while business was runnin' alright, he was workin' on a *scavengin'* two-cycle. It was an idea, you see, for gettin' all the advantage of a four-cycle without givin' up that middle stroke. The piston was double actin' y'see, it was quite complicated.

What was happening you see, is the four-cycles were startin' to come in, Palmers and that you see, and we could see the days of the two-cycle were numbered, because the four-cycle, it used less gas and it ran smoother. The fishermen didn't all see that yet, but we knew it. But Ernie, you see, bein' inventive, he wouldn't settle for just switchin' to four-cycle like the others were doin', he wanted a design that combined the advantages of both types of engine. You see, he didn't want to give up that middle stroke. If he could of made it work, he really would of had something. That's the inventor, you see. Shooting for the moon always. Later they got around to doing it by putting the blowers on the two-cycle but Ernie, he was goin' at it different.

All the time his mind was on this you see, it upset the workin' of the plant. Anyway he built a big two-cylinder model of this scavengin' two-cycle and got Bill Menshions to build a big sixty-footer to put 'er in. An 'e called 'er the *Konnomic*. She was on the coast here for long years. We built quite a few pleasure boats for the two-cycle days. Right in our plant there, in the back end.

That engine, well it worked *some times*. Heh heh heh. We entered 'er into the Seattle Motor Boat Race, in old days? They used to have it? We put 'er in on that.

Hah! One of the troubles was, the valves — it was pretty complicated, the scavengin' — the air cylinder was on the bottom side of the main power cylinder. She had two pistons, like — one pumping air, and one from the top, see? It was double actin', like it had a piston on the bottom to pump air in, to shoot it into the top cylinder see, to scavenge it out like they do now, see? But one of the things, it had rotary valves on it. Rotary valves along the side, and they were on a taper. Y'see. It was two-cycle, and these valves along at the top of the engine, they useta jam, they useta get heat, and the taper on 'em, it had to be very fine machined y'know, fine clearance on it, and when she got overheated a little bit, it'd swell up and jam and so on, and little things like that, but it was, it was a failure.

So, we lost out on that race. But we had a good trip. Well, they started to get kind of financially involved, y'see? Spent all his time experimentin' y'see? And then buildin' the boat, to put it in, to put it in, to demonstrate, y'see? It's one thing that put 'em financially behind.

Well then, my brother took in a couple of partners — I wasn't in the business then, I was on my own running a dairy business — he took in two partners, Cameron and Heskett.

Well, the two of them worked my brother out and the two of them took it over and eventually *they* failed. All the machinery was scattered and one thing another — it was quite a sad time. This took two, three, four years. It would be 1910, 11, somewhere in there.

Well now, I'd been doing pretty well on my own and my other brother George was engineer for Armstrong-Morrison, on his boats, he came to me and said whattya say we go into business again? Y'see?

So, we did that. Went into business again. The building next to our old place there was vacant and we put in a new set of ways and one thing another.

So! We didn't start in to make an engine right away, we had agencies. See? We took an agency for the Frisbee. It was a four-cycle, valve in head, but it had a weakness — it had a solid head and the valves were in cages. You could lift the cages outta there. It was a weakness because it used to overheat and one thing another. Well ennaway we had that and we worked up that into quite a business. Sold a lot of them to the Indians. Five horsepower, y'know? Single cylinder? Well ennaway, after we got that worked up into a pretty good business, they wanted us to buy their engines in carload lots. We didn't have that kind of money.

Ennaway, we got sore. And I said to George, I said, "George, why don't we make one on our own. We don't want to get stuck like this again." Workin' it all up, doin' all the advertisin', you see? Then they gave it to Lipsett. They gave the agency to Lipsett, after we'd built it up.

We said well, we'll cook up a little four-cycle engine of our own. Heh heh. See? And got thinkin' around, well, competition y'see? Like in everything else, in that business then. We gotta get up a little engine that we can undersell the others that are going round little bit, you know, and make a simple engine, y'see. So we can make it cheaper than the others.

There was Palmer, was the big competition, and Vivian in the meantime, he had started up too. He had worked for us in the two-cycle business, Bill Vivian did, so he got it into his head to start up. A four-cycle. Started right in with a four-cycle, y'see.

Besides Vivian there were, let's see — Shaake out in New Westminster made a four-cycle and so did John Cowie. Letson Burpee tried to build one too I think. So, there was competition there. Frisbee too, you see. They were competition now.

So that's how I got thinkin', I said to George well now look, we can't make a lot of these parts, so we said well now, what about that Ford? Ford connectin' rods, Ford piston, Ford valves — see? Those are all quantity manufactured y'see, we can get 'em for a quarter the price we could make 'em for. So, that's why we incorporated those in. Out of the Model T Ford. Three and three-quarters I think it was, three and three-quarters bore. Inch and a quarter main bearing. We thought that was a little small but we couldn't do anything about that.

There was no crankshafts around, we couldn't get any of that, so we used piece a flat steel, inch and three-quarters I think it was, by about two and a half. We bought it in the long size, cut it off the lengths we wanted, put it in the drill press and drilled it all through, put it in the lathe and turned it all up in the lathe. That's how we first made our crankshafts y'see. Otherwise we'd a had to get forging some way. The base was no problem there, just got a little pattern made for that n' had it cast.

So the problem was then, what to use for a timer y'see. On the old two-cycle we made our own timer, but this one we used the Bemis. Then the dry battery you see, and you're away. You've got a motor. Little four horsepower motor. There was a Bemis timer and a Cuno timer. Sometimes we used the one, sometimes the other.

Ennaway, that fixed that part of it. But — we wanted something to be independent of the batteries y'see, so we got this mag, y'see.

Wico. They could start the engine right on the Wico, and then they were independent of the battery. So that made a complete setup y'see. Right there. And, it worked fine. We didn't have a reverse gear and we put on some of them, the Gees. We brought those in from the States, so we were away. Later we got makin' our own.

It was a simple design. It was more simple than the others. And it did do the work, stood up better. Our castings n'that were a little heavier than these imported engines, they lasted longer. And another thing, like what we had over Vivian, he never balanced his engines. He didn't balance 'em. We balanced ours very fine, so single-cylinder engine we could rev 'er up to a thousand revolutions, we had 'er balanced so it kept the vibration down y'see.

Balanced the whole thing. We put it in with the piston-connecting rod, then we put it on the balancing stand and put the flywheel on and weighted the flywheel to offset the weight of the piston-connecting rod. See? Because that goin' up and down . . . We

cast that in the flywheel. A *lump* in the flywheel t'balance that, you see otherwise it would *jump* along like a rabbit. So that's where we had it over them — they said they wouldn't buy one of those Vivians because jumps right out of the boat. Vivian's flywheel was just straight, you see.

So, we worked up from one motor to another. Boats would get bigger and we'd make bigger motors. The fishin' industry kind of grew up, you see, from rowin' skiffs up to more sophisticated rigs, and we grew along with it.

The 8-12 was very popular, that was just two of the little fellas sittin' together, then the 15-18 for the bigger boats. The trollers. Then we went into a 30, a three-cylinder. That was very popular too. Worked good.

But on all those — the *dual ignition*. You see, that was a big selling point. We put on a mag and a battery system both. We called it "dual ignition." Then on the 30's, on those big ones, we fixed that up with a lighting system, the generation and a starter — and a Bosch magneto. If everything went dead they could just turn 'er over, click, and away she'd go.

That had a lot of attraction, especially for the trollers because out on the west coast there, all alone with those big breakers crashin' in on the rocks, you didn't want to be worryin' about the engine failing. So that was very good too.

And that trolling device, there's another thing. That was a lever we put on the valve shaft on the top, we put a cam on it so when you pulled the lever over it altered the gap between the rocker arm and the intake valves. Ordinary when yer running you have just clearance between the tappet, y'know? Well for slowin' down you pull that lever over, and it made a big gap in there so the valve only opened a little wee bit. That was a great thing for trolling y'see? They just pulled that lever over and they could go as slow as they wanted. Economical too, it only sucked in a little bit of a charge. Get the idea? We had those advantages you see.

And the half-compression cocks for starting. Halfway up the cylinder a cock that lets 'er blow out till she gets halfway up so the compression is only half. Makes it a lot easier to pull over to start. Haha. We couldn't give 'em electric starts always but we did make it easier to crank. Those features you see, those are the things that made it popular.

Vivian, he never did any of this kind of thing. He was sittin' right there, he had the same opportunity, but it didn't occur to him. He didn't think along these lines you see. With us, what it was, we all had a little bit of Dad's inventive stuff in us, and we could think along that line you know. What to do about a certain thing. We kept our eyes open you see.

And they could see that you see, the people who used the motors, because of these conveniences. Another thing along this line we used to do, instead of just putting out an operatin' manual, we gave 'em a tide book. Every year we'd send out the new tide book to anyone who had one of our motors. And you see we'd put with it all the mechanical information and pictures of all the new motors too y'see. All in one book. Everything they needed to know. It kinda kept us in touch. After one season you'd see those books of ours, just scraps.

Now if you ever see one of our books you'll see in the back there's some part from the Gospel. We always put in some section of the New Testament. This was another thing. Many's the time there'd be some old fella come tell me, out in some storm there off the west coast, he was glad he had that. We had an ad too, Jesus Light of the World. In the marine section there. Jesus Light of the World. It's what we believe you see, so we put it right out there where everyone can see it. In our ad in the paper. The boys kept it up for many years but I don't know if it's still there or not. That's all the promotin' we ever did, just the book and the ad in the boats column.

Our sellin' we handled right from the office. They'd come in and buy 'em right there. There were a couple agents too — Jimmy Dawson up in Rivers Inlet sold quite a few. Jimmy had quite a store there, Dawson's Landing they called it.

In the top years we'd sell, oh prittineer a hundred motors I guess. We made 'em all sizes you see, it was a lot of work. Had fifty men on. Forty-five in the shop, five in the foundry — we were doin' all our casting toward the end you see. Makin' everything right there in that shop in Coal Harbour, 1747 West Georgia. When we needed more room we just hung another piece on the end of the shop until it got to be quite a building. You can see it now, they're still using it.

I guess our best years were oh, '45, '50. Fifty I guess was the top, around there. By 1940 you see there were no rowin' skiffs left, then durin' the war we had war contracts — put motors in all the lifeboats for the shipyards. Went all over the world, those motors. After the war, there were a lotta people goin' fishin', goin' to bigger boats and one thing another. We made many many engines in those years.

Still goin' too, lots of 'em. They never wear out, you see. You have to get rid of them — they never go on their own. The operators go first. Ha ha. Funny story there. Up at Alert Bay, fella there had one of our old heavy duty nine horsepower. Great big single cylinder heavy duty. Oh, it was a monster that one. Great big flywheel half as tall as a man. Six by seven it was I believe. Take six men to lift it. Well, he had that. And he died. And he had to have that motor — his old friend y'see — he had to have that on his grave. They took that engine out of that boat and put it on his grave. Hahaha. Some boys I knew went up and saw it there. Old nine horsepower heavy duty sittin' up as a headstone. Probably still there.

Those were great years. Everybody was usin' our motors, right from one end of the coast to the other and we were right in the middle of everything that was goin' on. It was a wonderful time. I enjoyed every minute of it.

What happened was, Ford and Chrysler came out with the high speed marines and that kinda knocked ours, y'see. The Chrysler Crown. They claim that a lot of those motors, Chrysler marine, they were made out of rejects. Motors that had a little fault for a car you see, so they kicked them into marien production, you see. Sold 'em out here. Well I don't know, but I do know they were undersellin' us to beat the band. The price made a big difference.

See these Chryslers and so on, they had electric start and generator and everything all in there — you see there was a lot of 'em like to just look at the panel and push the starter button, they didn't want to go down and fool around with it anymore.

We tried to kind of modernize, took off the slowdown device, put covers on the head, speeded 'em up a little bit you know? Enclosed 'em a bit. Well, that was a mistake. Didn't sell. It was a bad thing. The old ones with the slowdown and the open valves so you could see what was up, that's what the fishermen liked. But ennaway it had to happen you see. Chrysler and Ford came with these high speed motors and that's what killed the heavy duty type of engine. It was the power, the speed they wanted. That's the way everything is moving these days. They went for bigger power, Faster boats. Now they've got 'em up, some of those gillnetters'll make 20 mile an hour I believe. Crazy.

It's the same thing wherever you look — faster, faster, more, more, y'see? Everybody's speeded up but they don't know where they're goin'. They've lost their way. Oh, it's a frightful thing to look at.

I tell you — this may surprise you, I don't know, but what we're looking at now is the end of this civilization.

Look at the violence, look at the murder. Things coming apart. Look how people are turning to dope all over the world. But you see what's gonna cap the whole thing, Russia is going to come down into Palestine. She's just gettin' ready now. Then we'll have a real war. She thinks she's doin' it herself, comin' in y'see — oil and that, and the Jews, you know they're all against the Jews. You see. But God said he'd put a hook in the nose of Russia and he would bring 'em down to accomplish what he got to do, so's to bring all nations there — you don't mind me doin' a little bit of preachin' now?

Well after this Battle of Armageddon see, after the Russians come in, people will get down on their knees and say, "Oh my God!" like when a man gets to the end of his tether he generally says that, y'see? And then — Jesus gonna return, set up his kingdom right there in Jerusalem. This is, this is — it's gonna happen. Can't get away from it. All this corruption, God says, "I'll wipe it out!"

You see he did that with the flood. There was violence and corruption before he came and wiped out the whole thing — and only one man and his family were left. But this time you see, he's gonna come in, Jesus is gonna come in, and all those born again Christians, or "converted" or whatever you like to call them, they're gonna be together and he's gonna set up his government right there — with *great power!* Not like he was before. Great power you see. Terrible power. Second coming. They call it second coming of the Lord. It's not too far away! It's all in the Bible and *the Bible is the word of God!* It's God talkin'! You see?

That's where we stand today, right in those end times. No doubt about that. We're in those end times.

Book Reviews

Fishing Literature

The sad truth is, there isn't very much. The writers who have been drawn by the balm and openness of the coast over the years have generally been too busy exclaiming over the blue mountains and indulging their imaginations in the Indian past to give much time to the present concerns of the people.

One who thought differently was Bertrand W. Sinclair, a Regina farm boy who went to Montana in the 1890's and together with magazine editor Betty Bower and painter Charles Russell helped launch the myth of the American cowboy. Tiring of that success, Sinclair came to Vancouver in 1908 and, seeing the trials of the small boat fisherman adventure equal to that of the cowboy, began writing a novel about the salmon industry which he hoped would catch on in the same way.

Poor Man's Rock still stands as one of the most popular novels ever written on the B.C. coast but fifty years later Sinclair was still complaining that the westcoasters lacked any sort of mythic dimension. "They take as much pride in their calling as men in other climes," he wrote in *The Fisherman* on his eightieth birthday, "but nowhere from California to Ketchikan is this pride embodied in song or simple homely story." His own life offers some clue as to the cause: in 1930 he went fishing himself and fished with passionate absorption until well past 80, sparing no further time or effort on his lucrative writing career. Living the life, he found, was better.

His only literary endeavour in later years was limited to songs and heroic verse about west coast fishermen which he wrote for "broadcast" over the radiophone when the boats were on the grounds. "Bank Trollers", printed in this issue, derives from this experiment in grassroots culture.

Poor Man's Rock is too melodramatic to inspire any thought of revival today, but it is realistic enough about the fishing industry of that time, from the handliners up to the cannery amalgamators, to have historical value. It is also an historical event in its own right, having left a deeper mark on people's imagination than its author perhaps gave it credit for.

In any case Sinclair was the first and last writer to conceive of a literature of B.C. coast fishing; apart from a children's book by Roderick Haig-Brown called *Salt Water Summer* and *Mist on the River* by Sinclair's old friend Hubert Evans which has a memorable section on cannery life, all subsequent work on the subject has been non-fictional and functional.

The most professional all-round history available is Hugh McKervill's *The Salmon People*, which begins with a discussion of aboriginal fishing customs and techniques and progresses through to modern times in a readable if not altogether thorough fashion. The book is dotted with cute anecdotes (it's family reading all the way) and the chapter on Rivers Inlet is especially knowledgeable and fascinating.

West coast fishing has proven one of the most political of Canada's industries, a fact that is evident in three well-produced histories, *Salmon: Our Heritage*, published by the major company, *A Ripple, a Wave*, published by the major union and *Tides of Change*, published by the major co-op, each rehashing old disputes and directing the march of history in its sponsor's favour.

Salmon: Our Heritage, published by B.C. Packers Ltd., is an encyclopedic work of 750 pages compiled by longtime company secretary Cecily Lyons, dealing mainly with the canning side of the industry. Lyons was more of a record keeper than a writer and the book is more useful as a source of statistical information than for reading, but it is limited even in this use by poor indexing.

A Ripple, a Wave, published only this year, is a compact little paperback as singular about its purpose as the Lyons book is rambling, offering a swift review of the long and only partially successful struggle to bring coast fishermen together in one strong union.

Tides of Change is the only one of these fishing books written by an actual fisherman, and what a difference it makes. Vic Hill's announced purpose is simply to tell the story of the rise of the Prince Rupert Co-op from a nickel-dime beginning with a few semi-literate Finns taking on the canning monopolies with a tacked-together shack on floats, through years of blunders and bankruptcy to the multi-million dollar international operation of today. That story is appealing enough in itself to hold most people's attention but in the course of telling it Hill manages to get over more of a feeling of what fishing is, from the overloaded troller in Hecate Straits trying to decide in face of a rising southeaster whether to risk the dangerous beam sea home to Rupert or run before it way out around Rose Spit, to the quirks of New York fish shoppers, than all the other books put together.

The only other books somewhat like it are *As the Sailor Loves the Sea*, a memoir by an Alaskan fisherman's wife named Ballard Hadman and *Guests Never Leave Hungry*, a tape-recorded autobiography containing recollections of fishing by the well-known B.C. seine skipper Jimmy Sewid. In these books the northwest coast, so often portrayed as desolate and unknowable, emerges with recognizable face, worn familiar by human use. This is the sort of awareness that exists in the fishing industry and it's too bad so few writers have ever discovered it.

PIONEERS IN PARADISE

Roy Padgett

AFTER CORTES ISLAND THE OLD MAN MOVED TO VANANDA and that's where I was born. Vananda was the place in those days — there was nothing on the mainland side but the logging camps — mind you they were big camps, big two and three hundred man railroad outfits — Stillwater, Lang Bay, Myrtle Point. But Vananda was a real city; had hotels, hospitals, an opera hall, its own newspaper, even had a Chinatown. Lots of mining going on.

Right after the First World War Vananda went flat. Price of copper dropped and what the mines had left wasn't very much so they pulled out for good. The town died in a matter of days.

Everybody started burning their houses down for the insurance till the insurance companies cancelled all insurance on Texada Island. Fire every day. One fellow living in Vancouver gave $50 to a guy to come up and burn his house down and the guy came up and burned down the wrong house. When the hotel went up everyone ran into the bar and grabbed all the booze so the whole town was soused.

We moved the following year. The old man had become disgusted with civilization all over again and decided to have another go at homesteading. There'd been a terrific fire in Paradise Valley just before that. It started in the logging camp above Myrtle Creek, swept over the hill towards Grief Point, right down to the back of the Atkinson place. Mr. Atkinson was throwing water on the shakes on the barn to keep them wet, and then suddenly the wind switched and threw it back over the hill and burned out the big camp just above where the Lamberts lived. Two or three people were trapped. They managed to get the women and kids out on the train to the beach and stood in the water while the flames raged around them. The fire covered a strip five or six miles long and five or six miles wide, right up to Cranberry Lake. It burned for about a month. September came, rains, and it burned itself out. It wasn't put out.

So you see the country was opened up by this fire. It came up all in grass, daisies and blackberry vine and there actually was a fair amount of sheep pasture — six miles by about two miles deep. Well the old man heard about this, came up and had a look, and took out land here.

We moved in 1919. We had some goats for milk, 200 chickens and about ten geese. We landed on the beach with our wagon and went up the ox road to the railroad grade and up the grade to this piece of land the old man had decided on, the goats and geese walking behind the wagon, following us up the trail.

It was some place. We couldn't even find a Christmas tree that Christmas, there wasn't a green tree in the valley. We had to go down to the beach to get a Christmas tree. No second-growth fir, no alder even, it was completely burned off. There was nothing except a very few patches of old-growth fir the fire didn't get into. We kids used to go down to West

Lake in the summer to go swimming. The temperature was very high because you had so much black absorbing the heat and at night it would radiate the heat out. It was like an oven up there. Soot and ash everywhere, and dust — then you'd be sweating and the dust would stick to you — sometimes my brother and I were like a couple of tar babies. But for us it was well, Paradise Valley. I remember down at the lake there was one alder tree about eight feet high and that was our tree. It was green! We used to sit under it and lick the leaves. There were aphids and they made that honey-dew, and it was sticky and sweet and we'd lick it off. We didn't have any candy.

We got along. It wasn't long before we had in a pretty good garden and there was meat to be had if you knew how to get it. Sometimes meat was quite scarce and when you're hungry it's a tremendous thrill to go out and make a kill. Not at all like doing it for the sport. When I read about the Eskimoes out waiting for that first caribou, I know just how they feel. The first meat we used to get in the spring were the blue grouse coming down from the mountains. The males came down first, around the beginning of March. The first signs of spring and you'd catch yourself listening. Then in a few days out in the bush there'd be the male blue grouse — hoot hoot hoot! — like a man blowing on a beerbottle, and your stomach would say: meat!

They were full of pine needles, you can imagine the strong turpentine flavour, but in those circumstances we'd find them most delectable. There was a

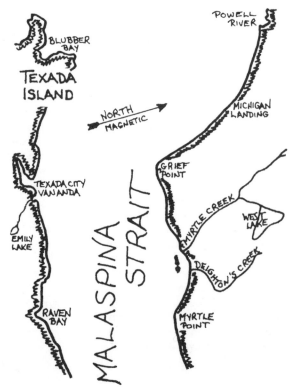

tremendous quantity of grouse. Just after the fire, with all the open space and all the clover, the black-berries and blueberries, it was ideal for them. The blue grouse and willow grouse started multiplying in such numbers that, walking the railroad grades behind West Lake, you'd come on hundreds at a time, dusting themselves and whump! off they'd go, you'd have to stop and wait for the dust to settle before you could see to go on.

The blue grouse migrate to higher altitudes through the season, from the early coastal berries up to the berries of the 2500-foot level, then in late November they move into the timber and live exclusively on fir needles until spring. The young are born in May. We'd hold off shooting during nesting, then around August we'd start again, taking one from each brood. That was a rule of the old man's.

There got to be thousands and thousands. For a long time we didn't have to shoot, we'd knock them over with a stick. I can remember as a very small boy, sitting right at the house and going hoot hoot hoot! hoot hoot hoot! And within a few minutes there'd be as many as maybe a dozen male grouse ringed around me going hoot hoot hoot! hoot hoot hoot!

You'll still hear a few blue grouse here, hooting up to July or August and everybody says oh boy! there's lots of grouse around! But the poor bastards have no hens! They keep hooting and they keep hooting but there is no mate. These are really the last of the hooters. The re-growth of the second-growth has choked their feed back off, but it was the Depression that really finished that tremendous population of grouse. Here'd be a man who'd earn perhaps a dollar-and-a-half a day, two dollars a day say, working *very* hard cutting hog fuel for the mill or cutting bolts for Jamieson's shingle mill, and over here you have a mother grouse sitting on a stump and there is only one thing on that fellow's mind. Free supper! He forgets that there are ten young ones underneath that will perish when the mother dies. It was remarkable how fast those grouse disappeared, with the indiscriminate shooting of the mother grouse, and they never came back. Not like they were.

There was other meat besides grouse. We had deer, there was a lot of deer in the valley, and trout from the creek, clams from the beach occasionally, and sometimes salmon. West Lake was the main source for Myrtle Point Creek and before the lake was tapped for a water supply in the thirties you had a run of creek sockeye, then coho, then in November a run of dog salmon. The run of creek sockeye, conservatively speaking, probably was between five and ten thousand. The coho run was probably fifteen thousand and the dog salmon run was probably twenty-five thousand, so thick that us kids coming home from school used to see if we could run across the creek on the beach flats on the backs of the fish, just like in the saying. It could be done too, they were wedged in there that tight.

When they cut off the West Lake stream Myrtle Point Creek went away down of course, the temperature of the water went up too high for the sockeye and coho fry, which have to stay a year in fresh water, and within two years the sockeye run was wiped out. The coho dwindled away too, and today all that's left is a run of perhaps a hundred dog salmon. But to us in those days what was more important than the salmon was the cutthroat trout, which lives on the salmon fry. When we first came you could go up to a pool, say fifteen feet long, ten feet wide and about four feet deep, and out of that one pool you could take between twenty-five and thirty cutthroat between nine and twelve inches. We never fished more than a hundred yards and we could have all the fish we could eat. All we had was a cedar pole, about ten feet of line, buckshot for weight, and an angleworm for bait. The angleworm was the hardest part. There weren't any under the primordial forest, even before the fire, and we had to come down to the beach to the logging camp pig pen. Angleworms were introduced to the area and they sorta spread.

The trout came back year after year because you had the ideal situation with the abundance of salmon fry and cold water. Now because the salmon have disappeared, and the lack of water, I doubt that you could catch at the best five or six trout in two miles. It was an incredibly beautiful creek. But it's gone forever, lost.

THE IDEA WAS, OF COURSE, TO RAISE SHEEP. My father was an Englishman. Vast green rolling acres dotted with sheep, that was the dream. No, I shouldn't say it that way. It's not fair or safe to look back at the oldtimers and laugh at their dreams. They were no more fools than we are fools, going on with old ideas in a new world. This whole idea of land, of *holding* land, it's still with us today, just not quite so pervasive.

You have to remember the first faculty when they built the University of B.C., and the biggest faculty, was the Faculty of Agriculture. The whole concept of government, from Hudson's Bay Company times till quite recently, was that this whole province, interior and coast both, was to be made secure for civilized man through agriculture. Encourage land clearing and planting wherever and whenever possible, and damn the difficulties. If you look at a land map of this district you will see from Westview to Lang Creek it's cut up into 40-acre blocks. I remember it getting surveyed by Burnett in the twenties with the idea it would be taken up by farmers. You could have bought that land up till not too long ago for two-and-a-half dollars an acre, before the government realized this was forest land with second-growth timber on it worth thousands of dollars to the acre.

But in the early days no one could wait to see the timber gone. I remember talking to old George Deighton, who owned this place. He came here from Ontario in 1893, to *farm*, and the first thing he did was to get the trees cut down and start burning them. He had 320 acres and it was all prime virgin timber, scaled 1500 feet to the log, so when one of the logging outfits heard about this they came over and offered him fifty cents a tree. Old George thought they were crazy, to clear off all this junk and give him fifty cents each besides. But there was more value in the timber he gave away than the land he was left with.

I can remember up on our own stump ranch when

the second growth fir began coming up, we'd set fires first thing in the fall and burn these seedlings with a real sense of indignation, that the forces of the wilds just refused to admit this was farmland now! But they had the edge when it came to persistence.

There was my father, Frank Graham, and Harry Scott, all had sheep, and they built shelters and ran them all together. They started to get a fair flock built up, but it was a frustrating business. The big thing was predators, cougars and wolves.

The wolves moved in on us quite suddenly in 1923 and were around only about one year. There were about fifteen or eighteen of them in three little packs. You could hear them moving around the house at night and in the morning we'd see the tracks in the snow. One night one howled right outside my window. It made me feel nervous but I was fascinated by them.

They made one large kill down towards Myrtle Point from our place and that sealed their fate. I wish I could have had a photograph of that but you couldn't because it wasn't the picture, it was the feeling.

There's the railroad grade that is now Padgett Road. The first half-mile you're on the ox road then you hit the railroad grade and the railroad grade runs south and comes out where the Stella subdivision is. My mother and I were walking one hot summer day and usually in the summer we had forest fires. So you start first of all with a picture of black snags, trees, stumps, logs – no green at all, nothing. Then you have a sky that is sort of leaden with smoke and through the smoke you have a round ball of fire, blood red, and that is the sun. And no wind. On the snags and on the stumps are sitting probably two hundred turkey vultures, and strewn around them are the bloated bodies of the sheep, twenty or thirty sheep and goats killed by these wolves. The vultures are so gorged and lethargic they just ruffle their feathers a little as you come up and occasionally make a low croaking AAAAAHHH! sound. For three hundred yards you're lined on either side by these grotesque-looking vultures and the sickly-sweet smell of decaying flesh. I can still smell that smell. And those gruesome birds, I can see them so plain: aaaahh!

At first we trapped the wolves. Wolves tend to run in a circuit so that made it easier. Later the government gave us a permit to use cyanide poisoning and strychnine. With strychnine they tend to run for water, gives them uncontrollable thirst, whereas with cynaide they just run, till they drop. It works on muscle tissue, pulls their muscles up into bunches. Rather an agonizing death, both of them.

Actually the method we used was not the best way. The best method was to kill an old goat, skin out the brisket, sprinkle on a mixture of strychnine and powdered glass and sew it back up. That way the glass lacerates the wolf's gums and he gets a direct jolt of the poison. Wolves will go for the brisket first because they want the fat. You kill them quicker that way, they don't suffer so much. The way we did it, we slit it and put poison in a hundred different places. It worked, because we trapped one wolf that had taken bait and by morning it died. And later we heard of people stumbling onto the odd rotting skeleton.

So they disappeared completely. Within months of the time we started poisoning, the wolves were all gone. Whether we killed them all or the ones that were left left the country I don't know. It's quite possible, because they are a highly intelligent creature, you can't help getting quite a feeling for them, even when you're just trying to exterminate them. I remember one we trapped. They would follow along the lake, down the creek, down Paradise Valley, around Rook Knoll, and then back again. So we had a trap there and one morning there was a little white female wolf in it. And as we walked up with our guns, she threw her head up and let out the longest, most mournful pathetic howl, right there in our sights. And perhaps two or three hundred yards off, there was another long mournful howl, almost human, the feeling in it. It was her mate I guess.

It didn't stop us, we went ahead and shot her, you know, we were so sure of our mission there to make this country safe for sheep. But that howl, it lingers in a person's memory. Now looking back, it's hard to see any point to it, us with our two-bit flock of sheep and big plans that didn't amount to anything, although that's not the way it looked at the time. There was no question that the wolves and cougars did massacre our livestock. There was no question about that at all. Except looking back, I wonder. We would often find sheep with just the hind quarters gone. We blamed it on the wolves at the time, but a wolf won't generally take just the hind that way. I think now it must have been some of the local loggers helping out. Shooting them, ones who had families here, for meat. Not that I'd blame them either.

The thing is, as soon as we had the wolves nicely out of the way the cougars started showing up. They won't share ground, cougars and wolves, so as long as the wolves were around the cougars kept clear but as soon as there were no wolves around they started moving in and within a year or two there got to be a real plague of cougar, and they weren't near as easy to get rid of.

I remember one time coming up from the logging camp, I was ahead of my father. About half a mile below where we lived the goats were all feeding and suddenly from behind a stump a cougar jumped out and launched an attack on a goat. It knocked the goat down about twenty feet from where I was standing and by the time it had the thing pinned I guess it wasn't more than five feet away from me. So here I am, a twelve-year-old kid, confronted with this cougar down on a goat, snarling and swishing its tail. No gun, no nothing. The old man didn't have anything either, so he picked up a dead cedar limb and came barging in hollering and waving this club and the cougar snarled a bit, then took off. We set the traps that afternoon and we had that cougar within a matter of hours.

Fences were no use. A cougar will go over a six-foot fence with a 150-pound sheep in his mouth and think nothing of it. Their strength is tremendous.

We trapped them at first, then later we got dogs. Poison was never used for cougars. There was no point. The cougar makes a kill, drags it away, then gets bark, ferns and wood and covers the whole thing up so that all you can see is a mound. You know where the kill was so you just follow the trail to the cache and set a few traps 'cause you know he'll be back. Cougar is like a house cat, he eats only a little at a time and saves the rest for later. Wolves gorge themselves on a kill and clear out, hit and run fashion, but the cougar is fastidious, he eats no more than three or four pounds at a time and hangs around. Mostly a cougar just kills what he's going to eat too, although he will occasionally kill for the fun of it. We had a couple of large kills by only one or two cougars.

Cougar will eat cougar. We shot a female once and skinned it and two days later when we came back we found a young one feeding off it. It went up the tree and we shot it.

We cooked some cougar up once — it was much like veal — and oddly enough the dogs wouldn't touch it. They just sniffed it and scuttled away behind the stove. I regret now that we didn't try it but we had an abhorrence of it. Actually there's nothing wrong with it. I've talked to several people who have had an excellent meal of cougar meat. And the Chinamen were always glad to get a cougar to eat. This idea of not eating meat that's eaten meat, we don't stick to it anyway — chickens and pigs eat anything.

Another way of trapping a cougar, if you don't have a fresh kill, is to get a kid goat and throw it in a burned-out stump. Then you set traps in front where he'll hit them, but you don't tie the traps down. You take and attach onto the trap five or six feet of chain and on the end of the chain you tie a couple of peavey hooks. So the cougar takes off and gets the hooks all snaffled up in the brush, wrestles around and gets loose and tangled a few more times maybe, till finally he's played out. You hope he's good and caught when you're walking up.

Biggest cougar we ever got we caught that way. Nine foot two inches tip to tip and close to two hundred pounds. Got him on the hind foot somehow — usually you get the front. He went for a tree, took trap, chain, hooks and all forty feet up a big alder. *Tremendous* strength! Then he came down the tree, eventually got snarled up, and we shot him in the trap.

The most cougar we ever got at once, we picked up a trail in the snow just beyond Lambert's place in Paradise Valley and we followed it into a stand of old growth fir just between Cranberry Lake and Haslam Lake. There were seven in that pack and we got four. It thawed then it snowed again and we picked up the three that were left on the far side of West Lake.

We'd pick up the tracks in the snow and then we'd go with the dogs following the tracks then we'd come to a stand of scrub, old growth fir that hadn't been logged. We'd let the dogs go, and as a rule the dogs surprised the cougar, began to bark, and the cougar ran up the tree. The dogs would sit at the foot of the tree and we'd come and look up till we found the cougar and shoot it. We got two that time so we got six out of the seven.

The best type of cougar hounds were the ones we had which are known as the "silent runner". They don't bark until they see. A lot of cougar hounds start to bark as soon as you let them off the leash. Even if the cougar is half a mile away. That type often gets killed because then the cougar is ready. And they will turn on a dog you know. One time my brother Rex let the dog go and all he heard was a YIPE! He ran to where it was and all you could see was the cougar crouched down and the dog's tail sticking out. So they fired a shot, the cougar took off, the dog staggered to his feet and took right back after him, treed him and they shot him.

But when the dog appears unexpectedly and starts barking, it seems to confuse the cougar and make him go up a tree quicker.

You want to know what you're doing when you go in to make your shot because you only get one. The best shot is behind the shoulder, that usually finishes them off, but it's hard to get. They're hard to shoot in the head too. They have a sloping forehead and unless you shoot very low, almost in the nose, the bullet will ricochet off the skull.

They're rarely dead when they come down. There's sort of a mixed-up melee when the dogs go in. The dogs are fairly cagey. They sort of jump and back off. Lot of snarling going on.

I remember shooting one underneath. The bullet ripped right through the stomach and really opened it up, and as it came down the entrails snagged and got yarded right out of it. It came right at me, so close it ripped the toe off my shoe getting past, all it wanted to do was get away, but it couldn't go very far and just got sorta down behind a log, and when my dog went in it grabbed him by the face with one paw. I ran in as a kid will to protect his dog and jammed my rifle into its mouth and shot it.

Oh, it's quite sporting you know. For a fourteen-year-old. Dogs, snow, open country, clumps of old growth timber, miles of burned stumps like a prairie, tearing around risking your neck . . . we thought we were pretty smart. We got write-ups in the local paper, "Local Padgetts Preserve Deer Population." Absolute drivel.

The last cougar I shot I guess was with a policeman, Jack Purdy, and he had some dogs. It was rather funny, that. I had no faith in him with the dogs because I guess I was anti-authority, but anyhow I went out with him and these damn dogs of his took off close to where we were living in Paradise Valley. They ran down towards the Myrtle Point Creek in the old growth timber and started barking and when we got there it looked like they had the cougar but I couldn't see just where it was. Well, this policeman spotted the damn thing in the tree right over my head but instead of saying anything — I guess he wanted to make sure he got the glory — the first thing I know BAM! and down comes the cougar, but not dead — just wounded. Well then it dove into a mess of salal and fallen logs and he was afraid to go in after it. I went in and all I could see was the yellow eyes in the gloom, so I had to get up quite close before I could place a shot, and got it in the throat. "Okay Jack," I says, "it's yours."

It's funny the feeling you get when you're hunting that you can't get hurt. A high I guess you'd call it, that you get from that moment of skirmish and kill.

But after, there's a kind of guilt or depression some-times – I can still remember the yellow eyes staring at me as I shot it, and then the film that ran across the eyes. You could see the life leaving just like pulling shutters. The life had gone out of it and instead of being bright yellow they were just empty.

You don't come to respect a cougar's intelligence the same way as a wolf, but there is something else about them, a vitality I guess you'd call it.

Well after we finished this cougar off of course this guy wanted to haul it down to the police station, and then at five o'clock when all the men were coming off shift he insisted on driving down to Powell River to show everybody the cougar that the police depart-ment had killed.

ALTOGETHER WE GOT THIRTY-SEVEN COU-GARS. We trapped eight or nine timber wolves and poisoned off an equal amount. It's hard to know just how to feel about it today. Whether to be proud or not.

The farming of course turned out to be hopeless. Stump ranchers live on what is known as "next year". Good old next year. But next year isn't any different, except you're a year older. Again though, it's only in retrospect you see the futility of it. Apart from the Fraser Valley and a few areas on Vancouver Island, there is no agricultural land on this coast. If you had money coming in and you wanted to live a secluded life you could do it, because you can grow a few vegetables, but as far as making a living at it, and that's what people wanted to do, it was hopeless. The land was here but it's not agricultural land. The flat land that starts south of Lund and ends at Saltery Bay is actually glacial till or moraine. Rock, clay, sand and gravel, all jumbled up. There's a thin skin of humus some places but for farming you need soil, deep soil. The oldtimers, all they could see was the top.

Kelly Creek was settled by a bunch of Ukranians from Saskatchewan. The provincial government coaxed them out to farm that area. I remember the four leaders coming up to our stump ranch in 1924 with the government agent, because we were fairly well established. We had fruit trees and the agent asked mother to open a can of plums to show what could be grown. And then I remember one of the Ukranians pointed to one of our more imposing stumps and asked this land settlement agent what you did with those things. The agent broke off a sliver and lit it with his lighter. "It's just wood," he says, "you burn it." You s.o.b., I thought. I knew even then it wasn't right what they were doing.

In the main I think the government was sincere but ignorant. Agriculture was all they knew and it stopped them from seeing conditions for what they were.

Like I say, you could get by. There was a day, on Cortes Island or in Paradise Valley for the first few years, if you had a good garden, fruit trees that were beginning to bear, with the game that was there, and especially if you lived on the water with the salmon and cod, you could get by on $150 a year. But again it was a submarginal life, who the hell wants that year after year? You can be sure your children won't.

We sold off our livestock and lived for some time on the cougar bounty. It was actually quite a hand-some sum, $40. A pair of caulk boots was $5 and a chokerman in the camps was only getting $3.50. Forty dollars was the equivalent of about two hundred dollars today. The reason they made the bounty so big was to protect the deer population, or more correctly, to leave the deer for man – get the predators out of the way so there would be more for the real predator – but it didn't work out, there just got to be less cougar.

I don't hunt at all anymore. A few years ago there were some blue grouse around this area, ten or twelve hooters, and I thought by God, I'm gonna get one, so I went out with the 22 and shot one. I could re-member what they tasted like when I was eight or nine but when my wife Florence cooked it, it didn't taste the same. I felt kind of bad about it. There was no damn need of it. You try to turn the clock back and just foul up your memories.

Index

269